MORE
confessions
of a forty-
something
f##k up

Alexandra Potter is the bestselling author of numerous romantic comedy fiction novels in the UK, including *One Good Thing* and *Confessions of a Forty-Something F##k Up*, one of the bestselling books of 2022 and 2023 and the basis of a major TV series. These titles have sold in twenty-five territories and achieved worldwide sales of more than one million copies, making the bestseller charts around the world.

Yorkshire born and raised, Alexandra lived for several years in LA before settling in London with her Californian husband and their Bosnian rescue dog. When she's not writing or travelling, she's getting out into nature, trying not to look at her phone and navigating this thing called mid-life.

Visit her at www.alexandrapotter.com
 @Alexandra.Potter.Author
 @alexandrapotter
 @40somethingfkup

Also by Alexandra Potter

What's New, Pussycat?
Going La La
Calling Romeo
Do You Come Here Often
Be Careful What You Wish For
Me and Mr Darcy
Who's That Girl?
You're The One That I Don't Want
Don't You Forget About Me
The Love Detective
Love From Paris
Confessions of a Forty-Something F##k Up
One Good Thing

MORE confessions of a forty-something f##k up

ALEXANDRA POTTER

PAN BOOKS

First published 2023 by Macmillan

This edition first published 2024 by Pan Books
an imprint of Pan Macmillan
The Smithson, 6 Briset Street, London EC1M 5NR
EU representative: Macmillan Publishers Ireland Ltd, 1st Floor,
The Liffey Trust Centre, 117–126 Sheriff Street Upper,
Dublin 1, D01 YC43
Associated companies throughout the world
www.panmacmillan.com

ISBN 978-1-5290-9883-9

1 3 5 7 9 8 6 4 2

A CIP catalogue record for this book is available from the British Library.

Typeset by Palimpsest Book Production Limited, Falkirk, Stirlingshire
Printed and bound by CPI Group (UK) Ltd, Croydon, CR0 4YY

MIX
Paper | Supporting
responsible forestry
FSC
www.fsc.org
FSC® C116313

Visit www.panmacmillan.com to read more about all our books
and to buy them. You will also find features, author interviews and
news of any author events, and you can sign up for e-newsletters
so that you're always first to hear about our new releases.

For all the Nells in this world

None of us want to be in calm waters all of our lives.

Jane Austen, *Persuasion*

Rubber gloves and determination can solve anything*

Cricket, *Confessions of a Forty-Something F##k Up*

---

* Failing that, tequila.

The Rules to Life

1. There are no rules.

Prologue

Hi, I'm Nell, and welcome to MORE Confessions of a Forty-Something F**k-Up, *the podcast for any woman who wonders how the hell she got here, and why life isn't quite how she imagined it was going to be.*

It's for anyone who has ever looked around at their life and thought this was never part of The Plan. Who has ever felt like they dropped a ball, or missed a boat, and is still desperately trying to figure it all out while everyone around them is baking gluten-free brownies.

But first a disclaimer: I don't pretend to be an expert in anything. I'm not a lifestyle guru, or an influencer, whatever that is, and I'm not here to sell a brand. Or flog a product. I'm just someone struggling to recognize their messy life in a world of perfect Instagram ones and feeling like a bit of a fuck-up. Even worse, a forty-something fuck-up. Someone who reads a life-affirming quote and feels exhausted, not inspired. Who isn't trying to achieve more goals, or set more challenges, because life is enough of a challenge as it is. And who does not feel #blessed and #winningatlife but mostly #noideawhatthefuckIamdoing and #canIgoogleit?

Which is why I started this podcast . . . to tell it like it is, for me anyway. Because Confessions *is a show about the daily trials and tribulations of what it's like to reach a point in your life when you thought everything would be sorted, only to discover it's the opposite. It's about what happens when shit happens and still being able to laugh in the face of it all. It's about being honest and real and telling it like it is. About friendship and love and disappointment. About asking the big questions and not getting any of the answers. About starting over, when you thought you would be finished already.*

In these episodes I'll also be talking to ordinary women who are quietly doing their thing but are no less extraordinary. In these honest and heart-warming conversations, we'll be sharing with you all the sad bits and the funny bits. We'll be talking about feeling flawed and confused and lonely and scared, about finding hope and joy in the unlikeliest of places, and how no amount of celebrity scented candles and smashed avocados are going to save you.

Because the message is clear: feeling like a fuck-up isn't about being *a failure, it's about* being made to feel like one. *It's the pressure and the panic to tick all the boxes and reach all the goals . . . and what happens when you don't. Because it doesn't matter whether you're twenty-something, forty-something or eighty-something, on some level, in some aspect of your life, it's so easy to feel like you're failing when everyone around you appears to be succeeding.*

So, if there's anyone out there who feels any of this too, this podcast will hopefully make you feel less alone and remind you we're all in this together.

And things are always better together.

JULY

#lifegoesbacktonormal

The Second Half of the Year Day

I can't believe it.

According to Google, today is the 182nd day of the year. Which means we're exactly halfway through. *Already!* Time to look back and take stock of all those resolutions you *didn't* make and goals you *didn't* achieve. (Or is that just me?) More importantly it marks exactly eighteen months since I kissed Edward on New Year's Eve and fell in love, not just with the man, but with my life. My messy, flawed, perfectly imperfect life. And for a brief moment everything felt sorted.

For like, two seconds.

Because if ever there was a lesson that life doesn't go to plan, no sooner had I finally managed to turn mine around, the world was struck by a global pandemic and everything changed overnight. It was surreal and scary. Collectively we lost loved ones, we missed our friends and family, we home-schooled and baked banana bread and clapped for carers. All the while enduring endless lockdowns, Zoom quizzes and a social media feed overflowing with Hollywood celebs singing 'Imagine' and doing the #stayathomechallenge. As if staying at home wasn't a challenge enough.

To add insult to injury, we also ran out of loo roll.

#imaginetheresnoloorollitseasyifyoutry.

In eighteen months, A LOT happened. Yet, conversely, in my world, a lot *un*-happened. Normal life was cancelled along with the West End production of Monty's play that I'd edited and my new newspaper column. 'Sorry, Stevens, but now is not the right time to be launching a new column,' Sadiq, my editor, had grimly told me over the phone. 'I need to keep you at the coalface, as it were, writing obituaries.' I also lost a big sponsorship deal for my podcast, and with it, some much-needed income.

In many ways it felt a lot like I'd gone right back to where I started all those moons ago when I'd moved back to London from America after everything fell apart. Any social life I had went out of the window, I couldn't visit The Parents (though this time it had nothing to do with them Airbnbing my old bedroom) and as for my love life . . . Well, let's just say it's difficult to have a romantic relationship when you're socially distancing.

And no, believe me when I say this, you can't do *everything* on Zoom.

Yet despite all the setbacks, I have *so much* to be grateful for. In fact, during the last eighteen months my daily gratitude lists got longer and longer. When times got tough I counted my blessings. And not just the big, life-or-death stuff, like our amazing NHS, or being healthy, or keeping my loved ones safe. But all the other things, like, for example:

1. *My listeners.*

Emerging red-faced from underneath my duvet, which is draped over my airer, I yank open the rickety old Victorian sash window and stick out my head to get some much-needed air.

It's Friday evening and I've just finished recording the latest episode of my podcast underneath the makeshift sound-proofing tent that I've rigged up in the corner of my tiny living room. Despite losing the sponsorship deal, my audience has continued to grow and I'm so grateful to be getting more downloads than ever.

When I first started my podcast, a couple of years ago, I thought I was the only one who worried life wasn't going to plan, but it seems during these troubled times a lot of listeners have identified with the confessions of a forty-something fuck-up. Because of course, I can still feel like a fuck-up. That's one thing that hasn't changed. Even in a pandemic, I think I was the only person who failed to learn a language or write a novel or give *Bake Off* a run for its money with all that banana bread and sourdough.

But seriously. No, I am being serious.

Because, honestly, for the most part I'm just someone stumbling through life and making it up as I go along. It's like the older I get, the less I know. My life still doesn't resemble what society would have us believe my life *should* look like. Never married. No children. Zero interest in yoga and making ceramics. Not one photo of me on social media killing it in a bikini. I'm still asking the big questions and struggling to find the answers and for every win, I still have my wobbles and challenges and demons yapping at my ankles.

In fact when we weren't allowed guests into our homes The Fear was a regular visitor. I didn't tell a soul, but I should've known it would break lockdown rules.

That said, who *hasn't* felt any of that during the last eighteen months?

Trying not to lean too far out of the window, as I'm two storeys up, I draw in a deep lungful of potted geraniums, traffic fumes and Thai food from the cafe across the street that has just reopened. But now summer has arrived, restrictions are being lifted and things are finally returning to normal.*

---

* But what is 'normal' any more? And, more importantly, do any of us want to go back to it?

2. *Not having to share a bathroom.*

OK, so getting back to basics.

Turning away from the window, I check my watch. Crikey, is it that time already? I need to get ready. Hurrying into the bathroom, I get undressed and jump in the shower. Steam quickly rises. I love a long, hot shower. The longer and hotter the better. Which is just one of the reasons I love having my own bathroom.

When I first moved back to London, I couldn't afford the sky-high rents for my own flat, not even with the help of a loan from dad, so I found a spare room to rent online. That's how I met Edward; it was his spare room. However, there was no spare bathroom, which meant sharing a flat with Edward also meant sharing the bathroom and it was always fraught. I was forever getting told off for using all the hot water and taking too long in the shower. Then there was the time I nearly killed him when I took a lovely, relaxing bath with my essential oils and didn't clean it afterwards, and he slipped taking a shower.

And don't even *get* me started on The Loo Roll Wars.

Shampooing my hair, I give a little shudder. Thank God we weren't living together during the toilet-roll shortage, when everyone got FOMO and started panic-buying and supermarkets began rationing. It doesn't even bear thinking about. Knowing Edward, he would have probably had me cutting up newspaper into little squares to use instead. Well, he does love to recycle.

Rinsing my hair, I stand for another five minutes, relishing the feeling of hot water blasting and the relief that no one is going to tell me off for getting hair down the plughole,* before turning it off and reaching for a towel. Rubbing on body lotion, I quickly get dressed. Cotton dress. Flip-flops. Smear of lip gloss. After so many months spent in sweatpants,

---

* Er hello, isn't that why God invented drain unblocker?

my hair in a messy bun, I'm out of practice when it comes to getting ready to go out on a date.

With my hair still damp, I pad into the living room and start hunting for my phone. But it's not just having my own bathroom that I love. It's having my own everything. Grabbing a cushion, I look underneath it, then give it a quick plump. Who would've thought plumping cushions would be such an act of joy? Every time I do it, it makes me smile like a loon. I grab another. Because they aren't just scatter cushions from IKEA, they're *my* scatter cushions from IKEA. I got to choose them, along with the sofa I'm stylishly arranging them on, just like you see in all those glossy home magazines.

OK, so admittedly I don't have the big fancy house, or bi-folding doors into the garden (or a garden, for that matter), or empty acres of countertop space (though, let's be honest, *we all know* they've stuffed everything in the cupboards for the photos and really it's chaos on those kitchen counters), but a tiny flat the size of a postage stamp – but it still gives me such a buzz of pride to think I'm a homeowner.

After so many years spent renting rooms and sharing bathrooms and staying with friends and moving in with boyfriends and making up sofa beds and arguing with landlords over deposits (though I have to say, Edward was very good about that) I finally get to own my own place. It's all mine. Well, mine and the bank's and the shared ownership scheme's.

And, like every man likes to point out, size really isn't important.

3. My iPhone.

After searching for several minutes, I eventually find it in a coat pocket. I feel a beat of relief. OK, so I know it's a bit materialistic to be feeling thankful for an electronic gadget that, frankly, we're all addicted to, but it's been a lifeline when I couldn't see family or friends.

I notice I've got several unread messages. I'm on a WhatsApp group chat with my friends, Fiona, Holly and Michelle. We've been trying to arrange to meet up to celebrate the much-awaited Freedom Day. I can't believe it's been over a year since we all got together. They're all married with children and it was hard enough arranging to see each other before the pandemic, what with babysitters and nap times and after-school activities. Luckily, my phone's kept me connected.

Grabbing my house keys, I race out of the flat.

Sometimes a little *too* connected.

'So we're Zooming at nine,' instructed Mum when she'd FaceTimed me earlier. 'On the dot. Don't be late. Your father's included a new round this week. Guess the age of the actor, but in Roman numerals.'

I'd groaned inwardly. Mum still hasn't got the memo that no one is doing Zoom quizzes any more. With the lifting of restrictions had come a national sigh of relief that we can now escape our living rooms and the weekly trivia night with relatives we normally only see once a year, at Christmas. Unlike now when Auntie Verity, who lives in Spain and drives Dad bonkers, and Mum's cousin Fred who refuses to wear his teeth, are in my living room every Sunday.

'Don't you think that maybe we should stop doing the quiz now—'

'Stop?' Mum had looked aghast. She was wearing her sequin top, hair blow-dried.

'Well, I was just thinking, now things are going back to normal.'

'But we do it every week. *As a family.*'

And now she looked hurt. And I felt guilty.

'Philip! Come and speak to your daughter. She says she's leaving . . .'

Oh God. Mum's gone all Empty Nester on me.

'I didn't say that exactly—' I began, but I was cut off as Dad's face loomed large on the screen.

'Hello, love.'

'Hi, Dad.'

We grinned at each other. We both knew what each other was thinking. That's one of the many things I love about my dad, the ability to have a whole conversation without actually saying a word.

'You look well.'

'Your mother says I need to lose weight,' he grumbled.

'Don't we all,' I commiserated, my hand instinctively going to my waistband.

Thing is, I'd started out with good intentions. During the first lockdown, I was doing PE sessions with Joe Wicks in my living room, along with the rest of the country. I'd felt inspired. Determined. Motivated. The sun was shining, my feed was full of celebs posting fitness videos and dance routines and healthy-eating regimes and I was embracing it whole-heartedly.

One minute I was working my triceps with Davina, the next I was disco dancing in my kitchen with Sophie Ellis-Bextor. And it was quinoa with everything.

But gradually the novelty had worn off. The lockdowns wore on. Summer turned into winter. I twisted something. I couldn't focus. I felt exhausted but couldn't sleep. Overwhelmed and anxious, I'd started comfort eating. But it gave me no comfort. Whilst everyone around me was #livingtheirbestlockdownlife I would lie on the sofa eating cheese puffs and doom scrolling.

Forget Couch to 5K, it was couch to the kitchen cupboards and back again.

Which probably explains why, as the world is opening up again, I am not rocking a kick-ass yoga body like my friend Liza in LA, but emerging blinking into the light, two years older, fifteen pounds heavier, wearing elasticated waists and thinking WTF.

'She's put me on another one of her diets.'

'I have not put you a diet!' I could hear Mum yelling in the background. 'It's a healthy-eating plan that's mostly plant-based.'

'*Plant-based*.' Dad shook his head in disgust. 'Honestly, what does she think I am? A bloody vegan?'

I stifled a smile and nodded sympathetically.

'I'll have you know it's full of superfoods!' Mum came back into view, the top of her hair-sprayed head reappearing behind Dad's, and there was a bit of a tussle over the iPad. 'If you don't believe me, ask Alexa!'

During lockdown, my parents got an Amazon Echo and it's been like having a new member of the family. I'll be on the phone to Mum, having a conversation, and she'll interrupt me to ask Alexa her opinion, or tell her to do something. Once I overheard Dad on his way out to his allotment, pausing to ask her if he needed a coat.

'Hi Carol, what can I do for you?' chimed Alexa cheerfully.

'Leave Alexa out of it,' Dad replied crossly.

It seemed Alexa was also being used to settle arguments.

'I'm just worried about your health, that's all. I don't want anything to happen to you, not after last time . . .'

A while back Dad was in a car accident and we nearly lost him. We rarely talk about it, but you never forget something like that. It changes you. As Mum's voice caught in her throat, I watched his face soften.

'Is that what all this is about?' Pulling her towards him,

he kissed her affectionately. 'In that case, I'll eat as many superfoods as you want, love.'

My parents have been married for nearly fifty years and the secret to a long relationship appears to be deep affection and irritation in equal measure.

'So we'll see you at nine,' she said, turning back to me.

Resistance was futile. 'On the dot.' I nodded, then braced myself for what was coming next.

'Will Edward be joining us?'

Mum asked me this every week, and every week I had to make an excuse.

'No, he's busy.'

'*Again?*' She frowned into the camera. 'He's always busy.'

'He's working.'

'*On a Sunday?*'

Oh God, this was ridiculous. I was going to have to tell her the truth.

Just not right now.

'Sorry, you're breaking up—'

Another wonderful thing about iPhones, is you can pretend the Wi-Fi signal is weak and you can't hear someone.

'I'm losing you, I better go—'

But of course Mum's not going to be deterred by something as trivial as a weak Wi-Fi signal, real or not, and launches into one of her stories about someone I don't know who has died, apparently caused by working on a Sunday. Fortunately Dad gets the message.

'All right, bye love.'

'Bye Dad, bye Mum.'

'Sorry, I'm having trouble with that,' chimed an electronic voice.

'Bye Alexa.'

4. *Date night.*

It's a gorgeous evening and outside the streets are busy. Heading away from the river, I climb upwards, past pavement cafes and restaurant terraces and beer gardens filled with people making the most of their newfound freedoms. It's heartening to see the city coming back to life.

After a few minutes I reach the top of Richmond Hill, which offers the most stunning view. I swear, you'd never think you were in London. Beneath me the trees and meadows sweep away with the River Thames as it winds its way towards the horizon. I once read it's the only view in London covered by an Act of Parliament. Lucky, as it's my favourite. Which is why we've arranged to meet here.

In front of me there's a wide gravelled path lined with benches, all of them filled with people enjoying both the view and drinks from the local pub. I cast my eyes along them, searching out his face as I continue walking. I feel a slight flutter of anticipation and excitement. He must be here somewhere.

And then I spot him. Just before he spots me and jumps up excitedly, licking my face and covering me in slobbery kisses.

'*Arthur!* Hello, boy!'

Arthur might be a dog but he's the size of a small pony and he almost knocks me over with his enthusiastic greeting.

'Someone's pleased to see you.'

In the middle of being bashed by Arthur's tail, I look down to see Edward sitting on the bench, smiling at me, his dark wavy hair falling over his glasses. He stands up and gives me a kiss. 'He's not the only one.'

'Hi,' I grin, kissing him back. 'You smell nice.'

'It's my new organic shower gel. Citrus and ginger.'

'Mmm,' I nod approvingly.

'Bit pricey, but I thought I'd push the boat out, what with it being date night.'

Edward says this with a completely earnest expression and I resist the urge to tease him. He takes our date nights very seriously. Instead, I wrap my arms around his waist as he gives me a hug. I'll never take hugging for granted again.

Date nights were originally Edward's idea. As a couple who don't live together, it had been hard to keep the romance alive during lockdown,* so once a week we'd get out of our respective flats and comfy clothes and meet up for a bike ride, or a walk along the river, or a picnic in the park.

Spending time together got easier after the government introduced support bubbles and I could join Edward's. Though, to be honest, there was rather a lot of bubble, bubble, toil and trouble from Mum who wanted me to join theirs, and Fiona, who said my god-daughter was desperate to see me, though I have a sneaking suspicion it was more Fiona who was desperate for help with childcare after her nanny went back to Brazil. As my friend Cricket said, single, childless women who live alone have never been so popular.

'So, shall we have a drink?'

'Have you ever known me to say no?' I laugh as we break apart, then glance across the street at the local pub where there's a long line forming out of the door. 'Damn, have you seen the queue?'

'How about a gin and tonic?'

'Seriously, Edward, it's halfway down the street. We'll be waiting ages to be served.'

I turn to him, but he doesn't seem to be listening and has

---

* Saying that, judging by the reported number of divorces caused by being cooped up 24/7, it might have been harder to keep the romance alive if we *were* living together.

sat back down on the bench and is rummaging inside his backpack. I feel a beat of exasperation. Edward has a dreadful habit of switching off, like my faulty kettle.

'Not if you bring your own,' he replies evenly, producing a bottle each of gin and tonic, two glasses and a lemon.

Exasperation is swiftly replaced by a swell of love. My observations of Mum and Dad were right. Irritation and affection. I think it's the cornerstone of any relationship.

'Why do you always think of everything?' I sit next to him on the bench.

'Be prepared,' he intones sternly, slicing the lemon with his Swiss Army knife.

'Huh?'

'Boy Scouts,' he explains and I notice he's even brought ice. Of course.

'I was banned from the Brownies,' I counter.

'Why does that not surprise me?'

'It was my first day and I was so excited I literally peed my pants. All the other Brownies sitting cross-legged next to me started screaming. Caused quite a scene.'

He laughs and adds a large slug of gin to each glass. Edward always pours large measures. It's one of the many reasons I love him.

'So, are you staying at mine tonight?' he asks as I tickle Arthur, who is sitting sphinx-like on the floor, staring down a squirrel. 'I don't have the boys this weekend.'

Since his divorce a couple of years previously, Edward's teenage sons have continued living with his ex-wife in the country during the week, which made sense as it's near their school, but spend a lot of the weekends with him in London.

'Fraid I can't. I've got the Zoom pub quiz at 9 p.m.'

He groans loudly.

'Don't worry, I made another excuse for you. Unless you

want to join us this week . . .' I trail off, but already know the answer.

'You know how much I hate pub quizzes. All those tedious anagrams and close-ups of household items. I'll never be able to eat a cornflake again.'

'You don't eat cornflakes, you eat organic porridge,' I remind him, but he pretends not to hear me and passes me a glass.

'What shall we drink to?' he asks, raising his in a toast.

'How about Freedom Day?' I suggest. 'It's in a couple of weeks.'

'How about freedom from your mother's weekly quiz,' he quips, only Edward doesn't quip and I laugh at his straight face. 'I know, how about to us,' he says simply, his eyes never leaving mine. 'And the future.'

For a split second my mind flashes back to when I first moved back to London a few years ago, single, forty-something and heartbroken, and I think how I never thought I'd get here. Unexpectedly I feel a twist of anxiety. I want us to just stay like this for ever, exactly where we are. Just a couple with their dog, sitting together on a bench, enjoying the simple pleasures of a warm summer's evening, a gorgeous view, stiff drinks and each other's company. But life's been on hold for long enough. It's time to start our lives again.

'To us and the future,' I repeat, smiling.

Because the future is always bright. *Right?*

More things I'm grateful for:
1. *The beautiful sunset this evening, because although I'm loving that there's been less pressure for perfection during the pandemic, since social media got all unfiltered and authentic I quite miss all those sunset shots and seeing what everyone's having for dinner.*

19

2. *Thermal underwear, for saving me and my octogenarian friend Cricket from freezing to death this winter when we could only meet up outside.*
3. *The mute button (alas my Uncle Fred has still not found it – or his teeth for that matter). OK, so he's technically not my Uncle, he's my first cousin once removed, but it's a bit of a mouthful – especially for Fred; try saying that with no teeth in.*
4. *Elasticated waists (see earlier).*
5. *Gin and tonics and cheese puffs – a.k.a 'How to Survive a Global Pandemic' by Nell Stevens.*
6. *Nature, for showing us that life goes on when things got really scary.*
7. *Feeling secretly relieved when the sponsorship deal for my podcast fell through. As much I needed the money, it didn't feel right to go into paid partnership with a big beauty brand that profits from telling women it's bad to age. Because, as Cricket says, the only antidote to ageing is death.*
8. *All those celebrities who posted selfies of themselves in bikinis in lockdown telling us to #staysafe. Because I felt a lot safer after seeing their bikini selfies.*
9. *My sense of humour.*

No Clapping Matter

On Sunday I get up early to meet Cricket for a walk in Hyde Park. We set off in trainers with good intentions, but the sun is out and so are the deckchairs, so it's not long before we find ourselves plonked in the stripy cotton hammocks, bare feet in the grass.

'You know, all this business of ten thousand steps a day was just a marketing ploy anyway,' she's saying now, as I sit with my eyes closed, face turned to the skies. 'It was to sell a pedometer called a Manpo-Kei to capitalize on the success of the 1964 Tokyo Olympics. In Japanese, *manpo-kei* literally means ten thousand steps.'

'Wow really? That's so cool you remember that.'

'Of course I don't remember. It was the sixties,' she snorts. 'No one who lived through the sixties remembers much of anything. That's why we have Google.'

I open my eyes and look across to see she's squinting at her iPhone, still wearing her leopard-print mask, which she refuses to take off.

'So it's all nonsense really.'

'Well, that's lucky,' I grin. 'I don't think I'm averaging anywhere near that. I spend most of my time in my flat.'

'According to this, if you go up and down the stairs forty-two times at home you'll do over a thousand,' she reads.

'I'd also need to buy new stair carpet,' I reply and she looks up at me from her phone and throws her head back with laughter.

It's good to see Cricket laughing again, even if it is in a mask. While it's been hard for everyone these past eighteen months, it's been especially hard for Cricket because her age made her particularly vulnerable. Though, from the outside you'd never have known it. 'Me! A vulnerable person!' she'd cried, when she first received the letters informing her she needed to shield at home. 'I'm not extremely vulnerable! How dare they!' She was furious and indignant. She was also eighty-something. And while she didn't seem remotely elderly or vulnerable to me, with her fashionable grey bob, sequined plimsolls and *joie de vivre*, the harsh statistics showed that she was very much at risk.

When Cricket and I had first met, we were both lost and lonely. She was recently widowed and I'd just broken up with my fiancé and moved back to London. I'd gone to interview her for an obituary I was writing about her late husband, Monty Williamson, a famous playwright. Both trying to start over in lives we didn't recognize, we struck up an unlikely friendship. Her girlfriends had passed away due to illness and old age and she missed them terribly; mine hadn't died, they'd just got married and had babies, but I missed them too.

We would meet up regularly. I helped her set up a free community library project, a network of little neighbourhood book exchanges called Monty's Mini Libraries, in honour of her late husband and she hired me to finish one of her husband's plays. We even went on holiday together to Spain to scatter his ashes. Despite our difference in age, we had lots in common and our outings were always the highlight of my week. Cricket had a lust for life. Her real name was

Catherine, but she'd been nicknamed Cricket as a child because she was so chirpy and it had stuck. She enjoyed doing new things and kept herself busy with various classes and projects and visits to art galleries and museums. And yet, much of it was as a way to cope with her grief.

'It's important to always have something in the diary,' she'd once told me. 'You need a reason to get out of bed. You need to keep up a routine.'

But then everything got wiped clean from her diary and life became a succession of blank pages. Empty day, followed by endless empty day. Without her daily routine Cricket soon began to suffer. Routine is a funny old thing. It gets such a bad rap. We think of it as dull and predictable and long to escape it. But routine is like a clothes hanger. You hang your days on it and it gives them shape. Without it life has no structure; if you're not careful it can collapse in a heap on the floor.

Before the pandemic, Cricket had downsized from her rambling old house in Notting Hill. At first she'd loved her smaller flat, which was only around the corner, but now, forced to stay at home it felt claustrophobic. We spoke regularly. Luckily, she had a smartphone and knew how to use it. Still, FaceTime couldn't compensate for human contact and the isolation soon began to take its toll.

'It won't be this wretched virus that kills me, it will be loneliness,' she'd complained.

She tried to keep her spirits up, but it was tough staring at the same four walls with only the TV for company. She missed Monty more than ever. While every week brought grim news about her contemporaries in care homes. 'I'm not afraid of death,' she told me, after attending yet another funeral on Zoom, 'but I don't want it to be while I'm standing on the doorstep with a torch, clapping.'

When Christmas was cancelled she lost weight and stopped

wearing her trademark red lipstick. I'd never put Cricket down as someone who could appear frail – her life force is so big – but her spirit seemed to diminish. As if she drew oxygen from the outside world, like a plant, and now she was being starved of it.

Watching her fade away on FaceTime, I knew I had to do something.

So we bought thermals.

People often say their lives are saved by many things; it's usually something spiritual or meaningful, like getting sober or walking the Camino de Santiago pilgrimage. In Cricket's case it was saved by thermal underwear from Marks & Spencer. I'm convinced of it. The change was remarkable.

'Do you think I should join TikTok?' she'd asked soon after, as we sat outside on opposite ends of a garden bench, obeying the two-metre rule.

It was the depths of winter but, thanks to thermals, we were now able to see each other again. Finding where to see each other had been a bit trickier. Both of us lived in flats and neither of us had our own garden. Cricket had a small balcony but it could only be accessed from inside. And during lock-down, park benches were strictly off limits, unless you were resting for five minutes during exercise. Which isn't very long when you're forty-something, never mind eighty-something.

But what Cricket did have was the key to one of the private communal gardens that Notting Hill is famous for. Which meant we could go and sit and have a chat without worrying the police were going to come and arrest us, or we were going to freeze to death.

'*TikTok?*'

'Well, if it's good enough for a Dame . . .'

As she spoke, Cricket straightened up a bit. Apparently

she and a certain famous English actress who was also a Dame had both been at The Old Vic theatre company as young actresses.

'Is it?'

'Yes, I read about it in the papers. Apparently she's been doing dance routines with her grandson on TikTok. I watched a few and she's very good. *Obviously*.'

'Obviously.' I nodded.

There was still a little bit of, how shall I put it, 'healthy rivalry' on Cricket's part.

'And you know how much I like to dance.'

I nod, remembering the time I'd taken her to an eighties concert and she had spent the whole evening bopping away, much to my delight and the annoyance of the grumpy woman seated behind her. Such a shame Cricket spilled that glass of red wine on her by total accident.

'Well, in that case, why not?' I encouraged. I was determined to be enthusiastic and supportive. Cricket once told me not to worry about growing older, but to worry about becoming dull. She was certainly never that. 'It sounds like a great idea. Who are you going to do dance routines with?'

She shot me a look.

Actually, on second thoughts.

'No, no way.' I shook my head, firmly. 'Have you never seen me dance?'

'Nonsense, my dear, you'll be marvellous.' She smiled brightly underneath her purple fedora. 'It will be like Zumba.'

'I thought you hated Zumba.'

'No, that was armchair yoga.'

'Why didn't you like armchair yoga?'

'Oh heavens, you should have seen it.' She rolled her eyes. 'It was full of old people!'

*

Thankfully The Winter of Our Discontent, as Cricket came to call it, was now firmly in the past, along with our thermals. We'd finally ditched them as the weather turned warmer and the evenings grew longer and, with the easing of restrictions, we'd taken to meeting up regularly in the park to go for a walk or just to sit and pass the time of day, like we were doing now.

'How about next time we meet we go to an exhibition,' I suggest. 'Now museums and galleries have been allowed to reopen.'

I thought Cricket would jump at the suggestion, but instead she just shrugs.

'Yes, maybe,' she says coolly.

'There must be lots of things you're dying to see.'

'Hmmm.'

I peer across at her in her deckchair but she steadfastly avoids my gaze and pretends to be absolutely fascinated by a jogger stretching his hamstrings.

'To get out and about again after being cooped up inside for all that time,' I persist.

'I am, it's just—' She hesitates, then exhales sharply and tuts. 'I just feel silly admitting it.'

'Admitting what?'

There's a pause.

'That I'm scared of life going back to normal,' she blurts. 'There! I've said it.'

She gives her shoulders a little shake and looks across at me, pushing her sunglasses on her head, and allowing our eyes to meet. Hers peer out over her mask, red-rimmed and glistening.

'That's not silly,' I say supportively. 'I think it's natural to feel a little anxious.' I think about my and Edward's toast to the future and how it all feels so uncertain.

'Well, I'm furious,' she says crossly, giving a sharp sniff. 'What on earth would Monty think?'

'I think he'd be understanding,' I reason.

She gives a little laugh. 'You didn't know Monty. He'd be furious with me too. Life's for living, he'd tell me. Get out there, my girl. Grab the bull by the horns. This is what we've all been waiting for.'

'I don't think you're going to find many bulls in Hyde Park,' I reply and watch the corners of her eyes crinkle up. 'OK, so I think you're smiling, but it's rather difficult to tell.'

She finally unhooks her mask from her ears to reveal her smile underneath.

'I never thought I'd get used to having to wear one of these dratted things, and now look at me! I'm nervous *not* to wear one.'

'Well, that one is rather snazzy,' I admit.

'I got it to match my bicycle helmet,' she says, looking rather pleased, then sighs. 'Not that I've been on my bicycle for a long time. Too many crowds.'

'Baby steps,' I say gently.

For a moment she looks thoughtful. 'You know, when Monty used to go away touring with his plays I'd miss him terribly at first, but after a while I'd get used to his absence. It became normal. Not having him around the house. So that when he came back it was a bit of a shock. To suddenly find the house filled with his music and cigarette smoke and mess. To find lights left on, doors flung open, red wine rings on the kitchen table . . .'

She breaks off and laughs. 'Sorry, I'm probably not painting a very good picture of him, am I? But I loved it all really. It just took me a little while to adjust and there was always a difficult period of trying to get used to each other again. It was like being strangers again and not in a good way.'

Listening to Cricket, I can see she's miles away.

'We'd argue and I would get upset. It happened at the end of every tour, so much so, I began to dread his return. So Monty decided to give it a name. He called it our "Re-Entry", like when the space shuttle returns from outer space to the earth's atmosphere. And somehow, just by acknowledging it, it became less worrying . . .' She breaks off, remembering. 'When it was difficult or hard, we'd just say, oh well, it's to be expected, it's our Re-Entry. And then we'd laugh about it, and it would all be all right.'

She smiles at the memory and her face brightens.

'I guess this is our Re-Entry,' I say, smiling. 'The whole world's Re-Entry.'

'Yes,' she nods, and I watch her mind returning reluctantly from the past to the present. 'Yes, I suppose it is.'

I'm grateful for:
1. *No one ever seeing those TikTok videos, thanks to Cricket not knowing how to upload them. Cricket was a natural but I was terrible at the routines. Seriously, I am never going on* Strictly.
2. *Being able to reassure Cricket about her fears, even just a little bit.* *
3. *Monty, for giving it a name and making it less scary, because Re-Entry is going to be different for all of us.*

---

* Forget FOMO (the Fear of Missing Out), now it's FOGO (the Fear of Going Out).

WhatsApp Group: Freedom Day Get-Together

Fiona
OK, so we still don't have a plan for 19 July.

Holly
What's happening on 19 July?

Fiona
Freedom Day! The government are lifting nearly all restrictions.
No more masks or social distancing!

Finally!

Holly
I've totally lost track of the days. Are we nearly there yet?

Michelle
Freddy used to ask that as soon as he got in the car. Now it's my husband. All he talks about is finally being able to stand at the bar and order a pint.

Ha ha, trust Max.

Holly
I've just looked at the calendar. 19 July is a Monday. Who celebrates on a Monday?

All the nightclubs are opening at midnight on Sunday.

Fiona

A nightclub! I can't remember the last time I was in a nightclub.

Holly

I am NOT going clubbing.

Michelle

I'm in bed by nine. Who's awake at midnight?!

Young people ☺

Holly

And puppies. Coco's six months but she still wakes up in the night. I swear it's harder than when Olivia was a baby.

Fiona

Izzy and Lucas can't wait to meet her!

I can't believe it's been over a year since we all got together.
I won't recognize you all!

Holly

I don't recognize myself ☹

Fiona

OK, I'm going to book a table at the pub for lunch next Saturday.
That way we can bring all the kids.

Michelle

I thought it was supposed to be Freedom Day?
Just kidding ☺

Edward's taking his sons to a cricket match.
OK if he comes for a drink later?

Fiona
Of course!

Michelle
Trust me, if Max has anything to do with it, it will be a liquid lunch.

Fab. Can't wait to see you all xx

Friends Reunited

On the Saturday following Freedom Day I wake up in a really good mood. Not just because it's another gorgeous day and the sun is pouring in through the gap in my blinds. Or because, at long last, all the restrictions have been lifted and life, officially at least, can now return to normal. But because I'm going to see my oldest group of friends.

And I cannot wait! I have been looking forward to this reunion for ages. It's unfathomable to think we've all been living in the same city yet it's over a year since we all got together. It's just bonkers. But then over the last eighteen months, time has taken on a weird elastic quality and it feels like both for ever and only yesterday that we all crammed into Max and Michelle's tiny terrace to eat home-cooked curry, get drunk and celebrate New Year's Eve together.

Buoyed up by the blue skies and sunshine and the thought of hugging my godchildren, I make my coffee then take it back into the bedroom where I have a quick rootle through my wardrobe. It's only lunch at the pub, but I'm thrilled to have an excuse to wear some of the clothes that have been hanging untouched for what feels like for ever. Plus, I want to make a bit of an effort as it's ages since I saw everyone.

An hour later my coffee's gone stone cold and I'm feeling a tad less excited. Nothing fits. Spaghetti straps are no longer my friend and instead are holding two little pockets of jiggly flesh hostage underneath my armpits. Probably as a ransom

32

for the safe return of my triceps, along with my waist, which appears to have been stolen during lockdown. As for shorts, I'm not sure it's Freedom Day for *these* legs.

Saying that, I can't blame everything on the pandemic. According to all these articles I keep reading, I am now officially in perimenopause. Which sounds like a lovely Caribbean island; one of those exotic, exclusive French-speaking ones frequented by rockstars and supermodels, where everyone wafts around in kaftans and all the furniture is made out of driftwood and shells.

Sadly perimenopause is not an exclusive Caribbean island, but the rather less exotic reality of finding I'm of an age where my hormones are starting to go haywire. Frankly, wafting around in kaftans sounds like so much more fun, which is lucky, as at this rate a kaftan is the only thing that's going to fit.

Thankfully, I find a pretty floral maxi dress in the back of my wardrobe that's both flattering and floor-length. God love a maxi dress! It even has cap sleeves. Talk about a win-win. All it needs is pockets and it would be the trifecta of wonderfulness. As for my hair, no amount of blow-drying and products can disguise the fact I'm in desperate need of a cut and some highlights, so instead I stick on a sunhat. Cricket always says hats are like the fourth emergency service, and looking in the mirror, I'm in total agreement.

'*Hola! Qué gusto de verte!*'

Fiona is the first to arrive, sweeping into the beer garden, her arms open wide and a huge smile on her tanned face.

'Since when did you start speaking Spanish?' I say in astonishment.

'During lockdown when I got furloughed,' she replies, coming in for a hug, then hesitating. 'Are we hugging?'

'I don't know, are we?' I proffer an elbow instead and try not to think about all those months sitting on my sofa eating crisps when I could have been conjugating.

Tucking her swingy blonde hair behind her ear (even during a pandemic, Fiona is no stranger to a professional blow-dry and a great colourist), she frowns, then throws her arms around me.

'*Oh, dame un abrazo!*'

'I suppose that means we are,' I laugh, hugging her back. Though, frankly I have no idea if that's what she said as I don't speak Spanish. Unlike Fiona, who sounds practically fluent. I make a mental note to download the Duolingo app later.

'It's so good to see you. You look amazing.'

'You too.'

'Auntie Nell!'

Hearing my name being yelled, I turn around to see Izzy hurtling towards us through the tables and chairs, like a ball in a pinball machine. She must have grown a foot taller since the last time I saw her.

'Oh my, you're huge!' I grin, scooping her up, though she's really quite heavy now. 'And you've lost more baby teeth!'

I've seen Izzy with Fiona a few times over the past eighteen months, but not nearly as much as I would like, and every time it's as if someone pressed the fast forward button and she's even more grown up. Gone are the cute fairy wings and blonde curls. Now her hair is cut into a bob and she's sporting a rather cool pair of denim dungarees.

'I'm seven and a half,' she says proudly, smiling to show off her new front teeth.

'Soon you'll catch up with me,' I tell her and she giggles loudly.

'No, I won't, silly, you're old!'

Fortunately at this point we're interrupted by the arrival of Fiona's husband, David, and Izzy's brother, Lucas, who appears to have morphed into David's mini-me more than ever, with their matching spectacles and taciturn demeanours; followed by Holly and Adam, their daughter, Olivia, and new rescue puppy, Coco, on a retractable lead that's getting tangled up around everything and causing chaos.

It's messy and loud and exactly the way a reunion between old friends should be. Only this time instead of cheek-kissing, there's lots of awkward elbow-and-fist-bumping while exclaiming how crazy it's all been and how grateful we all are to be able to see everyone again.

Because we are all grateful beyond measure, as is everyone who is seeing friends and family and loved ones again for the first time in for ever. And as we move chairs and order drinks and squash around the tables, sharing jokes and catching up and trading affectionate insults, we slip back into it as if we've never been apart, while thinking how we're never going to take this simple act of getting together for granted again.

'Where are Max and Michelle? Are they coming?' asks someone after a few minutes.

'Max texted to say they're running a bit late.'

'Well, they have got their hands full now with four . . .'

'Hang on . . . is that Max?'

We all look over as Max makes his entrance. At least I think it's Max. It's hard to tell as he's hidden underneath various bags, scooters and backpacks, with children hanging off every limb.

He reminds me of one of those one-man bands you see, with various instruments strapped to their back and chest. Only instead of playing a guitar with a base drum on his back and a mouth-organ round his neck, he's got Tom in a

35

toddler-carrier, Lily and Rose in each hand, Freddy, who's nearly a teenager, trailing behind him, and a dummy firmly between his gritted teeth.

Forget having a pair of cymbals strapped to his knees, Max looks like he's *on* his knees.

'Sorry I'm late, Michelle had to finish up an order, she sends her apologies and says she'll be here ASAP.'

'I saw her new online store, it looks amazing!'

'Yes, business is booming, she's now expanded into home-wares and soft furnishings.'

Max was made redundant just before the pandemic struck and wasn't able to find another job. Meanwhile, Michelle got out her sewing machine and started making masks, of all designs and colours. Demand was high and she was inundated with orders, so Max took over the childcare. It was only meant to be temporary, but she's been so successful, she decided to set up her own business.

'Wow, that's fantastic.'

Meanwhile Max still hasn't found a job so he's now a stay-at-home dad.

'It's great, as I get to spend time with the kids,' he's now saying, while making a start on his pint. He downs it in one go.

'Parenting's thirsty work,' jokes Adam.

'Yes, isn't it,' quips Max, coming up for air, though I have to say he seems a bit frazzled as he juggles Tom on his lap, loads up Lily's iPad, finds Rose's felt-tip pens and lets Freddy play games on his iPhone. 'Back in the office, David?' he asks, looking wistful.

'The home office,' replies David and I catch Fiona doing her Big Eyes, the ones she always thinks no one will notice, and the ones that everyone always notices. 'We had one built in the garden during lockdown.'

'We've never spent so much time together, especially now I'm working from home too. Though I'm on the kitchen table.' She gives a strained little laugh. 'But he's missing his colleagues and can't wait to get back, isn't that right, darling?'

'No, not really,' says David, rather cheerfully.

'Well, I for one can't wait to get back to work at the museum,' she says tightly.

'I'm quite enjoying the change,' continues David. 'That commute was murder.'

I glance at Fiona. Forget the commute, she looks like she's about to commit murder.

'Now I only have to walk into the garden to do a bit of alfresco Zooming.'

'*Por Dios*,' she mutters and drains her wine glass.

We order another round.

'How about you, Nell?'

As more beers and another bottle of rosé appears, the children decamp to the small playground at the bottom of the beer garden, supervised as usual by Freddy, who at twelve-going-on-teenager can no longer be bribed by his dad's phone and will only take cold hard cash.

'How's the podcast going?' asks Holly, who's been showing us the estate agent's brochure of a gorgeous cottage they've just put an offer on. After the last eighteen months, she and Adam have decided they're selling up and moving to the countryside. I'm happy for them but gutted for me. I'm really going to miss them. 'I loved last week's episode.'

Now all my friends know I'm the person behind the once-anonymous podcast, I feel a bit like Lady Whistledown in *Bridgerton*. My secret is out. Luckily, all my friends love it.

'Thanks. It's going really great,' I smile. 'I've got a lot of new listeners.'

'What about Edward?'

'Oh, he doesn't listen to it,' I laugh, amused at the thought. 'Edward's old school. He refuses to listen to any podcasts or do any social media. He says the whole world's addicted to their phones and keeps threatening to pull out his old Nokia.'

'No social media? How is that even possible?'

'He's right of course,' nods Adam, not looking up from his phone.

'Maybe he doesn't want to hear Nell moaning about him,' quips Max.

'Max!' gasps Michelle, suddenly appearing at his shoulder and swatting him.

'Oh, hi babe,' he grins, quickly handing over Tom, who's delighted to see his mum. Though not, I suspect, as much as Max, who now has both hands free for his beer.

'I take it you've never listened to Nell's podcast,' says Michelle loyally. 'Nell doesn't talk about Edward, she talks candidly *and humorously* about life –' she grins at me across the table '– and invites listeners onto the show to share their stories.'

'Honestly, why is it men always think we're talking about them?' tuts Fiona.

'Because you are,' grins Max, only this time he receives a look from Michelle that's so terrifying he looks suitably chastened.

'Sorry, Nell, I was only joking,' he apologizes.

'It's OK, I'm not offended,' I grin. 'Michelle's right, after I had my friend Cricket on the show, I got so many messages. So I thought why not invite more women on to share their stories? So many of them have said they felt like they didn't have a voice and being on my podcast gave them a real sense of power.'

'What about men? Can they share their stories too?' asks David.

'Um, yes . . . of course . . . everyone's welcome,' I smile, a little taken aback. David always makes me feel a bit intimidated as he's a partner at this major-league law firm and is both uber successful and uber serious. I didn't think he even *knew* I had a podcast.

'In that case, can I share my knee injury story,' chimes Max.

'Argh, Max, no!' yells the whole table, erupting rowdily into loud groans and hoots of laughter. Trust Max. He just can't help it. 'No one else needs to hear the knee story!'

And suddenly the conversation changes direction and we're back here again, making fun of Max for still insisting he could have turned professional and rivalled Beckham, were it not for his old football injury; old friends with their old jokes and the same old stories. It's reassuring to see that while so much has changed, nothing has changed.

Yet, something *has* changed. No longer am I the poor, feckless friend, with nothing to report but her broken engagement, rented room and unemployment. I might not have set up a successful business during the pandemic, become fluent in Spanish, or be moving to an amazing country pad, but I have a job! A boyfriend! My own flat and podcast! A life that warrants exclamation marks!

In fact, sipping my glass of rosé and enjoying the warm, fuzzy glow from the wine, being in the company of my friends, and looking forward to Edward soon arriving, I'm reminded of an article I once read. About how life is like trying to balance a three-legged stool: Career, Relationship, Self. And while I seem to have spent most of mine wobbling all over the place, trying not to topple over, finally, at long last I have all the legs of my life firmly on the floor.

I'm grateful for:

1. *Feeling inspired by Fiona to learn a second language. I've chosen French as I know a little bit from school and I've already whizzed through level one; I'm determined to be fluent in no time!*

2. *Ice: because the only thing chilled was Max after his fourth pint (is it just me, or is wine never cold enough?).*

3. *Ibuprofen and a hot water bottle as I put my back out lifting up Izzy.*

4. *Having someone to laugh and gossip with on the way home. It's OK being single, but after saying goodbye to everyone, it made a lovely change not going home alone.**

---

* Though Edward refuses to gossip and is absolutely no fun at all in that respect.

The Morning After

Oh my God, I love him, BUT THE SNORING.

After all that drinking, I'd planned on having a Sunday lie-in, but instead the next day I'm awoken at some ungodly hour by what sounds like a pneumatic drill in my ear. Groggy with sleep, I try to roll over to push him, but I'm pinned to the bed by his heavy body.

'Shurrup,' I groan, elbowing him in the ribs.

'Ouch,' protests Edward.

'Stop snoring.'

'I'm not the one that's snoring.'

'Huh?'

I blearily open my eyes to see it's not my boyfriend, but a huge hairy white lump squashed between us.

'Arthur,' I grumble, trying to shove him awake, but he's lying half across me, dead to the world.

'Who let him on the bed?' demands Edward, hoisting himself up on his elbows. He reaches for his glasses on the bedside table.

'Not me!' I fib, which is pointless as Edward knows I'm fibbing. I know I shouldn't, but I let Arthur sleep on the bed when Edward isn't here, and now he's got into a bit of a habit.

'I'll go make some tea,' he says, getting up and pulling on his boxer shorts. Leaving me lying in bed feeling a bit sorry for myself. I drank too much wine and I've got a bit of a hangover. After a few minutes he brings me in a cup of tea. All is forgiven.

'Thank you,' I smile appreciatively.

Edward doesn't drink coffee, but he does make a really good cup of tea. Exactly the right colour. I once dated someone who made it so weak it looked like washing-up water. We lasted less than two weeks as we soon discovered we had nothing in common. I've since wondered if instead of trawling through someone's dating profile, a good way of finding out if you're compatible would be to both look at a colour chart of cups of tea to see which one you are. If he's a weak and milky and you're a strong, stewed type, the chances are you're not a match. It's never going to work.

'I forgot to bring my toothbrush,' Edward is saying now, as he squashes onto the bed next to me.

'I think I've got a spare one underneath the sink in the bathroom.'

'Oh, thanks.'

'Are you staying here tonight?'

'Actually I was rather hoping you might come back to mine after we've taken Arthur for a walk in the park. I've got an early meeting and I don't have a change of clothes.'

'I've told you to leave things at mine.'

'I know, but I'm not sure where I'd put them . . .' He trails off as we survey my tiny bedroom. I just have room for a single wardrobe, which is already stuffed to the brim. Most of my clothes appear to be piled up on a chair. 'You know, if we moved in together we wouldn't have these problems,' he continues.

'I'm not sure we'll both be able to squeeze into my flat with Arthur. He takes up the whole bed as it is.' I laugh.

'You know he's not allowed on the bed,' he grumbles.

'At your flat, no, but at my flat the rules are different,' I smile, ruffling his hair. He really does look cute in his square-framed glasses and boxers. Edward runs and does yoga and has not succumbed to the Lockdown 15.*

'Anyway, I'm not talking about me moving into your flat, I'm talking about you moving into mine.'

'What, like before?'

'Well, no, I wouldn't expect you to be in the spare room.'

'Edward, that was a joke.'

'Oh, right, I see, yes of course,' he nods, then pauses, a deep furrow appearing between his eyebrows. 'Only, I'm not joking. I'm serious. It makes sense. All this forwards and backwards, to-ing and fro-ing. And financially. Paying two mortgages, two sets of bills, two sets of council tax . . .'

'You old romantic.'

He colours. 'I don't mean it like that. I love you.'

He says it so matter of factly. After a lifetime of complicated relationships, I'm still not used to that.

'I love you too.'

Leaning my head back against the pillow, I smile sideways at him and his face brightens. He reaches for my hand, slipping his strong, slim fingers between mine, and looks across at me, steadily.

'Let's get married.'

I take a gulp of tea, but it's too hot and burns my mouth.

'Married? What, now?'

'Well, we'd get engaged first,' he says, amused by my expression.

I'm rendered momentarily speechless by Edward's proposal. I hadn't been expecting it, which I know seems a bit daft when you think about it, as we've been together for eighteen

---

* Lockdown 15: otherwise known as the fifteen pounds I gained during lockdown.

months, but after his divorce I'd presumed he wouldn't want to get married again and somehow it didn't feel important.

'You don't look pleased.' Searching my face, Edward's own looks suddenly doubtful.

'Of course I'm pleased! I was just expecting tea not a proposal,' I quickly reassure him.

'It just feels like the next step,' he continues.

The. Next. Step.

As his words peg out in front of me, they unexpectedly trigger feelings I thought were dead and buried. I have a sudden, vivid memory of being engaged and pregnant with Ethan, my ex, and all the hope and anticipation and heartbreak that went with it. It comes from out of nowhere and it's as if someone has squeezed the air right out of my chest. Back then, that's all I wanted – to be married with a baby – but now things have changed. And I've changed with it.

Haven't I?

'What about the boys?' I force myself back to the present.

I've grown quite close to Edward's twin sons, who are lovely, albeit typical messy teenagers who drape wet towels and leave empty cups all over the flat, but it's all been really casual. I'm just their dad's girlfriend. Getting married to Edward would change all that. It would make me their stepmum. The thought feels a bit sobering.

'They love you,' he says confidently. 'And anyway, it's not like we'll all be living together as they'll both be heading off to uni soon. They have their own lives now.'

'Yes. Right.'

I grab hold of myself. Nell, you're being ridiculous. Edward loves you and you love Edward. You don't need to worry. Edward isn't Ethan. Nothing's going to go wrong. Things are different now. *I'm* different now.

'Sorry, I didn't do that properly, did I? I don't have a ring or anything—'

Edward looks troubled and, pushing away any doubts, I grab his face between both hands and kiss him. 'I think you did that wonderfully.'

'Really?'

'Really.' I nod and I think how much I love him. 'But there is just one thing.'

'Is it about the thermostat for the central heating?' He looks deadly serious. 'Because I'm sure we can reach a compromise.'

'OK, two things.'

He suddenly looks worried.

'Now you're going to have to do my family's Zoom quiz.'

'On second thoughts, maybe we should think about it,' he says. His expression is serious, but his eyes flash with amusement.

Grinning, I punch him on the shoulder and he yelps loudly, making Arthur wake up and start barking as he thinks we're fighting and we both fuss over him, telling him not to be silly. Of course we're not really fighting. We haven't moved in together yet.

'So will you say yes?'

Edward pulls me towards him and this time I don't hesitate. 'Yes.'

I'm grateful for:
1. *Do I need to spell it out? Edward and I are getting married!*

The Next Day

We tell everyone the good news. Mum still hasn't stopped screaming.

AUGUST

#rulesaremadetobebroken

FOR RENT

BEAUTIFUL BIJOU FLAT on the first floor of a period conversion. Wonderful location, close to the park and amenities. Furnished and recently decorated. Modern decor and fully equipped kitchen. One careful lady owner who, after years of renting, has enjoyed living in this lovely home and by her own rules, which include stacking the dishwasher any which way she wants and setting the thermostat to twenty-five degrees, but is now happily giving it all up to get married to the love of her life.

Long let (with a six month break clause ~~in case it all goes tits up again~~)

Outside the Box

'So on his profile it says he's six foot one, an architect, has green eyes and dark hair, and his interests including hiking, surfing and volunteering at his local homeless shelter.'

'Wow, he sounds great.'

'Oh, and it gets better. *He's a vegan!*'

It's Sunday evening and I'm FaceTiming Liza in LA. Apparently it was International Friendship Day a couple of days ago and she'd just been reminded, so she'd called to say hi. 'Better than a belated Hallmark card,' she'd beamed out at me from the screen of my phone, bright sunshine and palm trees swaying in the background. Meanwhile I was at home in my flat, surrounded by packing boxes with the central heating on. I mean, seriously. WTF is it about August and bad weather in England? As soon as the calendar flicks over, it's less White Rabbit and more Where's My Bloody Jumper?

Still, a bit of bad weather can't dampen my mood. Nothing can. I've just spent the last five minutes showing Liza my new engagement ring, a small, pink sapphire on my finger. Edward and I had gone to choose it a few days ago from our little local antique jewellers. I liked the idea of something vintage, as did Edward.

'What better for the environment than a recycled engagement ring?' I said, grinning, as he put it on my finger in the shop.

He promptly looked stricken. 'Oh God, should I be on bended knee?' he replied, and tried to take it off again.

And I laughed and said, 'Oh God no,' because whenever I see those staged videos of proposals on the internet, I always think, I would die of embarrassment if someone came down my street with a marching band.

So it's lucky it got stuck on my knuckle. Art deco rings are very small. Everyone must have had such tiny, delicate fingers back then, unlike my big, bulky-knuckle ones.

But anyway, Liza, like all my friends, is really pleased for me* – everyone, it seems, loves Edward – and now the conversation has turned from rings to sperm.

As you do.

'Only problem is he's a Scorpio.'

'So?'

'I'm a Taurus. We're totally incompatible.'

She says this with a completely straight face. Which is fair enough, I'm not averse to reading my horoscope to see how little comes true for guidance or finding comfort in the fact that when everything goes tits up you can blame it all on Mercury in retrograde. But after the last eighteen months, I'm not sure we should be looking for signs from the universe on which to base her decision.

'What does Tia think?'

'She really likes the high-school teacher with the strong jaw who has a passion for travelling and spent a year teaching in Malawi.'

'Oh I *loved* him.'

'Me too.' Lying on a sun lounger in a bikini, she looks suddenly disheartened. 'But so does every woman. He's already been reserved.'

*

---

* Or is it relieved for me?

So this is how my conversations with Liza go now. It reminds me a lot of when I was online dating and I would trawl through all the different profiles in search of The One. Only now instead of dating profiles, we're discussing donor profiles. Liza and her girlfriend Tia have decided to have a baby together and are hoping to get pregnant by using donor sperm.

But first they need to choose their donor, and it's proving difficult. For the past few months, ever since they made their decision to start a family, Liza's been sharing various profiles with me in their quest to find The One. Which we all know is a dangerous concept. Mr Perfect doesn't exist, be it as a donor or a date; worse still, by fixating on finding him you miss out on all the Mr Good Enoughs.

Which might sound like you're settling, but only if you think settling is choosing smart, decent, kind, attractive men who might not tick all the boxes but will give you what you need and make you happy. Even if he is the wrong star sign.

'I swear to God, all the good ones are taken.'

'You're being too fussy.' Grabbing a roll of bubble wrap, I start packaging up a vase, one of my vintage finds on eBay.

'Trust me, you've never dated a Scorpio,' she says darkly.

'But you're not going to date him.'

'True,' she agrees. 'But if we go for an identity-release donor he could potentially become part of our family and lives for ever.'

'So he won't stay anonymous?'

As I reach for the packing tape, she shakes her head.

'On their eighteenth birthday the child can find out the identity of their donor. Maybe they won't want to, but we want to give them that choice. At least that's one thing Tia and I agree on.'

'So can you see any photos?'

I can't find the scissors so tear the tape by biting it. Is it just me, or does everyone who does that hear the voice of their mum in their head yelling at them not to do it as they'll break their teeth?

'Only a baby picture. It's included for free along with their questionnaire. The other stuff is extra.'

'What other stuff?'

'Like a voice recording or extended profile. It's crazy how expensive it gets with all the add-ons.'

'Like flying budget,' I note, 'once you've paid for all the extras like checked luggage and an actual seat, it costs a fortune.'

It's my attempt to lighten the mood and I'm relieved when Liza grins. 'Who would have thought that fertility clinics and budget airlines would have so much in common?' she says, which makes us both laugh.

Liza knows all about my own IVF journey. She was a constant support when I was living in California and going loopy from injecting all those hormones. Other than Ethan, she was the only person that knew we were having fertility treatment. The only person other than Ethan who tried to comfort me when it failed. In fact, that's why she'd been so nervous to tell me about her decision to try and have a baby. She didn't want to upset me. To bring it all back.

And I'm not upset, I'm happy for her. Of course I am. I just didn't want to tell her that she needn't worry about bringing it all back: it never goes away.

'Hang on, I'll send you a baby picture of another donor . . .'

A photo pings up on my phone of a cute toddler with blond curls.

'He's on our shortlist.'

'Aww, look at those chubby cheeks!'

'I know, isn't he adorable? He kinda looks a bit like me when I was a baby, though I'm not sure if that's good or bad . . .' She breaks off and frowns. 'God, this is weird sometimes.'

I feel a shift, and pause what I'm doing.

'Don't get me wrong, I'm happy, but it's just not how I thought it would be.'

'I know,' I say gently, because if anyone understands what it's like to discover life isn't quite how you imagined it was going to be, it's me. 'Trust me, I get it.'

'My family still hasn't fully accepted it.'

I shoot her a look of sympathy. Liza's parents are deeply conservative and while she'd been nervous about introducing them to her girlfriend, she'd been both surprised and relieved when they'd welcomed her with open arms.

'They were great about Tia. They love her. But it's like this is a step too far.'

'They'll come round to the idea, just give them time.'

'I dunno. I hear Mom talking about her friends and all their daughters are leading these traditional lives. Mine doesn't look like that.'

'Neither does mine.' Finishing wrapping up the vase, I try putting it in the box, but it's an awkward shape. I try squashing it into another.

'Yes, it does, you're getting married.'

'True, but he's divorced with two kids and I'm forty-something. It's not the norm, is it? Look at all my friends, they found the right guy and settled down years ago.' I gasp loudly in frustration. 'I give up, this vase doesn't fit.'

'I guess not everything fits neatly inside the box.'

I look up to see Liza grinning and I start laughing.

'You know what no one ever tells us? Fitting in is *totally* overrated.'

I'm grateful for:
1. *Bin liners.*
2. *Friends, international or otherwise.*

Pivot with a Capital P

A couple of weeks after our reunion at the pub, I get a message from Fiona inviting me to go swimming at her private health club. She has a free guest pass and they have an outdoor pool, which sounds amazing, as it would appear the weather has jumped on the buzzword bandwagon and 'pivoted' from cold and wet to Costa del London. The city is sweltering, as am I in my tiny flat where I've been cocooned in bubble wrap packing for The Big Move.

It's amazing how you can amass so much stuff in such a short space of time. I arrived back in the UK from living in America with just a broken engagement, two suitcases and a carry-on. Fast forward less than three years and it has mushroomed into so many boxes my living room looks like the back of a delivery van (I'd say warehouse, but that would contravene trade descriptions, as seriously, you haven't seen the size of my living room) plus dozens of bulging bin liners.

At least I've managed to rent my flat out fully furnished, which means all the furniture is staying here. But still, how can one person have bought this many books? Or hair styling products that don't work? Or clothes I don't wear?

I text back immediately:

Yes! Absolutely! Thanks SO much

Great! See you tomorrow at 8.30 a.m.!

Crikey, that's a bit early. To be honest, I was hoping for something later in the day as I've got a pile of work to get through. Despite what some people might think, the life of a freelance writer does not involve wafting around enjoying endless coffees with your laptop somewhere instagrammable, with subway tiles, filament light bulbs and decent latte art.

Instead it's a cluttered kitchen table that doubles as a desk. Post-it notes everywhere. Frazzled nerves and several deadlines fast approaching. Hair that needs washing, up in a scrunchie. Elasticated joggers and a sweatshirt *with stains*. Probably hummus, as I've eaten it straight from the pot with a spoon at my laptop.

So, much less Insta-worthy.

This week I'm researching and writing several obituaries and I've got a new episode of my podcast to record. Still, I can't complain. I've been unemployed and it's no fun. Being a freelancer is either feast or famine, so I know I'm lucky.

That said, it's August and I'd love a summer holiday. Like most people I haven't been away for what feels like for ever; in fact I think the last time I put on a bikini and swam in the sea was when I went to Spain with Cricket, to scatter Monty's ashes. So I've decided. I'm going to look at this like I'm going on a little micro-vacation. I can go for a swim before work, close my eyes and pretend I'm in the Mediterranean, and still get home to meet my deadline.

Sorted.

As I push open the doors that lead out to the swimming pool area, I think it's the sound of children screaming that hits me first.

Or it could be Fiona, running towards me in a bathing suit and flip-flops, arms outstretched. She has that same look of exhausted relief that you see on people's faces in those TV programmes where they first spot the rescue team who are going to stretcher them off the mountain in a tinfoil blanket.

'Nell! You're here!'

Only we're not on a mountain, we're in a private health club in west London. Wrapped in a towel, I glance around me with alarm.

'Gosh, it's busy.'

I have a sudden, sinking sense that I'm the rescue team.

'It's the school holidays,' she cries in a strangulated voice.

Uh-oh. *School holidays*. A term used by my mum friends with the same wild-eyed fear you see in horror movies when the heroine runs screaming into the woods.

Fiona flings her arms around me with such brute force she almost tackles me to the ground like a rugby player. 'So glad you can make it! The children can't wait to see you! Look, Izzy and Lucas, it's Auntie Nell!'

Trying to make her voice heard above the din, Fiona yells across to the junior swimming pool, which is a blur of children splashing, neon foam noodles and floating plasters. It's quite hard to see as surrounding the edges are a crowd of stressed parents shuffling around in shoes wrapped in blue plastic bags, desperately trying not to get their iPhones wet. I finally spot Izzy being dive-bombed by a much older boy, while Lucas is locked in a deadly battle of tug of war over a pair of swimming goggles.

'Izzy! Lucas!'

But it's impossible to get their attention. Now I realize why Fiona's voice is hoarse; it's from all that yelling. It's bedlam.

'Um, are they OK?'

I feel a clutch of panic as Izzy disappears underneath the water and a terrified-looking young lifeguard blows his whistle and darts over.

'Oh yes, they're having lots of fun.'

Followed by relief as Izzy pops back up from underneath the water and waves gleefully at me, before shrieking with laughter and turning back to her enjoyable game of being dive-bombed.

'Oh good. For a moment there, I thought you needed me to go rescue them.'

'No, *not them*.' Fiona laughs at the very thought. 'I need you to *rescue me*!'

I watch as she turns and yells loudly over her shoulder. 'Mummy's just going to the big pool with Auntie Nell!' Then without waiting for an answer, grabs my hand. 'Come on, quick! Let's make a break for freedom!'

Thankfully the adult pool is set further away so, whilst you can still hear the cacophony in the background, you can also hear yourself think. Plus it's a gorgeous pool. Forget my local council-run offering. This is Olympic size. Heated. Lined with stylish, navy-blue sun loungers, canvas umbrellas and potted ferns. It really is something else. I feel as if I'm on some kind of luxury spa weekend, albeit in need of a pair of earplugs.

'So, gorgeous bride-to-be, have you set a date?' Fiona links arms and beams at me.

'No, not yet,' I smile at my friend's excitement. Fiona is over the moon for me.

'What about spring? I love spring weddings. All those gorgeous flowers, though you can never rely on the weather . . . Or how about one of those amazing winter weddings? You could have mulled wine and fur capes, though *not real fur* obviously.'

'Well, to be honest, we haven't really thought about it yet.'

'Oh, but you must, it takes for ever to organize a wedding.'

'Right, yes.'

'And have you thought bridesmaids?'

'Um . . .'

'Because I know Izzy would be over the moon!'

'Oh, yes, of course.'

'But no pressure, obviously,' she laughs and I smile, but I suddenly feel a bit panicky. Like I'm being swept up into something bigger than myself. Which is silly, as there are no rules, no rush, it's just Fiona being excited for me.

The pool's empty but for a couple of people swimming laps in the fast lanes. They all look very professional in their caps and goggles. Powering up and down doing the front crawl and butterfly. One woman's even wearing a snorkel and flippers. Watching them, I feel a little intimidated. I'm more your breaststroke, chin up, don't get my hair wet kind of swimmer.

Which is a shame as I know that wild swimming is all the rage for us mid-life ladies, though I have yet to see the appeal of going in the freezing cold sea. Whenever I see those posts on social media I always want to comment, 'If it's endorphins you're after, try cracking open a tub of salted caramel ice cream. Always works for me!'

Of course I'm only joking. Well, sort of.

I drop my towel. I couldn't find my bikini – everything's packed away in boxes, it's difficult to find anything – but I did manage to unearth an old swimming costume. It's not the most flattering as the elastic material has perished a bit and it's lost a bit of shape, but it's fine. It does the job. And it's not like I know anyone here, as it's a private club. So I'm just lowering myself into the slow lane, when I hear Fiona exclaim, 'Well, fancy seeing you here! Nell, look who it is!'

And feel a stab of horror. WTF! Is there anything more cringe than bumping into someone you know in your bathing suit? Especially when you've forgotten to shave your legs and are going backwards down the steps into the pool, bum first.

I wait until I'm safely submerged before I look over to see Fiona already in the pool and talking to one of the swimmers.

I feel a beat of relief. For a moment there I had a horrible feeling it might be Johnny, a date who once ghosted me, as I've suddenly remembered he used to teach at this club, but it's the woman with the flippers and snorkel. She's wearing one of those sporty racing costumes with so many cut-out bits to show off her amazingly toned figure it looks like it's being held together by strings of neon lycra.

Meanwhile, over in saggy, baggy, faded black, lost elasticity land . . .

'Nell, how wonderful to see you.'

It's only as she takes off her goggles I suddenly recognize her.

'Oh, hi Annabel.'

My heart sinks to the bottom of the pool. Oh God, Perfect Annabel is Fiona's friend. We met when I first moved back to London, and to be frank, there was little love lost between us.* That said, we put our differences behind us when she confessed to life not being that perfect, and made friends eventually. Well, it was more like a truce.

'You're looking well.' She flashes me a perfect white smile.

Still, I haven't seen her for eighteen months. Maybe she's changed. After all, the last eighteen months have changed a lot of people. Plus the last time I saw her she was getting divorced. That can knock the wind out of anyone's sails. She's probably much nicer now. More humble.

'Loving the new curves. I could never carry them off. So envious of people who can.'

I take it all back. She's still a complete cow.

---

* We don't talk about how she tried to sabotage my friendship with Fiona, humiliate me at Michelle's baby shower and caused me to face-plant at a fun run in front of my date.

'Nell's getting married,' announces Fiona, oblivious as always.

'Congratulations! Let's see the ring.' Her eyes swivel like lasers to my left hand, which she snatches out of the water like a pelican snatching a fish. 'Oh how cute and adorable.'

'Thanks,' I smile. Really it's amazing how Annabel can make a compliment sound like a criticism.

'Like I always used to say to Clive, size isn't everything.' Releasing my hand, she gives a little tinkly laugh.

'How is Clive?' asks Fiona while I seethe.

'He's with Clementine and his new girlfriend in the Bahamas.'

'He has a new girlfriend?'

'Clive always has a new girlfriend,' she smiles brightly. 'He likes to trade them in like his cars. But this one's lovely and Clementine adores her.'

'Oh, well, that's the most important thing.'

'Absolutely,' she nods and gives that little tinkly laugh again, though this time it sounds more forced. 'I think it's probably because they're so close in age.'

Despite the ring comments, I suddenly feel quite sorry for Annabel, trying to make light of a situation that can't be easy. Yet, I'm also aware of the steeliness that runs beneath. Unlike Fiona, who smiles supportively and gives her arm a reassuring squeeze.

'It's great to see you being so healthy about all of this.'

'Well, life is all about embracing change,' she nods, her face earnest. 'Did I tell you I've also changed career?'

'Gosh, really?' Fiona looks completely fascinated.

'Yes, during this last year I decided to close the boutique.'

'Oh, I'm sorry.'

'No, don't be. It just wasn't working for me any more and where I'm at in my life. What with everything happening in the world right now, I wanted to give back more.'

'I think we've all felt like that,' I nod, feeling my cynicism towards her thaw. 'I did some volunteering at the local food bank.'

She ignores me and continues talking. 'I thought, what do people really need?'

'More doctors and nurses?' I suggest.

'So I decided to become a life coach.'

'Wow, Annabel, that's amazing!' gasps Fiona in admiration. 'Isn't that amazing, Nell?'

'Um, yes,' I nod. 'Amazing.'

Well I suppose that's one word for it, though not necessarily the one I'd choose. Annabel? *A life coach?* I just can't imagine it. I've met a few life coaches in my time and they've always been really kind, supportive and compassionate people. Whereas Annabel's always been so . . . I reach for the right word . . . Well, a bit of a bitch, frankly.

'It just feels like the perfect fit for me.' She beams proudly at her announcement. 'I was feeling really dissatisfied and realized I needed to be more deeply engaged to find more fulfilment and that actually, I really wanted to help others.'

I want to believe she's genuine. I really do. It's just . . . I glance across at Fiona, she looks completely mesmerized. Maybe I'm just a bit biased.

'Like I say, it's all about self-care and knowing when life isn't working for us and when to pivot.'

Ah, that word again. Is it just me, or is everyone pivoting?

'And it's not just about the outward self, it's also about the inward. So as a coach I use healing crystals and guided meditation as well as practical workshops. In fact, I'm so passionate about helping people I even carry crystals with me at all times.'

Reaching inside her swimsuit, she pulls out two small crystals from her built-in bra.

'Here, have a citrine for positivity and optimism and an amethyst to relieve stress and anxiety.' She gives one each to me and Fiona. I'm not sure I want a crystal from her bra, but I smile and say thanks. I notice I get the one for stress and anxiety.

'I'm planning to do a weekend retreat in the autumn, you should come.'

'Oh, that sounds wonderful, doesn't it, Nell?'

Clutching my boob-warm crystal, I give a rictus smile.

'Fabulous! Well, ladies, I'll leave you to your swim.' And putting her goggles and snorkel back on, she dives back underneath the water.

I'm grateful for:

1. *Not drowning every time Annabel powered past me in her snorkel and flippers, sending a tidal wave crashing over me and causing me to choke from swallowing so much chlorinated water.*
2. *Finally getting my hearing back after a week of standing on each foot and jumping vigorously up and down to try to get the water out of my ears.*
3. *Edward treating me to dinner at our local pub, ahead of The Big Move on Friday, and not being disappointed when the waiter told me they were out of sticky toffee pudding . . . but pivoting to the cheese plate. See, I can pivot too!*
4. *My new swimming costume, thus freeing me from baggy, saggy, lost elasticity land. Well, only when it comes to swimsuits. Seriously, you should see my knees.*

Moving (Back) in Together

In my podcast I talk a lot about how life isn't always quite how you imagined it was going to be. Like, for example, you know all those smiley commercials that show newly engaged couples moving in together? The ones where the woman is wearing dungarees and up a stepladder with a roller and cute paint splashes on her nose while the man is in a vintage T-shirt having fun with cardboard boxes. And they are laughing and joking and putting their arms around each other in playful, homemaking bliss.

Well, now cut to the reality.

As Moving Day dawns I quickly discover Edward and I are *not* the young, playful couple I envisioned us to be. In fact when the removal van fails to show up and we're forced to spend all day traipsing backwards and forwards with everything piled in his car, fighting traffic on what is probably the hottest day of the year and arguing about directions, I realize that we are in fact a tired, grumpy, middle-aged couple and there is nothing remotely fun about him hurting his back trying to lift a heavy box of my books or me not having any space in his wardrobe to hang my clothes.

And that a week later we've spent an absolute fortune on designer paint tester pots and still can't agree on what colour to paint the bedroom.

'I don't see why we can't just stick with Dulux Trade White,' Edward is saying now with an exasperated expression.

'White's boring,' I argue.

Standing side by side in the bedroom we both stare at the various colour swatches I've painted on the far wall. In the corner of the room Arthur is lying on a pile of bin bags full of my clothes that I'm still yet to unpack.

'But there's plenty of room. Look, here's some spare hangers,' Edward had said, looking genuinely puzzled when I'd pointed out there was nowhere to hang anything. I counted them. There were five. *Five coat hangers!* Which right there is the reason men are from Mars and women are from Venus. Worse still, they were the wire ones you get back from the drycleaners that give all your tops shoulder bumps.

'No worries, I'll use the wardrobe in my old bedroom,' I'd suggested, which admittedly felt slightly weird, considering I was now Edward's fiancée and not his flatmate, but I was determined not to read too much into it. So what if he hadn't made space for me in his wardrobe? That didn't mean he hadn't made space for me in his life.

Except now he's divorced and shares custody of his twin boys, both extra bedrooms are full of their things for when they come to stay, so there's nowhere for me to put my stuff. Still, it's early days, I'm sure we'll figure it out.

'White's not boring, it's practical.'

Edward's voice interrupts my thoughts and I turn sideways to see his arms folded across his chest, hands tucked firmly up into his armpits. I'm no body language expert, but I'm sensing resistance.

'Why does everything have to be practical?'

Edward looks confounded by such a concept. 'Is that an actual question?'

My jaw sets. He's still sulking because I made him take down his beloved display of framed rugby shirts that hung above the bed.

'If white is so boring, why does all our bedding have to be white?' he persists, looking at our new set from The White Company. His mismatched bedding had been the first thing to go.

'That's different.'

'Why is that different?'

'Because everyone loves sleeping in white bedding.'

'That makes no sense. When you are asleep your eyes are closed so you can't see what colour it is,' he reasons.

'What about Breathless Ghost?' I suggest, changing the subject.

'Excuse me?'

And now he's looking at me like I'm completely bananas. Passing him the colour chart, I point to a particularly lovely shade of lilac grey.

'Honestly,' he grumbles. 'Who thinks of these names?'

Someone with an imagination, I want to say, but I don't, because we're supposed to be the fun, playful couple in dungarees and a vintage T-shirt, remember?

'Times have moved on since boring old magnolia,' I tease instead, slipping my hand around his waist. See, we can do happy, homemaking bliss.

'I like magnolia.' His face brightens. 'Actually, there's an idea.'

'Edward.' I shoot him a warning glare and take back the colour chart.

It had felt strange leaving my flat and moving back in with Edward. His place is so familiar and, since lockdown rules were lifted and we formed a bubble, I stay over all the time, but I hadn't prepared myself for how different it would be to move in with someone now I'm older.

When I was younger I was a blank slate. I didn't have any

baggage, except a futon and a cheese plant, and I hadn't the confidence to know what I liked. So I just liked whatever my boyfriend did. One loved heavy metal rock bands, so I loved them too and used to sit through concerts wearing earplugs. Another was into foreign films with subtitles, so I would trek along to the arthouse cinema in Soho, while secretly wishing I was at the local Odeon watching the latest one with Hugh Grant.

But now I know what I like and I've got plenty of baggage. Who doesn't by the time you get to this age? And it makes things a lot more complicated. Because it's not just the amount of stuff you bring with you – all the physical and emotional baggage that's hard to unpack and make room for – they've got all their stuff too. Over nearly five decades we've both accumulated an array of opinions and possessions and habits and hurts. Not to mention an ex-fiancé, an ex-wife and two children. Which together makes a lot of stuff for one relationship and a 1200 square foot flat.

'How about a French Kiss?'

'Is this you trying to be romantic?' I raise an eyebrow.

'No . . . it's on the chart,' he says, pointing at it over my shoulder.

I look at the colour and am pleasantly surprised. 'I hadn't noticed that one . . . yes, I like it.'

'OK, French Kiss it is,' he says, wrapping his arm around me and pulling me towards him. He gives me a kiss to prove it.

And now I feel a tad guilty about the magnolia. 'Are you sure?'

'If you like it, I like it,' he laughs, then his face falls serious and his eyes meet mine. 'I want this to work, for us to work.'

'Me too,' I nod, resting my head against his chest.

Because the truth is we've both been here before. We've both moved in with people and painted walls and had hopes for the future and we've both seen it all go wrong. And yet, despite the failed relationships behind us, we're both willing to take the leap of faith.

'It's just all about compromise,' continues Edward as we break apart.

'Absolutely,' I agree, turning to leave the bedroom. I'm going to get the paint now, before he changes his mind. 'And finding space for each other.'

'Definitely,' he nods, following me into the living room. 'We need to be able to communicate.'

'Totally,' I enthuse, feeling rather smug as I grab my handbag and head for the door. If you ask me, those commercials are completely overrated. Who needs to be the fun, playful couple when you can be the mature, sagacious couple, listening, accommodating, communicating—

'Ow, FFS!' I trip over Edward's rowing machine that's shoved in the hallway, along with several pairs of dumbbells and an exercise ball. Apparently when he lived with his ex-wife in the country, they had a home gym but after his divorce she turned it into a home office, and he turned his hallway into a sports centre. 'Edward, will you move all this gym equipment!' I yell, rubbing my ankle.

'What's wrong with it?' He appears in the hallway.

'What's right with it?' I cry, feeling a bruise fast appearing.

'I don't say that about any of your things.'

'Because my things are still in bin liners!' I retort, then remembering we're both adults and it's all about compromise, try to be reasonable. 'Look, I'm not saying you have to get rid of it, how about we put it in the spare room for now?'

'Oh, OK,' he nods and I smile to myself despite my throbbing ankle. There's a beat. 'But we don't have a spare room?'

'Exactly.' And kissing him on the cheek, I close the front door behind me.

I'm grateful for:
1. *The local charity shop who were delighted by the very generous donation of a rowing machine and gym equipment.*
2. *IKEA and our fab new fitted wardrobes and shelving system, so now we both have plenty of space.*
3. *Not having to put together the IKEA wardrobes and shelving system.*

One I Made Earlier

'My phone says it's this way.'

The following Tuesday afternoon I'm following Cricket as she leads me through a plethora of backstreets. I have no idea where we're heading. She'd phoned yesterday asking if I would meet her at Hammersmith station. Apparently as part of her Re-Entry mission she'd joined a new social club and asked if I would go with her. She wouldn't elaborate, but she didn't need to. After our conversation in the park I'd been a bit worried about her, so I was thrilled to hear she was getting back out there and more than happy to go with her for moral support.

Plus, to be honest, I'm struggling a bit with my own Re-Entry mission. Moving back in with Edward is lovely but not without its challenges, and having finally found room for all our things, it's now me that could do with a bit of space.

'What's the address?'

'I don't know. I put it in my phone.'

I turn to look at Cricket, who is striding along the pavement in a wide-brimmed hat and sunglasses, holding her phone in front of her like a divining rod. A young girl with a take-out coffee leaps out of her way.

'Sorry.' I turn to see the young girl dabbing the front of her blouse and throw her an apologetic look. 'Cricket, you need to look where you're going.'

'*Turn left,*' her phone suddenly instructs loudly.

'I am looking,' she replies, not looking up from her screen and taking a sharp left down a side street.

'Not at your phone, the pavement,' I cry, hurrying to catch up with her. It's always astonished me how a woman in her eighties who has never stepped foot in a gym or heard the word 'cardio' can walk so briskly. 'Watch out, there's a ladder.'

'So there is,' she says gaily, walking deliberately underneath it.

'So you're not superstitious,' I note, choosing to walk around it.

'Not about those things, no.' She shakes her head. 'I was raised Catholic, but I rejected the Church and all its religious superstitions. After all, what's the difference between a black cat and a Hail Mary? Of course, my mother was appalled. As children, my brother and I used to love scaring her to death by walking under them. Quite the adrenalin sport.'

'I didn't know you had a brother.'

'He died a long time ago. But not from walking underneath a ladder,' she adds, smiling ruefully.

'I'm sorry.'

'Me too,' she nods, with a stoicism that is so often mistaken for pragmatism in the older generation, and not a lifetime spent learning how to live with loss and still carry on.

'*Head north on Thorsbury Avenue towards Tindersticks Alley.*'

As we head underneath the railway bridge, she changes the subject. 'So, tell me, how has it been moving back in with Edward now you're engaged?'

'Fine.'

'So it's not fine.'

I laugh. Cricket, like all my friends, was delighted by my news, but whereas everyone else seems focused on the wedding, she seems to understand the challenges that come with it. 'Yes, of course it is, it's just . . .' I break off. 'Moving in with someone is different when you're older. We've both got baggage.'

'And I'm guessing it's not of the Louis Vuitton kind.' Glancing up from her phone, she flashes me a smile and I'm pleased to notice her red lipstick is firmly back on.

'No, sadly not,' I grin, 'and I've loved having my independence.'

'You can still have your independence and be married to someone,' she continues, this time more serious. 'And I speak from experience, you know I wasn't much older than you when I moved in with Monty.'

'It's just the last time we lived together, Edward had rather a lot of rules,' I say, remembering the ring binder he presented me with when I first moved in. It was filled with endless pages about being tidy, not playing loud music and being respectful, plus a whole section about being environmentally conscious and conserving energy; Edward owned his own environmental software company and was all about renewable energy solutions.*

'My dear girl, didn't anyone ever tell you rules are made to be broken?' Without waiting for the pedestrian crossing to turn green, she walks out into the road. A car brakes sharply and she waves cheerfully at the driver. 'That's part of the fun.'

She's right, of course, though I'm not sure breaking rules about how to stack the dishwasher are exactly what Cricket has in mind. Or how there's going to be anything fun about facing the knives upwards, unless of course Edward falls on them.

ONLY KIDDING! I love my fiancé. Even if he is driving me potty with the house rules. Dashing across the road, I hurry to catch up with her.

---

* I still don't really have a clue what this means, but it seems to involve being freezing cold and living in pitch darkness.

'Well, here we are.'

Cricket comes to a halt outside what looks like some kind of community centre. A narrow path leads to the entrance where the door is slightly ajar and I can see lights and activity. It must be some kind of seniors' club where you meet up for coffee mornings, or maybe play bridge or do other social activities.

'Great,' I smile enthusiastically. 'Do you want me to go ahead?'

She's obviously asked me along as she's a bit nervous, which is totally understandable. When you live alone, it's not always easy going to things by yourself, I know from experience.

'Oh, I'm sure it will be fine,' she says, slipping her phone into her pocket. 'I'm rather looking forward to it.'

I follow her into a large hall where we're greeted by a hive of activity. Several people are congregating by the entrance, where they're serving teas and coffees, and there's the hum of chatter and introductions and the clink of cups and saucers. Someone laughs nervously and a little too loudly. I glance around. I was expecting everyone to be Cricket's age so am surprised to see all ages. One girl even looks to be in her twenties.

'Welcome to the Tuesday Toodlepip Club.'

I turn back to see a rather jolly-looking woman with a clipboard swooping down on us.

'I'm Elaine, the organizer. And you are?'

'Nell and Cricket,' I say, quickly doing the introductions.

'Wonderful!' Crossing out our names, she proceeds to give us both elbow bumps. Elaine is a very enthusiastic elbow bumper.

'We're serving refreshments so if you'd like to get yourself acquainted with the rest of the members,' she continues.

'We're just waiting for two more and then we can begin. Oh, and help yourself to biscuits.'

'Splendid,' beams Cricket.

'Though don't eat too many or you won't fit in your coffin!' She wags a stern finger. 'Oh, look, here they are, do excuse me.' And waving at two women who have just arrived, she shoots off and leaves us.

'Bloody hell, that was a bit rude!' I turn to Cricket, who is already making her way over to refreshments. 'Did you hear what she just said?'

'Well, she does have a point.'

'Why? Because you're in your eighties?' I cry, offended on her behalf.

'No, because we're here to make our own coffins.' She turns to the woman serving teas. 'Just a little milk, if you don't mind.'

'Excuse me?' I must have misheard.

'It's once a fortnight for twelve weeks and by the end of it, you've made and decorated your own casket,' she says cheerfully. 'There's lots of choice: wood, cardboard, you can even weave one out of willow.'

With a beat of horror I suddenly notice all the tables set up at the back of the hall, each with their own workbench, and a pile of willow and flat-pack boxes.

'But I thought I was coming to one of those knit and natter clubs,' I blurt.

Which seems to tickle Cricket no end. 'Nell, can you ever imagine me knitting?' Holding her cup and saucer, she throws back her head and laughs heartily.

Which is true, but still.

'Oh, I'm sorry, have I shocked you?' Seeing my expression, her face abruptly falls. 'Have my tea –' she passes it to me '– you look a little pale. Here's some sugar.' Concerned, she passes me some packets.

'I'm fine, honestly,' I protest, but I take it from her. I'm surprised by how taken aback I am. 'It's just, not what I was expecting . . .'

Trailing off, I sit down on one of the fold-up chairs and take a few gulps of hot, sweet tea. I look around the hall at all the people smiling and chatting. Everyone looks so relaxed and cheerful, which seems rather at odds with why they're here.

'I thought you'd joined a club because you wanted some company,' I hear myself saying lamely.

'But I already have company. I have you and my books and all my memories to keep me company. What I need isn't company, it's peace of mind.' Sitting down next to me, she takes off her sunhat and smooths down her thick, grey bob. 'The last eighteen months made me feel powerless. I want to take back control.'

'Of your life?'

'Of my death.'

'Don't be silly, you're not going to die,' I say, quickly shutting down the very concept. 'You've got years left, you'll outlive me!'

'My dear girl,' she smiles, generously. 'That's very kind, but we both know that isn't true.'

'But you're as fit as a fiddle. You'll live to be a hundred.'

'Why on earth would I want to live to be a hundred? So I can get a telegram?' She waves her hand dismissively. 'But I do want to make sure that when my time comes, I'm prepared not scared,' she says, her face falling serious. 'And why not have some enjoyment in the process? Put the fun into funeral? Like Elaine says, it's not goodbye, it's toodlepip.'

I shift in my seat.

'I'm sorry, is all this talk of death making you uncomfortable?'

'I just hate thinking about it.'

'Says the woman who writes obituaries.'

'I know, but they're a celebration of life, not death,' I reason.

'Death is part of life. From the moment you're born only two things are inevitable. Death and taxes.'

I nod, listening. Being with Cricket always brings something unexpected.

'Unless of course you're a billionaire or an MP,' she quips drily.

'OK, ladies and gentlemen, now if you want to gather round . . .'

We're interrupted by the sound of someone clapping and look over to see Elaine with her clipboard, beckoning us all over.

'So, will you join me?'

I look across at Cricket and see her studying me, her bright blue eyes a little more crinkled around the edges with the passing of time. And yet, her spirit seems stronger than ever and I feel proud of her for facing up to what for many of us is the thing we are most afraid of. For finding a way to own it.

'Of course,' I smile and together we both stand up and walk over to where everyone is gathered.

At which point her phone in her pocket suddenly loudly announces, '*You have reached your final destination.*'

Oh God no. The irony. Did that just say—

The hall falls silent and everyone turns to us. Horrified, we look at each other. And then, without missing a beat, we both crack up laughing.

The Following Day

'How much is it?'

'Two hundred and fifty pounds. The coffin comes flat-pack. Or you can weave your own, but that's more expensive.'

Sadiq snorts coffee down his nose. 'That's terrible!'

'I thought it was quite reasonable, actually. It includes a free paintbrush and primer. Of course, decorations are extra.'

'No, I'm talking about this coffee.' He grimaces. Wiping his tie with a napkin, he lifts the microphone of his earphones closer to his mouth and lowers his voice. 'You can't get a decent flat white around here for love nor money.'

It's the next morning and I'm having a Zoom meeting with Sadiq, an old friend of over twenty years who is also the lifestyle editor on one of the big national papers and gave me my job writing obituaries, which effectively also makes him my boss.

'Stop being such a London snob.'

Not that I treat him as such. Our relationship hasn't changed from when we were flatmates in our twenties and would sit up half the night smoking cigarettes and drinking cheap white wine while bemoaning our terrible love lives. Now, however, Sadiq is happily married to Patrick, with whom he has two children, and last year they made the decision to quit the capital and escape to the country.

'Christ, I miss London.'

'I thought you loved living in the country.'

To tell you the truth, I couldn't believe it when he first told me. Sadiq leaving his urban life in London? It was unthinkable. Born and raised in the East End, the city was part of his DNA. I presumed he meant they were moving to the Cotswolds, which is basically Notting Hill in Hunter wellies, but no. They were swapping their trendy flat in Hackney for the *real* countryside, a thatched cottage with several acres in rural Devon. And with his office closed and working from home, I could see the advantage of all that extra space and fresh air. Plus, to be honest, what Londoner stuck in traffic doesn't secretly harbour fantasies of The Good Life.

'As a family, we're thriving. The kids love having a garden and Patrick's in heaven with his raised organic beds and rescue chickens.'

'How are the chickens?'

'Shitting everywhere.'

I get the feeling Sadiq is not sharing in his family's country idyll.

'And what about you?'

'All I want is a decent internet connection and real espresso—'

At least I think that's what he says, but the video freezes. The reception in Sadiq's local greasy spoon cafe isn't great. Still, it's better than it was in the chintzy tearooms by the castle (terrible) or the sixteenth-century village pub (non-existent) or the motorway service station that he drove to in desperation, and where all the other diners must have thought they were witnessing the end of a relationship as our entire conversation was spent saying 'I've lost you' and 'We're breaking up'.

Still, anything was better than his cottage, which has a dial-up internet speed so slow it would be quicker to use carrier pigeons.

'So anyway, as I was saying—' he unfreezes.

Oh no, what did I just miss?

I'd woken first thing to his text: 'Morning Stevens. You available to talk this morning?' but no mention of what it was about. Which begs the question: why do people do that? Why don't they just tell you what it is they want to talk about *in the text*. It would save hours of panic and worst-case scenarios.

'I'm sorry I had to put my offer, of you having your own column, on the backburner, but rest assured if ever there's an opportunity, I'll suggest it to our editor-in-chief.'

'Thank you.' I feel a blush of pride and a mix of surprise and relief. That's what he wanted to talk to me about?

'Plus it would pay a lot better than the obituaries. It's hard to make a living writing about dead people. There's a pun in there somewhere,' he adds cheerfully.

My stomach leaps at the thought of a bigger salary. Crikey, things really do seem to be looking up for me. First my engagement and now my career prospects. Perhaps Annabel isn't the only one who's pivoted their life. Mine's unrecognizable to when I first moved back from the States. But maybe it just takes some people longer than others to get their life sorted. Maybe we all go at different speeds.

'But that's not why I wanted to talk to you.'

'It's not?'

'We've received a complaint.'

'*A complaint?*' My stomach lurches.

'Yeah, apparently there was some kind of mistake in one of the obituaries you wrote a couple of weeks ago.'

And just like that, I pivot back again.

'Who complained?'

'Well, obviously not the deceased. Luckily the dead don't tend to complain about their obituaries.' Sadiq smiles wryly.

'No, it was an email from a relative. Quite an angry relative actually,' he adds, almost as an afterthought.

My mind is scrambling. I've always made sure I do my due diligence when it comes to researching and take great care to be respectful of the facts. That said, admittedly I've recently been distracted with everything going on in my personal life. I must have made some kind of mistake. Oh no.

'Is it OK if I put you in touch?'

'What? With the angry relative?'

Sadiq smiles as if this is amusing and not, in fact, my worst nightmare.

'Yes. Of course.'

'OK, great. I've got to go and try and find myself a coffee now.' Reaching for his jacket from over the back of the chair, he slips it on. 'I'll pass on the relative's email when I get home to my desk. The newspaper takes complaints very seriously but I'm sure you can sort it out. Just make sure they don't sue us—'

And then the screen freezes, along with my insides.

A Staycation

Twenty-four hours later and I still haven't read the email Sadiq forwarded from The Angry Relative. It sits in my inbox. Glaring at me. Still, it's August. Who replies to their inbox in August? Everyone's on their summer holidays.

Only this year, instead of a vacation abroad, it's all about the staycation, and the WhatsApp group chat with my friends is buzzing.

> *Fiona*
> We've rented a house on the beach in Cornwall. Can't wait!
>
> *Holly*
> Ooh, that sounds gorgeous. Adam booked a hotel in the Cotswolds.
> Hope it's dog friendly!
>
> *Michelle*
> We're going camping in Scotland. Six in a tent. We must be mad.
>
> *Holly*
> What about you Nell?

**We've been a bit busy, what with moving in together and getting engaged.
Haven't even started planning the wedding yet!**

We thought we'd book something last-minute.

Fiona
Last-minute! You'll be lucky! Cornwall's fully booked!

Fiona is prone to exaggeration. I ignore her exclamation marks.

Maybe we'll forget the coast and rent a cottage in the country instead.

Michelle
Cottages have doubled their prices, that's why we decided to camp.
But we had real trouble finding a campsite.

I am not staying in a tent.

Or a nice hotel.

Plus there's six of them and only two of us. I'm sure it will be much easier with us just being a couple and a dog. At the thought, I feel a buzz of excitement. It's going to be our first holiday together as a couple.

Holly
We booked months ago, have you tried Airbnb?

I'm sure we'll find something. We're not fussy.

Fiona
Good luck!

Thanks! I'm sure we'll be fine.

Date: The next day, after many fruitless hours searching online
To: Every boutique hotel, bed and breakfast, guesthouse, country cottage, Airbnb and campsite, including the depressing beige rental apartment that got terrible reviews and is daylight robbery but I'm desperate
Subject: Availability

Dear Sir/Madam,

I hope this email finds you well. I am enquiring about availability for one couple with a well-behaved dog during this month of August. I realize this is rather last-minute but we are flexible with dates. Ideally we would like a week but would consider a long weekend.

Look forward to hearing from you.

Best wishes,

Penelope Stevens

To: Penelope Stevens
Re: Availability

Dear Ms Stevens,

Unfortunately the whole of the UK is fully booked during this time. Including the depressing beige rental apartment. However, we do have a broom cupboard available for two thousand pounds a week, not including breakfast, in the middle of nowhere. This accommodation is offered to anyone who totally fucked up and didn't have the good sense to book their holiday ages ago. Please note, the mould around the bath is extra.

Best wishes,

Owner of broom cupboard who is making a killing

SEPTEMBER

#schooloflife

Our Engagement Party

Lots of things get better with age. Wine. Antiques. My taste in men. But one thing that gets much, *much* worse are hangovers. Waiting for my morning coffee to brew on the stove, I try to ignore my dull headache. Why did I have that second margarita? No, third. Hang on. *Did I have four?* And was that *before or after* the prosecco? Ugh. I can't remember. I stopped counting after we started doing tequila shots.

At the memory I suddenly feel quite nauseous.

Oh God. That's when it all got messy.

So two days ago Edward and I had a party. It was my idea. After my recent conversation with Cricket about death, it got me thinking about life. About how we should be celebrating it more. Why do we need to wait for a special occasion to gather our friends and family together and crack open the fizzy stuff? Plus, trust me, there's nothing like an afternoon spent making your own coffin to make you want to throw a party.

'A party?' Edward had replied to my suggestion with surprise. 'What are we celebrating? Our engagement?'

'Being alive.'

'*Alive?*'

'Yes, isn't that reason enough?'

Having just got back from a run, Edward leaned on the kitchen countertop and looked at me like this was a trick question.

'*And* our engagement,' I relent swiftly realizing if I'm to get Edward onboard, he needs something a little more traditional. 'How about August bank holiday?'

'But that's tomorrow.'

'So. Let's be spontaneous.'

'Isn't everyone away?'

'Go on, rub it in,' I laughed, because I was determined to laugh in the face of it all. After exhausting all attempts to find anywhere decent, we'd rejected the extortionate offer of the broom cupboard and decided to stay home. Well, they are always telling you to be authentic and what's more authentic about a staycation than staying put?

Plus, like Edward joked, who needed a Cornish beach when you had a garden and a hosepipe?* At least I think he was joking.

'We could have a barbecue.' I suggested. Now I could see I'd piqued his interest. What is it with men and barbecues? It must be some throwback to being cavemen as I can't get Edward near the oven.

'My barbecue skills are legendary. You should see me flip a burger.'

'I've seen you flip a pancake and that was impressive.'

'Ah yes,' he smiled, remembering our first Pancake Day together. 'It's all in the wrist action.'

'I'm sensing a schoolboy joke.'

Which made him laugh and grab me around the waist.

'Hey, you're all sweaty!'

But ignoring my protests, he pulled me towards him. 'I thought you wanted us to be spontaneous . . .'

*

* I posted (then quickly deleted) a selfie of our staycation. Trust me, not even a starburst filter could save us.

Sex in the kitchen and a party! How's that for celebrating life?

Luckily, as it turned out, lots of people were already back from their holidays and replied yes to the invite – only Fiona couldn't make it as they were still in Cornwall – so we spent the next twenty-four hours getting everything ready.

In the past my idea of having a party was to throw crisps in a bowl, open some wine and hope for the best, but Edward immediately swung into action and drew up a spreadsheet, complete with highlighter pens. There were strict instructions about filling up ice-cube trays, no single-use plastic glasses and only using compostable and biodegradable plates and cutlery.

As for the food and drink, he took it very seriously and carefully drew up a list of ingredients to make cocktails and calculated exactly how many burgers and sausages we needed by doing some kind of complicated algebraic equation. Think Einstein's $E = mc^2$, only this involved the number of meat eaters divided by vegetarians multiplied by the aforementioned cocktails consumed.

Only then did we go to the supermarket where he set off down the aisles on the kind of strategic operation that reminded me of the time I went on a school trip to Churchill's War Rooms. Meanwhile I randomly threw crisps in the trolley.

Still, I was excited. It was going to be the first time we'd hosted our friends in our home – and at our engagement party too – and I wanted everything to be perfect. Over the years I've been invited to so many gatherings by my lovely friends, with their lovely husbands, in their lovely homes, but now finally it was my turn. Stringing up carnival lights with Edward in our tiny garden, and watching him fire up the barbecue in his striped pinny, I didn't feel like I was on the outside any more, waiting for my happy ending, whatever that may be. This was it and it wasn't an ending, it was a beginning.

Even better, this beginning had cocktails. *Strong ones.*

First to arrive was Cricket. She came early, 'to avoid the crowds' and immediately informed me she'd only stay for one drink, 'but make it a strong one'. I was thrilled to see her. I knew she was still avoiding most social situations, but by some miracle we'd been forecast good weather, instead of the usual summer bank holiday washout, which meant we could be outside on the tiny patio and small patch of grass we called our garden.

Best of all, she finally got to meet Edward and he finally got to meet her. I'd told them so much about each other, it was almost surreal to see them both in the same place, heads bent together chatting, as Edward fixed her a whiskey and ginger, 'no ice, easy on the ginger'. I could tell immediately she liked him, by the way she held his gaze and gave him her full attention. How many of us do that these days? Checking phones and being distracted, talking when we should be listening.

A few of Edward's old rugby mates showed up next, carrying crates of beer and rowdily backslapping, followed by Max and Michelle without the children. 'We've got Max's parents staying and they offered to babysit,' she explained, looking quite worried for her in-laws. And well she might be. I babysat once, imagining lots of fun and cute snuggles with my godchildren, and instead it nearly broke me.*

And then about ten minutes later the doorbell started going and everyone seemed to arrive at once: Holly and Adam,

---

* Never underestimate a child in *Paw Patrol* pyjamas.

with Olivia and Coco; a few of our neighbours; Pazza, Edward's old friend from Bristol Uni, who was recently divorced. With my hands full of bunches of flowers and bottles of prosecco, I led them trooping through the flat and into the garden, where Edward was in charge of drinks.

I watched him greeting people through the window as I busied myself hunting for vases. I'd entertained friends before in my tiny flat and it had been fun, but having someone to fix drinks while I put flowers in water was a lovely feeling. I never minded so much being single, but having to do everything by yourself can get lonely and exhausting. It's nice to have someone to share both the load and – at the end of the night – the loading of the dishwasher. Because if there was one thing I could guarantee, it's that Edward would be in charge of stacking it later.

The barbecue was already in full swing when I opened the door and got a surprise.

'*Hola, chica preciosa!*'

'Fiona!'

Standing on my doorstep, she threw her arms wide and enveloped me in one of her bear hugs. 'Well, I wasn't going to miss your engagement party!'

'So pleased you could make it,' I grinned, hugging her back. 'How was Cornwall?'

'Amazing.'

'We learned to surf!' Without standing on ceremony, the children rushed into the hallway, yelling, 'Where's Arthur?'

'Begging for sausages,' I laughed as they disappeared through into the garden.

'Oh by the way, I hope you don't mind . . .'

I turned back to look at Fiona.

'. . . But Annabel called asking if I'd go over to hers. I think she's lonely, what with Clemmie being with Clive and her being on her own for the bank holiday . . . and did I mention her beloved French Bulldog died last year?'

'Oh no, that's awful! Of course, I totally understand if you need to leave early . . .'

I broke off as I saw another figure walking up the path with David.

'Well, no actually, what I meant was—'

But she's interrupted.

'Nell, hi. So kind of you to invite me to your party.'

It was Annabel, tanned and smiling, looking like she should be in Ibiza in denim cut-offs and woven wedge sandals that wrapped up her toned calves. Handing me a bottle of champagne, she flashed me her perfect smile while I stood frozen in the doorway feeling ambushed. I glanced at Fiona who did her Big Eyes and mouthed, 'Sorry.'

'Not at all, the more the merrier!' Swiftly changing gear, I pinned on a bright smile, while regretting my own flip-flops and shorts that, compared to Annabel's, now felt like something from *Dad's Army*.

Saying hello to David, I wafted everyone inside, to a look of gratitude from Fiona and obvious second thoughts from Annabel when she realized I lived in a flat and there was no professional catering.

'Oh Nell, the place looks amazing!' enthused Fiona, as they made their way through to the garden.

'So eclectic,' cooed Annabel. As a former interior designer, I could see her giving it the once-over. I said a silent prayer for taking the TK Maxx stickers off the bottom of the scented candles.

'I love the colours you chose. Do you know she painted it all herself?' said Fiona, turning to Annabel who looked both baffled and horrified by such a concept. 'I have such talented friends!'

'Oh, it was nothing,' I smiled, quick to dismiss. 'Mum used to do all the decorating growing up. I learned from the best.'

'A-*maz*-ing.' Annabel shook her head. 'Mummy only taught us piano and tennis.'

Outside on the patio, Edward was manning the barbecue in his pinny.

'Perfect timing, these are ready for the hungry masses.' As he handed me a plate piled high with sausages and burgers to pass around, I gestured to our new guests.

'Look who's here!'

For a split second I saw Edward quickly recalculating his complicated food computations, before his manners kicked in. He always did have good reflexes.

'Why hello!' He turned to greet Fiona and David, then spotted Annabel. 'Hi, I'm Edward,' he nodded politely. 'And you are . . . ?'

There was a split-second pause where I witnessed Annabel visibly straighten at the sight of a good-looking man. A bit like day-old tulips when you put them in water.

'Delighted to meet you,' she smiled, quickly adjusting her off-the-shoulder top, so that it was more off the shoulder than on.

Hang on a minute – *was she flirting with Edward?*

'Only teasing,' she giggled. 'I'm Annabel. I'm a friend of the host.'

Never has the word 'friend' been so open to interpretation.

'Ah, that would be my fiancée Penelope,' he smiled good-humouredly. 'Though technically, that would also be me.'

'Penelope, as in Nell? You mean she's your . . . *you're her fiancé?*'

I watched Annabel's expression change from confusion to disbelief, like a bruise changing colour.

'Are those sausages veggie?'

A loud voice snapped me back to see a couple pointing at the plate in my hand. They were our neighbours from the flat next door, but it took a moment to place them as they were both police officers and out of uniform.

'Because we're vegetarians.'

'Oh, yes, veggie. Definitely.' I gave a bright hostess smile and waited for them to help themselves so I could quickly move away. They were both burly men and blocking my view of Edward and Annabel.

'Blimey, these are delicious!' said one, taking a bite. 'Are they plant-based, or soy?'

'Umm . . .'

Damn. And now I couldn't hear what Annabel was saying to him.

'You know, I don't know why anyone needs to eat meat any more,' his partner was saying. 'I mean, give a meat eater these and they'd never know the difference.'

Please. For the love of God. Just take the sausages.

'Can we take more than two or is that being greedy?'

'Not greedy at all! Help yourself!'

Sod Edward's calculations.

After offloading several more, I tried to escape across the patio, but it was too late. I was now being swamped by several other hungry guests and while I could see Edward and Annabel, heads bent together, chatting, I couldn't hear what was going on.

'Great barbecue, Stevens!' Max appeared by my elbow with a large margarita and a squiffy grin that told me it wasn't his first. 'Cocktails aren't too bad either.'

'I can't take any credit for the cocktails, those were Edward's idea.'

'A man after my own heart.'

'And mine,' I laughed and Max's face softened.

'Glad to see you happy at last.'

'Got there in the end.'

'Is this the end?' He raised his eyebrows.

'You know what I mean,' I smiled.

'Yeah, I do,' he nodded and took another sip. 'Though I wonder, if it is for me with my career. That's it. It's the end. I'm doomed to be That Guy.'

'Who's That Guy?'

'Oh you know, the dad at the school gates pretending to be busy checking his phone for work emails but the only notifications he's got are WhatsApps about organizing the school disco.'

I've known Max a long time, ever since we met backpacking in Greece, when he was a long and lanky twenty-something with big hair and even bigger career ambitions. He was made redundant over two years ago now and I know how much it knocked his confidence. It was the same for me when the business I shared with my ex went bust and I had to move back to London.

'No luck with the interviews then?' I was trying to tread the delicate line between support and sympathy.

'What interviews,' he joked, only he wasn't laughing.

'I hear you have the burgers!'

We were suddenly interrupted by a hungry Pazza, Edward's old friend from Bristol Uni, and I quickly did the introductions as he filled his plate.

'Edward didn't mention you were a vegetarian,' I added.

'Me? A Veg Head? Nah, I'm a total meathead,' he snorted, taking a bite of his burger. 'These beef burgers are delicious by the way.'

Beef burgers? I felt a beat of anxiety.

'Are you sure they're not veggie? Because apparently these days you can't tell the difference.'

'Trust me, I know a good burger.' He grabbed a sausage. 'And the pork sausages aren't bad either.'

Oh fuck. I looked over at our neighbours, the vegetarian police officers, who had now eaten four pork sausages. Catching me looking they smiled and waved. Later, they'd probably arrest me when they found out. After all, meat is murder.

'OK, well, I'd better circulate.' And giving my excuses, I quickly ducked behind the hydrangea bushes.

Behind me I heard Pazza turn to Max.

'So, Max, what do you do?'

Poor Max. I felt bad for abandoning him. I've never much liked small talk with strangers at parties. Thankfully, the upside of throwing your own party is all the guests are your friends, so after saying goodbye to Adam and Holly, who left early because of Olivia's bedtime – 'And mine,' added Holly, rolling her eyes, 'we've just had a holiday and I'm still exhausted' – I went in search of Fiona and Michelle.

I found them behind the bike shed, smoking cigarettes.

'Since when did we start smoking again?'

'I've only had one tiny puff,' said Michelle, looking shame-faced and quickly stubbing it out. 'They're Fiona's.'

'Ooh, you snitch,' laughed Fiona, blowing smoke down her nostrils.

I've known Fiona since university, back when she had hair down to her bottom and smoked Marlboro lights and every boy was madly in love with her.

She held out the packet. 'Want one?'

I made a face, then feeling the effects of two strong margaritas, quickly surrendered. 'Oh go on then.'

'So come on, let's see the ring.' Michelle turned to me eagerly. I haven't seen her since we announced our engagement as she's been so busy. 'Wow, it's gorgeous, Nell.'

'Thanks,' I smiled, and wondered if I should mention my conversation with Max, then decided against it. I didn't want to worry her.

'I bet your mum's pleased,' she grinned.

'Just a little bit.' I rolled my eyes. 'She loves Edward.'

'What about his boys? Are they here?'

'No, they're at their mum's this weekend, one of their local friends was having an eighteenth birthday party. They're pleased for us, at least they said they were. Saying that, they're not boys any more, they're these giant men and they have these giant appetites. When they stay with us I seem to spend the whole time feeding them. I swear to God, they're *always* hungry.'

'I bet they're delighted. You'll be a really cool stepmum.'

'Thanks, I hope so.' I puffed on the cigarette.

'I remember when David and I first got engaged, I couldn't wait to spend the rest of my life with him.' As Fiona spoke, we both turned towards her. 'Now I'm hiding from him.'

'You are? Why?' I asked, surprised.

'Because I just can't stand spending any more time together!' she exploded suddenly, making me and Michelle jump. 'Now we're both working from home, I never get a moment's peace. He's either having video meetings on loudspeaker in the garden office with all the doors open so I can't hear myself think, or fixing himself lunch and leaving the kitchen a mess.'

'My kitchen's always a mess,' said Michelle supportively.

'Mine too,' I nodded, encouragingly. 'Well, perhaps, not now,' I added, as an afterthought. 'Edward's quite fastidious.'

But Fiona was on a bit of a rant. 'I know it's his house too, but he used to be out all day at his law firm. Now he never leaves! Except to go to Cornwall on holiday and of course we all went too. Don't get me wrong, I love David dearly but I need my own space.'

As she finished one cigarette and swiftly lit up another Michelle and I exchanged worried glances.

'Sorry, is that terrible of me?'

'No, of course not.' We both quickly rallied as Fiona looked a bit upset. 'It's totally normal, I'm sure lots of couples feel the same, now everyone's working from home.'

Michelle smiled brightly. 'It's hard spending so much time together.'

'Absolutely,' I agreed. 'Though I've barely seen Edward all night.'

'Oh, he's fine. He's talking to Annabel,' reassured Michelle, before catching my expression and realizing she'd just done the opposite.

'Maybe I should go circulate.' I quickly stubbed out my cigarette. It had actually made me feel quite sick.

'I'll come with you. I desperately need the loo,' grimaced Michelle. 'You know the score. Kids: four. Pelvic floor: zero,' she joked.

But it didn't raise a smile. Instead, Fiona tapped ash into an empty plant pot. 'Actually, I think I'll just stay here.'

After grabbing another glass of prosecco, I found Edward with a few friends sitting by the fire pit, with Annabel at his elbow, laughing loudly at something he was saying. As I approached, he looked up and smiled broadly.

'Ah, there you are! Our neighbours have been looking for you, something about the veggie sausages?'

'Oh, right yes . . . I think there might have been some kind of mix-up.'

As he made space for me, I sat down, forcing a wedge of my bottom in between him and Annabel. For the first time I was actually quite pleased about my Lockdown 15.

'So easy to make mistakes with the catering,' she consoled, lightly touching my arm. 'You should have asked for my help, I've hosted so many events.'

'That's very kind of you, Annabel,' thanked Edward.

'Very.' I smiled tightly.

'People always say what an amazing hostess I am, but I'm lucky, I think it just comes naturally to some people,' she continued earnestly. 'So I wouldn't beat yourself up, Nell.'

I tried not to choke on my prosecco.

'Ah Max, I see you've found the tequila.'

As Max appeared looking worse for wear, Edward quickly stood up so Max could sit down, before he fell down.

'Right, who's doing shots?' he demanded, waving the bottle of Jose Cuervo.

'I think I'm going to stick with beer,' said Edward. 'Anyone want anything?' After taking everyone's drinks orders he set off towards the kitchen.

'Oh, Eddie,' I heard Annabel call after him. 'Would you be a darling and get me another glass of rosé? The palest you have.'

Eddie?

I feel myself stiffen. No one calls Edward Eddie. He won't allow anyone to shorten his name – or mine. I know, I've tried hard enough. He still insists on calling me by my full name, Penelope. I waited for him to say something and correct her, but instead he just smiled.

'Côtes de Provence, coming right up.'

WTF?

'Nell, where *have* you been hiding him?' Annabel turned back to me. 'Eddie's adorable!'

Right, that's it. There was nothing else for it. 'Hey Max,' I said, turning to him. 'Pass me the tequila.'

I'm grateful for:

1. *Not throttling Annabel.*
2. *Edward and I having our first row later that evening when we were stacking the dishwasher and I accused Annabel of flirting with him and he accused me of being ridiculous and of not rinsing the plates, because it's really important in a relationship to clear the air and not go to bed angry.**
3. *Not being as drunk as Max, who had to be carried, legless, out of the party.*
4. *Not being arrested by our neighbours, the policemen, though I am still avoiding them and intend to lie under oath.*
5. *Paracetamol and Berocca.*
6. *All the lovely comments underneath the photos I posted on Instagram saying what a perfect party it was and what an adorable couple we make.*
7. *#lifeonthegram #instaversusreality #wearestillnotspeaking*

---

* I went to bed fuming.

Flirting With the Truth

'That's great that you had your first fight!'

'It is?'

A few days later Liza calls me when I'm out walking Arthur on the river, and I fill her in on all the gory details of the party.

'Totally. It's like losing your relationship virginity,' she encourages, hearing the doubt in my voice. 'Plus then you get the make-up sex.'

'Hmm, I think we missed that memo.'

'But that's the best bit. I think that was the only reason Brad and I ever used to fight.'

'That, and the fact he was an idiot,' I remind her.

Before meeting Tia, Liza used to date on-again-off-again Brad, her fellow yoga teacher who purported to be Mr Spiritual when, in actual fact, he was just an insecure, incense-burning bully.

'Well, I was an idiot in that relationship too,' she concedes, and quite generously if you ask my opinion. 'You're not still mad at him are you?'

'Who, Edward? No, of course not.'

'So what if she was flirting with him? He wasn't flirting with her, right?

'He said he was just being polite.'

A cocker spaniel runs up to greet Arthur and I watch as he stands politely as she sniffs his bum. I feel there's a metaphor in there somewhere.

'In that case maybe he should've politely told her to back the fuck off,' says Liza, with characteristic honesty, which makes me laugh.

It feels good to laugh. I haven't for a few days. Despite hoping we'd cleared the air, it still feels a bit strained between me and Edward.

'To be honest, I feel a bit silly for saying something. That's tequila for you.'

'That wasn't the tequila, it was your gut,' she corrects. 'Girlfriend has eyes.'

'Yes, well, I was pretty drunk.'

'Well, I won't be getting drunk any time soon, we finally did the insemination.'

'Oh wow, Liza, that's so exciting!'

'Yeah, we've got the two-week wait now.'

'So what donor did you choose in the end?

'Well, here's the thing, you know what's funny? After all those hours looking at eye colour and star signs and likes and dislikes, you were right. I'm not going to date him, so we just went with whoever was healthy and available.'

'That's actually probably the best dating advice ever,' I say and she laughs at the other end of the phone. And then there's a pause and in that moment of quiet I recognize all her hope and excitement and fear of disappointment. 'I'm keeping everything crossed for you,' I add quietly.

'Thanks, Nell. Love you. And don't worry about Edward and Annabel.'

'No, I won't. Love you too.'

Then we say our goodbyes and I keep walking, lost in thought, until I call Arthur and he emerges from the river, shaking wet mud all over me and shaking me from the past.

'Arthur!' I scream, laughing, and putting him on the lead we head home.

Face Your Fears

I've never been good at confrontation. If I can avoid things, I usually will, in the misguided hope that somehow this will make the problem miraculously go away. But of course it never does. An example being The Angry Relative whose unread email is still waiting to accost me every time I check my inbox.

By the end of the week I can't ignore it any longer. Which is so often the case with things in life. Sooner or later it becomes harder to put off that difficult conversation, or trip to the doctor, or nagging feeling, than it is to face your fears.

Plus, it's only an email, how bad can it be?

BAD. VERY BAD.

The Angry Relative has a name: Joe Lloyd, and he's the brother of a talented artist who won several prestigious awards, before tragically losing her battle with cancer earlier in the year. Apparently I'd not only mistakenly attributed a quote to her, but I'd incorrectly stated the inspiration for one of her most celebrated paintings, which he was most furious about, as it was deeply personal. That will teach me to trust what I read on the internet. Worse, the entire email is written entirely IN SHOUTY CAPITAL LETTERS.

Mortified by my mistakes, I write a sincere and grovelling email, re-read it about a million times, and then send it. I feel terrible, but hopefully he will accept my apology and that will be the end of it.

I close my laptop. It's gone six. Time to clock off. Only there's no such thing as clocking off these days. Not when you have a smartphone.

Ping.

Less than five minutes later a reply drops into my inbox.

Oh shit. *That's him*. I stare at my phone, feeling sick to my stomach, then click on it.

No. That's not the end of it. On the contrary, he's still furious and shouting and wants the newspaper to publish a correction.

UNDER THE CIRCUMSTANCES IT'S THE VERY LEAST YOU CAN DO.
  JOE LLOYD

After checking with Sadiq, my editor, I confirm that the newspaper will publish a fully corrected obituary in the online edition. I also promise to run it by Joe first for his approval.

  With very best wishes and sincerest apologies once again,
    Penelope Stevens

Pressing send, this time I wait nervously for his response. It swiftly arrives.

  MUCH OBLIGED. JOE LLOYD.

Phew. Crisis averted and job saved.

Relieved to have finally reached a resolution, I quickly shove my phone in my pocket, grab my jacket from over the back of the chair and dash out of the flat. It's my turn to cook dinner this evening. Usually my turn involves something to do with pasta, salad or a jacket potato – or, if I'm feeling adventurous, all three – but tonight I'm going to make an extra special effort.

After talking to Liza, I think she's right about the make-up sex. Everyone goes on about communication in terms of talking, but sometimes what you need between two people is that physical communication – i.e. Edward and I need to have a good old bonk to properly clear the air and get things back on track. So the plan is to get us both in the mood by cooking a romantic meal. I've found a recipe involving pan-fried this and truffle that and lots of fresh herbs and exotic-sounding spices. It will be so delicious we won't be able to resist each other.

I head to the delicatessen on the corner. I don't usually shop here as it's one of those expensive organic farm shops, filled with lots of women in designer sportswear and over-priced vegetables. That said, all the ingredients are fresh and delicious and I'm all about saving the planet, not to mention my relationship.

Making sure I have my credit card, I grab a trolley and set off around the aisles, trying not to look at the prices. It's a world away from my local express supermarket. Trust me, there's not a Meal Deal or packet of Monster Munch in sight. Instead, everything is perfectly curated with fresh flowers and scented candles and linen tea towels. Chia seeds and quinoa rub ancient grain shoulders with fresh juices and oat milk. There's even freshly baked vegan brownies to tempt you by the cash register.

It's as if Instagram and a supermarket had a baby. I float around, filling my trolley and trying not to think about when I'm going to have to pay for it all. In fact, I'm having the most wonderful shopping experience, when I hear a man's voice.

'Hello?'

It sounds like it's coming from behind me, so I turn around, but there's no one there, just another woman in yoga pants. I move over to the cheese counter and stare at the selection of triple creams and ripe Bries and heavily matured Manchegos, wondering which to choose. Is there such thing as sexy cheese?

'Hello? Penelope Stevens?'

As I hear a man's voice again, I suddenly realize it's coming from the back pocket of my jeans. Shit, I must have pocket-dialled someone. I quickly snatch out my phone and look at my screen. I don't recognize the number.

'Are you there? You just called me. This is Joe Lloyd.'

My chest constricts with horror. Oh my God. I've only gone and pocket-dialled Joe, the Angry Relative. Paralysed, I stare at my phone with horror. It's like holding a live hand grenade. It must be because I saved him to my contacts, or didn't close his email, or – oh fuck, I don't know, what happened to the screen lock function? I consider hanging up.

'Um, hi, Joe.'

But of course, I can't hang up, can I? Not unless I want to lose my job.

'Oh, hello. Finally.'

'Sorry, I put you on mute accidentally.' Silently I congratulate myself on my quick thinking. 'How are you?' I try to quickly untangle my headphones. WTF is it with headphones? As soon as I put them in my pocket, they spontaneously tangle themselves into knots like some kind of contortionist magic trick.

'Fine. And you?'

'Yes, super, thanks.' I give up and shove them, tangled, into my ears and then there's an excruciating pause as I try to think of something suitable to say. 'So I was thinking, perhaps we should meet,' I blurt.

'Excuse me?'

I can't believe I just said that. With both hands I clutch my forehead and drop it onto the handle of my trolley, in the kind of *Brace! Brace!* position you're advised to take to prepare for a crash landing.

'About your sister's obituary. It might be better, then we can talk, make sure you're happy with everything . . .' I can hear myself babbling.

'Right, yes.'

'I want to make sure I get it right this time. I'm really sorry. About before.' I draw breath and there's a moment's excruciating silence.

'Apology accepted,' he replies finally, his voice softening.

I'm both relieved and surprised. He sounds nothing like the shouting man on the email. Thankful to have survived, I lift myself up from the brace position.

'OK, well . . . um, how about a coffee next week?'

'Sounds good.'

'Wonderful. Well, I'd better get back to choosing a sexy cheese,' I reply, trying to be all light-hearted, then realize what I've just said and cringe. Talk about inappropriate. It's nerves. I always over-share.

'I recommend taleggio.'

'Oh.' It takes me by surprise. 'Great, thanks . . . Speak soon!'

I'm grateful for:
1. *Edward saying he liked spicy food to not hurt my feelings when his mouth was obviously on fire, and that using 1 tbsp of chilli flakes instead of 1 tsp is a very easy mistake to make.*
2. *Laughing in the face of it all being better at bringing us back together than any romantic meal ever could.*
3. *Joe, for recommending taleggio as it was delicious and*

for being so nice about everything, as it could have been a lot worse. I once ended a conversation with my mortgage broker by saying, 'Love you!' and sending an emoji of a cartoon mouse with love hearts for eyes (trust me, I have no idea where it came from!).
4. *Make-up sex and chocolate profiteroles.*

The Tuesday Toodlepip Club

Following on from Friday's theme of facing your fears, the following Tuesday I go to meet Cricket at the community centre. I'm running a bit late and as I push open the door and enter the hall, she looks up from sanding her coffin and waves cheerfully.

'Yoo hoo, Nell, over here!'

Seeing her, I'm quite taken aback. Seriously, I haven't seen my friend look so well in months. She's positively glowing.

Smiling, I wave back. 'Coffee?'

She gives me the thumbs-up. 'Milk, no sugar.'

Facing up to her death seems to have given her a new lease of life. Talk about ironic.

'Here you go.' Five minutes later I return with two polystyrene cups of coffee, to find her chatting to two other members of the club.

'Thank you, my dear.' Putting down the sandpaper and taking her coffee gratefully, she takes a sip, then rests it on the lid of her coffin. Made of chipboard, there's a fine coating of dust on everything, including Cricket. It brings a whole new meaning to the phrase 'powdering your nose'.

'Nell, have you met Diane and her daughter, Rosie?'

'Hi, pleased to meet you.'

We all smile and nod and say hello. Diane is rocking a short, spiky pink haircut and long, dangly earrings that seem to have a life of their own, while her daughter, Rosie, tells me they thought this might be a nice bonding experience.

'Usually we go for mani-pedis, but we thought we'd do something different this time, didn't we, Mum?'

Diane nods vigorously, her earrings sounding like wind-chimes. 'We were going to do a ceramics class, but like I said to Rosie, who needs another fruit bowl?'

Indeed.

Elaine runs the club with the help of her husband Seymour, an expert craftsman who is teaching Rosie and Diane and a few other people how to weave their caskets from willow. Our members are an eclectic mix of characters and we're still all getting to know each other. In the first week, Elaine did that thing where she went around the group and we all had to introduce ourselves and try not to look self-conscious. Everyone seemed very friendly. What was most surprising was how bizarrely cheerful everyone was. Initially I'd been worried it would be depressing and ghoulish, but the atmosphere has been fun and upbeat.

Leaving Cricket chatting to Diane and Rosie, I take off my coat and turn my attention to my own coffin. *My own coffin.* OK, so it's still surreal but strangely, it's beginning to feel a bit more normal. After all, it's just a box when you think about it. Except, to be honest, I'm trying *not* to think about it. There's cheerful and upbeat and there's a total head-fuck, so instead I busy myself with my paint tray and roller.

'So have you decided what colour you're going to paint it?'

It's Derek, my neighbour. Each of us have a table, or 'work station', and mine is positioned between his and Cricket's. Derek is a retired postman whose partner, Steve, died some years ago. Apparently he found the whole funeral experience cripplingly expensive and wants to ensure his daughter isn't faced with the same costs.

'Not yet, this is just the undercoat.'

'Don't you mean the undertaker?' He laughs, his lungs wheezing from a lifelong Embassy habit.

I laugh good-naturedly. I like Derek a lot, even if his jokes are terrible.

'What about yours?' I motion to his own casket. Derek is a keen carpenter and has decided to forgo one of the flat-pack options and make one from his own designs.

'I'm thinking I might cover it in stamps. Used ones, you know.' Holding a screwdriver, he stands back to survey his handiwork.

'Oh, that's a clever idea,' I nod. 'It's very personal too.'

'Well, I've always wanted to go first class,' he adds with a wink, then tuts loudly. 'Oh Gordon Bennett, I think my corners are wonky—'

Just then we're interrupted by Elaine who comes over to cheerfully remind us all that ours is only a twelve-week course and 'we don't have for ever' which seems a little on the nose, considering the course involves making your own coffin. Elaine reminds me of one of my teachers at school, telling us off for chatting at the back and chivvying us all along with a mixture of enthusiasm, compassion and sheer hands-on practicality. Apparently Elaine used to be a travel agent and after spending her whole life sending people around the world on package holidays, now she wants to help them on their final journey. 'But it's not goodbye, it's cheerio and toodlepip,' she keeps saying, with a smile.

As Elaine disappears with her clipboard and Derek starts taking apart his coffin, Cricket leans over. 'I forgot to say I very much enjoyed your party. Edward is lovely. I very much approve.'

I'm both amused and pleased by her blessing. It feels vaguely of another era. 'He approved of you too.'

'Great minds think alike,' she says, then frowns. 'I'm sorry I couldn't stay longer.'

'Oh, don't worry, I'm just glad you came.'

'I'm just still not used to going to parties without Monty. Even now, after more than two years, it always feels like there's something missing. I'm always absently reaching for him, but he's not there. Rather like that feeling when you've left your handbag at home.'

She smiles absently, then gives herself a shake. 'So anyway, I've been thinking how I might decorate mine.' She gestures to her coffin. 'How do you feel about graffiti art?'

'I love it. I can totally see you as the next Banksy.'

Her eyes flash with amusement. 'I've always rather fancied myself with spray paints. I tried oils, but they were never quite my thing.'

'Mine neither,' I grin, remembering the time she took me to her art class and I discovered that not only was it life drawing, but the nude model was The Hot Dad I'd fancied from the pub, who instead turned out to be The Fun Uncle, who turned out to be Johnny, my online date, who ended up ghosting me. Yes, I know, there's a lot to unpack there. 'And a graffiti coffin is certainly different.'

'Death may be inevitable, but I don't see why it has to be dull.' Reaching for her coffee, she takes a sip.

'Don't worry about getting old, worry about being dull,' I say, quoting her own words back to her.

Our eyes meet and we exchange smiles, both of us momentarily returning to that first time we met when I went to interview her for Monty's obituary and I felt a connection with someone who understood me for the first time in for ever.

'That's the problem, you see . . .'

I watch as Cricket's face falls.

'Monty's funeral *was* dull. He had a beige coffin. Lilies. People wore black. It was all very traditional and I worry that I let him down.' Absently she fingers the small gold locket that she always wears; a gift from him. 'I had to plan everything but the grief was so raw. So many decisions when you can't make a single one. In truth it was all such a blur . . .'

Her shoulders seem to sag, as if the memory itself is weighing heavily on them.

'I just remember the funeral directors with their fabric flowers and sombre music. I know it's not an easy job to do, but does it have to be so dour?' she gasps. 'All the ghastly brochures and hushed voices. The dreadful practicalities about what handles you want, or whether you prefer MDF, mahogany or a solid oak casket. None of it remotely reflected the person he was. Monty wasn't traditional in the slightest. He was eccentric. Flamboyant. Irreverent.'

I listen as she talks, not interrupting. I can't begin to imagine.

'He wouldn't have given a rat's arse about the type of handles,' she tuts, shaking her head, her face filled with self-reproach.

'I'm sorry you had to go through that, I wish I'd been there for you.'

'You're here now, that's all that matters.' Her eyes meet mine and I wish I could lift that heavy burden of guilt, the feeling that you let them down. And then I realize I'm no longer thinking about Cricket, I'm thinking about myself.

The sound of laughter echoes around the hall and we look over to see Rosie and Diane in fits of giggles with Seymour, who is in the middle of teaching them how to weave their lids. I watch Elaine darting over, arms circling like windmills, to find out what's going on.

'But anyway, let's not be gloomy.' Snapping back, Cricket

straightens up. 'I have some very exciting news. It's about Monty's play, the one you very cleverly finished.' I try to dismiss her compliment, but she bats me away. 'Christopher, the director called. The funding has been secured. We're hoping to open in the West End in June next year.'

'Oh, wow, that is exciting news!'

I know how disappointed she'd been when everything had been cancelled because of the pandemic.

'They're starting casting some of the roles next month, which I know is very early, but we've had so many setbacks we thought it might be prudent. I wondered if you wanted to sit in on the auditions? I thought it might be fun for you to see all the characters brought to life.'

'Gosh, yes that would be amazing.' I break off. 'But are you sure they won't mind? I mean, am I allowed? I just did a bit of editing.'

'My dear girl, don't be so modest, you did rather a lot more than that. If it wasn't for you, we wouldn't have a play to produce.'

'I only wrote the ending.'

'Perhaps the ending is the most important part,' she considers. 'Maybe we should approach life backwards. Decide how we want it to end so that then we know how to begin.'

She gestures around the hall, it's a hive of activity with everyone chatting and laughing as they work on their coffins.

'But isn't the whole point that we never know what's going to happen?' I reply. 'Even if we try, life hardly ever goes to plan, does it? Mine certainly didn't and neither did yours.'

'True,' she nods. Putting down her coffee, she picks up her sandpaper.

'And if we've learned anything from these past couple of years, it's that life has a habit of taking you by surprise,' I continue, as we both resume vigorously sanding. 'I for one certainly never expected to be spending my Tuesday afternoons making my own coffin,' I add and she laughs heartily.

We're interrupted by loud swearing coming from the next work station. 'Bugger it!' We look over to see Derek lying in his half-assembled casket, legs splayed out of the sides.

'Derek, are you all right?'

'Bloody Nora, they'll have to chop my legs off,' he groans loudly. 'I've got my measurements wrong. It's too sodding small.'

Hide and Seek

The next day I get a call from Max to apologize about being blind drunk at the party. 'I meant to call last week, but I haven't had a minute and didn't want to just send a text.'

'It's fine, don't worry. You weren't that drunk.'

'Nell, I was shitfaced. I can't remember anything that happened. Was I terrible?'

'How do you define terrible?'

'Well, there's wanker and there's total wanker.'

I laugh. I love Max. We've been friends for years and even though our lives couldn't be more different, we share the same sense of humour.

'In that case I'd just go for wanker.'

He laughs then and I sense his relief.

'You know, Michelle's still furious with me. Apparently I threw up all over the back seat of the Uber.'

'Classy.'

In the background I hear a commotion.

'Shit.'

I feel a beat of concern. 'Where are you?'

'Locked in the bathroom.' He lowers his voice to a whisper.

'Are you OK? It sounds like a hostage situation.'

'It is. Only I've temporarily escaped.'

'From where?'

'I'm hiding from the kids. The toilet's the only place I can get any peace,' he explains. He sounds like a desperate man.

'DADDY!!!!!!'

There's loud yelling in the background and the sound of thumping and banging on the door.

'Bollocks. They've found me. Better go.'

After he hangs up it gets me thinking. About Fiona hiding from David behind the bike shed at my party. About my conversation with Cricket, that day in Hyde Park a couple of months ago, when she confessed to wanting to hide from life. About how I'd hid from that email from Joe, The Angry Relative, until finally I'd been forced to face up to it. Which begs the question: are we all hiding from something? And, if so, can you hide from it for ever or will it always finally seek you out?

Wedding Plan Wars: the Battle of the Spreadsheet

Since moving back in with Edward, we haven't had any of our 'domestics' which characterized the last time we lived together. Instead we've compromised on the thermostat. I've remembered to turn the lights off and fill the ice-cube trays. We've even negotiated the stacking of the dishwasher – which, frankly, made Brexit look easy – so I'm feeling rather smug about planning a wedding together.*

Not that we've actually *planned* anything yet. We've had a few casual conversations, discounted a few ideas – it's Edward's second marriage and I'm not religious, so neither of us wants to do the whole vicar-and-church shebang – but nothing's been decided. Which is a bit worrying, as I just read an article about how you need at least a year to plan a wedding and *at least* six months to get your skin ready. *Six months!* To achieve a bridal glow? Crikey. I'm beginning to think Fiona was right.

So I was pleased and somewhat relieved when Edward suggested we set aside this evening to sit down together and make a start with the plans. He said he'd got something to show me. And now of course, I'm really excited. I wonder what it is? My first thought was he's asked his dad if we can

---

* OK, we're still in disagreement about the loo roll, and there was a tussle over whether the wooden spoons could go in the dishwasher, but nothing's perfect.

get married at his house in the South of France, which got me imagining romantic fairy-lit vineyards and Château de this and that, but then I thought maybe it's something else and . . . well, let's just say, my imagination's been going into overdrive.

It's funny, but when Edward first proposed, I had all these doubts. I'd been engaged before, but we never got as far as setting a date before it all fell apart, and I was worried that history might repeat itself. That it would jinx things between us. That perhaps I wasn't the marrying kind. Which sounds a bit ridiculous, but if ain't broke, why fix it? So for a long time I didn't look at anything to do with weddings. Not a google, not a hashtag search, not a bridal magazine for inspiration and ideas. Nothing.

But now I think I might have caught a case of wedding fever. It was quite accidental. A few weeks ago I just happened across the famous black-and-white image of Bianca Jagger in her famous Yves Saint Laurent wedding suit[†] and it was like lighting the touch paper. Soon after I found myself up late at night, watching *Four Weddings and a Funeral* for the millionth time, and a few days later I was flicking channels and came across *Married At First Sight* – and didn't flick over.

And before you knew it the fever had spread like a rash. I was online typing in #bohoweddings and scrolling through endless photos of rustic barns strung with carnival lights and brides with flower crowns walking through cornfields. Googling destination weddings; all palm trees and barefoot on the beach. Or what about something really cool and wacky, like those couples that get married abseiling down a

---

† Which has to be the best wedding outfit of all time – I mean seriously, sleeves AND pockets?!

mountain or dressed up like Vikings?* I was even tempted to get myself a Pinterest mood board.

I know. Me? I can hardly believe it!

And don't even get me started on the cake. I mean, hello, an excuse to eat cake and throw a big party and buy new shoes. Honestly, what's not to like about planning a wedding?

So it's with high spirits that I sit down opposite Edward at the kitchen table this evening. We've got a pizza, a bottle of wine and our laptops. Together with a huge sense of anticipation. Gosh, this is so much fun.

'OK, so I've got something to show you.' Opening his laptop, Edward makes a few taps on his keyboard.

'Me too,' I grin, putting down my slice of margherita pizza and turning round my screen to show him. OK, I confess. I actually did make a mood board. 'So I was thinking maybe a barn in the country, or even a destination wedding, there's some amazing ones I saw in the Maldives . . . or even the Caribbean,' I begin jabbering excitedly.

'The Caribbean?' Edward frowns.

Suddenly it registers. 'Oh, of course. You're worried about the carbon footprint! All the guests flying out . . . I know, maybe we can offset it by planting trees like all the celebrities do?'

Edward is looking at me blankly. All at once I realize I'm completely taking over.

'Sorry, I didn't mean to interrupt.' I reach across the table for his hand. 'I was just getting a bit carried away, what were you saying?'

And now I feel bad. He's probably planned this whole big reveal about having the wedding in France and here I am, blathering on about weddings in the Caribbean.

---

* That's why they call it wedding fever. I must have been delirious at that point.

'It's OK darling.'

Squeezing my hand, Edward smiles and we share a look across the top of our laptop screens. I feel myself relax. Seriously, could get this more romantic?

'I just wanted to show you something I've been working on . . .'

Oh my God, he *has* planned a surprise!

The South of France. Sunshine. Style. Glamour. Romance. Fairy lights. Vineyards. Rosé. French accents. It's all whizzing through my head like confetti. Wait till I tell Fiona or Liza. Or – even better – wait till Annabel finds out.

Edward turns his computer around so I can see. I can barely contain my excitement. I take a slug of wine and brace myself for a photo of a fairy-tale chateau.

It's an Excel spreadsheet.

Nonplussed I stare at it, then look at Edward. There must be some mistake. He must have hit on the wrong tab. Only instead of frowning and hitting his keyboard to open up the right window, he's smiling.

'It's a spreadsheet?' Confused, I state the obvious.

'It's not just any spreadsheet . . . it's our wedding spread-sheet!'

All that's missing is a 'Ta daah!!' He looks at me triumph-antly. I stare back, frozen. 'See, here's the column for the budget, so there's cost of hire, reception, drinks and food . . .' He pushes his glasses up his nose and leans closer, animatedly pointing at the miniscule row upon row upon never-ending row. 'And here's the guest list and seating plans. I've also used this really great software that let me put in the dates and cross reference . . .'

He lost me at budget and columns. I'm a large glass of rosé in and I honestly don't have a clue what he's talking about.

I try to focus but distant memories of terrible temping jobs come flooding back, struggling with spreadsheets with all those cells and figures and columns that were supposed to add up, *and never added up*. It was like maths, and I was always terrible at maths.

But here's Edward, joyfully engrossed.

'So what do you think?' he asks and I zone back in. He's almost bursting with pride. I feel a crash of disappointment, but try to hide it.

'Um . . . gosh, yes, very organized.'

And now I'm having flashbacks to when I first moved in as his flatmate and he produced a ring binder of house rules. What next, wedding rules?

'Well, yes, I think it's important to be meticulous with the planning so we keep to our budget.'

'But we haven't got a budget,' I say weakly.

The South of France and barefoot beaches in the Maldives have flown out of the window.

'Exactly! Which is what I wanted us to discuss tonight. But I thought it would be much easier for us to decide on finances and affordability now we have this spreadsheet.' He picks up his wine glass and leans back in his chair, beaming at me. I can tell he's really pleased with himself. 'In fact, I was thinking we should probably think about getting a joint account and then we can run all the expenses through it, make it much easier.'

All thoughts of romance are fast disappearing as practicality begins to congeal, like the melted cheese on the pizza. He offers me the last slice, but I shake my head and tell him to have it.

'It's not very romantic,' I say finally.

'Romantic?' Taking a bite of pizza, Edward looks puzzled at the concept. 'But we're planning a wedding.'

'Exactly!' I say finally with exasperation.

Caught off-guard by my reaction, he looks surprised. But in the middle of chewing, the penny seems to finally drop. 'Of course, you're right, I'm sorry, blinding you with all these numbers . . . What were you saying . . . something about the Caribbean? Was that about the honeymoon?'

At the mention of the honeymoon, it's like a bright light.

'Well, yes, maybe.'

'Sounds wonderful.'

Buoyed up by his enthusiasm, I feel my excitement returning. 'You know, I've always wanted to go on a safari on my honeymoon . . . though I know they're really expensive so we probably can't afford it,' I add quickly, but Edward silences my protestations by leaning over and kissing me. OK, I take it back, this is kind of romantic.

As we break apart, he strokes my cheek. 'Well, that's what's so genius –' he gestures to his screen '– this spreadsheet will tell us.' And breaking into a wide smile, he clinks his glass against mine. 'See, I've even got a column for the honeymoon!'

I'm grateful for:
1. *Having the maturity to know that it's OK not to see eye to eye with your partner when planning a wedding, and battles before the big day are very common.*
2. *Having the right Stain Devil to get the wine out of Edward's shirt when I throw it at him.*

University Challenge

According to my mum friends, there's nothing that makes you take stock of life like the first day your baby starts primary school.

To those mums I say, you give me a baby and primary school and I raise you a teenage stepson and university. Forget taking stock of life, it's a complete and total mind-fuck.

On Monday, Edward and I drive his son Ollie to Manchester. He's starting his first term at university and, by sheer co-incidence, he's chosen the same university I went to a few years ago. No, wait. It's been . . . let me add it up . . . *Twenty-something years ago?* Hang on. That must be wrong. It can't have been that long ago!

Can it?

How can that even be possible? Someone who went to university over a quarter of a century ago would be REALLY OLD now. They wouldn't be still shopping for bargains on eBay, and planning their first wedding and still trying to figure it all out. They're driving estate cars and checking the value of their pension plans and making noises when they get up and sit down on the sofa.

Oh God, but that's me. I caught myself doing it the other day. It's the weirdest thing. All these little sighs and moans and gasps that punctuate my every move. It's actually quite alarming. What I want to know is when did this start happening?

And, more importantly, *how can I make it stop?*

*

It's a long drive so we leave early.

'Are you sure it's OK for me to come?' I say from the back seat, where I'm sitting, squashed up next to Arthur and all Ollie's luggage. Edward's twin boys are both six foot five and so Ollie's in the front seat with his headphones on.

'Absolutely,' reassures Edward from the driver's seat. 'We're getting married, you're part of the family. Plus it's a good chance for you to meet Sophie, finally.'

At the mention of Edward's ex-wife my stomach churns. When I told Fiona I was going to meet her, she asked me what she was like and I replied, 'Petite, stylish and French.' To which there'd been silence on the other end of the phone. It's amazing, how much you can convey with silence. She rallied quickly, telling me it would be fine, and not to be nervous, that Edward loved me and to wear my new navy polka-dot jumpsuit as I looked amazing in it, but even Fiona sounded a bit worried.

'I know she's really looking forward to it.'

'Me too,' I say, trying to twist my wet hair into some kind of 'beach waves'. We'd all had to share a bathroom and Ollie had taken for ever, meaning I was the last in the shower and hadn't had time to dry my hair. I could already feel the frizz starting and my fringe was curling up at the edges like stale bread.

'Hopefully we won't hit traffic so we can all go and have lunch.'

Sophie was joining us there with her boyfriend, Jed. Apparently she'd just got back from taking their other son, Louis, to Paris where he was spending his gap year working as an intern at his uncle's law firm and improving his French.

'Sounds great.' I squash down the nerves and find a barrette in my handbag. I clip my hair up, then catch my reflection in the rear-view mirror (argh, is there a *worse* mirror than the rear-view?) and let it loose again.

'Then it's another two hours to your parents', so we should make it in plenty of time for dinner.'

'Tea,' I correct. 'Dinner's lunch, remember?'

Edward catches me looking in the rear-view and flashes me a smile. 'I better remember this stuff now I'm going to be the son-in-law.'

'Oh, you don't have to remember anything,' I grin. 'You're Prince Charming who's going to save their poor, feckless daughter from being a spinster *and* a vegetarian. You're golden.'

Edward laughs. He thinks I'm joking. And I am. Sort of. Mum and Dad live in a little village in the Lake District, and most of their friends' grown-up children live locally and are married with kids. Both me and my brother Richard moved away, but he got married a couple of years ago and now has Evie, who's nearly two, so no one thinks he's weird. Plus, no one ever really asked questions about Rich, because he's a man and Don't Get Me Started.*

But anyway, suffice to say Mum is beyond thrilled. In fact, I wouldn't surprised if she'd put a notice in the Post Office window.

Carol and Philip Stevens are proud and relieved to announce the engagement of their daughter Penelope to Edward Lewis.

'We'd almost given up hope,' added a delighted mother-of-the-forty-something-bride, 'but better late than never!'

After four hours we finally arrive in Manchester and pull

---

* Otherwise known as DGMS, which applies to all things my brother.

into the car park in front of the halls of residence. Having spent most of the journey with the window open so Arthur could get some fresh air, I get out of the car windswept and crumpled, covered in dog hair, my own hair like a bird's nest.

To meet Sophie, looking effortlessly chic in a trouser suit and converse high tops, her glossy blonde hair tied in a loose chignon, and a silk scarf – that is undoubtedly Hermès – knotted casually around her neck in that way French women always know how to do and I always look like I'm being strangled.

FFS. Not quite the first meeting with the ex-wife I had in mind.

But Sophie couldn't be lovelier. After hugging her son, who looks mortified by this public display of parental affection in a car park of his contemporaries, she greets me warmly, kissing me on both cheeks and congratulating me and Edward on our recent engagement.

It's a huge relief. I've heard so many horror stories about ex-wives (though it's always bugged me how they're always described as *crazy* ex-wives, and always by the men who married them). It's also reassuring to see Sophie and Edward being polite and friendly with each other. I knew their divorce had been amicable. According to Edward, both of them had simply fallen out of love with each other years before, but had stayed together for the boys.

Edward's relationship with his ex-wife's boyfriend, however, seems a little more on the strained side.

'Hello, Jed.'

'Wotcha, Edward.'

I'm not quite sure how I imagined Jed to look, but it's certainly not a shaved head, tattooed sleeves and the kind of facial hair that involves painstaking topiary. As Edward goes to shake his hand, Jed gives him an enthusiastic fist bump.

'So this is cool, huh? Little Ollie, flying the nest?'

Considering little Ollie is six foot five this seems to support Edward's suspicions that Jed was sniffing around Sophie, long before they divorced.

'Very cool,' agrees Edward, moving the words around in his mouth as if they're something unsavoury.

'Hey, can you give us a hand?'

Already busy unpacking, Ollie calls from the boot of the car. There's a tussle between the two men as they rush over and begin filling their arms, piling them up in a competition to see who can carry the most boxes. It's like Testosterone Jenga.

Meanwhile I turn my attentions to Arthur, clipping on his lead so he can sniff around and have a pee.

'Look, it's Sophie,' I enthuse, expecting his usual exuberant greeting when he spots his previous owner, but his tail barely wags. The feeling appears to be mutual. With an outstretched hand, she pats his head awkwardly.

'I'm allergic,' she explains, with a Gallic shrug of her shoulders.

'Yes, Edward told me, when I first moved in,' I nod.

'Ah, yes, of course, you were the flatmate, I forgot how you met,' she smiles, seemingly amused. 'The woman from America who broke up with her boyfriend and moved back to London and writes about dead people . . . what a funny story.'

I feel a slight rankle. 'Well, it wasn't exactly funny at the time.'

I like Sophie, she's really nice and doesn't mean any harm, but she has no idea. While I was flailing around on planet What The Fuck Am I Going To Do With My Life, she was ticking all the boxes: married, settled, twin boys, a lovely house in the country, not to mention a beautiful collection of Hermès silk scarves. Yet she wasn't happy either, I have to quickly remind myself. And she got divorced, which isn't very nice for anyone. Though I'm glad for me.

I look across at Edward, who's striding across the car park with Ollie, carrying a wobbling microwave balanced on a pile of bedding; racing alongside him is Jed with a precarious pile of kitchen utensils. As Jed's mug tree goes flying, Edward emerges the clear winner. I feel a blast of love towards him. I feel like a winner too.

After unloading the car, we all decamp to the local pub around the corner for lunch. Me, Edward, Sophie, Jed, Ollie and Arthur. This new blended family. We sit outside in the beer garden and raise a toast to Ollie's new student life with a bottle of champagne. It's pleasant enough, but I feel a bit like an actor who's joined a long-running soap, trying carefully to navigate the dynamics between the original cast members. I also sense a bit of tension between Edward and Jed.

'So Jed, how's photography these days?'

'I wouldn't know, mate. Anyone can take a photo with their phones and call themselves a photographer. I'm working on an app.'

'Oh yes? What kind of app?'

'It's for online shopping,' says Jed, cutting into his steak. I'd noticed he'd ordered the most expensive thing on the menu. 'Basically you can go on there and get anything you want, delivered to your door—'

'You mean like Amazon?'

'Well, I'm only at the design stage.' He takes a swig of the champagne and fills up his glass. 'But I've already had loads of interest. I've got a ton of meetings when we get back from our safari.'

'Wow, you're going on a safari?' I interrupt excitedly. 'I've always wanted to go on one, we were thinking maybe for our honeymoon, but they're so expensive . . .'

'Yeah, next week, for my birthday. Sophie's treat.' He flashes her a smile across the table.

'You mean my treat,' mutters Edward into his salad, but luckily they don't hear him as Jed is too busy stroking Sophie's arm and telling her about the balloon ride he's going to take her on across the Serengeti.

Which is probably the reason why Edward's spreadsheet wouldn't stretch to a safari and now we're thinking Rome for a few days.

'Can we get back soon, Dad? I want to unpack,' says Ollie, looking across at Edward.

'You mean to get rid of The Olds, eh?' laughs Jed.

'Of course,' nods Edward, ignoring Jed. As we leave, I notice Edward picks up the bill. Jed lets him.

When we return, the car park is full of teenagers and parents, in various states of unloading cars and saying goodbye. I look around at all the other eighteen-year-olds. They look so young now. Like kids, really, but when I was their age I felt so grown up. I thought I knew it all and yet, of course, I knew nothing at all. Not much has changed, and yet so much has changed.

As Edward and Sophie say goodbye to Ollie, I go round to the other side of the car to give them some space, where I catch the eye of a woman, blowing her nose and looking tearful.

'Back to the empty nest now, huh?'

'Oh, right, yes.' Realizing she's mistaken me for a parent too, I feel suddenly awkward.

'What's yours studying?'

'Oh, he's not mine . . . I mean . . . he's my stepson, sort

of . . .' I try to explain, but I feel myself getting tied up in knots. The woman stares at me blankly. 'Geography,' I add hastily, trying to rescue the situation.

'Jamil's doing law,' she smiles proudly, sniffing into her tissue.

'Congratulations.' I force a bright smile. 'You must be so proud.'

'You too,' she nods.

'Yes.'

But it's complicated. Watching Edward and Sophie with Ollie, I'm filled with mixed emotions. It's such a rite of passage, sending your child off to university, but as much as I share Edward's pride, I feel like an outsider. Where do I fit in? Being a stepmum can be hard to navigate. Harder still is navigating my own loss, of which today I can't help being reminded. Would that have been me, the proud mum trying not to cry?

'OK, come on everyone, time for photos.'

Ollie lets out a loud groan of embarrassment, as we all squash in for a series of selfies. Jed instructing everyone how to set the timer, Ollie just desperate to get on with it, Edward with his arm around me, and Sophie exclaiming, '*Dites ouistiti!*' as we all smile for the camera. And then we're all saying our goodbyes and climbing into our cars and waving at Ollie, who stands with his hands in his pockets, smiling bemusedly at these silly old people. Because I suppose that's what we are to an eighteen-year-old. Silly old people.

'Right, next stop, your parents' and plans for our wedding,' grins Edward, putting the car into gear.

Sitting next to him in the passenger seat, I smile and look out of the window.

And as we drive away, I look back at the familiar building, with its ugly sixties architecture, and it's as if time suddenly shifts and pulls back its curtain, and I see myself on my first day at uni, standing at the window of my old dorm room, watching me leave. Eighteen years old and no idea of what the future held.

'Who are you looking at?' asks Edward.

'Oh no one.' I shake my head.

And turning away from the ghosts of my past, I look firmly ahead to my future.

OCTOBER

#somethingoldsomethingnew

Something Old, Something New

'So have you thought any more about a date?'

It's the last day of our visit to my parents. Tomorrow we're due to drive back to London. It's been lovely to spend time with Mum and Dad again. And even with my annoying little brother Rich, who stayed over one night for dinner with his wife Nathalie, and little Evie, my adorable niece.

With everything that's been going on, it's been ages since the family has got together, and it's comforting to see that nothing has changed, apart from Dad's on a diet, Rich has lost even more hair and little Evie is now walking and talking and growing up so fast.

And Edward and I are getting married.

Something which Mum won't let anyone forget by going on about it 24/7. Which sounds a bit mean, as I know it's only because she's excited,* and I'm excited too, but you'd think it was her wedding. Only yesterday she came back from the supermarket with a pile of bridal magazines and suggested we make a vision board. Apparently it was Alexa's idea.

'You mean since you asked me yesterday? And the day before that?'

It's after lunch and I'm helping her clean up in the kitchen. It's just the two of us. Edward and Dad have gone out.

Mum bristles in her rubber gloves. 'Well, St Cuthbert's gets

---

* See! My daughter's not really a fuck-up!

booked up really quickly. Gordon, the vicar, says it's pandemonium, there's hardly a Saturday free. Alexa, open the calendar.'

'We're not getting married in a church, Edward's divorced.'

At which point Mum straightens up at the sink. 'Well, you'll be pleased to know, I've already had a word with Gordon, lovely man he is, very modern you know, and he says it's fine. They have lots of divorced people these days.'

'We were thinking London or France.'

'France!'

'France is a country in Europe,' chimes Alexa, cheerily.

'Edward's dad lives in Provence.'

Admittedly it's only been me that's been thinking France after Edward showed me photos of his dad's house, which is actually a chateau. Not a huge one, just a little one, but still, it even has its own vineyard. Alas Edward isn't particularly close to his father, so I doubt he'd want to get married there, even if we would save a fortune on wine.

'And have you thought about the dress yet?'

Mum, however, is not to be deterred and swiftly changes wedding topics. Of which, I am realizing, there are an infinite number.

'Only that I want to find something with sleeves and pockets.'

'Pockets?' She looks up from scrubbing the Yorkshire pudding tray with an appalled expression, then shakes her head. 'Oh, very funny, Nell.'

'I'm not joking.' Grabbing another pan, I continue drying. 'We all need pockets. Imagine making a pair of men's trousers and not giving them pockets, there'd be outrage.'

She bats me away with a rubber glove, dripping soapy foam on the floor. 'You were always difficult as a child.'

'I'm not being difficult, I'm being practical.'

'Well, your wedding day is one day you don't have to be,' she says firmly. And peeling off her rubber gloves with a snap, she hangs them over the sink and takes the tea towel out of my hands. 'Now, come upstairs, I want to show you something.'

I am not wearing a veil. Really. I cannot. I look ridiculous.

I'm standing in front of the full-length mirror on the back of the wardrobe in my parents' bedroom, my grandmother's veil draped over my head like an antimacassar.

Mum is fussing around me, adjusting the corners. I stare at myself through the tulle netting. I look like I'm a four-going-on-forty-something-year-old that's been let loose in the dressing-up box. I voice my concerns.

'Nonsense, you look lovely.' Mum has tears in her eyes.

'Seriously. I can't wear this.'

'But you must. It's Grandma Fairley's,' she insists. 'It's tradition.'

Oh God. The wedding traditions. Why does no one ever warn you? Getting engaged is a breeze. I should know, I've been engaged twice now, and it involves a ring and champagne and lots of people saying nice things. But once you get down to the *nitty gritty* of planning a wedding, this shit gets real.

I've heard my mum friends say there's a conspiracy of silence around the reality of childbirth, but I'm here to warn you that there's also one about weddings. This is not the fun, frothy experience I've been led to imagine my whole life. I've been sold a lie. I am not drinking champers with my friends, trying on gorgeous dresses, picking out beautiful flowers and laughing with gay abandon, all the while lighting scented candles.

I am in my parents' bedroom, with a bit of mouldy old lace on my head, arguing with my mother.

And my arms have gone.

FFS.

Meanwhile Edward is having a lovely time with Dad and Arthur at the pub. They made a quick exit after lunch with Dad jovially saying, 'Come on, son, I'm sure the girls have got lots to talk about.' In their defence, they both probably thought they were leaving us to have a lovely, emotional, mother–daughter bonding experience. At least I hope so, otherwise I'm going to kill them both.

And don't get me started on Edward's wedding spread-sheets.

'Something old, something new, something borrowed, something blue,' Mum is saying now. 'This is your something old.'

'It's just not me,' I try to reason.

'But you're a bride,' says Mum, looking bewildered. 'You're not supposed to look like you.'

I love Mum, but she's never understood me. My life and my choices have always been so different to hers. It's as if I've always been one of the clues in her crosswords she could never quite get. And as much as she's always tried to be supportive, I can tell she's relieved that her daughter has finally fitted into a trajectory she recognizes and understands. Like getting that final piece of a jigsaw to fit.

'I remember when I married your father, we barely recognized each other. We didn't live together and I'd never seen him all dressed up in a suit before and there was me in a long dress with my hair up, looking nothing like he was used to.'

There's a photo of them on their wedding day on her dressing table and she reaches over for it.

'Saying that, I wasn't wearing my glasses, so I could barely recognize anyone,' she laughs, pushing her bi-focals up her nose. 'I could have married a complete stranger.' Her face softens and she pauses, her mind miles away. 'Though, I suppose, he was a stranger really. We were both so young, we barely knew each other . . .'

It's hard to imagine my parents being a couple of nervous young newlyweds, but I suppose that's what everyone thinks about their mum and dad.

'And now look at us, we're like an old pair of slippers,' she laughs, shaking her head.

I smile, feeling both guilt and fondness. Maybe I'm being too hard on Mum.

'You both look lovely,' I say, peering at the familiar photo of Mum in a frilly, polyester seventies number with a high neck, and dad in his flared suit and sideburns.

'I felt like a princess.'

She looks at me, as if deciding whether or not to say something. 'You know, I always thought when I had a daughter, maybe one day . . .'

And then, without warning, she leaves me holding the photo frame and reaches underneath the bed. 'I had your father bring it down from the attic. I've kept it all these years, just in case . . .' Pulling out a big cardboard box, she places it on top of the eiderdown and opens it. Inside, nestled in yellowing tissue paper, is the very same frilly, white, polyester number.

'It's vintage, so it's something old,' she says, looking at me hopefully.

I feel a beat of horror. There's vintage, and there's looking like one of those toilet dollies my grandma used to have in the seventies to cover up her loo rolls.

Speaking of Grandma.

'Actually, on second thoughts, I think you're right. I'll wear the veil.'

141

I'm grateful for:

1. *My brother Rich, when he telephoned, for always being the joker and attempting to get me off the hook of having to wear Grandma's veil by suggesting 'something old' was the bride. At least, I think he was joking.*
2. *Not having to look like a toilet roll dolly.*
3. *That second pint, over which Dad begged Edward to put him out of his misery and set a date for the wedding as Mum was driving him round the bend.*
4. *My future father-in-law's swanky private members club in Mayfair, which offers fairy-tale weddings in a magical setting including a ballroom.*
5. *We've finally set a date!*†*

---

* Saturday, 5 Feb. Which has no significance, other than they had a free slot. Mum was right, of course. All the Saturdays in spring and summer were booked up already. Still, we don't want a long engagement and this way we can have a winter wedding, which is a great excuse to wear sleeves. Talk about a win-win.
† On googling, I have discovered 5 Feb is World Nutella Day. Which is pretty significant if you ask me, frankly.

Another Kind of Date

As soon as you get engaged, the first thing people ask you is, 'Have you set a date?' A date turns something imagined real. It gives us something to look forward to. To celebrate. Dates are important, but some are easy to forget – birthdays and anniversaries that you have to circle on the calendar, or write in your diary, or jot down in a notebook. And then there are other dates that need no reminders.

It hits me the moment I wake up. Before I open my eyes. 6 October.

It's not circled on the calendar but I'll never forget my due date. He or she would have been three years old today. I wonder what we would be doing together, in this alternate, imagined life. Maybe I'd be proudly picking them up from nursery with a big gold number-three balloon and we'd spend the afternoon on the swings at the park, pushing them 'Higher, Mummy, higher,' listening to their childish laughter and screams of delight.

Or maybe there would be tantrums and tears and they'd let go of the balloon and it would get caught in the branches of the tree, a deflated tangle of plastic that's terrible for wildlife and the environment. Maybe it wouldn't look anything like I imagined. But that's all I can do because I'll never get to find out for real.

I think about being in Spain, two years ago. When I sat with Cricket on a warm summer's evening, listening to music and watching a sunset and sharing with her a secret I'd kept buried deep inside. When I took the grainy black-and-white image of the ultrasound scan out of my purse, where I'd kept it hidden away, and talked about mine and Ethan's joy when we found out I was pregnant. How we called them Shrimp, because they looked like a little shrimp. And how my heart broke when just a week later they couldn't find a heartbeat.

I think back to that moment, high up at the lighthouse, when I finally let go of that piece of paper that was my baby, which I held fluttering in my fingers, and let it be carried away on the breeze. But I can't let go of the date.

Meanwhile I carry on. I count my blessings. Look forward, don't look back. Be grateful. There are so many terrible things happening in the world. So many tragedies. I have a great life. I'm lucky. Only today I don't feel lucky. I mute social media posts in case I see something that sets me off. I pass a woman on the street with a child that would have been about the same age and I feel rage at the unfairness of it all. Followed just as swiftly by deep shame.

There is no one to blame. It happens to lots of women. It's just one of those things. How many times have I read these words and heard these phrases. Reminded myself of them as I've battled through baby showers and Mother's Days and first days at university. Today slips past without ceremony. I mustn't make a fuss. But it's not lost on me that while I'm making my own coffin, they never got to have one.

I wonder if Ethan will be thinking about them today. If five thousand miles away, on the other side of the Atlantic, he too remembers the date. Perhaps. I don't know. He could barely remember his own birthday. I like to think he will. Apart from Cricket, Liza and the hospital staff, he's the only other person that knew Shrimp existed. I never told family or friends. After so much disappointment, we decided to wait until twelve weeks before we told everyone, but we never got there. I've never told Edward. When it happened it was too painful and now I wouldn't know how to find the words. I still don't.

Except to say, Happy Birthday, Shrimp.

Life goes on but I promise I'll never forget you.

A Coffee

So it's been a couple of weeks since I butt-dialled Joe and was so mortified I blurted out an invitation to meet for coffee.

I mean. FFS.

As my mother would say, 'Talk about from the frying pan into the fire.'

Anyway, since then, we've exchanged a few emails about the new, corrected obituary for his sister that I've been working on, but neither of us has mentioned that coffee, so I've been hoping he might have forgotten. Either that or he was just ignoring it and hoping it would quietly get dropped, in that way you do when you make an arrangement to see a friend, but as the date approaches you're both secretly hoping the other will cancel as neither of you can be bothered putting on make-up and schlepping halfway across town. Plus, it's much easier just to text anyway.

Alas, Joe is not of the friend mindset, and just when I think I'm off the hook, I get a text this morning: '*What happened to that coffee? I can meet today if you're free?*' And I know I'm busted. I think about making an excuse – to be honest, we could probably do everything over email – but it's probably more prudent and a lot more polite to meet up in person to go over the final piece together and make sure he's completely happy with everything. I daren't risk any more mistakes. He might not be so forgiving a second time.

'*Coffee sounds good. How about 1pm?*'

Not losing my job and getting sued has to be worth a flat white, right?

We arrange to meet at a cafe at the top of Portobello. It's his suggestion and I'm quite pleased as Cricket only lives around the corner. Earlier in the week she'd asked if I'd help with restocking a couple of the free little libraries in her local neighbourhood.

'I'll need a hand with these boxes. Monty once said books are heavy because they carry the weight of all our imaginations, but by golly our imaginations weigh a ton!'

I get there early and position myself in the window. It's a good old-fashioned greasy spoon, filled with workmen tucking into full English fry-ups washed down with strong tea. With the gentrification of the area, most cafes around here have gone the same way as the gastropubs: all chalkboards, filament lighting and succulents on tables, but there's something comfortingly honest about no-nonsense white Formica, strip lighting and plastic sauce bottles on tables. It's not trying to be anything. And in a world where everything is these days, it feels refreshing.

I pay for a mug of tea at the counter – this is not the place to order a flat white – then go sit in the window to wait. Outside it's started to rain. Someone has decided to dig up the street, put up signs, then disappear. On the pavement, people hurry by.

To be truthful, I'm not looking forward to this. Admittedly, Joe's been nicer on his emails, no more SHOUTY CAPS, but still, he's The Angry Relative who complained about me to my editor. Not that I blame him. Obituaries aren't there to simply report the death of a person, but to honour a person's life. Writing one carries a huge responsibility; not just to the person that has died and their loved ones, but to their legacy.

How do you want someone to be remembered? How, in just a few paragraphs, do you sum up a person's life? It's not a task I take lightly. I try to be sensitive but authentic. To write with candour and warmth and wit and kindness, to celebrate their highs but not shy away from their lows. To be life-affirming, not gloomy. And to always, *always* check my facts. Because if you don't you're going to end up in a greasy spoon on a rainy Monday afternoon, drinking tea so strong it's going to take the enamel off your teeth, while trying to ignore the jangle of anxiety in your stomach.

After five minutes I'm distracted by the sound of a motorbike and look up as one pulls up in front of the cafe. I watch as the rider dismounts and removes their helmet. I recognize him immediately. I couldn't find any photos of Joe online. Samantha, his sister, was intensely protective of her private life, though I did learn she had several half-siblings. The only pictures I could find of her family were a few paparazzi shots of her mum at the opening of one of her exhibitions. Of course I googled him, but nothing much came up. Still, the likeness to his sister is unmistakable.

Entering, he sweeps his gaze around the cafe. As it comes to rest on me I smile and give one of those embarrassed little hand signals you make when you're trying to attract the attention of the waiter. His face impassive, he gives a nod of recognition and makes his way over between the tables.

'Hi.'

'Hi.'

He puts his helmet and keys on the table.

'Want another?' He motions to my tea.

'Um . . . yes, please,' I nod, though to be honest, I've

had quite enough caffeine. I'm already jittery with nerves. I still feel terrible for making a mistake and the offence and upset it caused, and I'm worried there might be a confrontation. Emailing is very different to being face to face in real life.

He leaves me to order more drinks. They know him here and he chats with the woman serving him. I watch their easy banter. After a few moments he returns with two mugs of tea and passes me one.

'So.' Taking off his motorcycle jacket, he hangs it over the back of his chair, and sits down across from me. He's wearing a T-shirt and I notice he has a tattoo of a hawk on his forearm. 'Good to meet you, finally.'

'You too,' I nod.

He shares his sister's strong cheekbones. I'd marvelled at them in photographs, feeling envious, then ashamed. How can you be envious of a dead person?

'Find it OK? This place, I mean.' He sips his tea, lacing his fingers around the mug, to warm them.

'Yes . . . yes, fine,' I nod.

It's only small talk, but he's less intimidating in real life. Still, I brace myself. 'Look, before we start, I want to apologize again—'

'How was the taleggio?' he interrupts.

'Oh, you mean the cheese?' I smile, faintly embarrassed. 'Delicious.'

'Told you,' he smiles, his face relaxing. And just like that the ice is broken.

For the next hour we drink tea and he regales me with stories about his sister Samantha, 'but everyone called her Sam'. As her big brother, he remembers her coming home from hospital; 'I was ten years old and wanted a dog, I wasn't very

149

impressed,' he laughs. Theirs was a large family, he and Sam had different fathers, and although he left home to live with his dad as a teenager, they were always close. 'I'm so proud of Sam, we all are,' he says, leaning across the table to show me videos of her on his phone.

I notice he still slips into talking about his sister in the present tense, as if she's still alive. Like Cricket did about her late husband Monty, when I first interviewed her at her house in Notting Hill, in order to write his obituary. And listening to him speaking, in the same familiar way Cricket talks about Monty, it strikes me that while our bodies might be mortal, love never dies.

Which I know sounds like something you'd read on a fridge magnet, but when you hear it and see it with your own ears and eyes, it really hits home.

'She sounds like an amazing person.'

'You would have loved her, everyone did. She was special. I know everyone says that about the people they love, but Sam really was. She still is,' he says, after a beat.

There's a pause, but I don't try to fill it.

'Have you got any siblings?'

I nod. 'Yeah, a brother, Rich. He's my annoying little brother,' I add, and Joe laughs.

'Brothers always are. It's our job to be annoying. We always rag on our sisters.'

He leans back in his chair and grins at me across the table. He may have his sister's cheekbones, but he has the nose of a boxer. His face reminds me of a Picasso I once saw. All sharp, bent angles. But somehow it works.

'He'll always look out for you, though, your brother, I mean.'

'You obviously haven't met Rich,' I quip, but his face falls serious.

'Nah, trust me, he'd be there if you needed him. I was always there for Sam. I wanted to protect her, you know. I was her big brother. I did it my whole life. School bullies. Loser boyfriends. But it turns out you can't protect someone from cancer.'

His shoulders sink and he traces his thumb along the edge of the table. I watch him, wishing I could reach for some consolation or lesson to be learned or blessing to be found, and knowing there isn't one.

'She was only thirty-seven.'

'I'm so sorry,' I say simply.

'Me too,' he shrugs. 'Fucking cancer.'

'Fucking cancer,' I say, because there's nothing else to say, and then I reach into my handbag and pull out the few pages I've printed out. I feel absurdly nervous as I pass him his sister's new obituary to read. 'I hope I do her justice.'

It's still raining when we leave the cafe.

'It's wonderful, thank you. You've captured her completely,' he's saying now as we stand facing each other on the pavement.

I feel both relieved and gratified, and it has nothing to do with my job. 'Once my editor's signed it off, it will be uploaded online.'

'OK, great.' He smiles.

There's a beat and I feel suddenly compelled to speak.

'You know, you're different to how I imagined.' I just come out with it.

'How so?'

'I was dreading meeting you . . .'

'Dreading it?' His eyes widen. 'Why?'

'When you wrote those emails of complaint you were so angry . . . I mean, obviously I realize why—'

151

'Angry?' He doesn't let me finish. 'I wasn't angry, just upset. I was still being protective of Sam.'

'Yes, I know, but all the capitals—'

I break off as he frowns in confusion, a deep crevasse forming between his heavy eyebrows as he digs his phone out of his jeans to look back at our email exchange, then suddenly his face unscrews itself and out of nowhere, he explodes with a snort. 'My caps button got stuck. I wasn't shouting, did you think . . . ?' He lets out a loud bellowing laugh. 'That's funny.'

All at once I feel stupid and embarrassed and relieved.

'Not so funny for me,' I reply, which makes him laugh even harder and of course laughter is contagious, so I end up laughing too.

'You know, Sam always used to say, forget about cancer, if you lose your sense of humour, then you're really fucked.'

'I think me and Sam would have had a lot in common,' I smile.

'I think you would too,' he nods.

And then we say our goodbyes on the pavement and he leaves on his motorbike and I turn and walk away.

I'm grateful for:
1. *Hearing all about Sam, from someone who loved her; she really did sound amazing.*
2. *Brothers.*
3. *Joe Lloyd is no longer The Angry Relative – he's Mr Handsome.*
4. *Being an almost-married woman who notices these things purely on an observational basis, of course.*

A Leading Man

'Twice in two days, what a treat!'

The next day, Cricket and I leave The Toodlepip Club and head into the West End to watch the preliminary round of auditions for the play. We take the Piccadilly Line, spending much of the journey discussing various members' coffins:

'Glad to see Derek's finally got his handles on.'

'Diane's is really coming along, have you seen her tartan lining?'

'Rosie's casket is wonderful, I love all the glitter on the willow!'

Meanwhile Cricket tells me she's bought her aerosol paints: 'And I've been practising my graffiti at home in the kitchen.'

Not surprisingly, there are a few raised eyebrows around us from other passengers on the tube.

'The treat's all mine,' I say now, as we climb the steps to the station exit. 'I've never been to an audition before. It's exciting.'

'For us, yes,' she nods, 'but for the actors, it's a whole different experience. I used to be almost sick with nerves beforehand,' she confesses. 'My dear friend Ginny used to tell me to imagine the directors in their underpants.'

'Did it work?'

'Sort of.' Pausing on the steps, Cricket looks across at me and grimaces. 'I stopped feeling nervous and felt quite nauseous instead. Trust me, there are some people you never want to imagine in their underpants. Not that some poor girls had to imagine . . .'

As we cross Piccadilly, she shakes her head, remembering. 'This was a long time before the MeToo movement, I can tell you.'

'Did that ever happen to you?'

'No, I was very lucky. But I did hear tales. We all did.'

We continue walking through Theatreland, down narrow streets and alleys that lead off Shaftesbury Avenue and into Covent Garden. Cricket strides ahead without any need for a map. She knows where she's going. She lived her youth in these streets. A shortcut here. A passageway there. It's instinctive, like a language you never forget.

Until here we are at the back of the theatre and now we're walking inside and being met by Christopher, the renowned theatre director I've heard so much about. It's the first time I've met him and I'm ridiculously nervous. He's just how I imagined, with his silver hair, spotty red silk cravat and distinguished air. He greets Cricket warmly, then turns to shake my hand.

'Ah, we meet at last; our wonderful writer. Cricket's told me all about you.'

'All good I hope,' I reply, somewhat stunned by his compliment. *Did he just call me our wonderful writer?*

'Of course not.' Cricket tuts sharply. 'Wouldn't that be a bore?'

'Glad to see the fire hasn't dimmed,' he notes approvingly, smiling at Cricket. I can't tell if it's with admiration or fondness. I think it's both. '*Age cannot wither her, nor custom stale her infinite variety.*'

'*Anthony and Cleopatra*, Monty's favourite.' Cricket nods in appreciation. 'You remembered.'

'How could I forget? It's how we all met.' His eyes shine with the memory. 'And you made a wonderful Cleopatra.'

Watching them, I suddenly get an insight into Cricket's former life as an actress. She rarely talks about it; when she does, it's to be dismissive of her talents. Her late husband was the talented one, she always insists. She just went along for the ride. The only evidence I've seen is a few silver-framed photographs of her taken backstage, but now all at once I see her thirty-something years before as a formidable Cleopatra. Gosh, I wish I could have seen that.

'It's wonderful to be directing one of his plays again,' continues Christopher. 'Makes me feel like the old boy is back with us.'

'You know, the Ancient Egyptians believed if you continue to say someone's name, they can never die,' I interrupt. 'I read that once at a Tutankhamun exhibition,' I add, blushing.

'Why, this Cleopatra did not know that,' remarks Cricket with interest, then falls silent, absorbing the words. 'But I like that idea very much,' she adds, smiling.

'Please, if you'd like to come this way.'

Christopher's voice interrupts and we're taken backstage, along a rabbit warren of corridors that lead past wardrobe and dressing rooms, complete with mirrors surrounded by lightbulbs, just waiting for the cast and crew to bring them alive.

'So of course, we're still very much in the early stages with the production,' he explains, 'but we've overcome so many setbacks to get this far, we wanted to start our search early for our leading actors. Experience tells us it can take quite some time to get it just right . . .'

And now suddenly we're walking out onto the empty stage, our footsteps echoing.

'I thought you'd like to see where we're performing.'

I wasn't expecting this and I'm momentarily overwhelmed. I glance across at Cricket. She's standing centre stage, staring out at a sea of red velvet seats.

'How does it feel to be back treading the boards?' Christopher calls over to her, but she doesn't reply. I don't think she hears him. She seems lost in another world.

It's only later that I remember what she'd said to me as we'd passed the empty dressing rooms, where greasepaint and adrenalin still hung in the air. 'Smell that,' she'd whispered. 'It's the best perfume known to man.'

'What does it smell like?' I'd asked, curious.

'Life,' she'd said, her bright blue eyes flashing. 'It smells like life, my dear girl.'

The auditions start. Seated behind the director and producer, I watch, captivated, as various actors walk onto the stage and introduce themselves, before reading lines from the play. It's quite surreal to hear words I've only seen typewritten and covered in red wine stains and smudged thumbprints brought to life.

'This takes me back,' whispers Cricket.

'Isn't this how you met Monty?'

'It is indeed. I auditioned for one of his plays.'

'Which one?'

'I can't remember, I didn't get the part.' She smiles with amusement.

'But you got your leading man,' I whisper, and as she looks across at me in the dimly lit auditorium, I see her eyes shining.

'You know, just recently I've thought I'd quite like to meet someone.'

Her admission comes as a surprise, but a welcome one.

'That's wonderful,' I enthuse. 'But I thought you were happy being single.'

'I'm not *unhappy*,' she says evenly, after a pause. 'I've got plenty of things to keep me busy. The Toodlepip Club, Monty's Mini Libraries, seeing you.' She smiles at me. 'But it would be nice to have someone to do nothing with.'

There's a break in the auditions as the producer's assistant goes to get refreshments. Coffee? Water? No, thank you. Cricket declines then reaches into her handbag and pulls out a small, silver hip flask. 'Single malt. Much better for oiling the cogs.' And there was me thinking she was reaching for mints.

'Well, I think that's really positive,' I say encouragingly. 'It would be nice for you to have some companionship.'

'Good grief, I can get that from a hot water bottle,' she says, nearly spitting out her whisky. 'I'm not dead yet, you know.'

'Oh, sorry, I didn't mean . . .' I begin apologizing, embarrassed by my assumptions.

'Longing never really goes away, you know,' she says evenly and I feel my cheeks flame in the darkness of the theatre. Not because of her admission, but because of my own preconceived ideas. Why should growing older mean your feelings are diminished? When did society make up that ridiculous rule? She pulls her phone out from her pocket. 'In fact I have a confession.'

All that said, don't tell me she's going to show me a dick pic. I hang on to the hip flask.

'Oh yes?'

'I signed up to one of those online dating sites.'

The relief.

'You did? And?'

She gives me a look of horror. 'I had a look at my matches and they were all old men!'

I laugh. Now I don't feel so ashamed. Cricket's ageist too.

'I do wonder if I'm just being greedy. I got very lucky once. I can't hope for twice.'

'I don't think love is something to be rationed and used up.'

'Perhaps,' she nods. 'Though sometimes I worry love is like magic. That if you don't believe you'll find it, you never will.'

'Maybe it finds you.'

She's quiet as she absorbs the concept.

'We think we've got to do all this stuff, be all these things, go to all these places, but look at me and Edward. I met him in a kitchen and fell in love with him in a car park.'

My mind flicks back to when Dad had his car accident two years ago and Edward drove all the way up from London, without being asked, and waited for me in the hospital car park so I wouldn't be alone. If that's not love, I don't know what is.

She smiles then. 'And how are you and Edward?'

'We finally set a date for the wedding,' I say, passing her back the flask.

'Splendid.' She takes a sip and puts it back in her handbag, without asking me what the date is. And then the assistant returns and they resume the auditions.

In the end we didn't find our leading man today. But there's time yet.

I'm grateful for:

1. *Cricket; there are many reasons I love her, but one is she doesn't give a stuff about weddings. Which I know might sound odd, coming from a bride-to-be, but it's actually a relief.*

The Clocks Go Back

I've always found October to be a bit of a melancholy month. Some people love all that season of mists and mellow fruitfulness business. The turning of the leaves. The changing of seasons. The days getting shorter. Judging by social media, awash with reels of people in cute bobble hats and kicking up leaves, I'm very much in the minority. Our American friends even love fall so much, they celebrate by going leaf peeping and putting cinnamon on everything.

Personally, it serves only as a reminder that we're fast moving into winter and time is whizzing by, but on the flipside soon it will be the wedding. I still can't quite believe it. Me. A married woman. After a whole life spent ticking the single box on the many forms that make up our lives, I'm soon going to be ticking a different one. Not a better one. But definitely a different one. And it feels weird and wonderful all at the same time.

The next couple of weeks disappear like the leaves from the trees. Life becomes a series of to-do lists, decisions to be made and balls to be juggled, what with the wedding and work and all the general life admin. I also get an email from Joe thanking me for his sister's obituary.

'*Sam was notoriously private, but she would've loved it. The family are so grateful and it's the first time* in ages *I've seen Mum really smile. It was like bringing back Sam again. She even printed it out and framed it,*' he writes and I feel a profound sense of pride and gratitude. In a funny way, I'll be forever grateful for my mistakes in her obituary first time around, because if I hadn't made them, I wouldn't have got to meet Joe and a chance to get to know the real Sam.

I don't see any friends either. As usual everyone's busy and knackered. Busy & Knackered. It sounds like a cool R'n'B band but it's something that happens in your forties and, quite frankly, I'd do something about it if I wasn't so bloody exhausted. Luckily there's always WhatsApp so we keep in touch, but a funny meme isn't the same as seeing someone for a drink or having a proper conversation. I barely spoke to Holly at my party and to be honest I'm a bit worried about Max, after our last text exchange. I resolve to call both of them and add it to my to-do list, which is growing ever longer.

I'm also made aware of the changing of the seasons a bit closer to home by the arrival of Edward's son Louis, who returns from Paris, and comes to stay at the flat for a week. Accompanying him is his French girlfriend, Simone, all heavy fringe, kohl eyeliner and Dr. Martens.

Talk about the clocks going back. It's me circa 1995.

It's funny how getting older creeps up on you. It's gradual. Like the build-up of ice on your freezer. One day you're heading out to a club at 11 p.m., the next you're heading happily up to bed. That's if you're not already in it, fast asleep with your earplugs in. Apart from when you happen across an old photograph, or go to take a photo and have the camera turned the wrong way on your phone,* you still feel the same inside.

---

* And get the shock of your life. You don't look your age. You look like your grandmother!

But now, faced with Louis and Simone, it's quite clear that youth has flown out of the window. While Louis and Simone listen to music, talk about bands, and scroll their phones, Edward and I obsess over coasters on tables, wet towels on beds and lights left on (not only do I feel old, I've turned into Edward!). While they flirt and laugh and bite the end of each other's croissants, we argue about the dishwasher, the TV remote and the thermostat. In my defence, I do scroll my phone, but mostly it's to read scary news headlines or do online banking.

Most of all, I'm struck by how carefree they are. Like nothing matters. Well, apart from the state of the world, about which Louis and Simone are deeply passionate and vocal. Because of course, we Olds don't know anything about the world. That said, I can understand why they might come to that conclusion as we seem to be constantly engaged in conversations about the central heating and how to get the wedding guest list down to the right numbers.

Meanwhile, over in young, floppy fringe land they're lolling in a tangle of limbs on the living-room sofa, making me and Edward squash up on the other one, like two middle-aged parents. It's the most bizarre thing. Worse still, unlike Edward, I didn't get the cute toddler years, but as soon-to-be-stepmum I've been fast forwarded to dirty plates everywhere and tongues-down-throats years.

Worse still, there is the shagging.

Well, don't you remember those years with your first love? I know I do. It was all so new and fantastic, we couldn't get enough. Which is a bit like how I feel now when the new series of *Succession* drops. And it's the same for these two young lovers, but alas, they are in the bedroom next to ours.

Surprisingly, Edward is pragmatic. They're both eighteen and so adults. Asking them to sleep in separate rooms would

161

be ridiculous. And, most importantly, he doesn't want to be like his own father was, which was so authoritarian he left home and never went back. (At this point I resist the urge to remind him about the ring binder of house rules.)

Instead we laugh about it. But privately, I'm worried. I've always thought we had a healthy enough sex life, whatever that is, but now faced with the bedroom next door, it seems terminal. Furthermore, I start finding hand-washed scraps of exquisite French lingerie drying over the radiators. Delicate wisps of embroidered lace and gossamer silk in pretty pale eggshell colours and vibrant, hot pinks. Vacuuming the living room this morning, I pause from attacking the dog hair with my pet-hair attachment, to tentatively finger two tiny triangles of diaphanous lace, held together by a satin ribbon.

At which point, two thoughts strike:

1. When did I stop buying expensive lingerie and start buying expensive hoovers? Worse still, when did I start getting excited about my new hoover?
2. Hang on – *is that really a bra?*

I stare at it with a mixture of awe and astonishment. It's unrecognizable from my padded, flesh-coloured T-shirt bras that sit up by themselves like two jelly moulds.

And are those flimsy pieces of silk dental floss . . . knickers?
I wince. And not just because I'm imagining wearing them.

Right, that's it! The seasons might be changing, but I'm not sliding into the autumn of mid-life any time soon, thank you very much. On the contrary, I'm determined to put spring firmly back into our relationship by buying some sexy new lingerie and having more sex. I jab my foot on the vacuum and turn it off.

In fact, I'm going to add both to my to-do list right now.

I'm grateful for:

1. *The gorgeous lingerie boutique near Cricket's, where I spend an absolute fortune on the most beautiful silk balconette bra and matching satin-trimmed thong which makes my eyes water and not just because of the price.*

2. *My new sexy lingerie having the desired effect as Edward can't wait to take it off. Which is both wonderful and a blessed relief.*

3. *Being of an age where you realize that feeling sexy comes with being comfortable in your own skin (and your big knickers).*

4. *The flirty game I read about that's supposed to spice things up in the bedroom. All you need is to flip a coin – heads you get to have sex, tails you watch a movie – and we toss it in bed at night for a bit of fun. Though I think we're both secretly hoping it's a movie night because last night when it landed on heads, we both agreed to do best of three.*

The Hallowe'en Disco

On Wednesday afternoon I got an SOS from Max. A text. Just one word:

Help!

Only this time he wasn't hiding in the bathroom from his children, he was hiding from other parents.

'Nell, you're a lifesaver,' he said grimly as I hurried to his rescue and found him in the pub around the corner from his children's primary school. Tucked away in the back, he was hidden in the shadows with an empty pint glass.

'What's going on?'

Pulling up a chair, I looked across the table at him, worried.

'The Hallowe'en disco.'

I stared at him, nonplussed. 'So?'

'So I'm one of the class reps organizing it, but now the other two parents that were helping have had to drop out because they've both gone down with the flu.'

'You're kidding me.'

'No. I'm serious.'

'I don't mean it like that!' I snapped, suddenly infuriated. 'What I *mean*, Max, is is this why I've just dropped everything and raced across town? *Because of a children's disco?*' I was really quite pissed off. I had a million and one things to do, what with work and the wedding.

'Nell. Seriously. You have no idea.'

Folding my arms, I leaned back against the chair, furious. 'Oh really?'

Don't get me wrong, I know it's hard being a parent, but it's hard not being a parent too. Frankly, just being a human is a lot of hard work.

Looking furtively around the pub to make sure no one is watching, Max wordlessly slid his phone across the table, face down, towards me. I've never been a member of MI5 but I'm sure this is what it must feel like. With a quick nod, he gestured for me to pick it up. Talk about high drama. By that point I was in a real grump, but having caught two buses, I was there now, and so in the spirit of *Sod This** I played along and picked it up. As soon as I did it started vibrating.

'I've had to turn the sound off, but it doesn't stop the—'

I didn't let him finish. 'Doesn't stop who?' Confused, I glanced down at his screen. It was open at his WhatsApp. And that's when I saw them.

> Anyone got any tickets?
> Desperate for a ticket!
> Is there a black market for tickets?
> Can't be too hard to forge one!
> This is outrageous! How can the school have sold out of tickets?!
> Let's just turn up anyway!

He had hundreds of notifications pinging in. Many of them unread. And they were still coming, popping up on his screen at such a rate I couldn't scroll fast enough.

'What's all this?' I asked, bewildered.

---

* In times of need, my *Sod This* approach to life never fails me.

'What I've been trying to tell you,' groaned Max and for the first time I noticed the dark circles under his eyes. He'd aged about ten years since last time I saw him. 'Last year Hallowe'en got cancelled, along with pretty much everything, so this year the PTA voted to do a Hallowe'en disco on the Friday before half term—'

'Which is when?'

When my friends had kids they stopped talking in English and started talking in School Holidays.

'This Friday.'

'And?'

'And I'm nearly having a bloody nervous breakdown, Nell.' His frustration suddenly erupted. 'It's all on my shoulders and I can't cope! I swear to God, it's more stressful than when I was a creative director leading a team at work and we spearheaded the campaign for the Olympics.'

'Why? It's only a primary school disco.'

'Only a primary school disco!' he exploded. 'Haven't you seen the WhatsApp group? It's THE event of the year as everything last year was cancelled. Everyone's trying to get tickets and I totally screwed up.'

As he spoke another dozen pinged in.

> Is there a dark web? Willing to pay ££££
> Someone's head needs to roll over this! Little ones are devastated!
> OMG! Is it true distraught infants will be turned away at the door???
> Absolute shambles! This better not happen with the Nativity!
> Who's responsible for organizing this? NAME AND SHAME!
> Someone needs to go to the press!

Crikey. I saw Max had a point.

'And it's not just the cock-up with the tickets, it's all the organization required – the disco, refreshments, setting everything up, decorating the gymnasium, doing the tuck shop . . . Then there's all the supervision. I need someone on the door, the toilets, to judge the fancy dress competition.' He broke off to glance at his watch and jumped up from the table – 'Shit, I've got to pick up the kids' – then turned back to me. 'I don't suppose you could give me a hand?'

'On Friday night?'

'It finishes at eight.' He stared at me pleadingly. 'Nell, you're my oldest friend.'

I typed something on his phone, then passed it back to him. 'OK.'

'I knew you were a mate.' Stuffing it in his pocket, he beamed with relief, then frowned. 'Hang on, what did you just reply?'

I waved him goodbye. 'See you on Friday.'

So now it's Friday and we're at the disco and Max still hasn't forgiven me for sending a text that read, '*FFS calm down, it's not the fiftieth anniversary of Glastonbury*', to his group WhatsApp of thirty sets of parents.

'Well, honestly, if they can't take a joke,' I say, filling up the bowl of jelly eyeballs. 'Don't they have a sense of humour?'

But Max isn't having any of it and is still sulking.

'Not when it comes to the Hallowe'en disco. You wouldn't believe how much I got it in the neck for that text,' he's saying, swigging wine and handing me a jug of blackcurrant squash that's supposed to look like blood.

'Well, that's quite fitting, considering you've come as Dracula,' I joke, but he doesn't laugh and turns back to arranging the carved pumpkins.

We're standing on the edge of the school gymnasium, which

has been transformed into a sort of House of Horrors with the aid of a glitterball, strobe lights, a few cut-out skeletons and a smoke machine. Fortunately Max managed to rope in a few of the teachers while I asked Holly for help. Olivia's just started in reception and she immediately sprang into action, organizing and recruiting more volunteers, plus sorting out the necessary DBS checks. The big coup was that the caretaker's son has agreed to do the disco. Apparently he's quite big in Ibiza, though he's got a bit of a different set list for tonight.

'Monster Mash' is playing and children are dancing around in costumes, while their parents gather in groups, thrilled to be out and having a drink on a Friday evening without the need for a babysitter. Some of the parents have gone to a huge effort, with elaborate costumes that must have taken hours to make (or a fortune to hire), while others are from the last-minute camp and have obviously grabbed whatever mask they could find from the local newsagents on the corner. Case in point, I spot a dad wearing an old President Trump mask. Still, I suppose that is pretty scary.

Meanwhile, I've gone to even less effort and am wearing an old white bed sheet, which I'm just adjusting when I spot Holly and Olivia.

'What have you come as?' demands Max as she makes her way over to us. I don't think I've ever seen Holly not in her tracksuit and trainers, but today she's in jeans and a jumper.

'I've come as no sleep. That's always my nightmare.' Letting go of Olivia's hand, she watches as she runs onto the dance floor.

'Oh no, what's happened? Is it about the cottage in the country?'

'Don't ask,' she quickly bats my question away. 'How's it going with the wedding plans?'

'Don't ask,' I grin, handing her a book of raffle tickets. 'A pound each or six for a fiver. And it's cash only. No contactless.'

'You mean I can't get my Tesco Clubcard points?' she says drily, raising an eyebrow. 'You know there are going to be protests.'

'We've got some amazing prizes,' I enthuse, grinning.

'Ooh, what can you win? I fancy a Caribbean cruise.'

'We've got a giant teddy bear and a weekend Airbnb in Reigate,' snaps Max, who seems to have lost his sense of humour. 'Plus lots more.'

'Oh, by the way, Fiona's coming.' Holly swiftly changes the subject.

'*Fiona!* How did she get a ticket?' Max is indignant. 'She's not a parent.'

'Well, technically she *is* a parent,' I point out, 'but Izzy and Lucas go to the same private school as Annabel's daughter,' I add, remembering the sports day I once attended, when I had to compete in a race against Annabel and she deliberately tripped me up so she could win.

'I gave her Adam's,' says Holly, grabbing a glass of white wine. 'I think David's driving her crazy and she wanted to get out of the house by herself. It says a lot when you escape *to* a disco at a school your children don't even go to.' She rolls her eyes. 'Where's Michelle?'

'Busy building her empire.' Max tops up his glass.

'But she'll come later, right?'

'No, she's got a business deal she's putting together. A big catalogue company is wanting to invest.'

'Wow, that's amazing.'

'You must be really proud of her.'

Holly and I are full of praise and admiration and Max nods. 'Yeah, she's amazing,' he enthuses, sinking his fangs into a glass of wine. Maybe it's just me, but I sense something.

'*Hola!*'

We're interrupted by Fiona, who sweeps in wearing fangs and fake blood and looking impossibly glamorous. How on earth does she always do that?

'Oooh, gorgeous dress.'

'Vampire's Wife,' she smiles, giving a little twirl.

'Clever,' I nod approvingly. 'But be careful with a designer label and blackcurrant squash.' Picking up the jug, I fill up a few plastic cups.

'Oh don't worry, it's one of Annabel's cast-offs.'

Of course. Only Annabel could be casting off expensive designer dresses.

'Speak of the devil.' Hearing a ping on her phone, Fiona looks at her screen.

'Don't tell me Annabel's got a ticket too,' exclaims Max.

I feel my heart sink, though for different reasons to Max's. Then immediately feel guilty. I quickly remind myself she's got the same hang-ups as all of us. I'll always remember how she once said that we were all just like ducks – we may be gliding along on the surface but underneath the water our legs are paddling furiously trying to stay afloat.

Yeah, nice try, Annabel. Maybe, but hers are paddling in Jimmy Choos.

'It's about her retreat,' says Fiona, ignoring Max. 'She's got a few places left.'

'Fraid I'm too busy, what with planning the wedding,' I say quickly, nipping the idea in the bud.

'When is it?' asks Holly. 'Does it involve massages?'

'Next month.' Fiona checks her phone and then her eyes

light up. 'I know, let's all go! When was the last time we all went away together for the weekend?'

'Gosh, I dunno. We must have been in our twenties,' sighs Holly.

'Exactly!' Fiona is energized.

'Sounds amazing, but a whole weekend? I don't think Adam could cope if I left him home alone with Olivia.'

'Tell him it's Nell's hen weekend.'

My hen weekend? Er, hang on a minute. 'But I wasn't going to have a hen do,' I interrupt. 'You know me, I'm not really into them.'

'I know, but we can just say that as an excuse. That way all the men will look after the kids.' I can see Fiona's mind is already thundering ahead like a juggernaut.

'God, it would be nice. A whole weekend to recharge.' And now Holly is looking all dreamy.

'But I'm not getting married for three months,' I try protesting weakly, but it's hopeless.

'Better to get these things organized early,' says Fiona brightly, tapping a reply into her phone. 'Let's see if Michelle can come too.'

'And leave me with the kids all weekend? Over my dead body,' cries Max, who has been eavesdropping.

'Dead body, ha ha, very funny,' laughs Holly, but I don't think Max was joking.

'Brilliant, well, that's all sorted,' says Fiona, slipping her phone in her pocket. 'Right then, who's for the dance floor?'

I'm grateful for:
1. *Dancing to 'Ghost Town' with my friends and it feeling like old times – honestly when did we all stop dancing? And agreeing we must do it more, though next time it won't be in a bed sheet.*

171

2. *Someone's dad, who saved me when I tripped up and nearly went crashing into the display of pumpkins.*

3. *Paper towels for clearing spilled drinks, jelly eyeballs and vomit, and that was just the parents.*

4. *Being child-free so I can collapse exhausted into white bed sheets not covered in blackcurrant squash and sleep until the morning without a sugar-crazed primary-schooler.*

5. *The large bunch of flowers from Max that arrived the next day with the note: 'Fangs for Everything!'*

6. *Winning one of the amazing prizes in the raffle – I really needed a new cheese grater.*

7. *The confirmation email from Annabel – I'm going on a hen weekend and it's to Annabel's retreat, yay!*

8. *My sense of irony.*

WhatsApp Voicemail from Liza in LA

Hi Nell, it's me. I don't think you're awake yet but I want you to be one of the first to know – I'm pregnant. I didn't want to call or FaceTime with the news, because I always remember you saying a pregnancy announcement can trigger all kinds of emotions, that you can be really happy for them, but sad for you. And that makes it hard to pin on a big smile. So I wanted to give you the time and space. Best Friends should never have to do brave faces. Call me when you're ready. Love you.

I'm grateful for:
1. *Having a friend like Liza.*

NOVEMBER

#lifeisntafairytale

The Power of (No)vember

I'm a huge fan of Eckhart Tolle's *The Power of Now*, but I've recently discovered a different kind of power, and it's the power of saying no.

When I was younger I'd say yes to things I didn't want to do, out of guilt or duty, because I didn't want to offend, or look bad, or simply because I didn't have the courage to say no. And in doing that, I put the other person's feelings first.

But the beauty of getting older is finally realizing you don't have to say yes to stuff you don't want to do. Better still, you don't need to give complicated excuses. You just say no. It's so easy! And freeing. Seriously, why haven't I been doing this for years?

Which is handy, as by coincidence it's NOvember so I'm going to be doing lots of saying no. Starting with Annabel's retreat this weekend. I know it's supposed to be my hen weekend and I've agreed to go, but I've been thinking about it a lot. I don't want to let anyone down, but it's really not my thing. So I'll be practising the power of saying NO.

WhatsApp Group: Annabel's Weekend Retreat

Annabel
Just a reminder everyone, it's my self-care and life-coaching retreat this weekend, where I help guide you to transform your lives. Looking forward to seeing you all. 🙏

Fiona
Can't wait! So looking forward to the guided meditation and crystal workshop. I know it's going to be amazing!

Holly
What shall we bring?

Annabel
Please refer to the PDF I sent last week which includes all the information and directions to the yurts.

Holly
Sorry. Haven't read it yet. Been a bit distracted.

Michelle
You're turning into me, Holly! Glad to see you're not always organized ☺ I don't feel so bad now!

Annabel
Also, some of you still haven't returned the required forms ahead of the life-coaching workshop.
By some, I mean Nell.

OK, this is it. My time to practise the Power of No.

I'm not coming.

Fiona
What? But it's your hen weekend!

Holly
Oh no! What's wrong, Nell?

Michelle
WTF. Is everything OK?

Annabel
Ladies, let's not pressure Nell into doing something if she feels it's not beneficial to her wellbeing. My retreats are all about creating a safe soul space to clarify and achieve our goals, identify the obstacles holding us back and prepare for healing and transformation. As a life coach I combine practical guidance with a spiritual practice and together our circle will be manifesting energy and mirroring grace as we journey together to unblock, connect, align and expand into our new lives.

Annabel is typing

Also, Michelle sweetie, expletives create a negative vibration through our bodies; imagine toxic pebbles forming ripples on a lake.

You've got to be kidding. Toxic pebbles??

Annabel is typing

These unhelpful habits need to be cast off like those friendships that drain our energy.

179

Hang on a minute. Exactly which friendships is Annabel talking about casting off? I suddenly have second thoughts. It's one thing saying no to Annabel and her retreat, but that also means saying no to spending the weekend with all my best mates. Worse still, letting her loose amongst them. God knows what she'll try and manifest. Right. Sod This.*

Sorry. Predictive text. Meant to type I'M COMING.
See you Friday! 👍

* How's that for a Toxic Pebble?

The Retreat

OK, so I admit it. Despite agreeing to go to Annabel's life-coaching retreat, I still wasn't *exactly* looking forward it. I didn't want a hen do, and if I did, this certainly wouldn't be how I'd choose to spend it.

That said, after changing my mind, I decide I need to change my attitude as well. I need to put my cynicism and feelings towards Annabel aside. Be more open. Embrace the opportunity. Fiona is right. When was the last time I got to go away with all my friends? Usually everyone is so busy juggling work and childcare and commitments, putting a date in the diary is like organizing the G7 summit. This retreat means we get to spend the whole weekend together. So what if I have to do some yoga with Annabel and hug a few crystals?† It's a small price to pay.

Theoretically speaking, as the next day I referred to the PDF and saw the price of the retreat and nearly choked on my coffee – it's an absolute fortune! Which of course was no surprise, considering it was being run by Annabel.

'Oh don't worry, she's giving us mates' rates,' reassured

---

† For the record, I'm not bashing crystals. I actually love crystals. I mean, *hello*. I lived in LA. You can't walk down the street without tripping over a healing crystal workshop. I'd just rather they were under my pillow and not in Annabel's bra.

That said, I do not love yoga as I'm rubbish at it, but on the bright side, if this is going to be my hen do, it's better than stumbling around in L plates and a veil. Or playing crazy golf.

Fiona, when she called to apologize that her car's had to go into the garage so she wouldn't be able to give me a lift.

'I'm not sure you'd exactly call me and Annabel mates,' I replied.

'Don't be silly, of course you are. And anyway, you don't have to pay, it's your hen weekend. It's my treat.'

'Oh, Fiona, that's so kind of you,' I half groaned, half protested at my friend's generosity. 'But I don't expect you to pay for me.'

'Too late,' she laughed and I felt guilty for having mentioned the cost in the first place. 'And anyway, I owe you. For giving me a weekend away from David,' she joked. At least I think she was joking.

'Well, in that case, let me at least buy your train ticket,' I suggested, desperate to contribute. 'I'll book them now. Maybe we can all get the train together, share a table, have a few drinks from the trolley.' While I was talking, I opened my laptop and started googling trains to the New Forest. For the first time since the retreat had been mentioned, it was beginning to sound quite fun. 'We could start the party early.'

'Actually, Annabel offered me a lift,' replied Fiona awkwardly. 'She's bought herself a new sportscar.'

'Someone's been practising self-care,' I quipped, then realized that sounded a bit sarcastic and I was supposed to be putting aside all cynical thoughts, remember? 'Wow, how wonderful,' I embrace.

'She treated herself to a Porsche after the whole trauma of the divorce. I think she wants the company. Problem is, it's only a two-seater.'

I could tell Fiona was caught between the thrill of whizzing along the motorway in a sportscar and catching a cramped, delayed train that has no seat reservations and a blocked toilet. Only joking! Well, hopefully. Anyway, I told her not to worry, that of course she must drive with Annabel and I'd catch the train with Holly and Michelle.

'Are you sure?'

'Absolutely,' I said, grateful to be able to return the favour. 'I'll see you on Friday. Can't wait.'

On Friday, Edward offers to drop me at the station. He's been really encouraging and thinks it's a great idea. Secretly I think he's really pleased to have the flat to himself so he can take full control of the central-heating thermostat and TV remote.

'Go and have a lovely weekend; recharge the batteries,' he beams, helping me with my bag. 'Don't worry about work or the wedding or me and Arthur.' He gives me a kiss. 'We're going to have a boys' weekend.'

In the back of the car, Arthur wags his tail excitedly, sending fur flying. Luckily, Arthur has a thick fur coat like a polar bear so I'm not worried about him feeling the cold as no doubt Edward has plans to plunge the flat into a new ice age while they watch rugby together.

The train is booked for after lunch and I've arranged to meet Holly and Michelle at Waterloo, under the clock. However I arrive a bit early, so I take advantage of the opportunity to stock up on a few supplies for the journey; a selection of crisps and nibbles and my favourite little cans of pre-mixed gin and tonic. Gosh, I haven't had one of these for ages.

As I pop a few in my basket, I feel a sense of fondness. Since moving in with Edward, he insists on making me a G&T in a glass, with ice and lemon and those fancy bottles of speciality gin. Which are lovely and delicious. But there's something about these cans that makes me feel nostalgic. I joke that I owe my life to gin, but seriously, there have been times when one of those little cans really cheered me up. Or made me think, *Sod This*. Which sometimes was much better and just what I needed.

'Do you need a bag?'

I snap back to see the assistant has come over to punch a code into the self-scan checkout to say I'm over eighteen. She gives me a look as I realize how it might seem as *a few* has now turned into about a dozen.

'Oh, they're not all for me,' I blush, as they clank into the carrier. To be honest, I have a feeling that I might be needing a few this weekend. In the section on the PDF marked provisions it was all healthy juices and plant-based food, which sounds delicious, but it *is* sort of my hen weekend, surely I'm allowed a few contrabands. Plus the retreat is about 'self-care' so the way I look at it, I'm only making sure I'm taking care of myself.

Right?

Holly arrives first. I spot her sprinting through the station, zig-zagging through the crowds in her reflective running gear. Is it just me or is she even slimmer?

'I decided to jog from the office, it's only 5K,' she pants, taking off her headphones. 'I wanted to get some cardio in before we have to sit for hours, do you know what I mean?'

As someone who loves a train journey for the very reason they have an excuse to sit for hours and stare out of a window eating crisps, no I don't, but I nod anyway and offer her the bag of goodies. I've already started on the cheese puffs.

'No, I'm fine, thanks, I've got a protein bar,' she says, pulling one out of her backpack, then checks her heart rate. She wears one of those watches that tells you everything. Frankly, I'm not sure I want to know. 'OK, well, shall we board?'

'What about Michelle?'

'Didn't you get her text? She said she's really sorry but her business meeting ran over, so she's going to catch a later train.'

As she's telling me, I'm digging around in my bag for my phone. It must have been on silent as, sure enough, there's the message from Michelle on the group chat.

'So it's just you and me,' says Holly, almost apologetically.

'Never mind, more G&Ts for us,' I cheer, hiding a twinge of disappointment as we head towards the platform. It's fine. Really. We've got the whole weekend together. And this way I can have a proper catch-up with Holly. I can't remember the last time it was just the two of us.

Except, it's not. It's me, Holly and Colin, a chatty sales rep from Manchester who is off birdwatching for the weekend and sharing our table, and who proceeds to tell me his life story while showing me the thousands of photos of tits on his phone, no pun intended. Meanwhile Holly spends the whole time sending work calls to voicemail and replying to office emails.

As her phone buzzes for the umpteenth time, she goes to hit reject then frowns at her screen. 'Sorry, got to get this,' she says, swiftly getting up from her seat and making her way outside the carriage. Several minutes later she returns, looking a bit white-faced.

'Everything OK?'

'Yeah, fine . . . um . . . it was just the estate agent.'

'Bloody estate agents, they never leave you alone, do they?' chimes in Colin. 'Don't tell me. Bad news from the survey.'

'Something like that.' Holly nods, distracted.

'Oh no, what's wrong?'

'Nothing that can't be fixed.' She forces a bright smile. 'But I think I might have one of those cocktails if there's still one going spare.'

'Of course, I bought plenty,' I grin, getting out my bag of goodies and passing her one. 'Colin?' I offer and his face lights up.

'G&Ts, very posh,' he beams. 'Are we celebrating?'

'Nell's getting married, it's her hen weekend.'

'Congratulations, he's a lucky man,' he says, ripping off the ring pull. 'Hope he doesn't make a balls of it, like I did.'

Then we clink cans and Colin cheerfully tells me all about his painful divorce until it's his stop and Holly falls asleep for the rest of the journey, head resting against my shoulder. And it ends up just being me with my little cocktails in a can for company. Not quite how I imagined. I open another. Still, it's quite like old times, really.

I'm grateful for:

1. *The yurts, which are gorgeous and not really tents at all. But then, I shouldn't be surprised, as Fiona is forever telling me that Annabel has really good taste, which is proven by the fact she's chosen to stay in the luxury boutique farmhouse down the road.*
2. *The welcome pack of goodies that includes green tea, vegan sugar-free treats, organic exfoliating soap which reminds me a bit of those fat balls you feed birds in winter, white sage smudge sticks for clearing negative energy and a personalized leather-bound journal.*
3. *Bringing my own welcome pack of crisps, chocolate and gin.*
4. *The welcome chat in the bell tent, where I get to meet all the other women on the retreat, who all seem really lovely, and we sit in a circle with our green tea and woolly blankets as Annabel instructs us to turn off our mobile phones and devices, as 'there are no filters or hashtags here, ladies', and to hand in any contrabands,*

*such as sugar or alcohol, as this weekend is all about
cleaning our minds and bodies to illuminate, balance
and empower.*

5. *#hidingeverythingundermymattress*

Bride and the Bonfire

Saturday morning and I wake to the relaxing sounds of the forest and birdsong and—

FFS! What's that deafening noise?

I throw back the feather duvet and stumble out of bed – wow, I haven't had such a good sleep for ages – and pad across the bamboo floor towards the window to investigate. We all have our own individual yurts and, I have to say, they're extremely comfortable, with real beds, lovely linens and cosy sheepskin rugs and blankets draped here, there and everywhere. It's all very hygge.* They even have their own wood burners.

Boom . . . boom . . . boom . . .

The clocks have changed and the sun isn't even up yet. Peeling back the canvas shade, I peer blearily into the darkness, trying to make out where that incessant crashing noise is coming from . . . and spot a figure standing in the middle of a clearing. Wearing a long, white cashmere robe, they're bashing a gong.

Oh God, it's Annabel, signalling it's time for breakfast.

My body does a sort of knee-jerk internal groan and immediately wants to crawl back underneath the duvet for a lie-in, but I sharply remind myself of my determination to fully

---

* Well, it was when I arrived. Now it's a bit of a pigsty as the contents of my suitcase are strewn everywhere – so less hygge, more piggie.

embrace this weekend. So instead, I throw on some warm clothes and walk over to the farmhouse with Holly and Michelle and Fiona, where breakfast is being eaten around a large, communal table and a lovely lady called Josie is serving up organic porridge and fresh juices.

'Just a coffee for me,' I smile. Well, it is quite early.

'Ooh, no caffeine allowed here,' beams Annabel, sweeping into the room in her long white robe, looking like something from *Lord of the Rings*. Only hers is a cashmere dressing gown. 'It's one of the most addictive drugs in the world, on a par with heroin and cocaine.'

'Even if I have it with oat milk,' I joke feebly, but she wags a stern finger.

'Only wholesome and nutritious foods are welcome here. Remember, Nell, if we're to achieve clarity and balance, it's important we cleanse both our minds *and* bodies.' She thrusts a green juice at me, then turns to the rest of the women with a beatific smile. 'Now then, ladies, how are we all this morning?'

There's a murmuring of approval over the wonderful accommodation and how well everyone slept. Chastened, I sit down at the table to sip my juice. Annabel's right, of course. Coffee is a terrible habit. This is a good opportunity to be more healthy and I'm all for a green juice.

'How is it?' asks Babs, one of the women sitting next to me.

'Mmm,' I nod politely. 'Interesting texture.'

'That'll be the broccoli and minced garlic,' smiles Annabel.

I try not to gag.

'Wonderful!' Clapping her hands together, as if giving ~~herself~~ us a little round of applause, Annabel seats herself at the head of the table. 'In that case, I'll run through today's planned activities . . .'

ALEXANDRA POTTER

Producing several printed cards, she asks us to pass them around the table. I scan my eye down the detailed timetable. Gosh, that's rather a lot of activities.

'After breakfast, we'll start our day with a guided meditation, followed by a crystal workshop, breath exercises and a yoga session in our Divine Bliss bell tent to unblock our chakras, before enjoying a healthy lunch of my signature vegetable broth, which will give us lots of energy and fuel for our afternoon group workshops, where the real work will begin.'

I already feel exhausted. I try to perk up, but it's hard without my morning coffee. Honestly, I could murder a flat white.*

One of the women around the table sticks up her hand nervously. 'How can we tell if our chakras are blocked?'

Annabel seems to bristle at the interruption. 'That's something I'll be talking about in our class, Debbie.'

'I was wondering that too,' I say supportively as poor Debbie looks suitably told off.

Annabel shoots me a glare. 'Trust me. Your chakras are blocked, Nell.'

Right. OK. Well that put me in my place.

I glance across at Fiona, hoping for a bit of a conspiratorial eye-roll, but she's gazing earnestly at Annabel as if she's some kind of oracle. Out of nowhere, teenage giggles suddenly threaten to surface. This reminds me of when we were at uni and we'd sit in lectures together; Fiona would always be the serious one and there'd be me, the messing-about-at-the-back one.

'In the afternoon we'll be doing private written exercises and visualization to help identify both your goals and your

---

* Or Annabel. ONLY JOKING. #sortof

190

self-limiting beliefs. As a life coach I combine a spiritual and practical approach to help empower, invigorate and manifest the change you need . . .'

I stare back down at my timetable and try to compose myself. I'm being immature. I'm not eighteen any more and at a lecture, I'm forty-something at a life-coaching retreat. And actually that does sound really helpful. Maybe it will help with planning this wedding and getting married to Edward. Recently I've felt like a mess of self-limiting beliefs. I could do with some empowering.

As Annabel continues talking, I feel my suspicion and distrust begin to thaw. Perhaps I'm being too hard on her. Too sceptical. Perhaps she really has changed – people do – and now she genuinely wants to help people. Dare I say it, perhaps she is a really good life coach? So what if she drives a Porsche Boxster and is botoxed up to the eyeballs? It might not be very spiritual, but isn't that a form of self-empowerment?

Plus it is a really lovely retreat and I love the energy of all the women together. Moreover, having this time away to reflect and work on yourself can only be a good thing. Right?

'. . . Before tonight's powerful and closing fire ceremony where we will set our intentions, release negativity and create healing.'

And who doesn't love a bonfire? Yesterday was Guy Fawkes Night, so it's perfect timing. I start to feel quite cheered up. I wonder if there'll be fireworks?

We start with a guided meditation, which is actually really relaxing. So relaxing in fact, I fall asleep and wake myself up with a snort, which is a bit embarrassing, but I don't think anyone noticed. Except for Annabel, who glares at me, but then, that's nothing new. Followed by the breathing exercises

191

(it transpires I've been doing it all wrong, though I console myself that I can't have been doing it *that* wrong, as I'm still alive) and the crystal workshop, which turns out to be fascinating. Apparently each crystal has a different energy and we can talk to them. Who knew?*

Next on the list of activities is yoga, but thankfully Annabel offers 'forest bathing' as an alternative for those of us less downward-dog inclined. This basically involves going for a lovely relaxing walk amongst the trees, taking the time to really switch off and enjoy being in nature. Which is pretty much one of my favourite things, only usually I'm with Arthur, who tends to make it a little *less* relaxing by attempting a mass murder of squirrels.

But with Arthur safely at home with Edward, I go for a walk by myself. It really is stunning here, the leaves on the trees have started to turn and I wander along the woodland paths, absorbing all the sights and the smells and enjoying my own company. However I soon discover I'm not alone in the forest, when I stumble upon a tall, rather glamorous woman talking to herself in a clearing.

'Hi.' I quickly change direction as she looks up and sees me, a look of shock flashing across her face.

'Phew, I thought you were Annabel and I'd been caught.' She smiles and waves her phone at me. 'It's Nell, isn't it? I'm Emma.'

I suddenly realize she's at the same retreat. 'Sorry, I didn't recognize you.'

'I'm wearing make-up,' she laughs. 'I was just making a reel.'

'Right, I see,' I smile, though to be honest, I don't really.

---

* Which I know sounds totally bonkers, but hello, so does the fact you make vodka from potatoes, so I can believe anything.

I've only just got my head around stories. Are they the same as reels? Or is that TikTok? Honestly, sometimes I dream of the days of my old Nokia when all we had to worry about was what ringtone to have.

'I managed to find some 4G so I could get online. I know we're supposed to be switching off, but I needed to do a sponsored post. I'm an influencer,' she adds in explanation.

'Don't worry, I won't tell anyone.'

Which comes out a bit wrong, but never mind. Smiling, I leave her posting a selfie and head back to the campsite, but I've only walked about five minutes along the path when I spot Michelle. Crikey, this forest is busy. She's holding her phone out in front of her like a divining rod and almost bumps into me.

'I have to make a work call.' She looks sheepish.

'4G's that way,' I smile. 'Just don't be late for lunch.'

Lunch is a vegetable broth in the farmhouse kitchen, and then it's an afternoon of workshops, which, on first glance, aren't really the kind of fun activities you'd choose for a hen weekend, but turn out to be really interesting. Though I'm not sure they're going to help empower me to manifest change in Edward's spreadsheets.

Afterwards there's a break in the schedule and we all head back to our yurts for a bit of R&R. I think everyone's tired. It's been non-stop all day with the workshops and activities and, personally, I could do with a bit of a lie down. Who knew creating change, finding empowerment and challenging yourself could be so exhausting? Poor Holly looked shattered at lunch.

But I've only just closed my eyes when I hear a rustling sound outside the door of my yurt. My heart sinks. Oh God, don't tell me it's Annabel with another session of some kind.

I pretend not to hear and ignore it, but the rustling gets louder. Then I hear a whisper.

'Nell, it's me, let me in.'

It's Michelle. Swiftly followed by Fiona then Holly. I quickly usher them all inside.

'What's going on?'

'Someone told me this was supposed to be a hen party,' she grins, producing a bottle of champagne from her bag. 'So I thought we should get the party started.'

'Champagne *and* chocolate teacakes,' I grin, as she hands me two packets of her favourites. OK, so I know I said I wasn't into hen dos, but this looks like a lot more fun than a breath workshop.

'Isn't that against the rules?' whispers Fiona, looking worried.

We all round on her, groaning.

'Have you been on the crystals again?' laughs Michelle, attacking the foil on the cork.

'I'm just saying, we're supposed to be cleansing our minds and bodies.'

'Oh FFS, what happened to the F**k Avocados T-shirt?' demands Holly, in reference to the time we all got a bit drunk once and Holly yelled the bit about avocadoes and Fiona said it should be printed on a T-shirt.* Before seeing Fiona's face and swiftly apologizing. 'Sorry, I didn't mean . . . I've just been a bit stressed recently . . .'

'Which is why we need to crack this open,' placates Michelle, popping open the cork with a jumper to muffle the sound and filling up four plastic glasses. Trust Michelle to think of everything. 'I mean, come on, we're away for the

---

* So I got her a T-shirt printed for Christmas and she proudly sent me a selfie wearing it.

weekend, together for the first time *in for ever*, we've got to have a bit of fun.'

'Didn't you enjoy the crystal workshop and guided meditation?' Fiona looks upset.

'The whole retreat's been great, honestly, thanks so much for suggesting it,' I swiftly interrupt, passing around champagne.

'Ooh, and it's chilled,' wide-eyes Holly.

'Hung it from a tree. An old trick from when I used to live in a squat and we didn't have a fridge . . .' Grinning, Michelle holds her glass aloft. 'Here's to you, Nell. Our bloody fabulous bride-to-be.'

As everyone raises a toast, I feel myself blush. Up until now, the fact I'm getting married to Edward hasn't seemed real. *Correction*: it's seemed real in a stressful, loads-to-do, Edward's-spreadsheets and mother-breathing-down-my-neck kind of way. But not this fun stuff with your friends, being toasted with champagne. I take a sip of the delicious golden bubbles. I take it back, I'm really enjoying this hen-do business.

'I've also got another surprise . . .'

'Don't tell me you booked a stripper,' I laugh.

'*A stripper?*' Holly nearly chokes on her champagne.

'Jesus, Michelle. You didn't, did you? Annabel will freak.' Fiona looks apoplectic.

'No, of course not. Though I think some of the other women might have enjoyed it. Debbie particularly,' grins Michelle, raising an eyebrow. 'It's just a little something.'

She hands me a package and I quickly unwrap it. 'I know it's a bit early, but it's part of a new wedding range I'm doing.' Inside are garlands of exquisitely embroidered silver-and-white bunting made from the most beautiful linen, with mine and Edward's initials intertwined.

'Oh wow, you made this? It's really lovely, thank you.' I feel my eyes well up. And now I'm getting all teary.

'Well, it was either that or a knitted penis,' she says as I go to give her a hug and we all laugh and someone breaks out the chocolate teacakes.

'Oh God, do you remember when someone brought those penis straws to your hen do, Holly?'

There are shrieks and Holly groans at the memory. 'I wouldn't mind but they were useless, you had to suck really hard or nothing happened.'

'Are you sure you're talking about the straws?' quips Michelle and there are cackles of laughter. I think the champagne has gone straight to everyone's heads. Well, we did only have that vegetable broth for lunch.

'Gosh, I've been to some awful hen nights,' remarks Fiona, taking a gulp of champagne. She seems more relaxed now. 'I remember one where the bride kept going on about wedding customs. Apparently it was customary for friends to have to pay for a crazy expensive weekend to Monte Carlo, a five-star hotel, a helicopter ride and a stretch limo.'

'I once knew a bride who had three hen nights!'

'God, the agony!'

'The money!'

'The emails!'

'Death by Reply All,' I let out a groan, which turns into a collective one.

'I was already pregnant when Max and I tied the knot, so I didn't bother with a hen night as I couldn't drink,' says Michelle.

'I remember. I was invited to Max's stag,' I nod. 'Though mostly I think it was just to make sure he got home in one piece.'

'You could have done a spa weekend or crafting, like I

did,' suggests Fiona. 'It was so much fun, we made our own fascinators. Do you still have yours, Nell?'

'Absolutely. I wear it all the time,' I fib.

'I don't know about all these games and activities.' Michelle drains her glass. 'Can't we just do what the men normally do?'

'What's that?' asks Holly.

'Get hammered!' Reaching for the champagne bottle, she tops up everyone's glasses and we continue having a merry old time, until we realize we've run out of champagne and we're miles from the nearest off-licence. And then I remember my stash of gin-in-a-tins – see, I knew they'd come in useful – and produce them from underneath the mattress, along with all the nibbles, to lots of whooping and cheering, as we're all starving after only eating vegetable broth, and we all carry on drinking and laughing and eating—

'Hello, ladies? Are you in there?'

A loud voice outside the tent causes Fiona to sit up like a meerkat.

'It's Annabel!' she hisses, doing her Big Eyes.

Abruptly we all fall silent, except for Michelle who's totally got the giggles.

'You missed dinner, is everything all right?'

There's a pause as we all hold our breath, then the sound of a zip being unfastened on the door covering.

Oh shit. Stuffed full of chocolate teacakes and crisps and copious amounts of booze, no one is hungry. What we are is blind drunk. There's a mass scramble to stuff everything under the bed as Annabel appears, lumbering into the yurt, dressed in a white full-length duvet coat, like a cross between an abominable snowman and a teacher who's just caught her pupils misbehaving.

Of course it's all terrifically hilarious.

'Oh, we were just er—'

'Manifesting,' says Michelle, with a hiccup. I shoot a look at her and she quickly wipes off the chocolate at the side of her mouth.

Annabel narrows her eyes, unconvinced.

'Well, it's time for the circle of light. The fire ritual, which is our closing ceremony, so bring cushions and blankets, and something to write on, as we'll be setting our intentions.'

There's a murmuring of obedience and I resist the temptation to say, 'Yes, Miss,' as we gather everything up and follow her outside. God, it's FREEZING. It had been warm inside the yurt with the log burner on, but now it's dark and the temperature has plummeted and my breath makes white, puffy clouds. More than that, it's only when you go outside that you realize just how drunk you actually are.

Fortunately a large bonfire is already burning, around which are gathered the rest of the women in a circle, and there are lots of blankets to keep us warm.

'Ooh, it's like bonfire night,' gasps Fiona loudly. She's really quite pissed and swaying ominously. Annabel looks furious. 'Has anyone got any sparklers?'

'Let's sit down,' I whisper, easing her onto the cushion before there's fireworks, *but of a different kind*.

'We are here in this healing circle to honour ourselves for the work we have done today to mark the beginning of our new lives,' intones Annabel.

As we join the circle, I glance around at the rest of the women, their faces glowing orange from the fire, like an old Dutch painting. Several catch my eye and smile in greeting and I feel a warmth, and it's not just from the fire or the alcohol.

'By performing this powerful cleansing ritual, we commit to ridding ourselves of anything negative in our lives . . . it could be a bad relationship, a painful memory, an unresolved conflict, or self-limiting belief . . . and we do this by writing it down on a piece of paper and throwing it in the fire . . .'

I notice Holly and Fiona and Michelle have grown quiet and know they're feeling the energy too. All joking aside, there's something very powerful about coming together in a circle, with its ancient and spiritual symbolism. Sitting here in the darkness, with the flames and the stars and the vast skies above us, and the sudden sense of perspective it brings, I feel both an insignificance and a strength I've never experienced before.*

For a few moments there's silence. Just the crackling sounds of the fire. Everyone has fallen deep into thought. Some women write quickly, others take their time to decide what to put on their piece of paper. Until after a few minutes, Annabel speaks.

'OK, if everyone has written something, I'd like to go around the circle . . .'

Babs goes first. Babs seems like a pro and needs no instruction. Standing up, she reads aloud her intention, then throws it into the fire.

Next up is Debbie, who looks horribly self-conscious, and mumbles something unintelligible before quickly sitting back down.

I look at my piece of paper. I didn't realize we were reading out loud what we'd written. I decide to leave out the bit about Annabel.

One by one we go around the circle. Some things are specific and deeply personal, others more general, or seemingly trivial. (Or, in the case of one woman who wants to get rid of the indiscriminate rage she feels when her partner doesn't

---

* In hindsight it could have been the gin talking, but I really don't think it was.

hang up their wet towel, quite funny.) Listening to everyone, it's amazing how different we all are, but how we all hold on to things that we need to let go of.

'Holly?'

And now it's the last person in the circle and I look up to see my friend stand up with her piece of paper. Her breath forming a little white cloud as she clears her throat and exhales. The blink-and-you-miss-it tremble in her voice as she speaks.

'I want to get rid of my breast cancer.'

Life Isn't a Fairy Tale

Back in London a few days later I go to meet Cricket at Kensington Palace to see an exhibition of Princess Diana's wedding dress. I'd bought tickets ages ago in the summer, as part of Cricket's Re-Entry plan, and I've been really looking forward to it. Plus, now it's only a few months until I'm a bride myself, so the timing feels serendipitous.

However, as the day dawns I'm not much in the mood to be looking at wedding dresses, even if it's one as iconic as Diana's. I'm still reeling from Holly's news at the weekend, and haven't been able to think of anything else. It was all such a shock. There were so many questions. So many hugs. But Holly didn't want any fuss. She assured us she was going to be fine, that she had a great doctor, and that it was all under control. Typical Holly.

I know she's right to be positive. Treatments and survival rates are better than ever. The NHS is amazing. We have some of the leading cancer hospitals and specialists in the world. But cancer is still a word that strikes fear into you. As soon as Holly told us, my mind immediately went to Joe and his sister Sam. She'd had breast cancer and I'd just written her obituary. It doesn't get more sobering than that.

'She told us not to worry, but I'm scared.'

'Of course you're scared.'

As we make our way through the lavish rooms of the

King's State Apartments, Cricket is sympathetic, but matter of fact.

'We are all walking around like everything is normal, but inside we're all secretly terrified of losing those we love.' She pauses in front of a glass case of jewellery. 'But we have to juggle fear and joy every day. Now look at that tiara? Isn't it stunning?'

I am, however, always in the mood to spend time with Cricket.

'But me being scared isn't going to help Holly, is it?' I've spent the last fifteen minutes telling her all about Holly and her diagnosis. It's been good to get it all off my chest. 'I want to be supportive, but I don't know what to say.'

'The problem with us humans is we want to try and fix things. To feel like we have some control over things we have no control over.'

Leaving the state rooms, we begin descending the staircase that leads outside.

'I remember when my friend Ginny was diagnosed with cancer, all the advice and miracle cures people would offer up – it was quite incredible how everyone suddenly became an oncologist. Rather like how everyone suddenly became a specialist in infectious diseases during the pandemic.'

Cricket raises an eyebrow and I smile. I think it's the first time I've smiled since I got back from the retreat, despite Edward and Arthur's best efforts.

'All you have to do is be there. And to listen. It's quite simple really.'

Reaching the bottom of the staircase, we set off walking across the grounds of the palace, our feet crunching on the gravel, as we make our way across to the Orangery, which houses Diana's dress. At the entrance, I hesitate. There's comfort in being with someone who's weathered the storms and knows what's ahead, but with it brings truths you might not want to hear.

'What happened to your friend Ginny?' I'm almost too scared to ask.

'She survived and went on to marry and divorce three times and give birth to five children.'

It's only when I exhale with relief, that I realize I've been holding my breath tight inside of me.

'She always used to joke, "I've lost two breasts and three husbands, but I never lost my sense of humour."' Cricket laughs fondly, her face reflective. 'You would have loved Ginny. She was such a hoot.'

I know how much Cricket still misses her girlfriends and, reaching out, I slip my arm supportively through hers and together we walk through the exhibition until we finally come upon a huge illuminated glass case. Talk about saving the best for last. As we approach from the back, the train reaches out towards us in full. Even now, it takes your breath away.

'Do you know the train is twenty-five feet long,' marvels Cricket, 'and the designers, Elizabeth and David Emanuel, measured the width of the aisle at St Paul's Cathedral to make sure it would fit perfectly.'

'Wow.' It's all I can say.

Letting go of Cricket's arm, I move nearer the glass. As a little girl, watching the wedding on a tiny portable TV, I thought she looked like a princess from a fairy tale. Forty years later, a lot more than just the fashions have changed, but the magic remains. Up close the dress sparkles. Hand-embroidered silk taffeta. Hundreds of thousands of seed pearls. Antique lace. Minute detail of the embroidery, only seen up close, reveals crowns and motifs. I actually feel quite emotional.

'I always thought it was a little over the top, but it's actually rather beautiful isn't it,' marvels Cricket, then tuts loudly.

'I'm sorry, I've been terribly remiss. I haven't even thought to ask you about your dress.'

'There's nothing to tell.'

'Ooh, is it a secret?' Her eyes flash with curiosity.

'No, there's no secret,' I smile, then shake my head. 'I still haven't found anything I like.' I turn away from Diana's dress. 'What did you wear?'

'Black.'

'*Black?*' I look at her astonished.

She nods, as if this is perfectly normal for a bride. 'Well, this wouldn't suit me –' gesturing to Diana's confection, she looks amused '– and I thought white seemed a little misleading, considering I was hardly a virgin bride.'

'Me too. I'm worried I might look silly in white.' We move towards the front of the dress. It really is a long train. 'According to an article I read the other day, I'm what they call "an older bride".'

Cricket lets out a loud snort.

'I was seventy-five and I didn't feel like an older bride, I felt like a teenager,' she dismisses. 'You know, that's the brilliant thing about love, it never gets old, unlike us, and it has a magical ability to make you feel young again. All those beauty companies should realize that. Forget a face cream, fall in love.'

As her face lights up I smile. It's true. Sometimes Edward looks at me and I feel like a teenager.*

'So exactly what did you wear?' I'm still curious about the black.

'A cocktail dress I'd had in my wardrobe for years. Every woman should have a little black dress they can wheel out on occasion. Very practical.'

'I've never known you be practical.'

---

* Particularly when he's telling me off about leaving the lights on.

'Not when it comes to what colour to paint my living room, how to decorate my coffin, or what shoes to wear, no –' she glances down at her silver plimsolls '– but those are things I care about. Monty and I didn't care a jot about getting married. We only did it to avoid all that tax nonsense and paperwork when Monty's health was failing.'

We stand at the front of the dress now, trying to navigate the small crowd that's gathered in front of it.

'It was meant to be just an exercise in form filling, a way of cutting through the red tape. That it turned out to be rather wonderful took us both quite by surprise.' She smiles then, her face lighting up.

'So tell me, any wedding tips?'

'Just remember that it's about the two of you. Don't be distracted by all the pomp and ceremony. The flowers and the fuss.' She beckons to Di's wedding dress. 'It was just the two of us at City Hall and it was just about me and Monty and our life together.' She pauses. 'You know a marriage is about more than a wedding. Or a dress. A marriage is about what comes after the wedding.'

I nod, thinking of all the millions of things on my wedding to-do list. Listening to Cricket, it all seems so unnecessary.

'I always think it's easy to fall in love, but it's staying in love when that love is tested that's hard. Life isn't a fairy tale.'

A space clears and as we both turn to gaze upon the dress, I think about being a little girl, playing dress-up as a bride, making my little brother be bridesmaid and carry my train. All the childhood fairy tales of happy ever after. Of course, now I'm grown up, I know the reality. Is it one in two, or one in three, marriages that fail?

And yet still we make the leap of faith. Look at me and Edward; he's divorced and I was engaged before, we both know there are no guarantees. So why do people still get married? Is it faith or hope or simply because you love each other? Is it about making a commitment or the power of tradition or just an excuse to throw a big party for all your family and friends? And why is there still so much emphasis on the dress and the whole idea of 'the big day'?

'There is one thing I do regret about my wedding day.'

I snap back. 'Oh no – what?'

'Not having a cake.'

'You can rest assured I won't be making that mistake.' I grin and she laughs, before her expression turns thoughtful.

'You know, we're here to look at a dress worn by a woman marrying a prince, but look around you, it's all women here with their friends.' She turns, her gaze sweeping around the exhibition. 'So much is made of romantic love, but I've always been of the opinion that one's girlfriends are our real soulmates.'

I follow her gaze around the Orangery. She's right. The room is full of female friendships. I think about all my friends. I think about Holly.

Cricket catches my expression as it clouds. 'I'm not going to tell you not to worry about your friend Holly, because I know you will. But remember, you can't worry someone well. You can only be there for them.' She smiles and links her arm through mine. 'Now, let's go to the cafe. I hear they do marvellous cake.'

I'm grateful for:
1. *Cake and Cricket; the lemon meringue pie was as delicious as the company.*
2. *Knowing that when I eventually find a dress, it won't have mutton sleeves and a twenty-five-foot train.*
3. *That life isn't a fairy tale and I'm marrying Edward, not a prince.*
4. *Female friendships.*

Like Mother Like Daughter

OK, so I owe my mother an apology.

For years I've teased my mother about her habit of telling me about the ins and outs of people I don't know. Stories about people I've never met, who are related to more people I've never met, who live next door to someone I have truly never heard of. Usually when we're on the telephone and I've got to get back to work.

But then this morning I found myself scrolling social media, watching cute videos of strangers' dogs, flicking through stories featuring house makeovers and far-flung adventures, reading posts about break-ups and fertility journeys and mental health updates, whilst liking, sharing and love heart emoji-ing. And suddenly realized two things:

1. I don't know any of these people and have never met them.
2. I've turned into my mother!

An Unexpected Item in the Baggage Area*

First thing this morning I have an appointment to see my GP. I can't remember the last time I actually saw a doctor face to face, everything's online these days, but recently I got a phone call from a new doctor who's just joined the practice.

'Nothing to worry about, I'm just inviting all our female patients to come in to run through a few health checks as part of my well-women clinic.'

People like to bash the NHS, but really it's so fab.

On arriving, I'm informed there are several patients ahead of me and she's running late. Finally she appears in the waiting room with the kind of frazzled but determined expression you see on marathon runners.

'Penelope Stevens? I'm Dr Harris. If you'd like to come on through.' She wafts me through to her office with a warm smile. 'Sorry to keep you waiting.'

'Oh, no worries.' I smile back. Already I'm lying to my lovely new doctor. I have lots of worries.

'So, I've just been reading through your notes and wanted to have a chat about the suitability of continuing with your current combined hormonal contraception.'

Sitting behind her desk, she peers at her computer screen.

---

* FYI this is not a typo: we're talking emotional baggage here.

'It says you started taking it almost two years ago. Was that just to alleviate the symptoms of perimenopause? I can see here a mention that your periods were becoming heavy and erratic?'

She's describing my menstrual cycle, but frankly, with my old jeans no longer fitting and my see-saw moods I'm beginning to feel that could also be a description of me these days. *Heavy and erratic.*

'Well, yes, and I also started a new relationship.'

She briefly glances up from reading her computer screen.

'And I didn't want to get pregnant.'

It's the first time I've said it out loud. When I got together with Edward, we didn't really talk about contraception. I offered to go on the pill and that was that. I'd hoped it would help with my increasingly painful periods, and it did. But hearing myself say those words is a jolt.

'Our guidelines recommend that women over forty should be counselled about alternative effective methods—'

I snap back, 'Counselled?'

'Although the pill is very safe, there are risks and these increase with age. Especially as I see there is a family history of thrombosis?'

I nod. 'My mum had a blood clot in her leg. Luckily they caught it and she's fine. They think it was caused by a long flight.'

'A DVT.' Dr Harris's face is serious.

'Yes,' I nod, 'though Mum calls it a DVD.'

I see a flicker of amusement on my GP's face, but she remains entirely professional.

'So in cases such as yours, I would recommend an intra-uterine device. Not only is it a very effective contraceptive but it can cure painful heavy periods.'

'Sounds great.'

'Better still, once it's inserted it stays in place for up to five to ten years so you can forget about it.' She smiles brightly. 'Of course, just one thing, you'd need to be certain about not wanting to get pregnant as it would likely take you up to the age of menopause.' She starts tapping something into her keyboard. 'So, would you like me to make an appointment for you to have one fitted?'

One minute you're sailing along at a well-women clinic, chatting to the nice doctor and now, without warning, you're hurtling towards menopause and a sudden sense of finality.

'Actually. No.'

'I'm sorry?' Abruptly she stops tapping and looks up from her keyboard.

I feel my cheeks flame with embarrassment. 'I mean, I'm not sure . . .'

Out of the blue, this appointment has taken an entirely unforeseen, and rather startling, direction and I'm trying to articulate what's going on inside. Which is hard, as all at once there's a lot going on inside. I thought I was at peace with not being a mother. That I was going to have a different kind of life to the one I had planned; one I was meant to have. But now, suddenly, it's like there's an Unexpected Item in the Baggage Area.

'About switching to the coil?'

'About wanting a baby.'

'Oh. I see.'

Though, really, I'm not sure she does. How can she. I don't.

'I see in your notes you had a miscarriage a few years ago. I'm sorry.'

She's being so nice but it makes me feel like a fraud. It wasn't a baby, it was a miscarriage. Just the prefix makes me feel I did something wrong. That it was my fault somehow.

That I made a *mis*take. That I shouldn't make a fuss.

'I haven't tried to get pregnant since.'

'Pregnancy after loss can be very difficult and, as I'm sure you're aware, over forty it can be harder to get pregnant and stay pregnant, but it's certainly not impossible . . .'

And then, without warning, something else happens. Listening to her, it's as if the door of possibility that I've kept firmly shut unexpectedly cracks open. Not much, but just enough to let in a chink of light that shines into the dark recesses.

'. . . A woman is still fertile up until she's had her last period, so equally, if you are *not* wanting to get pregnant, contraception is still necessary.'

'Yes, of course,' I reply calmly, but inside I feel weirdly disorientated.

'Obviously, it's something you'd want to discuss with your partner,' she continues, smiling. 'But, Penelope, if you want to try for a baby, I would strongly encourage you do it now and not to wait any longer. This could be your last chance.'

Two Weddings and a Funeral

Weddings are like buses; you don't get one for ages and then two come along at once. A few days later Liza calls to invite me to hers. We haven't spoken since I FaceTimed her to congratulate her on her baby news. I'm so happy for her and Tia; there were no brave faces, only genuine smiles. Now she and Tia have decided to get married ahead of the birth and it's going to be in LA in January.

'I know it's a bit short notice, but can you come?'

'To California in the winter? Try stopping me,' I laugh.

'And Edward too, of course, I'm dying to meet him!'

Who would've thought it? Both me and my friend Liza getting married just weeks apart. There was a time when neither of us could've imagined it, but now here we both are talking wedding plans, and life feels suddenly full of all these new beginnings.

Which contrasts sharply a few days later when Cricket and I both attend our last session at The Toodlepip Club and I'm faced with the flipside. As we all put the finishing touches to our coffins, Elaine gathers all the members around and we raise a toast and celebrate everyone's achievements and hug everyone cheerio and toodlepip. It's very emotional and there's lots of tears and laughter. And a reminder that with beginnings we get endings too, and they're ones we made ourselves with glitter and spray paints.

A Weekend Away

It's Edward's birthday and to celebrate we go away for a romantic weekend. I'm beyond excited. It's our first trip away to somewhere that isn't my parents' and I'm really looking forward to getting away from the city, work, his kids and my mother and for it to be just the two of us, and Arthur of course.

(I'm planning on turning my phone off – no more texts from Mum about the ever-changing guest list – he's planning on not worrying about Louis and Simone, who are staying at the flat again, setting the place on fire.)

I can't wait!

I've also been thinking a lot about what the doctor said and I want to talk to Edward about everything I've been feeling, and which I'm still trying to make sense of, and this will be a great opportunity.

So we splurge and book ourselves into one of those fancy boutique hotels in the countryside, where we drink delicious cocktails, eat fresh, organic, plant-based this, that and the other, have lots of sex and try not to goggle at the A-list celebrity couple we star-spot in the spa but instead remain totally cool.*

---

* Or rather, I spot the aforementioned Hollywood couple in the jacuzzi and discreetly whisper in Edward's ear with strict instructions not to look. Only for Edward to loudly repeat their names, demand 'Where?' and then stare right over at them.

Suffice to say we have an absolutely wonderful time celebrating, until I decide to try the oysters – and discover I'm allergic – and end up spending the next twenty-four hours throwing up, while poor Edward hovers around the bed with a bucket and sleeps on the sofa.

Happy Birthday, babe!

I'm grateful for:
1. *Being able to finally find our room as the hotel is so trendy and dimly lit that we spend most of the time fumbling around in the dark. Which is a bit of a metaphor for life, frankly.*
2. *Being in charge of choosing the hotel as Edward was insistent that a hotel is 'just a bed for the night, so why spend a fortune?'**
3. *It being dog-friendly and Arthur for not peeing on the furniture.*
4. *Spending quality time together and having fun before Oyster-Gate; that said, I never got the chance to talk to Edward about the conversation with the doctor as I was too busy throwing up.*
5. *Edward for passing me my sick bucket.*
6. *Romance not being dead.*

---

* Note to men everywhere, a woman will never, ever view a hotel as 'just a bed for the night'.

DECEMBER

#(s)elfonashelf

Skating on Thin Ice

'So surgery is scheduled for next week.'

It's a Saturday morning and I've come to meet Holly at the Natural History Museum's ice rink where Olivia, who's now turned four and is old enough to join the penguin skating club, is having her first lesson with an instructor who's wearing reindeer antlers.

Jingly Christmas music is playing. Lights are twinkling. And watching from the side of the rink, we're drinking mulled wine and waving and cheering every time Olivia goes past the giant Christmas tree. Anyone looking at us would think we're a couple of friends getting into the festive spirit, without a care in the world.

Just shows.

'Results of the biopsy showed the type and grade of cancer, so I'm having what the surgeon called a wide local excision, to remove the tumour as well as a margin of healthy breast tissue to check for any cancer cells. Followed by six rounds of chemo, plus thirty daily rounds of radiotherapy . . .'

I listen as Holly reels off her treatment as if it were a grocery list. Always practical and extremely organized, she seems to be approaching her diagnosis with the same business-like attitude she has towards everything in life.

'Or is it thirty-three? I need to check that. Anyway, I've written it all down, including the combination of drugs I'll be taking so I can cross reference – WOO-HOO, LIVVY! You're doing AMAZING!'

She breaks off to wave at Olivia.

'Yay, way to go!' I cheer alongside her.

The rink is full of children whizzing around with their plastic penguins and as Olivia comes into view with her yellow pom-pom hat, rosy cheeks, and same look of determination as her mother, we grin like loons and whoop with encouragement. As she sees us, her face lights up like the Christmas tree.

'How's Olivia taking it?' I turn to Holly once she's skated past.

'She's been incredible. I was honest with her, I didn't want her to hear us talking about it, or hide anything from her. I told her Mummy is poorly but she's going to get better. That I have to have an operation and it might be a bit sore afterwards. She asked me if I wanted her stickers—'

Her voice catches and tears spring up. She quickly wipes them with her mittened hand.

'Olivia always gets stickers when she's had a bump or a scrape. To make it better.'

I give her arm a squeeze.

'How's Adam?'

'He's struggling, but won't admit it. You know Adam, he's always so emotional about everything, but feels he has to be strong for me. I think he feels a bit useless. Of course all the house moves are on hold now. I need to be here, near my doctors and specialists and the hospital.'

'Well, that's my silver lining,' I smile. 'I didn't want to lose you to the Cotswolds.'

'Oh, we could never afford the Cotswolds, but Adam calls it Cotswolds adjacent,' she corrects and we both laugh.

'To be honest, I'm still trying to get my head around it all,' she admits as we turn our attentions back to the rink. 'Once I was diagnosed, it all happened so fast. One minute life's normal, and then suddenly you've got breast cancer. It's a lot to take in . . . like trying to run a race you haven't trained for.'

'It must be overwhelming.'

'You know me, I'm very much like, OK, here's a problem, now how do we fix it?'

I've been absently watching the skaters, but now I glance sideways at Holly. In her full-length duvet coat, woollen beanie and mittened hands, she's protected from the cold. But she suddenly seems so vulnerable.

'I have to fix it. It's non-negotiable.'

We both look over at Olivia skating past. Seeing her mum, she waves excitedly.

'It has to be.'

My mind flashes to Joe's sister Sam. I drag it back again.

'Yes,' I nod, feeling my insides twist. I want to offer encouragement, to tell her she's going to beat this, but I resist the urge to reach for all those tropes and platitudes and remember Cricket's advice to just listen and be there for her.

'So, how's the wedding planning coming on?'

'Oh you don't want to hear about that,' I say dismissively. 'It's all so trivial and unimportant compared to what you're having to deal with.'

'Are you kidding me? I love trivial.' She looks at me, her eyes wide. 'I want trivial right now. And that's not true, it is important,' she says firmly. 'Please distract me with details about wedding favours and flower arrangements and what tiara you're going to wear . . .'

I look at her, askance.

'That was a joke,' she adds, and I feel a beat of relief.

'Phew, because I haven't got anywhere near that far yet.

219

I'll be honest, I had no idea there was so much to think about when planning a wedding. My to-do list is forever getting longer.'

'Can I just ask you one favour?'

'Of course, what?' I ask curiously.

'Promise me you won't ask me to be a bridesmaid,' she grimaces and I laugh.

'Promise.'

'I'll probably be bald by then anyway.'

Her words slip out into the frozen air and she gives a little shiver and warms her hands on her mulled wine. For a split second I think I see a flicker of fear but it's quickly replaced with a determined indifference.

'Whatever. It's only hair,' she shrugs.

'Mummy!' interrupts Olivia, waving from the rink to tell us the lesson is over.

'Coming, darling!'

'Exactly, it's only hair,' I agree, though we both know it's a lot more than that.

Afterwards we celebrate Olivia's first lesson with hot chocolate and warm hugs and excited chatter. The ice rink at the museum is one of London's loveliest and most magical traditions but later, when I get home, I read that after fifteen years, it's going to be its last year. Today feels bittersweet, in more ways than one.

Dear Santa

Nativity plays, Elf on a Shelf, Santa's Grotto, Winter Wonderland . . . with the festive season fast approaching, it's been non-stop fun activities for my godchildren and little niece. Being a kid at Christmas is so much more fun compared to being an adult. I seem to spend mine in a state of panic ordering things online, making endless to-do lists and locking myself in the bedroom yelling, 'DON'T COME IN,' while furiously trying to wrap (though Fiona confessed to me she just *pretends* to wrap so she can go into the bedroom and have a lie down).

This afternoon, I offered to pick Izzy up from school. What with everything going on, I haven't seen her for ages and she's growing up so fast. I'm worried the next time I see her she'll have a tattoo and be clubbing. I take her for a hot chocolate and help her write her letter to Santa, not that she needs help any more. She's nearly eight now and already asking questions like, for example, how is it possible that Santa can deliver everyone in the world's presents in one night, 'because Santa doesn't even have Amazon Prime?'.

Fiona says this is probably the last year she'll still believe in Santa, which makes me feel a bit sad. Christmas is so magical when you're little. It's a shame that stops when you get older. Which got me thinking, why does it have to? Unlike a lot of things, Christmas doesn't have an age limit. So this year, I've decided I'm going to write my own letter to Santa . . .

Dear Santa,

My name is Nell and I'm forty-something years old and I live in London. This year I have been:

1) Very good.
2) A bit grumpy.
3) Perimenopausal.
4) A total f**k-up.

I hope I am on the nice list (even if I've been a bit cranky sometimes) and I know you're really busy, so I've written you a list of things I would like for Christmas:

- My neck back.
- Ditto my waist, my eyesight and my upper arms.
- Eight hours of uninterrupted sleep.
- Somewhere fancy to go so I can wear all my gorgeous high heels that are gathering dust in my wardrobe.
- To be able to walk in aforementioned high heels (and not to have to change into flats after five minutes as my feet are killing me).
- Pockets and sleeves in everything.
- To actually use my gym membership and not just pay for it every month, thus deluding myself I am going to the gym and being healthy.
- To be able to drink more than one glass of wine without having a raging hangover.
- To remember why I went upstairs.
- Or opened the fridge.
- To already have all the ingredients necessary to follow a recipe in all the cookery books I will no doubt get for Christmas, so I can make a homemade lasagne that

doesn't end up costing forty-five pounds and several trips to the supermarket.

- Ice-cube trays that fill themselves up and don't dribble all over the freezer tray (seriously, how do you do that?).
- Full control of the smart meter.

Actually, scrap all those. I only have one thing on my Christmas list this year:

- For my friend Holly to get well again.

The Dress

So a couple of days ago an email from Annabel popped into my inbox. Unlike her weekly newsletter, which I was ~~forced~~ invited to subscribe to at her retreat, and which usually goes straight into my junk mail, this one was addressed to me personally.

I opened it like a bomb disposal expert might approach a suspicious package. No encounter with Annabel is without its dangers – if she's not trying to steal my best friend, flirt with my fiancé or invite me to one of her retreats, she's sending me motivational tips and weekly affirmations, together with a photo of her in tree pose – and so I approached with due caution.

So you can imagine my surprise when I discovered she wanted to make amends for being frosty with me at the retreat. According to her email, she felt like we got off on the wrong foot and there was '*a miscommunication*'* and she conceded that, while '*emotions were running high as we were releasing and empowering*', as Fiona's friend, she wanted us to be closer.

At which point I was reminded of that saying, 'Keep your friends close, but your enemies closer,' but then maybe I was just being paranoid.

Especially as she went on to write in the rest of her email:

---

* That'll be the bit when she accused me of being drunk.

Fiona told me you haven't got a dress yet and I would love to help! Due to my incredible contacts, I've been able to do THE IMPOSSIBLE and arrange for you to have a fitting with an exclusive wedding dress designer in Mayfair. Usually her waiting list is years long, but I explained you were a friend. How amazing is that?

P.S. No need to thank me for this amazing opportunity. Helping you be the bride you want to be is thank you enough. Better still, it's a chance for us to bond!

'Apparently she did one of the royals,' said Fiona, when I rang her up to tell her. 'She's a super exclusive designer.'

'I'm sure the prices are super exclusive too.'

'Annabel assures me she can get you a huge discount.'

'It'd have to be 99 per cent,' I replied, unconvinced, but Fiona was very excited.

'Wow, lucky you, Nell. Her dresses are just beautiful,' she enthused.

'Why don't you come too?' I suggested.

Safety in numbers, I wanted to add, with it being Annabel. But of course, I don't.

'Oh, I wish I could, but I'm finally back at the museum. No more working from home, thank goodness.' She heaved a sigh of relief down the phone. 'But this is great, you two will get to know each other better. Seriously, I think you've always got Annabel wrong. Once you get to really know her you'll love her. Plus, it will be fun!'

Fiona has a habit of thinking things are fun when she isn't the one doing them, but my curiosity was piqued. Plus I still hadn't found a dress yet. I'd looked at so many and nothing seemed right, I was beginning to lose hope and motivation. Maybe this super swanky designer would have something perfect and affordable. Or maybe I was just desperate. Either way, I emailed Annabel back and arranged to meet.

So now we're here, in a particularly chi-chi part of Mayfair, in a magical world of white tulle netting, swathes of ivory silk and shimmering embroidery. It's Procol Harum. Everything is a whiter shade of pale. From the velvet sofas, fresh flowers and ornate antique mirrors to the veils and accessories. Glass cabinets line the walls, filled with exquisite pearl earrings, glittering necklaces and, crikey, *is that a real tiara?*

I don't know what I was expecting, but it's all quite over-whelming. Having rung the bell and been allowed to enter, we're immediately swooped upon by Cressida, the owner and designer, who appears to be best friends with Annabel. There's a flurry of cheek-kissing and flutes of champagne appear from invisible assistants, while Cressida congratulates me on my engagement.

'So, what kind of gown do you have in mind?' asks Cressida, sitting next to me on the velvet sofa. I notice she refers to them as gowns, not dresses.

'Just something simple, really.'

I'm determined not to get carried away.

'Classic,' nods Cressida, subtly correcting me in the language of Bridal.

'Yes, classic, exactly. I just want something flattering and not fussy. No sequins or lace or anything like that—' I break off, realizing that, in fact, the entire shop is full of sequins and lace and stuff like that. 'I don't want to look like a big meringue,' I quip, light-heartedly.

There's a sharp intake of breath. That was meant to be a joke, but Cressida looks mortally offended. This wedding dress stuff is serious business. Annabel glares at me.

'Nell's just nervous,' she says quickly, soothing her friend.

'Of course, I understand,' nods Cressida, placated. 'We're here to bring joy and magic to what can be a very stressful time for a bride . . .'

'Thank you,' I smile, suitably chastised.

'We're here to make your day extra special. To make you feel like a princess.'

Having seen the Princess Diana exhibition a few weeks ago, I'm not sure I want to feel like a princess, but I nod anyway and sip my champagne. To be honest, I feel a bit out of my depth. This might be my second engagement, but I haven't got this far before, and I actually feel quite nervous. Reaching the dress – sorry, gown – stage makes it feel all very real.

'And of course, it's even more special for Nell . . .'

I snap back, to see Annabel smiling sweetly and sipping her champagne, as all eyes turn to me.

'. . . being a later-life bride,' she coos.

FFS. Is this what she calls bonding?

'Not that you'd ever know, as she looks amazing.' Reaching over, she gives my arm a supportive squeeze. Or maybe it's just to prevent me chucking my champagne all over her. I'm not quite sure.

'Amazing,' enthuses Cressida.

'But still, I'm sure Nell won't mind me telling you, she's waited a long time for her special day,' continues Annabel, sticking the knife in, 'which is why I told her we absolutely have to come and see you, Cressida.'

'Absolutely, and you came to the right place. We'd suggest cap or flutter sleeves and high necklines as a very flattering way of covering arms and chests, but of course, there are no rules, it's whatever you feel comfortable in.'

Jeans and a T-shirt, I'm tempted to reply, but instead I

smile dazedly as an invisible assistant tops up my empty flute. I seem to have gone from blushing bride to ancient old crone in the time it took me to down a glass of champagne.

'It's all in the details, and we offer a completely exclusive and bespoke couture service, as well as a selection off the peg that we can alter to create the perfect gown for you.'

As she's talking, Cressida starts pulling out dresses, but frankly by this point I've decided this is a bad idea. I don't need some fancy designer wedding dress that I'm only going to wear for one day. I only came out of curiosity (and desperation) but it's obvious that everything is going to be out of my price range. There are no prices on anything, and everyone knows if you have to ask you can't afford it. Plus, Annabel is right. I'm not some blushing, young bride. I'm older. Wiser.

And I've had enough.

'Thanks, Cressida, but I don't want to waste your time. I don't think these dresses are really me.' Putting down my champagne flute, I rise up from the velvet sofa. 'So I'm going to go.'

'*Go?*' chorus Annabel and Cressida.

'I'll show myself out.'

Cressida looks slightly bewildered. I don't think I'm *quite* the breathless bride she's used to. Meanwhile Annabel looks furious. I have a sudden suspicion she might be on commission.

'Are you sure you wouldn't like to try on just one gown?' Cressida's arms are full of frothy white tulle.

'No, honestly, I'm fine, thank you.' I begin putting on my jacket.

'Don't you want to see the look on Edward's face?'

Annabel's mention of Edward makes me pause.

'When he turns and sees you in your gown, walking up the aisle.'

'We're not getting married in a church,' I counter, but doubt prickles.

'It doesn't matter,' chimes Cressida. 'You know, you never forget the look on your husband's face when he sees you for the first time . . .'

'I've never forgotten Clive's,' nods Annabel, dabbing her eyes.

'*The look of love*,' whispers Cressida and there's an audible sigh.

Both women look at me. I feel my resolve wavering. I don't know if it's the mention of Edward, the heady mix of two glasses of champagne and all those seed pearls, or the desire to be on the receiving end of my own look of love, but suddenly I'm taking off my jacket, sitting back on the sofa, and picking up my champagne.

'OK then, just one.'

I'm grateful for:
1. *The collective gasp when I try on my first dress (sorry, gown) and turn to look at myself in the mirror. Even I gasp at the transformation. I take it all back, Cressida's creations are truly stunning and so flattering. But like I said, I'm just trying it on.*
2. *Not getting completely carried away and trying on half a dozen more; luckily I'm not someone who would ever be seduced by a sequin or antique Chantilly lace. Or find themselves in a changing room, being helped into acres of tulle and an exquisitely embroidered bodice.*
3. *Absolutely knowing I would never wear a veil, but just going along with it for a bit of silly fun and having one attached to my head with a diamante tiara.*
4. *Changing my mind about veils, they're actually not silly at all and really quite symbolic. You can have them*

personally embroidered with motifs or messages of your choice. In fact, I'm totally digging veils. Veils are gorgeous, how could I have ever thought otherwise?

5. Feeling quite giddy as my common sense and budget go flying out of the window, as it means I'm truly alive and living in the moment and absolutely nothing to do with that fourth glass of champagne and catching Wedding Dress Fever.

6. That tears-rolling-down-the-cheeks moment when I find The One.

7. Paracetamol, for when I wake up nauseous the next morning with a Wedding Dress Hangover and realize the mist has lifted and I've spent several thousand pounds on a dress I'm only going to wear for one day. Oh God. Edward's going to kill me. And it doesn't even have sleeves!

Christmas Spirit

'Another snowball?'

'Mmm, yes, please.'

Plucking the maraschino cherry out of my empty coupe glass, I savour its sweetness as Cricket reaches for the silver cocktail shaker and gives it a vigorous shake. As the ice rattles inside I decide there is no better sound.

'What are these made of? They're delicious.'

'Advocaat, sparking lemonade, lime cordial . . .' Reeling off the ingredients, she tops up our glasses with frothy yellow liquid. 'They used to be all the rage in the forties when I was a little girl. I remember my parents drinking them every Christmas.'

'Very retro.' I nod approvingly as she garnishes them both with a toothpick threaded with cherries, balanced on the rim.

'Like me,' she says with a mischievous smile, clinking my glass against hers.

It's a few days before Christmas and I'm at Cricket's flat, enjoying a Christmas cocktail and getting into the festive spirit. Which isn't difficult. The tree is up, shimmering and sparkling against the inky-dark walls. The fire in the grate is burning, much to the delight of Arthur, who I brought with me as Edward is working late at the office, and who is passed out in front of it. Meanwhile, on her old record player, Bing Crosby is crooning above the comforting crackle of the stylus against the vinyl. I love Spotify, but somehow so much of

ALEXANDRA POTTER

the magic is lost. But maybe that's just the cocktails and age talking.

I've also brought Cricket's presents as she is refusing to accept my invitation to spend Christmas at my parents' and is insisting on staying in London.

'I don't know why you won't come up to the Lake District with us,' I'm saying now, as she sits down next to me on her sofa. It's one of those squidgy feather ones, the deep crimson velvet worn and soft, and she sinks into it. 'Edward's driving and Mum and Dad would love for you to join us again.'

'I've told you, it's very kind of you, but Christmas is a time for families.'

'But you *are* family.'

Reaching out, she pats my hand, the rings on her fingers catching in the lights from the tree. 'That's terribly kind.'

But I'm insistent. 'I'm not being terribly kind. Or sweet. *Or patronizing,*' I rebuke, throwing her a firm look. 'Family doesn't just include relatives, thank God,' I add, thinking about Uncle Fred and his teeth, 'It's about the people you love.'

She tuts sharply. 'Are you deliberately trying to make me cry?'

'No, I'm being serious.' Smiling, I squeeze her fingers. 'It's like that saying. Family is what you make it.'

'Well, thank you. And I couldn't agree more.' Her eyes meet mine. 'But I'm perfectly happy here.'

'But you can't be by yourself for Christmas.'

'Heavens, no! Whatever gave you that idea? I'm not going to be on my own. I'm going to be with dozens of people.'

'Dozens?' I frown, confused.

'Possibly even more,' she nods, her face brightening. 'I'm helping out at the local homeless shelter, they need volunteers to cook Christmas dinner.'

'You are? Wow, that's amazing.'

232

'Well, I don't know about that. You haven't been witness to my woeful attempts at doing a turkey. One year Monty and I ended up with potted meat and pickle sandwiches.' Raising an eyebrow, she shakes her head. 'But when I saw their appeal for volunteers, I thought why not?'

My mind casts itself back to when I first met Cricket and she responded to a question with, 'Why not?' I thought then it was a good philosophy for life. Now after the events of recent years, it seems even more pertinent.

'Don't get me wrong, it's not a completely unselfish act,' she confesses. 'I will be receiving as much as I am giving, if not more. By helping those in times of need, I will be helping myself in time of need.'

She turns her head slightly, her gaze falling onto the fire. Her thick grey hair is swept up, away from her face, and the flickering light from the flames dances across her cheekbones.

'Christmas was Monty's favourite time of the year, which always makes it the most difficult for me. This will be my third without him, yet I still find it hard to believe he's not here to hang mistletoe and fuss over the decorations. I used to call him a sentimental old fool, but I loved it all really . . .'

She breaks off and smiles, Bing Crosby's voice and memories filling the living room.

'He had a place for every bauble on that tree. We'd buy one wherever we went. The purple glass one is from our trip to Vienna to see the opera. The wooden ornament is carved from a piece of oak from Richmond Park where we used to walk sometimes. The silver bells came from a Parisian flea market. It was snowing and I remember thinking I've never seen a city look so pretty. Like being in a snow globe. It was magical . . . Every single one has a memory attached. The story of our life together is hanging on that tree.'

As she speaks, I notice her eyes are glistening.

'You know, I thought by selling the old house and moving here, it would be a fresh start. That I'd leave a lot of the old ghosts behind me, but you never really do, do you? The past still haunts me.'

She turns to me now and gives a little shrug.

'What's more, I can't decide if that's good or bad.'

Our eyes meet as her words resonate. It's almost three years since my life fell apart and now I have a whole new one and yet still the ghosts of my old one haunt me, too. Broken hearts heal, but you never forget. And yet, for all their pain, there are some things I never want to forget.

'I'm sorry.'

I snap back to see Cricket studying me, her face apologetic.

'I'm being horribly gloomy.'

'No, you're not.' I try to reassure her. 'You're just being honest.'

'But I wanted it to be festive.' She looks upset.

'Fuck festive.'

It comes out too quickly. There's a brief pause and I fear I've said too much, but then her face lights up and she smiles wickedly.

'Now that should be a Christmas card greeting if ever there was one.'

'Cheers to that,' I laugh and we go to clink our now-empty glasses, when we're suddenly interrupted by the loud commotion of Arthur leaping up from in front of the fire and racing over to the window, barking.

'What on earth – Arthur, stop it!'

I call him over. But he has his nose pressed up against the long, full-length windows that face out onto the street, his paws scrabbling against the glass.

'Sorry, he must have seen something – probably a reflection – I'll draw the curtains.'

'Let me –' Cricket stops me as I'm about to get up '– I need the exercise.'

'I'm taking a Christmas break from my ten thousand steps,' I confess, grinning.

But Cricket isn't listening. I notice she's paused by the window, twitching at the curtains.

'It's him again.'

'Who?' I ask, curious.

'The man who's been stalking me.'

I jump up from the sofa, my idle curiosity suddenly taking on a much darker turn, and hurry over to the window. 'Where?'

'Standing underneath the lamppost.'

Quickly pulling back the curtains, I peer out into the darkened street. The pavement is empty. All I can see are parked cars.

'There's no one there.'

'Well, there was. I just saw him. And he was there last night too.'

'What did he look like?'

'I can never see his face. He wears a hoodie.'

'*A hoodie?*'

'Yes, it's like a sweater with a hood,' she explains, 'for some reason the baddies seem to wear them in all the television dramas.'

'Yes, I know what that is.' I feel a beat of alarm. God, I hope no one's looking to burgle Cricket's flat, knowing she lives here by herself.

I watch as a lone fox skittishly crosses the road, and then I see him. Or rather, I hear his dog barking. Further ahead up the street; a man with a spaniel. With the hood of his coat up to protect against the cold, he stops to let his dog sniff a lamppost.

'Oh, it's just a dog walker.' I feel a beat of relief.

'It is?'

'Yes, don't worry.' Feeling a bit silly, I close the curtains and turn back to Cricket. I swear she looks a bit disappointed. 'Well, now that's sorted, I think we need a drink, don't you?'

Her face immediately brightens and she reaches for our empty glasses. 'Another snowball?'

'Why not?' I reply, using her well-coined phrase. She smiles delightedly and I watch as she goes over to the drinks cabinet. It's in the far corner of the adjoining dining room and I hadn't paid attention to it before, but as she takes the bottles from the shelves, suddenly I recognize it. 'Hang on, is that—?'

'My coffin, yes,' she says briskly, busying herself. 'A local carpenter added some shelves. Isn't it marvellous? I thought I'd put it to good use until I needed it.' Rattling the cocktail shaker, she pours the drinks and turns to me. 'Now then. One cherry or two?'

I'm grateful for:
1. *Cricket's ingenious way of recycling her coffin. Maybe I should suggest it to Edward as God knows he loves to find ways to recycle. Instead of a drinks cabinet, how about a bookshelf?*
2. *Our toast to Monty.*
3. *It not being a burglar.*

Ghost of Christmas Past

Talking of Christmas spirits, today I was out buying presents, when I got a text.

> Hi, how are you?

It was from a number I didn't recognize. Normally I'd ignore it, but I've just got a new phone and I've had problems transferring across my contacts.

> Sorry, who is this?

> Ouch.

> No, really, I don't know this number.

> Johnny.

WTF! *Johnny!* I feel myself reel. Are you kidding me? Hot Dad turned Fun Uncle turned Absolute Shitbag who ghosted me! I thought I'd blocked him. It must be this new phone.

> It's been a long time ☺

A long time? It's over two years! Talk about transparent. He's obviously just broken up with someone and going through his old address book. What is it about this time of year? It's not just Christmas cards you get from people you haven't heard of all year, but old flames who suddenly appear, haunting you like the ghosts of Christmas past.

Cue lots of indignant outrage. *And lots of delighted satisfaction too.*

How are you?

Engaged.

Finally, *finally*, after years of never being able to think of a witty comeback when it comes to men, I've just aced it. There's a pause, then I see him typing.

Congratulations. Who's the lucky guy?

For a brief unexpected moment, the wind is taken out of my sails and I'm reminded of all those disastrous online dates and relationships that didn't work out; all that panic and potential, all that bravery and hope, all that agonizing hurt and disappointment. I think about how they always say ageing is not for sissies, but try dating too. Then I think about Edward and how thankful I am Johnny ghosted me.

And then I think 'what a prat' and type.

Not you 😊 Merry Christmas!

And block him again.

The Shortest Day

So today is 21 December, which means there is good news and bad news.

Bad news: it's the first day of winter and only four days until Christmas Day (!) and I've still got loads of presents to buy. Good news: today marks the winter solstice, so from tomorrow, the nights will be getting shorter and the days longer. Hurrah! We are literally heading into the light.

I've always loved this date, and this year it feels particularly symbolic. Not in a hippy dippy Stonehenge stone circle kind of a way. But we're coming to the end of this old year, and looking towards the New Year and all the hope for the future. My wedding to Edward, Liza's baby, Holly finishing her treatment and getting the all clear. I spoke to her last week after her surgery. Her doctor said it was a success; they've removed the tumour and several lymph nodes, and now the focus is on her recovery so she's ready to start chemo in the New Year.

I'm grateful for:
1. *Everything.*

A Family Christmas

I've always loved going home for Christmas, even when I lived in America and would make the ten-thousand-mile round trip by myself so I could eat Mum's roast potatoes and curl up on the sofa next to Dad's scratchy wool jumper and watch *Love Actually* for the millionth time. But this is particularly special, not just because, like so many families, we weren't able to spend it together last year, but because it's the first Christmas that Edward comes too.

His sons are spending the holidays with their mum. They were invited too, but Edward says it's more important for Sophie that she spends it with the boys. He's going skiing with them in the New Year. I worry he'll miss them, but he assures me he's happy with the arrangement.

'It was different when they were little, but if it was up to Ollie and Louis they wouldn't be spending Christmas with either of their parents, they'd be spending it with their phones,' he laughs on Christmas Eve, as we pack everything up in the car. 'Believe me, I'll see much more of them on the slopes.'

Arthur is pleased, it means he gets to stretch out on the back seat, while we sit in the front singing along to Wham's 'Last Christmas' and eating homemade cheese-and-piccalilli sandwiches. Edward has forbidden us to buy things in plastic from service stations, and brings snacks like nuts and tangerines. It's like eating the contents of my childhood Christmas stocking.

Ahh, the good old 1970s. Things have changed a lot since

then. I try to imagine my godson Freddy's reaction to finding those in his Christmas stocking today. He'd think the world had gone bonkers. Though to be honest, that's how I often feel, and it's got nothing to do with a few Brazil nuts and satsumas.

On Christmas Day it snows – hurrah, a white Christmas – and we play charades and that game of pretending we love all our presents. Only joking, I really do love my heated gloves, cashmere dressing gown and microwavable slippers from Edward, which of course has everything to do with wanting to keep his sweetheart warm and nothing to do with keeping my hands off the central-heating thermostat. And he's completely thrilled with his tickets to a West End show I've been dying to see.

On Boxing Day Uncle Fred arrives, along with his teeth,* and my little brother Rich and Nathalie and Evie, who we all fuss over. She has everyone eating out of her chubby little hands, even Edward who, after lunch, walks around the living room on all fours, pretending to be an elephant, while she rides on his back, giggling delightedly. It's the cutest thing ever. Watching him with Evie, it's not just the snow that melts. My heart does too.

Then, later that night we all cram on the sofas to watch *Love Actually* again and hand around tins of Quality Street. It's a family tradition. Only this time I'm squashed up next to Edward and there's a point in the film when I take my eyes off the screen and take in my own scene. It feels magical, and not just because of the fairy lights. There've been so many bumps to get here and I have this moment of just being completely happy exactly where I am. Like everything makes sense. It's a lovely feeling. The best gift of all.

Happy Christmas, everyone.

---

* Which, we all agree, is a Christmas miracle.

I'm grateful for:

1. *Not being the family who takes photos in matching pyjamas. Since when did that become a thing?*
2. *Edward not eating all the best Quality Street, but saving me the fudge squares (if that's not love actually, I don't know what is).*
3. *Being on the winning team of Mum's Christmas quiz. Like I said to Edward, it's not all doom and Zoom!*
4. *The group photos Cricket sends me of her in a pinny and pair of reindeer antlers, surrounded by pots and pans and lots of smiles.*
5. *Edward's dishwasher-stacking skills and fitting everything inside like a jigsaw, which impressed the whole family. So much so, he's now been roped in to finishing Dad's thousand-piece puzzle of the Houses of Parliament which has been spread out on the sideboard for years as he's only managed to do the corners.*
6. *Calories not counting at Christmas, or comparisons; who needs to be on a beach in Barbados posting bikini selfies when you could be eating your own bodyweight in mince pies?*

Two Pink Lines

We drive back to London on the 27th. Edward has got some work to do. That's the thing with being self-employed and setting up your own environmental software agency. As Edward says, the environment doesn't take time off for Christmas.

I always think the days in between Christmas and New Year are a weird time, where you lose track of the days and what you've eaten. It's a bit like mid-life, really.

When we get back to the flat, Edward's son Louis is there with his girlfriend, Simone. The two young lovebirds. I like Simone, she seems sweet, but somewhat subdued. Apparently she's not feeling too well. A stomach bug. I tell her I think there's something going round. I've felt a bit off too, but put it down to the ridiculous amount of Stilton and Quality Street I've consumed. I make us both a hot lemon drink, my mum's cure-all, then nip to the loo. After the long journey I'm bursting.

Five minutes later I'm staring in disbelief and astonishment at the two pink lines on the pregnancy test. My mind is reeling. That explains feeling off.

Suddenly the door opens. We all share a bathroom and I've forgotten to lock it.

'I'm in the loo!' I call out as Edward appears in the doorway.

'Oh sorry –' he begins to back out again '– the door wasn't

locked, I thought it was free—' He suddenly breaks off when he sees what I'm holding in my hands. The pregnancy test. His eyes go quickly to it, then to mine.

A look flashes between us. Everything seems to freeze for a moment.

'Is that—?'

'Yes, it's positive.' I stare at it.

I'm suddenly transported back to that moment several years ago in California. I sit down on the toilet seat, hand shaking, heart pounding, my reaction has taken me completely by surprise.

'Oh my God, Penelope.'

I snap back to see Edward, still standing in the doorway, a shocked expression on his face. And something else I can't place. 'I thought you were on the pill?'

As he speaks I'm suddenly realizing his mistake.

'No . . . no . . . you've misunderstood,' I shake my head, mind scrabbling. 'It's not mine.'

'It's not?' Edward frowns and looks totally confused. Entering the bathroom, he closes the door behind him. He's ashen-faced.

'I found it in the wastepaper basket, in the bin –' I motion to the little pedal bin that's kept next to the loo '– I saw the packaging first, the box . . .' All my words are tumbling out as I remember coming into the bathroom to go for a pee, going to put the tampon wrapper in the bin and then seeing the packaging, and underneath something wrapped in tissue paper.

'It must be Simone's,' I say in a hushed voice.

'Simone?' he whispers.

I nod, our eyes meeting, as the reality begins to dawn.

'Yes, Simone's pregnant.'

There's a split-second pause as Edward registers and I

expect him to be upset, or horrified, or even angry. For any of these emotions to kick in before the obvious worry and concern that will come later from the parent of a teenage son who has got his teenage girlfriend pregnant. But what I don't expect to see is *relief*.

'God, Penelope, for a moment there . . .' Sitting down on the edge of the bath, he lets out a deep exhale. And I suddenly realize that the expression on his face that I couldn't place was terror. He was terrified.

'What?' I look at him. '*For a moment there, what, Edward?*'

'I thought it was you.' His face breaks with relief and he actually smiles. 'I thought you were pregnant. I was like, fuck.'

I think that's probably the first time I've heard Edward swear. He never swears. But now, realizing his fiancée isn't pregnant, he's used the F word.

'Why, would that really be so awful?'

'Excuse me?'

'To think that I might be pregnant?'

Confused by my reaction to this turn in events, Edward looks at me blankly. 'Well, yes.'

'Instead of your teenage son's teenage girlfriend?'

I feel anger coming from somewhere deep inside of me, erupting.

'Well, no, that's not ideal either,' he says, with typical understatement, then seeing my expression, frowns. 'Look, this is obviously something I'm going to have to talk to Louis about, any parent would be shocked, It's just—'

'Just what?' I break off. I can't quite believe it.

'Penelope, I don't know what you want me to say. I don't know where you're coming from—'

'I'm coming from the point that you looked relieved to find out it wasn't me that's pregnant, but would rather it was your son's girlfriend.'

'Well, neither's ideal.'

'Really?'

'Well, yes, you don't want to have a baby any more than I do—'

As he's talking he's looking at me, and it's as if suddenly it registers and it's no longer a statement but a question.

'*Do you?*'

I stare at him, thinking about the feelings that had been triggered by my visit to the doctor – the unexpected item in the baggage area – and the conversation I wanted to have with Edward but could never find the right time for. Oh hello – is this the right time? When you've just found his teenage son's girlfriend's pregnancy test and you're both huddled in the bathroom, talking in whispers so they can't hear you? And yet, I don't feel like I've got much choice.

'That's something I wanted to talk to you about,' I begin, falteringly. 'I've been trying to find the right time . . .'

'Oh, and you think *this* is the right time?' Edward's incredulous.

He's impatient and angry and it feels like a slap. This is all wrong. It's coming out all wrong. Not how I hoped at all. I try again.

'I went to the doctor, we were talking about changing my contraception, she said that if I wanted to try and have a baby this was my last chance, that I should talk to you about it . . .'

Edward's peering at me, bewildered and perplexed, like he's trying to make sense of the small print.

'But I always assumed we were in agreement. You're on the pill.'

'I know but—'

I want to tell him about being pregnant before, about losing the baby, about why I've never told him. How I was worried about bringing my old relationship into this relationship, only to recently discover I couldn't leave it behind. But now it seems more impossible than ever.

'Penelope – I always thought I'd made it clear I don't want any more children.'

It's his tone. It's so dismissive. Instead of feeling upset, now I'm angry. My mouth sets tight. 'Well, I don't remember that conversation.'

Now Edward looks exasperated. 'But isn't it obvious?'

'Obvious? How is it obvious?' Something snaps inside of me. 'If it was that obvious you should have put it in your ring binder with all the house rules, so there's no room for miscommunication.'

'Well, that's a bit unfair,' Edward retaliates. 'I'm not the one changing my mind.'

'People change their minds, people are allowed to change their minds!'

Gone are the hushed voices and whispers.

'Well, clearly!'

'Well, I'm sorry for being human, but life doesn't fit neatly into boxes! This isn't one of your fucking spreadsheets, Edward.'

'You need to calm down.'

'Calm down? I need to calm down!'

I've never thrown things before, but I'm sorely tempted. But all there is is a couple of electric toothbrushes and some paraben-free handwash. It's as comical as it's terrible.

'I'm nearly fifty. I have two children already. Two grown-up children. Well, they're not children if one of them is getting his girlfriend pregnant.' He breaks off, scraping his hands through his hair.

He looks so broken that for a brief moment I deflate and all I want to do is hug him. To tell him it'll be OK and support him. But then my hurt and angry side kicks in.

'I don't though,' I point out.

'I'm sorry, but I'm too old. I've done it. I've raised two boys.'

'But I haven't.'

'You're telling me you want to have a baby?!'

'I don't know—'

'Well, I don't,' he says firmly, shutting me down.

'Edward—'

'Look, I can't do this now. I need to talk to Louis.'

And with that he leaves me in the bathroom and storms out, slamming the door.

The Big Talk

I learn a lot of things over the next two days, but one of them is that there is no perfect moment. All that time I'd been waiting to find this elusive moment when I could talk to Edward about all my feelings that have been triggered. Putting it off, thinking we were too tired, or too busy, or in the wrong mood. That I wasn't sure, or couldn't find the right words, or was afraid of his reaction, of what he might say, what *I* might say.

But let me tell you that moment doesn't exist. There is only now.

Even if it means having a showdown in a tiny, fogged-up bathroom, while your teenage son and pregnant girlfriend are listening outside.

So while Louis and Simone's world was imploding, Edward and I found ours was too. Thrown into our most difficult conversation ever, there began long tearful talks into the night. A conversation we should have had when we first got together, instead of after two years of building a life with each other. And yet, how could we, when the conversation didn't exist then?

When we first got together I thought I'd fully made peace with the past. Having surrended the life I thought I was going to live, I was embracing the life I was meant to live. And it was messy and unconventional and brilliant and all mine. Edward was right, we'd made a tacit agreement not to have kids. But things change and life is ever-evolving and it had thrown me a curveball. Suddenly, there was the unexpected item in the baggage area. And it opened a door again I thought I'd closed.

Edward's door, however, was still firmly closed. He was still resolute, but now the shock had worn off about both his son and my admission, he'd had time to think about everything. To try and see things from my point of view and not just his own.

'I love you but that doesn't change the fact that I don't want any more kids. I'm too old, I don't want to start all over again, but I don't want to rob you of your chance of being a mother, Penelope, if that's what you want. That would be terribly unfair of me, I couldn't live with myself . . . But moreover, you would come to hate me and resent me . . . and that would be even worse.'

In truth, part of me wanted him to be a dick about it, so I could be angry. At least that was better than being upset. But while Edward could be tactless, he wasn't unkind. I told him how confused I was, how I wasn't sure what I wanted. As a man who worked in certainties and absolutes, Edward said I needed to be sure.

'A marriage can't work if two people want different things. You've got to be on the same path, otherwise it just won't survive. Trust me, that's something I learned from the failure of my first marriage.'

Because of course, while he might not show it like I did, Edward was upset too. While I wore my heart on my sleeve, he was much more reserved, but there was no denying he'd been blindsided by this sudden turn in events. He'd been through a divorce and didn't want to go through another one.

'If you want something different, you need to go away and

explore that. We can't get married if you have any doubts,' he said firmly. 'It wouldn't be fair on either of us.'

Of course, I knew he was right. He was being calm and rational while I felt panicky and emotional. And yet, I also knew I loved him and I didn't want to lose him. So I tried to swallow my feelings and convince us both I'd been mistaken. That it would be crazy to throw away what we had on a silly panic, no doubt caused by my haywire hormones and the last gasps of my biological clock screaming out at me. Give it a few days and everything would go back to normal.

But in the middle of the night, I awoke feeling anxious and unsettled. The moon was shining through the blinds, illuminating the darkness. Finding the pregnancy test had been like a laser focus. Triggering feelings and bringing it all back. All the loss and the grief, but also the hope and excitement. And I couldn't ignore it. I couldn't shove it under the proverbial carpet and hope it would go away. To do so would be foolish. *Dangerous*. Unfair to both of us. The genie was out of the bottle and, try as I might, I couldn't stuff it back in.

NYE

The next day. Two years since we got together. Edward and I broke up.

JANUARY

#goinglala

The New Year

How the hell did I get here – *AGAIN*?

Woken by the alarm on my phone, I fling my arm out of my sleeping bag and scrabble around in the dark, trying to find it.

It's another New Year, and while everyone on Instagram seems to be jetting off to the Caribbean, I have once again found myself somewhere much less exotic: single, homeless and forty-something (and it's getting to be *a really big something*) I'm enjoying an all-inclusive at the destination of What The Fuck Am I Going To Do With My Life: The Sequel. As for Dry January, there's nothing dry about mine – due to copious amounts of both alcohol and tears.

But I'm making light of it. Trying to find humour where, really, there isn't any. Laughing in the face of it all. Only this time, not really. The wedding plans are off, I've moved out of Edward's, and I'm right back where I started a few years ago. Only it's worse second time around. Not just because I'm older, or supposed to be wiser, but because this time there's no one to blame. No guilty party. No cheating ex. Just two people who love each other; and for whom it got really complicated.

And with the absence of blame and anger to distract you, it really doesn't get any sadder than that.

My fingers fumble against my phone and, snatching it up, I turn off the alarm. The room falls silent. I look around me as the weak winter-morning sunlight squeezes between the heavy, damask curtains, catching on the chandelier hanging above my head and casting rainbows of light on the deep turquoise walls.

I'm in the spare bedroom at Cricket's. I've been sleeping here for the past two weeks, ever since I packed a few belongings and left Edward's on New Year's Day. There was no drama, no flouncing off, no slamming of doors and hurled insults, the way you see couples breaking up in movies and on TV. But then real life never is like how it's portrayed on the screen, is it? With its hair and make-up and designer wardrobe and cleverly crafted dialogue. It's messier and more mundane, but no less devastating. And everyone always looks like shit.

My phone starts ringing. I look at the caller ID. It's Mum. *Again.* I feel my chest tighten, and turn off the ringer. When I called to tell them the wedding was off, Dad answered the phone. I could hear Mum in the background, wanting to know what was going on, but I didn't want to go into details. Later she'd left me a message, asking me if that meant the wedding was cancelled or just postponed. I was tempted to tell her to ask Alexa. Instead I just said I didn't know.

Last week it was my birthday, and for once I was pleased my friends were either away or too busy dealing with their own lives as I was in no mood to celebrate. I just wanted the day to disappear. Mum FaceTimed me. She'd obviously been schooled by Dad and sat rigidly in front of the camera, smiling fixedly and repeating well-rehearsed, tactful speeches about how she hoped I would have a lovely day, regardless. There was no mention of Edward . . . or from him.

Still I can't avoid Mum's phone calls for ever. Or my friends. I haven't told them yet, about Edward and I splitting up. I just can't face it yet, so I'm hiding away here at Cricket's.

But I know I need to face up to some things, so I've already given my tenant notice. Thankfully I have a six-month break clause in the rental agreement, and a very understanding tenant, so I can move back into my flat by the end of January.

Oh God, the awful practicalities.

In the meantime, Edward has gone on his annual father-and-son skiing trip. Initially he wanted to cancel and stay and support Louis, but when he and Simone both went back to Paris so she could be with her parents, Edward didn't think it was fair on Ollie to miss out, so he just took him instead.

As for me, I get to be Cricket's new housemate, along with Arthur who's staying too until Edward returns. To be honest, I could have stayed at the flat while he's away, but I knew being there would only make me feel worse.

Leaning over to tickle Arthur, I hear the door to the flat open, and Cricket pops her head around the bedroom door, looking resplendent in her caramel-coloured cashmere coat, silk scarf and purple fedora.

'Oh splendid, you're awake. I thought I'd pop out and fetch us both fresh coffee and croissants.'

Trust me, that is not how I look when I 'pop' out. It's not even 8 a.m. I swear, I don't know how she does it.

'Oh, thank you.' I push myself up on my elbows, feeling somewhat embarrassed. My hair is all over the place, and I'm wearing an old T-shirt.

Entering the darkened bedroom, she puts the take-out tray on the side and goes to draw back the curtains. Weak winter sunshine fills the room. 'Sleep well?'

'Not really . . .'

She follows my gaze to the floor, where I'm surrounded by snotty tissues from crying.

'You think I'm an idiot, don't you?'

'We're all idiots, my dear.' She smiles kindly. Still wearing her coat, she perches on the end of the bed and studies me. 'For what it's worth, I think you're being very brave. It takes a great deal of courage to cast off from safe shores into uncertain waters.'

'I don't feel very brave. I feel like I just suck at relationships, as my friend Liza would say.'

'Well, I don't know your friend Liza, but just remember, the longest and the most important relationship you will have in your life is the one you have with yourself.'

I smile gratefully.

'Now, speaking of important relationships. *Coffee.*' Taking off her hat and coat, she passes me a coffee and croissant. 'I got the pain au chocolat that are terribly bad for us.' She pulls a face. 'Why are the things that are so bad for you always so wickedly delicious?'

I sip the hot coffee and bite into the croissant. Both are delicious and cheer me up.

'Oh, and I meant to give you something else.' She reaches into her handbag and pulls out something shaped like a small, golden bullet. 'I bought it a few days ago and forgot to give it to you.' As she passes it across to me, I realize what it is.

'Lipstick?'

'Red lipstick,' she corrects.

I swivel the case. I usually wear a nude lip gloss, but this is a proper pillar-box red. Bold and unapologetic.

'You know in the war, they didn't ration lipstick. Churchill knew how important it was for morale. Red lipstick isn't about vanity, it's empowering.' She smiles widely, showing off her own red-lipsticked mouth. 'After Monty died, it was the first thing I put on every morning.'

'Thank you,' I say, touched.

My phone beeps, interrupting us, and I pick it up and let out a groan.

'Oh no.'

'What's wrong? Is it Edward?'

I shake my head, reading the text alert. 'It's a reminder from the airline about my upcoming flight to LA. I totally forgot. It's Liza's wedding, Edward and I are supposed to be flying out there. I've booked the Airbnb and got a companion ticket . . . it just slipped my mind, with everything . . .' I rub my forehead with a groan. 'Even worse, the tickets are non-refundable.'

Stricken, I look at Cricket. There's a beat.

'Well, if it's a companion you need . . .'

I'm grateful for:
1. *Croissants and red lipstick.*
2. *Being able to change the ticket to Cricket's name.*
3. *Flying to LA at the weekend!*

Ready for Take-Off

On Saturday morning, Cricket and I find ourselves at Heathrow, waiting to board a flight to Los Angeles. I'd WhatsApped Liza to tell her Edward wouldn't be coming as we'd broken up and could I bring my friend Cricket instead? I didn't go into details, and she didn't ask for any. Instead she replied with just one word: *Absolutely*.

Which explains, right there, why Liza and I are best friends.

It's amazing how one word can convey so much. No judgement. No reaction. No need for explanation. Just unequivocal support and understanding. In that one word, she said everything she needed to say and I loved her for it.

'Well, isn't this fabulous?'

I turn to Cricket. She's beside herself with excitement. We're flying premium economy, as I've still got some air miles left, and I've managed to use my points to get us into the club lounge, and she's like a kid in a candy store.

'You mean everything is complimentary?' she's asking now, eyes wide.

'Everything,' I nod, smiling, my red lipstick firmly in place. Which is quite something, as I really haven't felt like smiling much at all the last two weeks. Which makes Cricket smile too as she's probably sick to death of seeing me moping around her flat, subdued and red-eyed. I know I am.

'Well in that case –' she turns to the barman '– two flutes of champagne, please.'

'Isn't it a bit early?'

At which point Cricket looks at me askance. 'My dear girl, it is *never* too early for champagne.'

Edward had arrived back from skiing yesterday and driven over to collect Arthur. It had been the first time I'd seen or spoken to him since I'd moved out, and it was an awkward, but brief exchange. Believe you me, it brought a whole new meaning to The Doorstep Challenge. I'd invited him in, but he said he couldn't, due to him being parked on a double yellow.

Which of course was a complete fib as Edward is probably the last person on earth to illegally park, even if he was picking up his beloved dog from his ex-fiancée. It was obviously an excuse. But then, considering I'd only extended the invitation out of politeness, I was relieved. And sad. Meanwhile Edward was cold and detached, his face and thoughts unreadable. Standing on the doorstep, I was struck by how quickly two people who were once so close can feel like strangers. And then I felt even more sad. So I was glad that our meeting was brief. I felt relieved when he left.

Soon it's time to board the flight. Being in premium economy, we have two seats together; I get the window as Cricket wants the aisle.

'It's my bladder,' she confides, 'it's not what it used to be.' With her eyes trained on the toilet like a sniper, waiting for it to become unoccupied, she tuts in annoyance. 'Let me tell you, ageing is not for sissies, it really can be quite bothersome at times.'

Cricket rarely complains about getting older. 'How can I? When so many don't get the privilege,' she's forever saying. Stoicism and a stiff drink, rather than anyone's sympathy, is how she likes to deal with any aches and pains.

261

'According to the doctor, it's over-active.'

'Like your imagination,' I note, as the toilet becomes free and she dives into it.

Left alone, I turn my attentions to something difficult that I need to deal with. I can't put it off any longer. Digging out my phone, I click on my email and open up a new message. As I do, I'm reminded of why I first started my podcast. Of being someone who looked around at their life and thought, this was never part of The Plan.

Which, despite the circumstances, makes me smile. Seriously, Nell, you've really gone and outdone yourself this time.

Because while I thought I was going to be flying back to America with my fiancé, to be a guest at the wedding of my best friend, just weeks before my own – here I am instead, crafting an email to all my friends and wedding guests. And as Cricket returns to her seat and the stewards ask us to turn off all our devices so we can prepare for take-off, I think about how you can think life is sorted, but it never is. Which can be both a good thing or a bad thing, depending how you look at it.

'All good?' asks Cricket, and I turn to see her looking at me, her bright blue eyes filled with both concern and encouragement.

'All good,' I nod, because I'm determined to try to look at it that way.

And then I press send.

YOUR INVITATION
to

NOT ATTEND NELL & EDWARD'S WEDDING!

Mr & Mrs Stevens are delighted to announce:
Their daughter has fucked up again!
The wedding is off!
There will be absolutely no drinking
and dancing!

So FFS please don't join us to celebrate
on 5 February
At the super swanky private members club in Mayfair

But it's not all bad news! Now you won't have to buy a wedding gift they'll never use, wedding outfits you'll never wear again and spend a fortune on a babysitter who will eat the entire contents of your fridge while you get drunk at the evening disco and embarrass yourself on the dance floor to 'Come on Eileen'.

(No need to RSVP as the bride-not-to-be is currently offline and ~~running away~~ winging her way across the Atlantic, gin-sozzled and watching a bad in-flight movie, whilst the child behind her repeatedly kicks the back of her seat making her seriously question motherhood and wonder how on earth she got here)*

---

* Alas, I didn't send this, despite being sorely tempted, but sent a very sensible email instead.

Nothing to Declare

Over eleven hours later, we land in Los Angeles. Flying really is incredible, isn't it? No matter how many times I do it, it never ceases to amaze me how we can board a metal bird, spend a few hours watching movies, drinking gin and tonics, failing to get any sleep and being shocked by your reflection in the toilet mirrors (while squirting the expensive foundation you just bought in duty free everywhere because of the pressurized cabin) and then boom, you're suddenly in a completely different country.

And when it comes to LA, a completely different world.

Luckily, we whizz through immigration. A first, if ever there was one, but I have a sneaking suspicion that could be down to Cricket, who suddenly transforms from the sprightly, capable eighty-something I know, to a frail little old lady who can barely walk and has to be whisked through in a wheelchair, accompanied by her carer which, she informs me in a whisper, is me. Now I can see how Cricket was an actress, I've never seen such a performance. It was quite remarkable.

Once on the other side of baggage claim, she swiftly returns to her perfectly able-bodied self, and we collect our rental car. I've booked a compact, but we're upgraded to a large SUV, which immediately makes me think of the environment and how Edward would kill me. But Edward's not here, I remind myself, firmly shoving all thoughts of him to the back of my mind. Along with our suitcases and Cricket's duty-free packages, of which there are a ridiculous amount, into the large trunk (see, we're in America now!) and then we're off!

Only when I'm driving along the highway, on the right (or should that be wrong) side of the road, do I pause to think about how strange it feels to be back. It's so familiar it's surreal, like slipping back into your old life, right back where you left off. What I didn't realize is, I'm not the only one feeling this way.

'I've been trying to work it out, and I think it's forty years since I was last here, yet now I'm here it feels like yesterday.'

Surprised, I glance across at Cricket who has the vanity mirror pulled down in the passenger-seat sun visor and is applying a slick of red lipstick. Wearing a pair of oversized sunglasses that she purchased in duty free, she looks like she's just come straight out of Beverly Hills, not off a long-haul flight from grey, cold, rainy London.

'I didn't know you'd been to LA before?'

'Oh, yes, many times,' she nods, and I can feel there's something she's not telling me.

'You're a dark horse.' My eyes dart between the traffic ahead and the expression on her face. 'How come you never said?'

She gives a little shrug of her shoulders. 'You never asked,' she smiles impishly.

Indicating to pull into another lane, I quickly do the calculations. Cricket has told me she was nearly fifty when she met Monty, which can only mean . . .

'OK, so who was he?' I demand and I can tell immediately by her face that my suspicions are correct. Even behind those over-sized sunnies.

'Jack.'

I raise an eyebrow. 'That's all you're going to tell me, his name?'

I brake sharply. The traffic is doing that strange thing it always does in LA, constant braking and accelerating, which strikes me as a metaphor for my life. Cricket rolls down the window and turns her face towards the late-afternoon sunshine. Despite the traffic fumes, you can smell the distant ocean.

'He was an actor,' she says, after a pause. 'Quite a good one, too. We met when I was doing *Death of a Salesman* in Edinburgh. He was in the audience, not the cast.' Her pearl-drop earrings catch the sun as she gives a little shake of her head, refracting light around the car, like tiny glitterballs. 'Jack didn't do theatre, he just happened to be visiting a friend in Scotland who had tickets for the play. He lived and worked here, in Hollywood.'

'A Hollywood actor!' I glance sideways at her, agog. 'You mean, like a movie star?'

'Well, he did a few films, but mostly television. He was in a long-running American television show. Soaps, they like to call them. You know the term originated from radio dramas being sponsored by soap manufacturers—'

'Is he famous?' I interrupt.

While Cricket's been talking, I've been wracking my brains, trying to think of famous actors called Jack, but not getting very far. To be honest, I'm pretty useless when it comes to actors. I mean, obviously I know who Brad Pitt is, but I'm always that person wondering where I've seen that face before and groping around for a name. Unlike Edward, who's like the IMDB database and can give you so many details it's as if he's describing a suspect to the police.

Catching myself thinking about Edward again, my eyes prickle and I blink rapidly, simultaneously both upset and furious at myself. *Sod This.* I'm here in LA for my best friend's wedding. To celebrate, not ruminate. Moreover, I'm here with Cricket, my other BFF who, after the last couple of years, could really do with a holiday. For the next two weeks I just really want us to have a good time and for nothing to spoil it.

Feeling a resolve, I tighten my grip on the steering wheel. OK, so my life in London has all gone tits up, but I didn't come all this way to bring my emotional baggage with me. In fact, the only baggage that's coming on this holiday is in the trunk of this car. And putting my foot on the accelerator, I shove Edward firmly out of my mind.

'He was quite famous in America.'

Cricket's voice interrupts my thoughts. I glance across at her.

'Though I had no idea who he was when he waited for me backstage, to tell me how much he loved my performance . . .'

She trails off then and I can see she's not quite here any more, but back in Edinburgh, all those years ago.

'And?' I prompt, after a few moments.

With a sharp intake of breath, she straightens up and turns to me.

'And that was how it began,' she says simply.

Her words are just left hanging there, in the air, between us. In all the time I've known Cricket, she's never talked about any of the men that came before Monty, whom she met when she was about to turn fifty and had given up on love. I knew she'd been engaged several times, once to a man who, days before the wedding, confessed to being already married, much to her relief. When we first met, she told me that by the time she met Monty, she'd had her fill of passionate love affairs and doomed romances. But she'd never gone into detail and I'd never asked.

But now, as I look at her in complete fascination, I can't help wondering. Was Jack one of her doomed romances, or one of her passionate love affairs?

Soon after, we arrive at our Airbnb. I've booked a cute little cottage in Venice, just a few minutes' walk from the beach. Which in itself is a rarity, as nobody walks in LA. Actually, that's not completely true, people *do* walk, but usually it's only to their cars, unless it's in activewear and then it's called hiking.

But then LA is a funny old city in lots of ways. Home to Hollywood and its many famous filmstars, it's everything and nothing like you imagine. For starters, this city is huge! I remember first moving here and being perplexed by a city that had no centre and was so spread out you had to drive everywhere. And the traffic was always terrible.

But while first impressions felt less glitz and glamour and more gridlock, I soon fell for its charms: the endless sunshine and palm trees, being able to wear flip-flops in January and the dreams and opportunity that hang seductively in the air. Unfortunately my own dreams didn't work out. Soon after arriving, I left LA to set up a business with my boyfriend, Ethan, which would later go bust, along with our relationship, and I ended up moving back to London.

But I loved those few short months I lived at the beach. Which is why I wanted to come back and stay here with Cricket. Not just because this place holds such happy memories, but for practical reasons: Venice is such a walkable neighbourhood, which is important as Cricket doesn't drive.

'Oh look, they have bikes,' says Cricket, a few hours later after we've finished unpacking and are relaxing in the small backyard on a couple of sun loungers. She points to two brightly coloured bicycles and their baskets, propped up against the barbecue.

I look up from using Cricket's phone. I deliberately borrowed hers to avoid turning on my own – I wasn't ready just yet to deal with the fallout from my email – and I've just finished speaking to an excited Liza who kept saying, 'I can't believe you're actually here!' over and over, while both of us shrieked with delight down the phone. Neither of us can wait to see each other, but because she's on the Eastside and we're on the Westside, which is miles away, '*and, you know, traffic*,' we've arranged to all meet tomorrow for lunch. I should've probably been sensible and booked to stay somewhere closer to Liza, but when I saw this cottage I couldn't resist. Plus, whenever have I been sensible?

'They call them beach cruisers here,' I say, in reference to the bicycles.

Cricket's face lights up. 'I rather like the sound of that.'

'I knew you would,' I smile, pleased that I'd remembered what a keen cyclist Cricket used to be when I'd booked this place. She'd lost her confidence during the pandemic and I wanted to get her back in the saddle – after all, it was *literally* like riding a bike. 'There's a bike path that runs all the way along the side of the ocean, you can cycle for miles along the beach.'

'Oh, that sounds wonderful, shall we go?'

'Don't you want to rest?'

'My dear girl, I know I've got forty years on you, but there's only so much resting a person can do before one atrophies. And anyway, I slept most of the way on the plane.'

Which is true. While I tossed and turned and stared out of the window, Cricket slept like a baby and snored like a train.

Standing up, she walks over to the lime-green bike and

rings the bell. Despite its cheerful ring, she tuts. 'Bugger, I should have brought my bicycle helmet.'

'Hang on, they might have them.' I get up off the sun lounger and go to look inside the back porch.

'Not like my leopard-skin one,' she points out, in reference to the helmet she bought a few years ago; after a near-miss with a motorist she decided that perhaps, at eighty-something, it was time to start wearing one.

'No, you're right,' I call from inside, 'but they have these instead.' I return with two straw cowboy hats and plonk one on both of our heads.

'How do we look?' she laughs.

'Like Thelma and Louise,' I laugh. Reaching for my phone, I take a selfie.

'Right, come on then, let's go.'

'Hang on, I thought you wanted a helmet,' I call after her.

But Cricket is already in the saddle and pushing off on her pedals. 'What have I always told you? Live dangerously!' And ringing her bell, she sets off down the street.

I'm grateful for:
1. *The bike path being on the beach so we didn't have to worry about motorists or motorbikes, just the pedestrians who walked out in front of Cricket and nearly got run over. Thank God for bicycle bells.*
2. *Cricket getting her confidence back.*
3. *The delicious sundowner we enjoyed on the terrace at a gorgeous hotel looking out onto the Pacific Ocean.*
4. *Sunshine and twenty-eight degrees in January, and a best friend to share it with.*
5. *Google and the Wi-Fi password. Jack's alive, widowed and living in Hollywood!*

Going La La

The next day we wake up with the California sunshine streaming in through the blinds. Back in the UK, the dark, cold winter mornings make it almost impossible to get out of bed, but here it's impossible to *stay in bed*. Throwing back the duvet, I make coffee on the stove, slip on my flip-flops and go to drink it in the garden.

I won't lie. It's heaven. Sunshine and flip-flops in January never gets old.*

I also wake up to a flurry of voicemails and concerned messages on my WhatsApp from worried friends who've received my email. After sending it, I turned off my phone on the plane and didn't turn it back on until this morning, when I could brace myself with a coffee. I just hadn't wanted to deal with it.

> Oh my God, what happened?
> Are you OK?
> What's going on?
> Call me!
> Did the bastard cheat?! (That one was from Max.)

I start to type out one of those celebrity break-up statements, about how Edward and I are still good friends but

---

* I post a photo then delete it as there's nothing more annoying than flip-flop feet when you're in London in January. Plus, I am in desperate need of a pedicure and nobody needs to see these horrors on the Gram.

have decided to go our separate ways (though I miss the bit out about magical journeys), but then I change my mind and delete it. In the end I just send a group text back telling everyone not to worry, that I'm fine (that old chestnut) and alive and well and in LA for Liza's wedding.

Then I add a few happy face and sunshine and beach emojis to prove it. Because everything's always a lot better with a few emojis.

Cricket rises soon after and makes freshly squeezed juice from the oranges and grapefruits growing on the trees in the garden, which we eat with the yoghurt and honey the Airbnb host thoughtfully provided, while being lulled by the gentle sounds of the windchimes in the warm morning breeze.*

Seriously, it's like we've landed on another planet.

It almost makes you want to roll out the yoga mat (there are two provided – well, this is LA) and start doing my morning asanas.

I say *almost*. Let's not get too carried away.

After spending the rest of the morning catching up with a bit of work, otherwise known as a self-employed holiday, while Cricket reads her book and relaxes in the hammock (which later becomes less relaxing and more hilarious when she realizes she can't get out of it . . . luckily, the grass is a soft landing), we shower and change and head out to meet Liza and Tia.

We've arranged to have lunch at a popular cafe and on arrival we're shown to our table on the patio by a super friendly waiter who hands us our menus and takes our drinks

---

* Windchimes are a good example of how California is different to the UK. Growing up, I remember our village being tortured by a neighbour's windchimes that would clang incessantly in the howling gales, until the local farmer silenced them with a shot gun.

order. Cricket orders an iced tea, while I order a green juice called The Detox, which I need after all the drinks on the plane and the beach last night, and which thankfully is much more delicious than the one I had at Annabel's retreat.

'Well, this is rather wonderful,' beams Cricket, settling back underneath the parasol and sipping her tea. 'What a shame everyone's too busy working to enjoy it.' She gestures around us at all the people sitting at tables, tapping away on their laptops, heads buried behind their screens.

'They're probably all working on their screenplays,' I grin. 'Here in LA, all the cafes are filled with people writing film scripts, hoping it's going to be the next blockbuster.'

'Really?' Cricket looks at me wide-eyed and I nod.

'When I lived here everyone I knew was writing one.'

'Perhaps we should write one.' Her eyes flash. 'You did such a wonderful job of Monty's play, we should do a movie next.'

'How about we eat lunch first,' I laugh, as I see her mind racing ahead. I swear to God, there's no stopping her.

'Monty would have loved it here,' she says after a moment. 'He used to write at the local library. In winter he'd take a hot water bottle and ask the librarians to fill it from their kettle.' She smiles at the memory. 'I think he could've got used to this.'

We're suddenly interrupted by Liza arriving. Holding hands with a woman who must be Tia, Liza has a tiny, but visible, bump.

'Oh my God, look at you!' I cry, jumping up and giving her a hug.

There's lots of squealing with delight and a flurry of intro-ductions. It's the first time I've met Tia and seen Liza pregnant and if I was nervous about how I would feel, I needn't have been. Seeing her now, I'm just so happy for my friend.

Tia is lovely, but then I never doubted she would be. As

they join us at our table, I watch the easy affection between them. They look so much in love, so together, so on the same path, it throws into stark contrast how it was with Edward in the few days before I left, how we felt so far apart, both of us talking but not hearing each other. I listen to them chattering excitedly, their voices running over each other, finishing each other's sentences. Both are excited for the baby and their upcoming wedding at the weekend.

'It's all very low-key. We're having it in the garden, much to the dismay of my family who wanted a religious ceremony,' Tia tells us.

'Good for you, it's not about what anyone else wants,' says Cricket with approval and Liza smiles.

'I'm so pleased you can join us.'

'And I'm so pleased to be invited,' replies Cricket, graciously, 'though I realize I'm the understudy,' she says, in reference to Edward.

'Cricket was an actress,' I explain, hoping to change the subject.

'Well, in that case, you've come to the right place,' smiles Tia. 'There's a few of those in Hollywood.'

'Oh, I'm getting a little long in the tooth now.'

'Rubbish,' I protest. 'What did you once to say to me? You're not too old, it's not too late and yes you can.'

'Hell yeah! Up high,' cries Tia, going to give Cricket a high-five.

For a split second there's a pause as Tia holds up her palm and I wonder if I should explain to Cricket what a high-five is.

But of course, that's not necessary.

'Down low,' beams Cricket, slapping her hand with gusto as Tia whoops with delight and I laugh at myself and with my friend who never fails to surprise me.

274

'So, how are you?' A few minutes later there's a lull in the conversation and Liza turns to me. 'I got your email.'

A look passes between us. With Liza, I don't even have to say anything.

'All the better for seeing you,' I say, giving her a big smile.

'You don't have to put on a brave face for me,' she reminds me.

'I know, but I'm here to celebrate your wedding, not talk about me calling off mine,' I tell her firmly, and she smiles and squeezes my arm.

'Why don't you come to one of my yoga classes while you're here?' she suggests, 'I'm still teaching.'

Which makes me laugh as Liza is a yoga instructor, and we first met when I went to one of her classes. Thankfully she's never held it against me.

'You won't be if I scare all your other students away.'

'On second thoughts.' She wrinkles her nose, laughing. 'Well, I'm here if you decide you do want to talk about it.'

'Thanks.' I smile gratefully. To be honest, I wouldn't know where to start.

We're interrupted by the waiter who appears at the end of the table, and takes our order.

'I'll have the eggs, please,' I say when it's my turn.

'Alrighty, and how would you like your eggs?' he asks cheerfully. 'There's a list of options on your menu. Scrambled, boiled, poached, over easy, sunny side up . . .'

I look at the menu. The list is so long I feel a bit overwhelmed. Who knew there were so many ways to cook eggs.

'Sunny side up,' I say, finally choosing one.

What the hell. Sunny side up sounds like a good place to start.

To Age or Not to Age

After a couple of days spent getting over our jet lag, Cricket and I go to Beverly Hills where we do a bit of shopping, spot a few celebrities and notice a lot of cosmetic surgery.

'Golly, I've never seen so many facelifts,' remarks Cricket later, as we stop for a bite to eat and sit at a table outside on the pavement, people watching. 'It's fascinating!'

Sitting across from Cricket, I watch her trying to demolish a giant steak. When the waiter asked her if she'd like any sauces on the side, she'd misunderstood, and asked for a vodka martini.

'Though it makes me feel a bit of a dodo,' she adds, as an afterthought.

'A dodo?'

'Or a woolly mammoth.'

'Sorry, you've lost me.'

'Something that's gone extinct,' she says, then adds firmly, 'that is no longer in existence.'

I'm beginning to wonder if the heat has got to Cricket. It is about thirty degrees. I quickly top up her water glass. 'Are you sure you're feeling OK?'

'I'm fine. I'm just an old woman who looks her age.' She waves her fork like a conductor's baton. 'Look around, can you see another one?'

Several women walk past with impossibly smooth faces and plumped lips.

'Rubbish, you don't look your age,' I admonish, but she quickly shushes me.

'Nonsense, of course I do,' she says briskly. Her face creases into a smile. 'And believe you me, when you've sat through as many Zoom funerals as I have, you're delighted to be ageing, because it means you're still alive.'

Quite unexpectedly my mind flicks to Holly. I drag it back again.

'Yes, you're right . . . of course,' I nod in agreement, prodding at my rice bowl. 'But I still hate the wrinkles I'm getting around my eyes,' I confess. 'Is that terrible of me?'

I lift my sunglasses and lean closer so she can see.

'My dear girl, what's terrible is we're taught to hate them. That somewhere along the line, someone made up the rule that women shouldn't be allowed to age.' Abandoning the effort of trying to finish her giant steak, she puts down her fork and reaches for her Martini. 'You know, I had Botox once.'

'You did?'

'Of course. I'm not immune to wanting to look fresher.' Sitting back in her chair, she smiles amusedly at my expression. 'Don't look so surprised.'

'Well, now you've said that, I've been thinking of getting some myself,' I admit and she nods, understandingly.

'Well if you want to try it, why not? There's enough judgement on women, without putting any more on yourself. I tried it once, years ago now, when I wasn't getting the parts. Being an actor is quite brutal for a woman, the roles dry up as you get older. Unlike the men of course, who simply become distinguished and grow a beard,' she adds with a smile.

She says it all matter of factly and without a hint of bitterness, but I can't help thinking how unfair it all is.

'But it wasn't for me. It turns out that being able to move

your face to show expression and emotion, are quite important for an actress. So I thought the hell with it, I'm going
to stick with the wrinkles.'

She laughs and takes another sip of her cocktail. 'But I
wouldn't judge anyone who wants to look more youthful,'
she continues. 'I've been applying for jobs and I can't get
one. No one will hire me because of my age.'

'I didn't know you were looking for a job?' I look at her
in surprise.

'Yes,' she nods. 'Now Monty's libraries are set up, I don't
want to just sit around twiddling my thumbs. For a while
now I've been thinking I'd like a job and so I started replying
to a few adverts for vacancies. I've even had a couple of
interviews. But as soon as they ask for my date of birth, I
never hear back.'

'But they can't do that, that's ageism!' I protest.

'They can and they do,' shrugs Cricket. 'The only thing
I've been offered is voluntary work in a charity shop.'

'And you wouldn't want to do that?'

'It's not that I don't want to, I just feel I want more of a
challenge than putting clothes on hangers.'

'To be honest, I find that pretty challenging,' I say, trying
to cheer her up. 'Have you seen my bedroom?'

Which makes her laugh and me resolved to find her a job.
Sod society trying to tell us that our worth decreases as our
years increase – all I see sitting across from me is a woman
who is funny and wise and more vibrant than ever. Cricket
has a lifetime of experience to offer and any company would
be lucky to have her. There must be *something*.

I'm grateful for:
1. *Knowing there's a weird dichotomy when it comes to*
   growing older. You can be feeling grateful and saying

ageing is a privilege, and at the same time be looking in the bathroom mirror and pulling your face back with your hands. And that's OK.

2. *Botox. I haven't had it yet, but if and when I do I know there's nothing to be scared of. It's just a few little pricks. And frankly, what woman hasn't dealt with a few of those by the time they get to my age?*

3. *The super fabulous Cricket, for showing me there's no age limit to fun, it's never too late, and there's a power in growing older – but you've got to stop looking at the outsides as it all happens on the inside.*

4. *All those amazing cosmetic surgeons offering all that amazing cosmetic surgery, because it's your face and body and if you want a boob job or a facelift, you go, girl!*

5. *Not having a facelift; in fact I actually feel terrified just thinking about it.*

Ghosts of the Past

OK, so I have a confession.

Originally, when I booked this trip to Los Angeles, I was supposed to be going with Edward. Cricket was a last-minute substitution and, while I was grateful of her company, I'd been disappointed it wasn't going to be how I'd imagined. All romantic sunset walks on the beach . . . and of course, being guests at Liza's wedding, where Edward would charm everyone with his English accent and I would feel a ridiculous pride that I was soon going to be his wife.

That, after what has felt like a lifetime of attending other people's weddings, it was finally going to be my turn.

But now I feel a bit like a manager of a football team must feel when their star player is injured and they bring on the substitute not expecting much *and they totally ace it*. Not that Cricket could ever be a substitute for anyone. But instead of feeling disappointed, or quietly crushed, that I'm not here with Edward, I'm having The Best Time Ever with Cricket.

We've been here a week and every day we do something fun. Staying by the beach, we quickly turn into a couple of California beach bums, cycling there at all times of day with our bathing suits and the books that we find in the free little library at the end of our street.

'How wonderful to see where it all started,' says Cricket with delight, when I show it to her and tell her it's the inspiration for Monty's Mini Libraries.

Enjoying breakfast in the sunny backyard, which we make together in our pyjamas like we're in the classic Morecambe and Wise sketch, with Cricket squeezing fresh grapefruits and me in charge of the coffee and pancakes. Though alas, I'll never be as good at catching them as Eric.

We also fit in a bit of tourist stuff. As well as our trip to Beverly Hills, we walk along the Venice canals, visit the Getty Villa Museum and spot dolphins in Malibu. We even go on a graveyard tour (which, of course, is Cricket's idea) at the Hollywood Forever Cemetery, the final resting place of many famous legends, including Cricket's idol, Judy Garland. Trust me, I'm beginning to think romantic sunset strolls are *seriously* overrated.

In fact, I've barely had time to miss Edward or think about any big decisions since I've been here. I know real life is lurking like a ghost in the shadows, waiting for me back in London, but for now I'm in la la land. Quite literally.

Speaking of ghosts.

'You know this hotel is supposed to be haunted, don't you?' says Cricket, as we arrive at one of Hollywood's most iconic hotels and sweep up the palm-tree-lined driveway. It's Friday night and we're here for the rehearsal dinner ahead of the wedding at the weekend.

'By who?'

'By *whom*,' she tsks, grammatically rapping me on the knuckles. 'Take your pick, all the Hollywood greats stayed here . . . I used to stay here with Jack.'

'You did?'

It's the first time she's mentioned him. After googling him and discovering he was still alive, and a widower no less, I'd suggested she try to get in touch, but she'd been resolute. 'We had some wonderful times together, but some things are better left in the past,' she'd said firmly. I hadn't tried to change her mind.

I remember the time I'd met my ex Ethan for a drink, a year after we'd broken up, and as lovely as it was to see him, it was like trying to hold on to a moment that had already slipped through our fingers. I didn't meet up with him again and thankfully I don't have to worry about bumping into him while I'm here, as he now lives in San Francisco.

'There are so many stories of scandals and secrets,' she continues, as we walk into the atmospheric lobby. With its velvet couches, tasselled lampshades and dimly lit corners, it oozes a faded glamour.

'Are any of those yours?' I ask, and she laughs mischievously.

'Now, that would be telling.'

We find Liza and Tia and their family and friends seated outside in the romantic courtyard garden. Lit by twinkling fairy lights, and with just the sound of fountains, the restaurant feels almost magical. The conversation is already flowing about the wedding on Sunday. Liza's parents have flown in from Austin, while Tia's beloved grandmother, a tiny woman with the widest smile, has travelled all the way from the Philippines.

'We always joke about how much we love staying home, so we thought why not just get married in our backyard?' laughs Tia.

'Is that legal?' asks Cricket, curiously.

'Absolutely. I'm here to make sure of it, ma'am.'

A distinctive Southern accent from the other end of the table causes us all to turn. It belongs to one of those ridiculously handsome actor-types you see everywhere in LA.

'Tia's best friend Josh has kindly offered to become an officiant for the day so he can marry us,' smiles Liza.

'I've got my certificate and everything.' His voice is like velvet and he flashes his Hollywood smile.

'Wow, how amazing.' He catches my eye and I smile.

'It's going to be a very different kind of wedding to the ones we're used to back home, that's for sure,' nods Liza's mum, offering up the bread basket. Liza has told me how supportive her parents have been from the very beginning, by welcoming Tia into their family, but tonight her mum seems nervous.

'Me and your mom couldn't be more proud,' says her dad, and as I watch him patting his wife's hand, I realize it's just normal mother-of-the-bride nerves.

And I think of my own mum and feel horribly guilty and say yes to another bread roll.

It's a really lovely evening. Not just because the food is divine and the setting is beautiful, but because we all have such fun getting to know each other. It's amazing how such a random collection of different people, from all over the world, can find so much in common, if given the opportunity.

Which makes me think we should all constantly be having rehearsal dinners – groups of strangers coming together, to talk and laugh and share good food. And not to celebrate upcoming weddings, but to celebrate this thing called life.

Soon it's time to say our goodbyes. Tia and Liza leave with their families, while the gorgeous Josh hugs both me and Cricket, saying how lovely it was to meet us and how grateful he was not to be the only single person at the wedding, as he's just broken up with his boyfriend. Which makes two of us.

'His loss,' says Cricket, cheerfully waving goodbye.

'Well, thank you, ma'am, I like to think so,' he smiles, heading off to valet parking while we head off to the ladies'. Cricket needed the loo before the drive home.

Five minutes later we walk back into the lobby, engrossed in conversation about the evening that's gone and the wedding on Sunday, me trying to find the valet parking ticket in my handbag, Cricket suggesting I've left it in the ladies' and should she go back to look—

'Catherine?'

A voice from behind causes Cricket to stop in her tracks.

'Is that really you?'

As I watch her turn, I wonder what she's looking at, before remembering that's her proper name, and then seeing a man standing behind us, his figure half-hidden in the shadows. I look at her face. She looks like she's seen a ghost.

There's a beat, and then she speaks.

'Hello, Jack.'

I'm grateful for:

1. *A wonderful evening spent celebrating love.*
2. *The waiter for taking some lovely group shots of us all at dinner, together with a photo of me and Cricket and Jack later enjoying a nightcap, which I post along with the hashtags #newfriends #oldflames*

Before Sunrise

At 5 a.m. I'm woken by my phone ringing and a hysterical Liza. Josh has broken his ankle and is at the hospital, waiting to go into surgery.

'Oh my God, what happened?'

'He was rebounding.'

'From the break-up with his boyfriend?' I'm still half-asleep.

'No! He was on his rebounder!' she cries and then sensing my confusion adds, 'It's like a mini trampoline. It's great for all your joints as it's super low impact.'

Obviously not *that* low impact, as poor Josh has broken his ankle.

'He's so upset as not only will it ruin his chance of auditions, now he can't officiate our wedding.'

I'm tempted to ask what on earth he was doing on a mini trampoline at some ungodly hour in the morning, but now is not the time to go into details as Liza has suddenly gone from chilled-out yogi to full-on Bridezilla.

'We're fucked!'

'Don't panic—'

'But everything's going to be ruined!' she shrieks and I have to hold the phone away from my ear. She's almost hyperventilating and I'm a bit worried about the baby. I think about suggesting she do that breathing thing through her nose that she always used to go on about in class. On second thoughts, maybe not.

'Surely someone else can legally marry you.'

'Like who?'

But before either of us can answer, we're interrupted by a soft knocking on my bedroom door and a voice. 'Nell, it's Cricket. Is everything OK?'

My Best Friend's Wedding

It was just like in the movies, only better as it's real life. OK, seeing as everyone in LA is writing a screenplay, here's mine.

Fade in . . .

ACT ONE

Girl meets girl. They fall in love, and pregnant with a sperm donor. Overjoyed, they plan a barefoot wedding in their backyard.

ACT TWO

Disaster strikes! There is no one to marry them! All is lost until they are rescued by our Superhero, an octogenarian actress, who fills in a form online and gets ordained for the day, so she can take on the biggest and best role of her life and save the day!

ACT THREE

Surrounded by balloons and carnival lights and a whole lot of love, the happy couple wear faded jeans and a silk dress as they hold hands and are married by our Superhero who in her best Shakespearean tones declares, 'You

287

may now kiss the brides!' Eyes are dabbed, fizzy wine is drunk and pizza is eaten, the delicious kind with the bagel crust that causes waistbands to be loosened and diets to be started on Monday.

FINAL CREDITS

Dusk falls, the firepit is lit, someone brings out a guitar and the adults try to remember all the verses to 'American Pie' while our Superhero rests and the children play on the trampoline. Where they are joined by the funny British lady who might yet still be single and childless and forty-something, but is happy in this moment, and makes them laugh by bouncing higher and higher without a care in the world or fear of bladder leakage. Proving there is always something to be grateful for, even if it's an intact peri-neum, as we fade to black and the credits roll . . .

FEBRUARY

#whatslovegottodowithit

Back to Life, Back to Reality

It's Friday night and I'm home doing laundry. Outside, it's cold, dark and drizzly; inside, condensation has steamed up the windows and I'm surrounded by damp clothes, hanging on airers or stuffed onto radiators. I don't have room for a dryer in my tiny flat, so I've whacked up the heating. Edward would have a conniption.

Emptying another load from the washing machine, I hunt around for any free space to dry them, then admit defeat and start lassoing knickers and bras around mirrors and picture frames, like you do at Christmas with tinsel.

So *not exactly* the glitz and glamour of Hollywood.

I catch sight of my reflection in the mirror. My tan's fading fast and LA, with its blue skies and sunshine, feels like a million light years away.

I've been back in London for a week. Talk about coming back to earth with a bump. And I'm not just talking about landing at Heathrow in the middle of a gale, where we hit the ground with an almighty thud and bounced screeching along the runway, while I white-knuckled Cricket. My tenant's moved out of my flat and, with the help of my friends, I've been able to move back in. Which is lucky, though to be honest, it doesn't feel that lucky. It feels a bit depressing, like life's gone backwards.

I had a long chat about everything with Liza when I was

in LA. The days following her wedding we got to spend a lot of time together. Tia is a TV producer and had to go straight back to the studios, meanwhile Cricket was busy with Jack. After bumping into each other in the hotel lobby, he'd asked for her number. Both were in shock. Neither could believe it. *After all this time*, they kept saying over and over.

But it was like no time had passed. The moment I saw them together, I felt their connection. That rare, magical energy you get between two people, like trapping lightning in a mason jar. Some things might be better left in the past, but this wasn't one of them.

So while Cricket went out for lovely lunches and memory-lane dinners with her ex-lover, catching up on the last forty years, I hung out with Liza at the beach, where after a while talk moved from weddings to babies. Both real and imagined.

'So Edward definitely doesn't want any more kids.'

'Definitely.'

'And you've tried talking to him about it?'

Gazing out at the ocean, I watched the waves hitting the shore. 'We talked about nothing else,' I nod, my mind flicking back to those awful few days before I moved out. 'He said if I wanted to try to have a baby, it wouldn't be fair to stop me, but his mind's made up. I'd be on my own.'

'Not necessarily.' She shook her head. 'Edward's not the only man in the world . . .'

I let out a groan. 'Please, don't make me go back out there. Me and online dating broke up too. It was all a disaster. Remember Mr Fitbit?'

She laughed at my woeful expression. 'I'm being serious. You might meet someone. There's still time.'

'Is there?' I fell silent and let the sand trickle through my fingers. The symbolism wasn't lost on me.

'Would you do it by yourself?'

I shrug. 'I don't know, I've never thought . . . I mean, it's not how I imagined it.'

'Having a baby with my wife using donor sperm isn't either,' said Liza, then she grinned and rubbed her belly. 'But I couldn't be happier. '

I smile fondly at my friend. 'I'm so happy for you. How it's all turned out.'

'Me too.'

It's funny. That day, when I saw Princess Diana's wedding dress, I'd questioned the whole concept of marriage – it had seemed like an outdated fairy tale that had no place in the modern world – but witnessing Liza and Tia saying their vows had proved it could be real and inclusive and look any way you want it to. However much society changes, there will always be a place for two people in love wanting to spend the rest of their lives together.

Reaching for my hand, Liza squeezed it. 'Now I want it for you too.'

'I think I've given up hope,' I admitted.

'Well I have lots of hope, so you can have some of mine,' she replied firmly.

I smiled gratefully.

'You're a great person, Nell. Any man would be lucky to have you . . . and luckily we live in a world today where there are many different routes to motherhood. Donor sperm, donor eggs, surrogacy, adoption . . .'

As she began reeling them off I must have looked a bit overwhelmed, because she paused.

'Look, what I'm saying is you have lots of options.' Her voice was quiet but firm. 'But there's only you who can make the decision about what you want.'

I'm grateful for:
1. *Some straight-talking.*
2. *Options, even if they do seem scary and confusing.*

My Wedding Day

At twelve noon today I was due to marry Edward at an exclusive private members club in Mayfair. Instead I'm at Tesco's, determined to carry on, business as usual.

It's only when I'm pushing my trolley down the loo roll aisle that I check the time and get a bit choked up. Tears prickle my eyelashes and, blinking furiously, I'm suddenly reminded of The Loo Roll Wars* and defiantly shove loads in my trolley. Whereas most people would drown their sorrows in a bottle of Sauvignon, I choose a six-pack of two-ply quilted.

'Are you OK, love?' A rogue tear escapes when I'm unloading my trolley onto the conveyor belt and is noticed by the kind woman on the checkout.

'I'm supposed to be getting married today,' I sniff.

'Better get a bloody move on then,' says the grumpy man behind me in the queue.

In the end all day is spent trying to distract myself from checking the time and imagining what would have been happening. It's like there's an alternate universe consisting of confetti and cake and kissing the bride – while I'm pricking the sleeve of a meals-for-one and putting it into the micro-wave. Mum crying happy tears in a bad hat and Dad looking all proud as he walks me down the aisle – as I sit on the sofa flicking channels with the remote.

---

* The Loo Roll Wars – when my life was, literally, in pieces.

Getting drunk with all my friends and hitting the dance floor with Edward in the gorgeous ballroom, laughing and twirling around and trying not to trip over my dress – while watching *Mamma Mia!* for the umpteenth time, only this time it doesn't cheer me up. Not even when Pierce Brosnan starts singing.

At midnight I find myself lying awake listening to the rain on the bedroom window, imagining us being spooned up in bed in a lovely hotel, drunk and happy and calling each other husband and wife, while laughing with delighted disbelief that it's real and we did it.

Trust me. I've had better days.

And no, I don't hear from Edward. I didn't expect to.

I'm grateful for:
1. *Today being also World Nutella Day, so I decide to mark the occasion with a large jar and no self-control.*
2. *Being able to use as much loo roll as I like.*
3. *Not having to spend the day in control pants. (Believe me, it's the little things.)*
4. *My friends, for their kind and thoughtful messages; sometimes all you need is a love heart emoji to know someone is thinking about you.*

Valentine's Day

Thought for the day: *you've got to be fucking kidding me.*

Following swiftly on the heels of my wedding day that never was, today is another fun day on my social calendar to make me feel like I'm winning at life. Hurrah! So I practise self-care and stay off social media and try steadfastly to ignore it, after all it's just a lot of silly commercial nonsense.

But actually, it's quite hard to ignore it.

After working at my laptop all morning I pop out for lunch at my local Thai cafe – they do great lunchtime specials – and am ambushed by love and romance: shops selling Valentine-themed this, that and the other; window displays of love hearts; bouquets of red roses outside the florist; and every restaurant I pass offering romantic-two-for-one lunches and dinners. Even my favourite cafe.

Table for two? No, table for one, please.

Maybe I'm just a bit fragile, but it stings a bit, so instead of eating in, I change my mind and order my noodles as take-out. Last year Edward and I exchanged cards; his was homemade, which was sweet. He'd made a collage from old birthday cards. Typical Edward. Always recycling. Less sweet was discovering the cards were all from his ex-wife Sophie.

'But I was trying to save the planet!' he protested, genuinely bewildered by my reaction.

'Save the planet! You better start trying to save your relationship!' I yelled back, shoving my card in the bin. And not the recycling, which infuriated him, so it was all a bit of a disaster. But then it's been like that with every boyfriend. I guess I'm just not the Valentine's type.

Which is why this year, I've offered to babysit for Holly and Adam. With everything that's been going on since her diagnosis, the last thing on either of their minds has been a date night.

After Holly's surgery in December, they've both been solely focused on her recovery and trying to keep things normal for Olivia. The operation went really well and she started chemo last month, but she hasn't felt much like seeing people, so Adam regularly sends updates to our WhatsApp group. It was only a few days ago that I finally got her on the phone and offered my babysitting services so they could both have a break. I've learned from Cricket never to say to someone, 'Let me know if there's anything I can do,' because if someone has to ask, they never will; at least this way I feel like I'm helping in some small way.

'Are you going anywhere romantic?'

I'm in the bathroom, sitting on the edge of the bath as Olivia splashes soapy bubbles and Holly tries to do something with her hair, which she's had cut short.

'On Valentine's Day?' she scoffs. 'I'm sure the restaurant will be rammed and overpriced, plus I've got mouth ulcers and horrible constipation. That's one of the side effects of chemo no one tells you about—'

She breaks off and looks across at Olivia to see if she's heard, but she's engrossed in trying to shampoo her octopus.

'Sorry, that's probably too much information.'

'You know, if you've changed your mind and don't feel up to going out, I'll babysit another time.'

But Holly shakes her head firmly. 'No, I'm looking forward to it, plus it's important to Adam. He says he wants to take

his wife out for dinner. He even bought me a dozen red roses.'
She turns back to her reflection and tries to tease her fringe
with her fingertips.

'He's never bought me roses before. You know Adam, he's
hardly the romantic type.' She catches my eye in the mirror
and pulls a face. 'I said to him, is that what I have to do
around here to be sent flowers? Get cancer—'

She's joking, trying to make light of it, but her voice catches
in her throat, and she breaks off, swallowing hard.

We haven't seen each other since the skating rink because
Holly hasn't felt like seeing anyone, and it's been quite a
shock. Holly's always seemed so invincible, but as she opened
the front door this evening there was a fragility I've never
seen before. And it wasn't just the outward physical changes,
such as the weight loss and haircut, it came from within.

'I give up,' she gasps with a loud tut. 'I can't do anything
with it.'

'Your hair looks fine,' I say supportively. She pulls it back
with her hands and I notice its thinning and see her scalp
under the bright bathroom spotlights. 'You look great,' I add,
then feel clumsy; we both know she doesn't look great, but
I don't know the right thing to say.

We're interrupted by footsteps on the stairs and then –
'Daddy!'

Adam appears, back from the office, with Coco at his
heels.

'So this is where all my favourite girls are hiding,' he grins,
giving me and Holly a kiss, before swooping down on his
daughter, grabbing his tie to keep it out of the water as he
scoops up bubbles, balancing them on both their noses as
she giggles delightedly. I glance at Holly, her face lit up, as
I take in the scene. All of us, squashed into this tiny bathroom. And I think how we're taught it's the big moments in

life that are important, but it's in the gaps in between where the real magic happens.

Scooping Olivia out of the bath, Adam wraps her in her towelling dinosaur bathrobe. 'I'll dry her off and start getting her into bed while you finish up.' Squeezing his wife's hand, he smiles. 'Cheers for tonight, Nell, really appreciate it.'

'Oh, it's nothing.' I bat him away. 'Go drink an overpriced cocktail.'

He laughs and disappears with Olivia.

As he disappears, Holly turns to me. 'Seriously. Thank you.'

She looks tired and pale, despite the copious amounts of blusher. I know tonight's a huge effort, but it's also hugely important; for both of them.

'Are you kidding me? I should be thanking *you*,' I protest. 'It's the first night I've been out since I got back from LA.'

'What, babysitting?' she looks at me with mock horror.

'Hey, don't knock it. I get to eat the contents of your fridge and hang out with Olivia and Coco . . . and an eight-legged sea creature.' Still sitting on the edge of the bath, I give the rubber octopus a squeeze and we both start laughing as it squirts water all over us.

Since getting back from LA, I haven't been very social. It's not that I don't want to see my friends or they don't want to see me, in fact they've been constantly in touch, checking I'm OK, reminding me they're here if I want to talk, which is so kind and I'm so grateful. But that's just it, I haven't felt like talking or being social. On the contrary, I've needed time alone to try to figure things out for myself first, to get some clarity. Trust me, I'm still trying.

The last time I saw Max and Fiona was when they helped me move out of Edward's flat and back into mine. Edward had been there as we loaded boxes into Fiona's huge four-by-four and it had all been so awkward. Max had spent the whole day cracking terrible jokes and trying to lighten the leaden atmosphere while Fiona had fussed with the soft furnishings.

'It's no one's fault, it's just a lot more complicated when you meet someone when you're older,' is all I would say. 'We're coming from different places.'

'Too much baggage,' nodded Fiona supportively.

'Bloody hell, I'll say,' grunted Max as he lugged my heavy suitcases up the stairs to my flat.

Meanwhile Fiona had invited me over for dinner last week – 'I'll order your favourite dim sum and the dipping sauce you love' – which was kind of her, but I wasn't in the mood. Not even if it meant seeing Izzy, who'd been so excited to be a bridesmaid and had proudly presented us with a drawing of me in a top hat and Edward in a veil. I couldn't bear the thought of disappointing her, but Fiona had assured me she was fine.

'As long as she gets to keep the dress.'

'I see she takes after her mother,' I'd replied, which had made Fiona laugh.

'You and Adam seem really good.'

'Yeah, we are.' Pulling out the plug, Holly lets the water drain out of the bath and begins tidying up the bathroom. 'One of the surprising positives. Cancer couples therapy. Who knew?'

'I once read it's the big stuff that either brings you closer together or pushes you apart.' As I hear myself saying it, I realize I'm not just talking about Holly and Adam.

'Sorry about you and Edward.'

'Me too.' I shrug. Scooping the octopus out of the bath, I look up to see her studying me with concern.

'Sorry for being a crap friend.'

I blink in astonishment. 'What are you talking about?'

'I've been meaning to call you, ever since I got your email about the wedding, it's just what with everything going on . . .'

'Don't be silly, I'm fine honestly,' I try quickly to reassure her. I didn't come here to talk about Edward. This evening isn't about me, it's about Holly.

'I've been worried about you.'

'*You're* worried about *me*?'

I feel a rush of guilt. Here's Holly, facing a life-or-death situation. And here's me with another relationship gone wrong. Like she doesn't have enough on her plate to worry about, without me adding to it.

'Just because we're going through different shit, it's still shit.'

'You've always had a way with words.'

She smiles broadly, and I remember why we connected all those years ago over baked potatoes in the microwave when we worked our first office job.

'So, how's your shit?' Meeting her eyes, I smile.

'Pretty brutal.' She picks up a hairbrush and waves it at me. It's full of strands of hair. 'Lost part of my boob, hair next.'

'I thought the hospital said you could wear a cold cap to help prevent that.'

'You can and I am doing it, but it's pretty uncomfortable and there are no guarantees. I wonder if it's worth it. I've got enough of a battle on my hands, without worrying about my hair—' She stops herself. '*Battle*. God, I hate that word. *Battling cancer*. Makes you feel like if you don't fight hard enough it will be your fault. It's so much pressure.'

'I'm sorry you've got to go through all this.'

'Me and millions of other women.'

Our eyes meet, and I think about all the other women out

there going through this, having these conversations with their best friends.

'What do the doctors say?'

She smiles briskly. 'My margins were clear and the drugs I'm on are meant to be amazing at getting rid of any trace of cancer, so they're pleased, but cautious. We've still got a long way to go yet. It's a marathon, not a sprint.' Picking up a towel, she hugs it to her chest.

'Well, you've won a few of those,' I reassure.

'I don't want a medal for this one, I just want to cross the finishing line.'

'You will.'

'But what if I don't?'

'You're going to be fine.'

'Nell, please.' She suddenly interrupts me, her face imploring. 'Let me be scared. I can't be scared in front of Adam or Olivia or the rest of my family. I don't want to frighten or worry them.'

I fall silent, as she continues talking.

'At the hospital, when I go for chemo, there are all these incredible, amazing women, being so positive, running marathons, raising money for charity, like I should be. Like I thought I *would* be. I feel like a total failure in front of them.'

'Oh Holly.' I feel my heart ache for her.

'People keep telling me I'm brave, but I don't feel brave, I feel the opposite.' She breaks off. 'Please, just give me that space. Just allow me to be scared in front of you. Will you do that for me?'

'OK.' I nod. 'You can be scared with me.'

'Thank you.'

I stand in that tiny bathroom, with one of my oldest friends. What I don't tell her is that I'm scared too.

*

Later, after they've left for the restaurant, I tuck Olivia into bed to read her a bedtime story.

'What about this one,' I suggest, randomly selecting a title from her bursting bookshelves. She has quite the library for a four-year-old. 'It's about elephants.'

'No.' Diving out from underneath her duvet, she grabs a book from a pile on the side and shoves it at me with her chubby fist. 'Read this one.'

I have to smile. Talk about like mother like daughter. Olivia certainly knows her own mind.

'*The Magic Faraway Tree*,' I read the title. 'Oh, I love this one. It was one of my favourites as a child too,' I say, but Olivia isn't listening. She's already back in bed, thumb firmly in her mouth, teddy clutched to her chest, waiting.

Seriously. Kids are a tough audience.

'Right, OK, here goes.' And settling myself next to her on the bed, I open the book and start reading.

Afterwards, when she's fallen asleep, I go downstairs to watch some TV, but my mind won't focus. I keep thinking about life and how it's not like in the books we read as children. There are no magical faraway lands when we grow up.

But for so long, I believed there was one. Some mythical place I'd finally arrive at once I'd passed those exams, or he told me he loved me, or I got the job, or lost the weight, or could afford a nicer apartment. Where everything would be perfect and all sorted out, and now life, the life I wanted to live, could finally start.

But here's the thing I'm fast realizing. You never get there. There is no such place. It doesn't exist. There will always be something – another goal to achieve, or hurdle to overcome, or issue to deal with – because that's just life.

I think about me and Edward and how life suddenly did

a handbrake turn. About Holly and Adam and how they got through the problems in their marriage, they were moving to the country, everything had worked out. And then boom, she found a lump. Who knows what's ahead for any of us. All we have is here and now.

It's late, I'm tired. I hope my friends are having a nice time. Lying on the sofa with Coco, I eat some leftovers I found in the fridge and flick through the TV.

I'm grateful for:
1. *Dad, who sends me his annual Valentine text: SWALK.*
2. *Holly's smile when she got back, exhausted, but happy.*
3. *The bottle of tequila I found had been delivered when I got home, along with a handwritten note: 'Happy Galentine's, love Cricket.'*

The Blame Game

It's the weekend and I wake up this morning to discover I've been kidnapped. My captors? Why, Guilt and Self-blame, of course.

Held prisoner underneath my duvet, these unwelcome feelings tell me that I deserve to be unhappy, with my life a mess. To be alone again. Lonely and unloved. That the break-up with Edward is all my fault and I'm an idiot. That I've thrown away the chance to marry an amazing man, to gamble on something I'm uncertain about.

Plus I'm forty-something – er hello, TICK TOCK, pipes up their best mate, Panic.

Put like that, it does sound like madness.

Self-blame decides that Edward has every right to hate me. He's a poor innocent victim, who has had his life ruined and his heart broken by his fuck-up of a fiancée.

While Guilt fills me with regret and lists all the ways I should feel bad about myself:

- I did things wrong.
- Made mistakes.
- Changed my mind.
- Over-reacted.
- Was too emotional.
- Too ridiculous.
- Too selfish.

- That I want too much.
- That I am too much.
- That it's all my fault.

That phrase again.

I try protesting. Why are women always made to feel like it's their fault? But you can't argue with your abusive emotions, they don't want to hear. After Edward has dropped off Arthur for the weekend, I find myself worrying about him. I hope he's OK. And his son, Louis, too. After they went back to Paris, I texted Simone but never got a reply. It's a family matter and I'm no longer family. Edward shut me out. But like I said, I don't blame him. I was the one that screwed everything up.

Later, after I've finished beating myself up, I continue the downward spiral by lying on the sofa and looking at my phone. Well, why not do a bit of doom scrolling to make myself feel even worse? Of course my rational brain knows not to compare my life to anyone else's, especially when it's their highlights reel, but trust me, I'm not feeling rational.

If I was, I wouldn't be scrolling through Annabel's stories about self-care while coveting her fabulous designer wardrobe. She's at some swanky fundraiser event looking amazing as always. Still, at least I'm grateful Edward doesn't use social media. There's nothing worse than seeing your ex out having fun at some party with another woman while you're lying on the sofa feeling depressed—

Hang on a minute.

There's a group shot and I see Annabel's arm draped around a man in a dinner jacket. They're laughing and smiling and holding champagne glasses. Is that a new boyfriend? I pinch the screen and zoom in.

WTF! It's Edward!

WhatsApp Chat with Fiona

I can't believe Edward!

Ooh, what's happened? You two back together? I knew it would be temporary!

No we are not!
He's with Annabel!

What?

I saw it on Instagram!

I thought he wasn't on Instagram.

He's not!

????
Am confused

But Annabel is! I looked at her account last night. They were at some charity thing together!

It's an old photo.

What?
You knew about this?!

It's nothing.

Nothing!

Fiona is typing

> **They're at a ball!**
> **He's wearing a DJ!**

Fiona is typing

It was a couple of weeks ago. You were in LA. I only found out afterwards. I didn't say anything as I didn't want you to get the wrong idea.

> **I HAVE THE WRONG IDEA.**
> **Am calling you.**

Call declined at 9.06

Can't pick up. In a meeting at museum about new exhibition.

> **I can't ducking believe it!!**

I know, some of the Byzantine mosaics
are incredible.

> **Not the exhibition!**
> **Edward and Annabel!**

Sorry . . . curator's head on . . .

Fiona is typing

She invited him to a charity fundraiser against climate change.

> **I didn't know she was into climate change.**

She's into lots of things.

> **And one of them's my ex-fiancé!**

309

Don't be silly. She said she thought it might be a good opportunity for Edward to network.

Hmmm. OK. Maybe I jumped to conclusions.

Annabel's got a really big heart you know. That's why she became a life coach. To help people.

And now I feel bad.

She asked if you were OK. I mentioned you two had broken up.

Fiona!

Oops. Sorry. Is it a secret?

No. Of course not.

She said to tell you she's here if you need her.

That's nice of her.

And that she's got 15 per cent off her life-coaching courses.

She did not say that!

I know, isn't that generous?
OK, better go. Boss giving me daggers. Literally Greek Byzantine ones.
Speak later xxx

Xxx

I'm grateful for:
1. *Having the life experience and maturity of my years to know how to deal with these things, instead of doing something silly and immature, like leaving a string of poo emojis underneath THAT photo.*

2. *Being able to override my time lock on Instagram so that I can spend hours doing a deep dive into Annabel's social media, scrutinizing every post, comment, reel, story and motivational message. Of which there are many.*

3. *The freedom to whack up the central heating without having to deal with Chief Inspector of the Thermostat. Thus consoling myself that he can go to charity balls with perfect Annabel and drink champagne, but the future is bright. Literally, as I've also left all the lights on.*

4. *Spending the rest of the evening listening to empowering podcasts about women doing it for themselves and living in the moment, while eating an entire bag of cheese puffs and having one too many gins. Because tomorrow I will not feel empowered, I will feel hungover. And my energy bills are going to be fucking huge.*

Kintsugi

Today I read a fascinating article about Kintsugi, which is the Japanese art of repairing broken pottery pieces with gold – the idea being that, by celebrating flaws and imperfections, you can create an even stronger, more beautiful and unique piece of art. Accompanying the text were lots of photos of repaired vases and bowls and they were just so incredibly beautiful, and it was because of their golden scars, not despite them.

Isn't that just the most wonderful idea?

I love that instead of being upset that something is broken and trying to hide the damage, you proudly embrace the bits that are broken.

So from now on, I'm no longer going to think of myself as a fuck-up, I'm going to imagine myself as a beautiful Japanese Kintsugi vase. One that has been knocked around a bit by life and isn't perfect or flawless, but is showing more than a few cracks and chips. And is stronger and more wonderful for it. In fact, the more bashed about you are, the better.

See. Everything is perspective. It's just about the way you look at it.

I'm grateful for:
1. *Not really being a Japanese vase as I'm so clumsy I would drop myself immediately and be smashed into a million pieces.**

---

* There's Kintsugi, and there's a dustpan and brush.

To: Penelope Stevens
Subject: CALL ME

Dear Forty-Something F**k-Up,
   I have good news and bad news. Bad news: our columnist just quit.
   Good news: the job's yours if you want it. Call me ASAP.
   Sadiq

A Word of Advice

'I am not wearing that hideous monstrosity.'

'It's a royal-blue shift dress.'

'It's Margaret Thatcher!'

Poppy, the stylist, looks worried. 'How about a nice twinset, instead? You could wear it with this purple scarf for a pop of colour.'

'A twinset!' Cricket explodes. 'What next? A tweed skirt and lace-up brogues?'

'Well, actually . . .' The stylist pulls one off the rail with a flourish – 'How about this Harris tweed? It's very country chic' – before seeing Cricket's glaring expression, and shoves it back again. 'Or how about we keep looking, shall we?'

Oh dear. I feel a bit sorry for poor Poppy.

When we first arrived at the newspaper offices, she was all bouncy and enthusiastic. In her white vegan trainers and palazzo pants, she greeted us in reception, bearing a wide smile and a lanyard. Escorting us through security and into the lift, she took us to the third floor where the photographer and her assistant were busy setting up the lights.

That was over two hours ago. Since then, watching her trying and failing to pick out an outfit for Cricket, I've witnessed Poppy's exuberance slowly drain, like the battery on my iPhone. The problem isn't so much the actual clothes, as society's presumption of what women in their eighties wear. Not having met Cricket before, Poppy has chosen a series of sensible, classic and, let's face it, rather dull outfits, that Cricket, in her silver plimsolls and dungarees, wouldn't be seen dead in.

I brace myself as Poppy reaches for something else on a hanger.

'Beige? Over my dead body!'

See what I mean?

We're here today to have our photographs done for our new column. Yes, that's right. *Our* new column. Since receiving Sadiq's email out of the blue a few days ago, a lot has happened. After calling him straight back to check that this wasn't some kind of joke or elaborate scam email to extract my pitiful savings, he'd confirmed that, yes, he was indeed offering me my own column in the weekend magazine of a national newspaper.

'So what's your answer, Stevens?' Sadiq had finally asked, after several moments of me being stunned into silence. Which rather says a lot, for me.

The answer of course was yes, except the moment I got off the phone, I found Imposter Syndrome waiting for me, demanding to know if I was up to the job and making me doubt myself. The editor wanted the new column to take the form of an agony aunt column. Readers would write in with their confessions; various problems and dilemmas and perceived failures and I would give advice.

'People can relate to you, Nell, you make them feel less like a fuck-up,' said Sadiq cheerily, which was a compliment, *I think*. Only, I wasn't qualified to give advice. What did I know? If anything, the older I get, the less I feel I know the answers to any of the big questions in life. Except, there *was* one thing I can tell people: they're not alone. That whatever they are feeling, there is someone out there that feels the same too. And that's a pretty big thing, I think.

As for the rest? Well, that got me thinking about the person I've learned so much from. And she desperately needed a job.

'So I called him straight back and suggested we did it together and he loved the idea,' I'm saying now, as I sit in front of the mirror, having my hair tonged by the hairstylist. Fortunately for Poppy the stylist, I chose the first thing she picked out. A fabulous, emerald-green trouser suit.

'Wow, that's awesome.' Siobhan, the photographer, looks up from her tripod. 'What's the name of the column.'

'I wanted to call it "Failing That, Tequila",' pipes up Cricket, who's getting her make-up done. 'Which is always my advice, when all else fails.'

'But the editor thought that wasn't *quite* the right message,' I add hastily.

'Well, the world would be a better place if it was,' grumbles Cricket. 'That and a pair of rubber gloves and some determination and you've cracked it.'

Hair and make-up both giggle. 'I love this column already!'

'I suggested "Laughing in the Face of it All",' I grin.

'Umph . . . yes,' nods Poppy, appearing from underneath the rolling rack with an armful of hangers and her hair all over the place. 'Great advice.'

'But they thought that was too long,' tuts Cricket, suspiciously eyeballing a skirt being offered to her.

'So we went with "Confessions",' I finish cheerfully. 'Short and sweet and it refers to the title of my podcast. Only now they're not *my* confessions, they're from the readers who write in.'

'Wow, cool,' nods the photographer. 'I love your podcast by the way. I listen to it every week. I can't wait to read the new column.'

'And we can't wait to start writing it,' beams Cricket. 'Now, if I can just find something to wear. Oh, what about this darling suit?'

'You mean the hot-pink tuxedo with the satin trim?'

Dropping everything she's holding, Poppy pulls it from the rack. 'Hang on, let me check it's your size . . .' She holds it up to Cricket. 'Yes, it is!' She's triumphant.

'Wonderful. And it will go with my silver plimsolls.'

Cricket looks delighted. As does Poppy. Actually, she looks more exhausted.

'Brilliant. So once you've finished hair and make-up we're ready to go. Have we decided what we're doing with your hair?'

'How about I pop in a few hot rollers,' suggests the hair-stylist brightly, but Cricket looks horrified

'I might be in my eighties but I am not having a cauliflower head.'

There's a room full of blank faces.

'That's what my friend Una called old-lady hair,' she explains. 'At my age, you have to be on your guard against a short curly perm.'

'Isn't that the same friend who said never to join the Blue Rinse Brigade, they might kill you,' I smile, remembering our first meeting.

'Indeed she did. And if it's not them, it's the natter of cauliflower heads,' she warns comically, and the whole room erupts into laughter.

I can't help feeling this column will be popular, though frankly I don't think it's going to be because of me.

In the end the photoshoot turns out to be a lot of fun. The photographer does lots of different poses of the two of us sitting on stools or lounging on a sofa. It's all terribly posed and professional with the backdrop and the large reflector lights. At one point I even think they're going to bring out a wind machine. Honestly, several times I have to pinch myself. Me! With my own column in a national newspaper! I've got total Imposter Syndrome.

Unlike Cricket, who is in her element. Being in front of an audience and in front of a camera. She says it's like her old theatre days when she used to get her headshots done. At one point Sadiq pops in to see how it's all going and meet Cricket. He's thrilled to be back in the office. Apparently his husband is planting up his raised beds and there's only so much *Gardeners' World* and Monty Don a man can take. Even if he does have fabulous herbaceous borders.

'You know he bought us matching Crocs?' he tells us, rolling his eyes and shuddering, much to the commiseration of Cricket.

'I've got a pair and I love mine!' I interrupt. 'They're *so* comfy.'

'So are your pyjamas but you don't wear them outside,' retorts Cricket, to which Sadiq roars with laughter.

I don't think I've seen Sadiq roar with laughter before, so I decide best not to add that actually, I have been known to wear my pyjamas to pop to the corner shop to buy a pint of milk. Underneath my coat of course, but still. I can see how our advice column is going to pan out. It's going to be Cricket telling everyone to walk on the wild side and me suggesting slippers and an early night.

Afterwards, Siobhan shows us the photos on her laptop. They're fantastic. Both in our bright suits, we really complement each other.

'I think we make a good double act,' says Cricket when it's all over and we take the lift back down to the ground floor.

'Me too,' I smile, as together we walk through reception. 'And that was the idea. Two for the price of one.'

Which is true. By sharing the column with Cricket it's half the money, but the upshot is I get to keep writing the obituaries. They don't pay much, but I've realized that I don't want to give them up. Everyone has a story and I want to be the one to tell it. Plus, I'm excited for us to be working together.

'So do you fancy getting a quick drink?' As we head out onto the street, I turn to Cricket. 'Seems a shame to waste all this hair and make-up.'

She checks her watch. 'I'd love to, but I have to be home by six. I'm FaceTiming with Jack.'

It's the first time she's mentioned him since we got back from Los Angeles and I notice her blush. Which is quite something as I don't think I've ever seen Cricket blush before, and especially not underneath all that foundation.

'I wondered what was happening between the two of you.'

'Well, I realized when I got back to London that I quite missed him.'

'So is this a *romantic* thing?' I tease but Cricket won't be drawn.

'I don't know. It's a thing. That's all I can say.' She shrugs and smiles. 'There's a lot of freedom in travelling without a destination.'

I know she's talking about her own life, but listening, I think about my own. 'See, you give good advice. That's why I asked you to do this job.'

She laughs and turns to hail a taxi. One immediately swings around and pulls up at the kerb. I wait as she climbs inside and pulls down the window.

'By the way, I forgot to tell you. We've found our leading man.'

'Oh wow, who is it?'

'An actor, goes by the stage name of Lloyd G Joseph.'

'I don't think I know him . . .'

'Me neither. But Christopher says he's wonderful.'

As the cab pulls away she waves goodbye, her arm out of the window. It's only then I realize she's still wearing the hot-pink tuxedo.

I'm grateful for:
1. *Cricket's life advice.*
2. *Smoke and mirrors; I look so amazing in my headshot I don't even recognize myself.*
3. *Eye make-up remover. Now I realize why everyone looks so fabulous in photoshoots, my make-up is literally trowelled on.*
4. *Our first column comes out next month. Woo-hoo!*

Timing

I've always known that so much about life is all about timing. Today I receive a voicemail that makes me realize it more than ever.

It's from Simone.

After I heard she'd gone back to Paris, I tried to contact her. I had her number from when she'd once called me, after locking herself out of the flat in London. I sent a text but received no reply. I thought about calling Louis but decided against it. We haven't spoken since his dad and I broke up and I wasn't sure he'd welcome me getting in touch. I was worried he'd tell me it was none of my business.

Yet still, I kept thinking about Simone. Kept wondering if she was OK. For all her rock'n'roll swagger and cool Parisian chic, she was still only eighteen. I tried to imagine myself at that age, faced with the decision she had to make, and felt fiercely protective of her.

She calls me when I'm working and my phone is turned off. I play her voicemail on speaker phone. Her distinctive French accent filling my tiny flat, she begins by apologizing for not replying sooner, 'but things have been a little crazy', and goes on to tell me that, with the support of Louis and her family, she'd had a termination a few weeks ago. They'd both given it a lot of thought and it was completely the right choice. They were both too young and she wasn't ready. There was so much she wanted to do first . . . 'to finish my studies and go to college . . . travel and see the world . . . have a career . . . get my own place . . .'

She says she's relieved and now she just wants to put it all behind her and get on with the rest of her life. 'It wasn't the right time to have a baby.' And listening to her, I think there it is again. *Timing.* How difficult it is to get it right. Perhaps you never do. Perhaps there is no such thing as perfect timing.

She ends the message by telling me that she and Louis have broken up, but that it's OK, it probably would've happened anyway. She sounds in a good place and I'm glad. Then she hopes I'm OK, because Louis had told her I'd broken up with his dad. 'That sucks, you made a cute couple,' she says, which makes me feel sad.

She signs off with a kiss. '*Au revoir, Nellie, gros bisous.*'

Later, I look at Instagram and see a photo of her. She's with her friends on a sailing boat and they're all salty and wet and laughing. It makes me smile. I feel happy for her, this young French girl, who's just starting out in life. It's not easy for any us. Simone. Me. Cricket. Three different generations. Three different times of life. All trying to navigate these choppy waters as best we can, trying to make the right choices. I press the love heart on the photo. It turns red.

MARCH

#decisionsdecisions

Owning It

Sod This. Sod This. Sod This.

It's 1 March. Traditionally, on the first of every month, you're supposed to say three white rabbits for good luck. Apparently, for the charm to work, it has to be the first thing you say as soon as you wake up, but of course, I always forget.

This month, however, I remember. Only I'm less white rabbits and more mad March hare – and the person I'm mad with is myself.

Ever since I got back from LA, I've been mooning around, feeling a bit sorry for myself. February felt particularly gloomy, not just because of the endless grey skies, but because it was the month Edward and I were supposed to get married, and even the brilliant news about my and Cricket's new column couldn't lift me out of the doldrums for more than a few hours.

But now I give myself a stern talking to. Whatever happened, has happened and I need to own it. No more second-guessing myself, no more doom scrolling, no more hiding away and slobbing on the sofa of an evening with crisps and gin.* It's a brand new month and I'm determined to have a brand new attitude. Fresh start. Clean page. Rest of my life and all that malarkey. (Well, I've been here before,

---

* On second thoughts, perhaps that's being a little too hasty.

so I do know the drill.) Plus, if I've got a new advice column in the glossy magazine of a national newspaper, I need to start by giving myself some advice and putting my own life in order.

My phone starts ringing. I'm in the kitchen in my pyjamas making coffee. I look at the screen. Withheld number. Who's calling so early? I never answer a withheld number, no matter what time of day it is. Seriously. Does *anyone*? But in the spirit of my new can-do, face-things-head-on attitude, I pick up.

'Hello. Penelope Stevens,' I say confidently.

See. I'm *totally* owning it. Even in slippers!

'Ah. Ms Stevens. Finally we speak! I've been trying to get hold of you for several weeks now. I was beginning to think you were avoiding me. It's Cressida, your bridal couturier.'

Oh bollocks. I *have* been avoiding her. Along with a lot of things.

'Cressida! Good Morning. How wonderful to hear from you.' Not only can I own it, I can lie through my teeth. 'How can I help you?'

'It's about your wedding gown.'

'Ah yes. My dress.'

The messages had started in January, after Edward and I had called off the wedding and before I'd paid for the dress in full. Which of course I did, as soon as I received their invoice and almost fainted. *How much?* But then in my short-lived experience of being a bride-to-be, once you put 'wedding' in front of anything, you add several noughts on the other end.

And it was a beautiful dress, truly it was. The thing is. I didn't want the dress any more.

Neither, it appeared, did Cressida.

'Yes, the gown you were supposed to pick up six weeks ago?'

Her messages had started out terribly polite and gushing. All breathless excitement and endless hyperbole. Everything was extraordinarily wonderful, or incredibly delightful or indescribably breathtaking. It was like she was speaking in diamante.

And she was very sympathetic when I'd emailed to tell her the news that the wedding was off. She even signed off, 'Hugs, Cressida'.

But in recent weeks her voicemails and emails had turned increasingly fraught and annoyed, demanding I call her back. Which, to my shame, I hadn't. Like I said, I haven't been facing up to a lot of things in my life the past couple of months, but all that's going to change now.

'I'm so sorry, I've been away.'

'But now you're back. And the gown needs to go,' she said firmly.

'Absolutely.'

'No one wants to see a gown hanging here for a wedding that didn't happen. It's bad energy!' Her voice is getting higher and more urgent. 'Brides can be *very* superstitious. Have you any idea how this reflects on us? A jilted bride is the kiss of death for a bridal boutique!'

'Well actually, I wasn't jilted—'

'The gown needs to be gone ASAP!' she shrieks.

There were definitely no more hugs from Cressida.

Cut to a couple of hours later. Mayfair. Me trying to fit through the doorway of Cressida's bridal boutique, my arms filled with sequins and tulle. The dress is in one of those zip-up bags that reminds me a bit of a body bag you see on those crime dramas on TV. And it weighs a tonne. Who knew sequins could be so heavy? It's like carrying a dead body.

Or a dead bride, pipes up my gallows humour.

Trying to manoeuvre, I find myself wedged in the arch of fake flowers around the doorway. A bridal party have gathered on the pavement, unable to enter for their appointment and are goggle-eyed. Inside the boutique, Cressida is almost apoplectic. I think back to all the smiles and offers of flutes of champagne when Annabel had taken me for the first dress appointment. Now Cressida practically has her knee in my back shoving me out of the door.

I'm joking.

Actually, no, I think that really is her knee in my back.

Finally I pop through the doorway, like a cork from the bottles of my wedding champagne that were never popped, and am showered by fake blossoms, like plastic confetti. Cressida looks thunderous. Quickly ushering in her customers, she closes the door behind them and pulls down the blind.

Alone on the pavement, I feel less triumphant and more relieved. Not quite how I imagined collecting my wedding dress would be, but then so much of my life hasn't been how I imagined it, so why change the habit of a lifetime? I go to hail a cab, then considering the extortionate amount of money the dress cost, change my mind. I'll take the bus instead.

Lugging my dress, I head off towards the bus stop. I'm reminded of when I used to do the walk of shame in my twenties. Only now I'm in my forties and I haven't left some boy's bedroom after spending the night, I've left a bridal shop after a cancelled wedding. Talk about the goalposts moving. It's a different sort of walk of shame.

Finally at the bus stop, one of those new routemasters appears and I climb on board. Only it's a bit difficult to get on as the dress is so heavy and cumbersome. I'm really seeing now why Cricket went for the little black cocktail dress. Finally I manage to get on, and walk down the aisle, looking for a spare seat. I notice all the passengers are staring and then I realize it's at the dress. It's in a big cover with 'Bridal Couture' emblazoned across it. Everyone on the bus is looking and staring and smiling. Women of all ages have gone all misty-eyed.

I smile awkwardly, feeling like a complete fraud. I might as well be wearing a 'Bride on Board' badge. Only I'm not, and putting the dress next to me on the seat, I pull out my phone and try to avoid all eye contact.

Twenty minutes later I nearly miss my stop. Pressing the bell, I quickly scramble to get off, when I hear a voice from the back of the bus.

'Hey love, you're forgetting something.'

Oh shit! The dress!

'Thank you.' Grabbing it, I smile gratefully at the stranger for reminding me.

'You can't have a bride without her dress!' they call out jovially and I wave and smile and clamber off the bus, my arms full and my heart heavy.

And now it's pulling away and I'm left standing alone on the pavement. Which begs the question: but what happens if you have a dress without a bride?

I'm grateful for:
1. *The charity shop, Cancer Research, for providing me with an answer by being right there by the bus stop when I get off, which immediately makes me think about Holly.*
2. *The lovely manageress who gives my hand a little squeeze and says someone will love the dress as it's beautiful.*
3. *Not crying until I leave the shop.*
4. *Spending the evening in the company of my frying pan,*

*as today is also Pancake Day, which means stuffing
myself with pancakes in an attempt to eat my emotions
as today also reminds me of Edward, which fails,
obviously, but my God they were delicious.*

Co-Parenting

In the past, when I've broken up with boyfriends, it's been a clean break. But with Edward it's different – we have Arthur. OK, so *technically* speaking Arthur isn't my dog, but he was the reason I agreed to rent Edward's spare room, all those many moons ago, and now I couldn't imagine life without him. Breaking up with Edward is one thing, but I could never break up with Arthur.

Fortunately, Edward doesn't expect me to and has agreed to share custody of Arthur. Weeks are to be split – handover day is Wednesday – and we do alternate weekends, unless one of us is busy, like for example going away on business (or to fundraiser balls with Annabel!). We're like a divorced couple, sharing custody of the children. Only our canine child weighs forty kilos and sheds hair and mud everywhere.

Today is Wednesday. So, as agreed, I walk Arthur back to Edward's flat. Drop-offs and pick-ups have been brief and excessively civil and are shared as per the Excel spreadsheet that Edward drew up after I moved out. 'So there's no room for confusion,' he'd told me, handing over the laminated version. Edward doesn't do confusion. Sticking the spreadsheet on my fridge had reinforced just how different – and incompatible – we are.

Nearing what used to be my home and anticipating seeing Edward again, I feel the usual whole host of conflicting emotions. Absently I wonder if I could spreadsheet my whole life, as it is *nothing but* confusion.

'Hello.'

As I walk up the path, he's out front, putting out the rubbish and recycling. Today is collection day. Arthur launches on him, jumping up and wagging his tail excitedly. They look so cute together. My heart swells. Pushing his glasses up his nose, he peers at me.

'You're late.'

'Am I?' Instantly my heart shrinks back.

'Yes. By fifteen minutes.' He checks his watch.

And now I just feel plain irritated.

'Not at another party with Annabel then?'

OK, so not quite the genial, civilized conversation I was aiming for, but I can't help it. It just comes out.

Meanwhile Edward's face remains impassive, but I notice a twitch of his cheek muscles as his jaw clenches. 'It was a climate change fundraiser. Annabel kindly invited me in my capacity as CEO of a software company dealing in renewable energy solutions, as a networking opportunity.'

I force a bright smile. 'Sounds wonderful. Shame I wasn't invited.'

Networking my arse. You can't pull the organic wool over my eyes.

'You were in Los Angeles,' he replies, diligently folding cardboard.

Unlike me, Edward is not one to order things online and half-heartedly squash up the box in the hope that the bin workers will take pity and take it. But instead, will diligently remove all the tape, take it apart and stack it neatly. Not that Edward would order anything online, of course, as he shops local.

'Reconnecting with old flames, apparently,' he mutters under his breath.

'Excuse me?'

He refuses to elaborate. 'And anyway, you wouldn't be interested.'

'How do you know I wouldn't be interested?

'Penelope, whenever have you been interested in environmental issues?'

'What are you talking about?' And now I'm indignant. 'I recycle. I know all about sustainable fashion . . . I'm always on eBay and in charity shops! I walk everywhere or take public transport, unlike *you*, who has a car—'

'It's electric.'

'Big deal.'

The conversation is getting heated.

'Well it is a big deal, actually. Reducing your carbon footprint is about more than shopping on eBay.'

'Oh don't be so bloody pompous!'

'Pompous! I'm just stating the facts about CO_2 emissions and ways to reduce them.'

'Says the man with two children,' I retort.

'Says the woman who wanted me to have more!' he fires back.

As the words fly out of our mouths, we both suddenly fall silent. God, what has happened to us? How did we get here? Underneath my jacket, I feel my chest heaving. Edward looks pale and furious. Arthur starts whining. For a few moments we stand motionless, staring at each other. Just a few feet apart, yet we might as well be worlds apart.

Briefly, I think Edward is going to say something, but then he seems to change his mind and reaches for a bin bag. I watch as he goes to put it into the dustbin. They're made of recycled corn starch and, according to Edward, are a much greener alternative to the evil plastic drawstring ones I used to buy from the supermarket when we first moved in together.

So what if they didn't fit properly and tore every time you took them out, when you were saving the planet? Or burst open at the bottom and scatter food waste all over the garden path . . .

As Edward begins picking up broken eggshells and teabags, he shoots me a look, daring me to say something. I watch him for a moment, then unclip Arthur from his lead and tickle his ears goodbye. Before turning, walking down the path and closing the gate behind me.

I don't say anything.

I'm grateful for:

1. *If you're going to walk on eggshells, it's probably good that they're already broken. I think there's a metaphor in there somewhere.*
2. *Having the bright idea of just leaving Edward a key in future; I can't face seeing him every week.*
3. *Being able to buy my own bin liners (which not only fit my swing bin perfectly but also happen to be biodegradable, so take that and stick it in your compost bin, Edward).*

To: Penelope Stevens
Subject: Exhibition

Dear Nell,
　　Long time no speak. Hope all is well.
　　I wanted to send you an invite to Sam's exhibition at The
Gilpin Gallery next Friday. It's kind of a memorial to her and I
thought you'd like to come and raise a glass to my little sis.
　　I've attached the invite to the email; the address and all
the details are on there.
　　It would be great to see you.
　　Joe x

I'm grateful for:
1. *The chance to celebrate Sam and see her paintings in real life.*
2. *The chance to see her handsome brother again.*
3. *I'm not dead yet.*

A Day Later

And I still haven't replied to Joe's email.

Luckily emails are not like WhatsApp. There are no blue ticks to inform the recipient you've read it and are ignoring them. Not that I'm ignoring Joe. It's just that now, in the cold light of day, my initial excitement has been replaced by doubts. I'm not sure how to reply or even if it's a good idea to go. It's a bit out of the blue.

Do I . . . ?

A) Agonize about it for hours.

B) Make an excuse and say I'm busy.

C) FaceTime Liza in LA, who gets all excited and says it's A SIGN! The universe is trying to tell me something.

D) Dismiss that as being too woo woo.

E) Secretly think she might have a point, maybe it's true and the universe does work in mysterious ways? Maybe I was always meant to meet Joe, maybe that's the reason it didn't work out with Edward, maybe it's like that movie, *Serendipity*!

F) Pull myself together, sharpish; I sound like a loon.

G) Tell myself I'm being ridiculous, I'm reading far too much into this.

H) Remind myself that Joe's just a friend. Actually more like an acquaintance. Who's really handsome.

I) Feel disloyal to Edward.

J) Remember we've broken up. And he went to a fund-raiser with Annabel.

K) Wonder when this gets any easier.

L) Call Cricket, who tells me it never gets easier, you just get less time to worry about it.

M) WhatsApp Fiona, the married voice of reason, but she doesn't answer.

N) Give up asking everyone else and imagine what advice I would give if this was a letter to our new 'Confessions' column.

O) Take it at face value; remind myself it's purely platonic and it's not a date, but it would be nice to get dressed up and go out. And I really need to stop overthinking things.*

P) Say yes, I'd like to come and raise a glass to Samantha.

Q) All of the above.

---

* He signed off with a kiss. According to Liza this is the universal sign of a man flirting, so now I'm even more confused than ever.

A Birthday Surprise

On Sunday it's Izzy, my god-daughter's, eighth birthday. Fiona is throwing a party at her house and she's invited all the usual suspects. However with this invitation, unlike with Joe's when I was wracked with indecision, I didn't need to think how to reply.

'I wouldn't miss it for the world,' I say, when she calls first thing this morning to check I'm still coming.

'Oh good. Izzy will be delighted. I was just a bit worried . . .'

'Sorry, I know I've been a bit absent recently, but don't worry, I take my godmother duties very seriously.'

'No, it's not that.'

'Rest assured, I'll be taking her for her first tattoo on her eighteenth,' I continue, referring to a joke we've always had. Well, I think it's funny, though Fiona always looks a bit horrified. 'Wow, I just realized, that's only in ten years!'

'I invited Annabel,' she interrupts awkwardly.

I can tell she's stressed about the situation. Immediately I feel lots of different things, none of which I want to share with her, and most of which begin with Fuck.

'Of course you did,' I say breezily. 'She's Clemmie's mum and Clemmie is Izzy's best friend.'

There was a point, a couple of years ago, when Clementine confessed to bullying Izzy, but all that's in the past now.

'And you're fine with it?'

'Course I am, silly. We're all adults.'

'Exactly.' Fiona sounds relieved. 'Well, brilliant. See you later then.'

'See you later.'

Of course I'm lying. I'm an adult; I'm not a bloody saint.

Thing is, I still haven't figured out how you're supposed to do this adulting business. In fact, if I look at my track record so far, I'm really not very good at it.

As I turn into Fiona's wide, tree-lined street, my stomach does that thing Arthur always does when he's trying to get comfy in his basket and keeps turning around in circles. I'm a bit apprehensive. Earlier, on the tube journey over here, it struck me that it's the first social event I've been to back home since calling off the wedding, and everyone will be here. I haven't wanted to talk about what happened, so I haven't been out much. I feel a bit embarrassed. One broken engagement is unlucky. But two?

That said, they're my oldest friends and it's only a children's birthday party. No one's going to judge me. Still, I just feel a bit, 'Here comes Nell, the forty-something fuck-up with another failed relationship under her belt, what's wrong with her?' Because they might not judge me but I can do a pretty good job of doing that myself.

But as I reach Fiona's large, Victorian red-brick semi, all self-sabotaging thoughts disappear and I do a double take. A large 'For Sale' sign is fastened to the gate post. Hang on. Have I got the right house? I double-check the number on the door. No, this is right. Plus there are party balloons tied to the letterbox. Confused, I ring the doorbell, and moments later it's opened by Fiona, looking gorgeous as usual, all swingy blonde hair and fine cashmere knits, without *even a hint* of a bobble.

'I didn't know you were selling the house!'

'Neither did I –' ushering me inside the entrance hall, she

closes the door behind me '– until this morning when the estate agent appeared with his board.'

Loud, blood-curdling shrieking wafts in from the garden.

'I got a bouncy castle,' she explains. 'I don't know what I was thinking. With all that sugar it's a lethal combination.'

She leads me through into her large, open-plan kitchen. God, who would sell a house with a kitchen like this? It really is to die for. Decorated with streamers and large gold helium balloons that spell out Happy Birthday, it boasts a huge island filled with all different kinds of party food, around which several parents are gathered. I spot Annabel talking to Michelle, who waves a cupcake at me and mouths something unintelligible, the universal signal that she'll be over in a minute. While at the far end, sleek, steel-framed doors lead out onto the garden, where a dozen under-nines are going crazy.

'So where are you moving to?' I ask.

As I turn back to Fiona I'm reminded of that duck analogy. She looks her usual serene self, floating around the kitchen island, filling up the tray of Colin the Caterpillar cupcakes, but I have a feeling her feet are paddling furiously under the water. It's weird. I've never seen Fiona like this before. She normally has this adulting business completely sussed.

'Ask David.'

At that moment, David appears in the kitchen and walks over to the fridge. At least, I think it's David. Gone are his suit and side parting. Instead he's barefoot, wearing frayed cut-off jeans. And wait – *is that a man bun?*

'Oh, hi Nell.' He gives a casual wave. 'Can I get you anything to drink?'

Rooted to the limestone flooring with underfloor heating, I stare, astonished. 'Um . . . wine, thanks.'

As he takes a bottle of something expensive from the fridge and pours me a glass, I notice that in place of his Rolex, he's wearing woven bracelets and a string of beads looped around his wrist. I feel as if I've stepped into a parallel universe.

'So, um, I notice the house is for sale,' I say, taking a large gulp of ice-cold Chablis, while he takes a swig from a bottle of craft beer.

Craft beer! Swigging from a bottle! What the hell is going on? It's as if David has been body-snatched.

'Yeah, we're moving to Cornwall.'

'*Cornwall?*' I almost choke on the wine and Fiona abandons the cupcakes to quickly thump me on the back.

'David wants to surf.' Taking my wine glass so I don't spill it, Fiona takes a large gulp herself.

'Wow, really? Amazing. Cornwall's stunning—' I catch her expression. Shit. No. Not Amazing. 'I mean, interesting.' I swiftly change adjectives. 'I didn't know you surfed.'

'I've just started learning,' he grins broadly, which in itself is quite something as I've never seen David look anything but serious. 'On our summer holidays there last year, I tried it for the first time and it was a totally life-changing experience. I swear, I found a freedom I've never felt before. It felt like a sign we had to change our lives.'

'Gosh.'

And there was me thinking I'd be under scrutiny. What was I worrying about a little thing like a broken engagement for? This was apocalyptic.

'David wants to resign from his partnership at one of London's top law firms, for me to give up my dream job at the museum, to sacrifice the children's private education, to up-end our lives, to leave our lovely home and move to the ends of the earth so he can devote his life to the waves.' Fiona says this all at once, without drawing breath. I can't make up my mind whether she's furious or panic-stricken. I decide on both.

341

'Really sorry, I'm going to have to shoot off.'

We're interrupted by Michelle, oblivious to the fact she's just walked into a Code Red situation, with David appearing to have his finger on the nuke button. I haven't seen Michelle for ages, not since the retreat, and as she gives her apologies to Fiona about some emergency with the suppliers and how running your own business means working weekends, I think how different she looks.

For as long as I can remember, Michelle always had a chaotic, fly-by-the-seat-of-your-pants-ness about her, with her messy hair and crumpled clothes and mountains of Tupperware filled with blueberries and rice cakes. But now she's pressed and blow-dried and carrying one of those tiny, Duchess of Cambridge-type clutch bags, that only have room for a lipstick and your phone. Talk about a transformation!

We quickly hug each other and I tell her she looks amazing; she tells me it's because she's finally lost the baby weight, to which I protest, because Michelle has always been tiny. She says she's sorry about the break-up; I say me too, which makes her hug me again.

'Promise me you'll come over for dinner,' she insists as she shoots out of the front door and hurries down the path to her waiting cab. I promise I will, though we both know I won't. She's always so busy now with the new business and I haven't spoken to Max since he helped me move back into my flat, apart from a few texts. I resolve to try and have a proper catch-up with him, as now Michelle is leaving, he'll be on pick-up duty.

After leaving Fiona deep in frantic discussions with David, I search for Holly, but she hasn't arrived yet, so make polite chit-chat with some of the other parents over a bowl of crisps and some crudités, until I'm inevitably unmasked as not being a parent, and one of them makes a joke about how I can have one of their moody teenagers.

'Thanks, but no thanks,' I laugh, as I think they were trying to make me feel better.

But now the dad of the moody teenager looks a bit put out.

'Well, actually, she's a good kid really and it is only a stage,' he says defensively.

'Right. Yes.' And now it's all a bit awkward. I reach for a carrot stick.

'She doesn't mean to be rude and ungrateful and shut herself in her bedroom and ignore us the whole time and make her mother cry,' he continues tensely, his voice getting louder and louder. 'And who wasn't drinking and smoking weed at that age?'

He looks to one of the other parents, who quickly takes up the baton. 'Absolutely, I was forever throwing up. I mean, honestly, vomit everywhere!'

On second thoughts, I decide against the humous.

Making my excuses, I head over to the presents table, which has been set up at the other side of the room. I've bought Izzy a gift, and am just digging it out of my bag to add to all the other brightly coloured packages, when I'm suddenly hijacked by Annabel.

'Hi, Nell!'

It had been fully my intention to avoid her, but she swoops up on me from behind like a fighter pilot in a satin dress and heels. She looks as if she's at a cocktail party in Mayfair, not a children's birthday party.

'How are you? How was LA?'

For a split second I consider ignoring her, then decide to face matters head on.

'Wonderful, thanks.' I force a bright smile. 'How was your fundraiser?'

ALEXANDRA POTTER

'Oh, you heard about that.' She pretends to look sheepish. 'I hope you didn't mind me inviting Eddie to be my plus one.'

I don't so much mind as want to murder her for making such a blatant play for my ex-fiancé.

However, I remain cool and calm. It's my pride really. I can't let her see she's getting to me.

'Not at all. So kind of you to think of him. Such a brilliant networking opportunity.'

She looks thrown off course. But swiftly recovers.

'Oh, my pleasure. He charmed everyone. And I had no idea he was such a good dancer!'

My smile has turned rictus. Edward has never danced with me. Well, maybe once, on NYE when we first got together, but you couldn't really call it dancing. More like drunken kissing and swaying. I feel suddenly discombobulated by the memory.

'Or how much we had in common. Both being divorced and single parents.'

I swear to God, there's no stopping her. She's like the Terminator.

'You must have had lots to talk about,' I say drily and make a move towards the gift table but I'm blocked by her resting a perfectly manicured hand on my arm in a ~~gloating~~ supportive gesture.

'By the way, I was really sorry to hear about the wedding being called off. Must have been such a blow.'

'Actually, it's been all very amicable.' I force an upbeat voice. 'We're still very good friends and love each other very much.' Well, if it's good enough for the Hollywood celebrities.*

'That's what I love about you, Nell. Always such a trooper.' She flashes me a huge smile. 'And what a wonderful attitude.

---

* Though I stop short of us both going on separate magical adventures.

344

Some women might have taken it personally. Especially with it being your second broken engagement.'

It's like a cartoon bubble appears above my head.

FORTY-SOMETHING FINALLY SNAPS
It was supposed to be a children's birthday party, say shocked partygoers, not a murder scene!

'I want you to know I'm always here. As both a friend and a life coach.'

I grit my teeth. 'Thanks, Annabel. Now, if you'll excuse me I've got Izzy's birthday present . . .'

Holding my gift, I turn my attention to trying to find a space for it on the table. Honestly you wouldn't believe how many gifts an eight-year-old gets these days. 'Wow, look at all these presents and cards . . .' My eyes sweep over all the dozens of packages wrapped in brightly coloured children's wrapping paper . . . and then land on a GIANT green bag with distinctive gold lettering that's taking up most of the room. 'Crikey, who bought something from Harrods?' I gasp.

'Oh, that one's from me and Clementine,' beams Annabel, stroking it like a pet.

I should've known.

'Didn't anyone ever tell you the best things come in small packages,' I quip, putting my little gift next to it, which looks TINY by comparison.

Annabel looks at me blankly.

'Oh, never mind,' I smile. I forgot. One thing Perfect Annabel doesn't have is a sense of humour. Which suddenly makes me feel a bit sorry for her. Because really, you can have everything, but without that, life can't be much fun.

Or even survivable. I mean, how do you even begin to get

through the tough, scary, darkest bits of life without being able to laugh in the face of it all?

'Sorry I'm late, I had a date with an electric razor.'

Turning, I see Holly. As she walks over to me, I see everyone's eyes fall upon her. She'd finally given up using the cold cap and, rather than spend several agonizing days watching her hair rapidly fall out, she's shaved her head and her baldness is visibly shocking. Yet, at the same time, I've never seen my friend look more beautiful.

'Nits,' she says loudly, to everyone in the kitchen, pretending not to look.

And boom – just like that – the mood lifts and I burst out laughing.

Unlike Annabel who looks stricken.

'No one mentioned anything about an outbreak.' Automatically she scratches her scalp.

'Relax, I'm joking.' Giving me a hug, Holly turns to her, smiling. 'I don't have nits. I have cancer, remember.'

Which causes Annabel to look like she wants the ground to swallow her up. 'Oh, um, yes . . . of course . . . silly me . . .' And I think I couldn't love my friend more.

'OK, so who's joining me on the bouncy castle?' Holly looks at me.

'Like you have to ask,' I smile.

'Right, come on then, why should the kids have all the fun.'

And looping her arm through mine, we leave Annabel standing by the gift table and go outside.

I'm grateful for:
1. *Holly, for being so brave. Afterwards she told me that shaving her head gave her back some sense of control and also a feeling of empowerment; by embracing her*

baldness she wanted to show her daughter, Olivia, there was no need to be afraid.

2. *Putting life in perspective; seriously, who cares about Annabel, the silly *?%!?!*
3. *Not swearing in front of the children.*
4. *NOT being a fly on the wall at Fiona and David's later.*
5. *Bouncy castles, who knew they were so much fun?*
6. *Izzy, for declaring me 'the coolest godmum' and telling me to 'keep jumping, Auntie Nell, KEEP JUMPING' and not to worry, 'because if you get knocked down, you just get up again'.*
7. *Life advice from an eight-year-old.*

Emergency Talks

The next day Fiona calls me. This is unusual. Fiona rarely calls. She always texts. When we were in our twenties we would chat for hours on the phone, but no one does that any more, do they? Who has the time? Or the partners that don't get annoyed at them being on the phone? When I lived with Edward, I was forever sitting on the loo, covertly WhatsApping.*

Luckily Cricket loves to chat. And then, of course, there's Mum. Though with Mum it's hard to get her *off* the phone.

Anyway, it appears This Is An Emergency and a text won't cut it.

'I think David is having a mid-life crisis.'

She calls me from the car on the way to do school pick-up.

'Is it because of the man bun?'

'No, it's not just the man bun, it's everything. He's still insisting we move to Cornwall to "rewild our lives".'

'Ooh, like that show on TV. I love that show.' I try to be positive.

However, Fiona is not in the mood for positive.

'Why can't he just take hormones like everyone else?' she demands.

'You're taking hormones?'

---

* Bathrooms, it seems, are big for secret phone calls. Look at Max, hiding from his kids.

'I've just started. My GP said it will help with the hot flushes and mood swings. You know, sometimes I just get these feelings of rage, but she said these will make me feel calm— No! Don't you dare cut me up!' There's a loud honking as she yells at a driver. 'Sorry, where was I?'

'Feeling calm.'

There's a heavy sigh on the other end of the phone. 'Look, don't get me wrong. I love Cornwall. It's beautiful. But our life is here in London. We can't just uproot it because he wants to take up surfing. He's being ridiculous and selfish—' She breaks off, sounding furious, before adding with a quiet frustration, 'He's not the only one to want something different, to be bored and want a bit of excitement.'

It's the way she says it. Without anger. Just honesty. And for the first time I feel genuinely worried.

'So what are you going to do?'

'I've suggested a couples therapist.'

'And what did he say?'

'He suggested *ayahuasca*.'

Which makes us both laugh, probably because neither of us knows what else to do, except laugh at it all, and I feel the mood lighten. It's like a reset.

'What about you and Edward?' she asks, after a few moments.

'There is no me and Edward,' I say simply.

'Really, Nell?' Fiona's voice is full of concern. 'You can't really mean that.'

Sitting at my laptop, I look across at a photo on my shelf. It's of me and Edward just after we first got together. I've put most of them away, but for some reason I kept this one out. I remember I made him do a selfie, despite his protestations, and we look so happy and carefree. I feel a beat of sadness. It feels like a million years ago. Like looking at two strangers.

'Maybe some people just aren't right for each other, after all.'

There's silence on the other end of the phone, then the sound of car doors opening and children's voices.

'Hi darlings, I'm on the phone to Auntie Nell, say hello . . .' There's a babble of noise from Izzy and her brother Lucas as I ask them questions about school, and then Fiona comes back on the phone. 'OK, I better go.'

Only after she hangs up, do I worry she might misinterpret what I said to be about her and David. I was talking about my own situation. So I send her a WhatsApp to try to explain. It's when I'm going to bed that I see the ticks turn blue and she replies.

> But that's the problem.

I watch her typing.

> I don't know what's right for me any more. Do you?

The Exhibition

I almost change my mind and don't go.

Friday evening and I've been getting ready for hours. I can't find anything to wear. It's not a date, but it feels like a date, and everything in my wardrobe is wrong. I want to look fashionably hip and cool, but everything I try on is either too revealing. Too job interview. Too trying to be sexy. Too *meh*.

I finally opt for high-waisted flares and a new neon jacket from the high street that delivers both sleeves *and* pockets – and Liza asks me to send her a selfie, so I take a photo in the full-length mirror in the bathroom.

Only it's less 'Felt cute. Might delete later' and more 'Feel completely ridiculous. Will delete pronto'. What was I thinking? It definitely looked cute on the model on the website, but everything looks cute when you're half my age and size. Just the other day I saw an amazing dress in a shop window, but when I tried it on I looked like a potato sack. It was only when I looked at the back of the shop window dummy, I realized they'd used bulldog clips to cinch in the waist and make everything perky and tight.

Alas, there are no bulldog clips in real life.

I look at my reflection. This neon jacket might be on trend but I feel like I should be working for the council and moving traffic cones.

Oh God. Maybe it's just easier to send my apologies and

forget the whole thing. After all, the exhibition is miles away, it's going to take me for ever to get there, I don't know anyone and Joe will probably be too busy to talk to me. Liza texts in the middle of me falling down the rabbit hole of finding excuses not to go. I tell her I've changed my mind. She sends a firm text back.

> Go. At least you don't have swollen ankles the size of elephants.

And a smiley face emoji. I reply with a bicep emoji and console myself that at least I still have biceps in emoji land.

In the end I ditch the heels for trainers, wipe off most of the make-up (I followed a tutorial online to achieve a 'strong brow' but there's strong and there's Groucho Marx) and let my hair loose. I don't want to look like I've made a huge effort, when clearly I've made a huge effort.

The exhibition is in a gallery in a Hackney warehouse and it takes several tubes, a bus and a lot of walking. I'm thankful I wore my trainers. In fact, I can't remember a time when I *wasn't* thankful I've worn my trainers (note to self: give all my high heels away, they are instruments of torture). The address is hard to find, down a narrow back street that eventually leads to a graffitied door. I almost walk right past it when abruptly it opens and someone steps outside to light up a cigarette and I hear a waft of music and chatter coming from inside.

Summoning up my courage, I push open the door and enter. It's a large space. Exactly how you imagine an art gallery exhibition in an East End warehouse to be. Industrial windows, exposed brick, white blank canvas walls hung with artwork, around which lots of people are milling, holding glasses of wine. I notice a lot of hats and statement glasses and what fashion shoots always call bold accessories. I watch a group of Beautiful People having their photo taken by an official photographer. I bet no one deletes those later.

Everyone looks desperately young and achingly cool and my confidence, which has been threatening mutiny the whole way here, nearly deserts me and I almost bolt for the door. But somethings stops me. When has not fitting in ever held me back before?

I'm suddenly reminded of when I first met Cricket. That feeling of being alone, of feeling different to all my friends, of walking past all those houses on my birthday, me on the outside, looking in on everyone on the inside. And I remember how she gave me the courage to embrace that, how she showed me how great the view from the outside can be.

And so I grab a drink and circulate and end up having a lovely time chatting to Ziggy, Bowie and Hendrix, who are all really sweet and funny and interesting and, I'm guessing, have parents who really love music.

'Nell. You came.'

I turn to see Joe at my elbow, smiling warmly. He's casually dressed in jeans and a linen shirt. He looks pleased to see me.

'Hi. Yes.' I smile back, doubts instantly evaporating.

'Let me get you a drink.' He looks at the glass in my hand which is already empty.

'Thanks. White wine please.'

As he busies himself getting drinks I get the chance to observe him. He's taller than I remembered. Broader. Someone walks over and pats him on the back. He turns, smiling, as they try to engage him. He's holding two glasses. One for me. One for him. He glances over, briefly, as if to say *sorry*. My stomach flutters, unexpectedly.

He returns a few moments later and passes me my wine. 'Sorry about that.'

'You're very popular,' I say, taking a sip. It's warm. For the first time in my life I don't care about ice.

'Nah. Not me.' He shakes his head. 'They all want to talk about Sam's art.' He gestures around the room, at the artwork. 'Can I give you a guided tour?'

'Yes. Please,' I nod, glancing around at the huge canvases with their bold colours and large graphics. 'I'm afraid I don't know much about art.'

'Neither do I.' He grins. 'But I'll do my best.'

We walk slowly around the exhibition, pausing in front of each piece of artwork so he can explain the inspiration, subject matter and different techniques used.

'Wow, this one's incredible,' I gasp.

'This depicts two nudes using wet and dry mixed media . . . newspaper clippings, old postcards, rolls of film negatives, over which were painted layers of acrylic, oils, even crayon . . .'

'Hang on, I thought you didn't know much about art,' I protest and he laughs modestly.

'I think it must have gone in by osmosis. Being around my sister, she was passionate . . .'

His eyes meet mine. We're in a warehouse full of people but it feels bizarrely intimate. His hand lightly brushes against the bottom of my spine to lead me on to the next painting and my breath seems to catch in the back of my throat. Hang on, is something going on here?

'Hey, congratulations man, I just heard.'

We're interrupted by a loud voice and I turn to see a guest go to shake Joe's hand. 'Can't wait to see you in the West End.'

'Thanks.' Joe looks bemused as his hand is pumped enthusiastically.

'Are you going to tell me that was about your sister's art too?' I ask a few moments later, as he's finally released and we move on to a new set of paintings.

'He's an old friend. He heard I got a part.' He shrugs like it's nothing.

'In the West End?' I repeat and he looks abashed.

'Look, tonight's supposed to be about my sister. It's Sam's evening.'

'So you're an actor?'

'Yeah, though I retired from acting a while ago. After the success of my TV show, things got a little crazy, I needed some time out.'

'You had a TV show?' I look at him curiously and when he tells me the name I shake my head. 'I was living in the States then, I never saw it.'

'That's why you don't recognize me,' he laughs then blushes. 'Though it's probably the extra weight and the beard.'

'I didn't realize you were an actor.'

'I go by a different stage name so you wouldn't find me on Google.'

I feel my face flush.

'I don't know about you, but that's the first thing I do when I meet someone,' he confides, grinning.

'Me? No. Never,' I frown, shaking my head and as he laughs loudly, I can't help feeling a connection.

'To be honest, I haven't worked in a long time. I got disillusioned with the industry. Sam's death made me want to try again.' He pauses in reflection, then looks at me and smiles. 'So are you going to come and see me?'

'Of course,' I nod. 'Which play?'

'A Paris Raincoat. It's Monty Williamson's last play. Well, it's sort of his first really, he wrote most of it when he lived in Paris in the fifties . . .'

And now I'm staring at him in disbelief.

'I'm the lead.'

'No way.'

'What? You don't think I'm leading man material?'

'No, it's not that.' My mind flicks backwards, to that day at the newspaper, Cricket telling me they'd finally found their actor. 'I'm best friends with the playwright's widow. I wrote his obituary. I helped edit that play . . .'

'You're kidding.'

'No.' And now I'm grinning. 'Wow, that's crazy. What a coincidence.'

Joe's mouth curls up with amusement, like he's just heard something funny.

'Did nobody ever tell you? There's no such thing as a coincidence.'

I'm grateful for:
1. *His Wikipedia page; now I have the right acting name (Lloyd G Joseph instead of Joe Lloyd), it throws up lots of fascinating information, for example:*
    (i) *He was in a hit TV show but turned his back on fame and hasn't worked in a decade.*
    (ii) *His sister was the celebrated painter, Samantha Davies, winner of the prestigious Lyons Prize. Fiercely private, Davies was determined her success should be independent of her brother's and never spoke publicly of her famous connection.*
    (iii) *He's never been married and has no children.*
    (iv) *He's currently single.*

The Mother of All Dilemmas

Today is Mother's Day. As usual I ring Mum, who is thrilled with her card and flowers. As usual I send both from me and my little brother Rich. When he was single he always conveniently forgot; now he's married and a dad, it's a different excuse.

'Sorry, sis, but I've just so much to organize. I've got to make a glitter-glue card and breakfast in bed and organize flowers and take Evie to the park so Nathalie gets to lie in . . . I mean, you've no idea. Mother's Day is exhausting!'

I don't point out that every day is probably exhausting for Nathalie, who's a stay-at-home mum.

After getting off the phone to mum, I go to dial Cricket. Unlike the rest of my friends, she doesn't have kids, so we usually spend the day together. Even after Edward and I got together; it's become something of a ritual. We always do something fun; one year we went to a life drawing class, and got rather more than I bargained for. Put it this way, it was a *lot* more than a handmade glitter-glue card.

But in the middle of dialling her number, I pause. The significance of the day isn't lost on me. It's already three months since Edward and I broke up and I still haven't made any big decisions. For weeks now it had been going around and around in my head; I have been thinking about it, but not doing anything. And yet, if I wanted to be a mother, what was stopping me? What was I waiting for? The right man? The right time?

Because of course, it's never the right time. There's always a good reason to wait or an obstacle to get over. There was the trip to LA and Liza's wedding. Moving back into the flat. The new column. *Life*. I've been so busy, dealing with so many things, I haven't had the time or headspace to deal with such a huge life decision.

Except, in recent weeks I've caught myself wondering if they are reasons, or just excuses. I read stories about women who will go to any length to be a mother, for whom it's all they've ever wanted, ever since they were little girls, and while I'm happy for them, I'm confused for me. I don't recognize myself in these stories. Where are the women like me? The ones for whom it was a lot more complicated.

There are so many different ways to live a life. I look at my friends with their children and then I look at Cricket. Both are happy in their choices; there is no right and wrong, whatever society might like to try and tell us. Because of course, everyone has an opinion about it. Frankly, judging by the media headlines, I don't know how women find the time to do anything, when we're supposed to be busy freezing eggs, looking hot in a bikini, giving birth, but not leaving it too late, or starting too early, while smashing it at our careers and baking gluten-free brownies.

As a teenager, I was taught at school that a pregnancy would ruin my life and I was terrified. In my twenties, busy trying to climb the work ladder, afford my rent and date all the wrong men, having kids was part of some far-distant grown-up future; in my thirties, as friends got married and started having babies, I was still trying to find the guy whilst trying not to panic. Then finally I'd met Ethan and we tried and failed. And then I was terrified again, but in a different way.

When I fell in love with Edward, I also fell in love with

my life. Yet, still I feel confused. I thought I'd made peace with my choice, but then suddenly there it was, the unexpected item in the baggage area.

To be honest, I wish it hadn't been. It's caused my relationship to fall apart and endless sleepless nights. Moreover, I'm still plagued with doubts. Did I throw away something wonderful, for something I might never have? After all, I'd tried and failed to have a baby. Could I dare to try again? More importantly, deep down, is that what I really wanted? Was it desire I was feeling or the fear of regret?

And lying awake at night, I blink back tears in the darkness, a voice whispering in the very heart of me. *Was it a future baby I wanted, or the baby I lost?*

A wise friend once told me that it's OK, you don't *have* to know. You don't have to know how you feel, or what you want. But one thing I do know is I can't deny the feelings that were triggered that day in the bathroom when I held Simone's positive pregnancy test. Because it wasn't just the loss and the grief that came rushing back, it was something even more painful; it was all that hope and longing. And sitting here now on Mother's Day, it finally hits me.

Fear.

Fear is what's been stopping me. Fear made me try to bury my feelings. Fear stopped me telling Edward about my miscarriage. Fear made me avoid thinking about motherhood. I just wanted it to all go away. For so long I've been so scared of having to go there again, of having to face up to a lot of stuff I thought I'd let go of. All that grief and hope and loss. But eventually you reach a point, where you can't live in fear any longer.

So instead of calling Cricket, I sit down at my little kitchen table, open my laptop and go online. I need to shine a light into that darkness. To start being brave and stop being scared.

To stop avoiding. I'm going to do some research, speak to some people, explore my options, arm myself with the facts . . . and then do what feels right.

I pause, my mind racing ahead. I don't know what comes next. What discoveries and decisions I'll make. And that's OK. Because what I've realized is what I want most of all is to have the choice. As a woman, isn't that all we want when it comes to having kids or not? *A choice.*

I'm grateful for:
1. *Getting an appointment at one of London's leading fertility clinics next month. First things first, I need to find out if I can even have a baby. After all, I'm not getting any younger, and with my age and history, the odds are stacked against me.*
2. *The woman at the adoption agency who is super nice and books me in for their next virtual information event. Liza was right, there are lots of ways to be a mum, not just the traditional ones, and I want to explore my options. After all, life has never been quite how I imagined it was going to be, so why would motherhood be any different?*
3. *Spending a wonderful Mother's Day at Kenwood Ladies' pond with Cricket, who isn't a mother, but as an eighty-something in a bathing suit on a freezing cold day in March, is a goddam ass-kicking superwoman.*
4. *All the amazing mums out there doing an incredible job, including my own, and all those mothering in so many different ways.*
5. *The dictionary definition of mothering, which is being caring, loving and kind. Today can be difficult for so many, so today, I do that to myself.*

Fast Forward

Why is it that celebrities can move on so quickly in the relationship stakes? One minute they're getting married and talking about their undying love and how they've found The One, and the next they're splitting up and they're single for, like, two minutes and they've found another soulmate.

Today I went to the hairdressers and while she was covering my head in tinfoil and I was trying not to look at my reflection (oh the agony of having to stare at yourself for two hours in overhead lighting, wearing a severe black cape; is it just me, or are hairdresser's mirrors *the worst*?), I flicked through a few gossip magazines.

I mean, seriously, celebrities are literally tripping over soulmates in the street! Oooh, be careful, mind your step, or you'll bump into another true love.

I can't keep up. Engagement rings are flying around left, right and centre. Twitter spats are exploding. Cryptic Instagram posts abound with quotations about moving on and seizing the day and #feelingempowered. Then before you know it they're coupled up again, getting married and having a baby! It's like life on fast forward.

Meanwhile I haven't remotely moved on. Joe called today but I missed his call. He left a voicemail, thanking me for coming to the exhibition and asking if I'd like to have dinner at his friend's new pop-up. 'I know I'm biased, but the food's out of this world.'

I haven't called him back yet, as I don't know what to say. I'm both flattered and confused. I like Joe. He's cool and interesting and handsome. I mean, honestly, what's not to like? The other night I thought I felt something; that said, it could have been the copious amount of warm white wine. And yet, I'm just not in *that* place. I'm still licking my wounds and trying to sort out my head. Good job I'm not a celebrity. I'd be hopeless. I am not seizing my dreams and jumping into bed with someone else whilst getting matching tattoos. Maybe I should?*

---

* Not the matching tattoos part *obviously*.

Dear Confessions:
I feel so much pressure.
Is this normal? Help!

Our new advice column about love, life and everything in between, for any woman who wonders why life isn't quite how she imagined it was going to be.

NELL STEVENS (a forty-something f**k-up) AND
CRICKET WILLIAMSON (her eighty-something BFF)
THE SUNDAY MAGAZINE

Hi and welcome. In this, our first column, we talk about feeling under pressure – and no, it's not a catchy David Bowie song. Our letter this week is from a woman in her twenties who is feeling a huge amount of pressure from her parents to settle down and get married. But she's not alone. We've also received similar letters from readers in their thirties, forties, fifties and beyond, who are also experiencing huge amounts of pressure, but in lots of different ways. For once, it seems age is truly irrelevant.

Because pressure has no age limit – and we should know, as one of us is in their eighties and still feeling it! All through life there are those boxes you're supposed to tick. It starts when you're a baby with milestones that send panicked parents to the paediatrician. You have to walk at a certain age. Talk at a certain age. Ride a bike. Do long division. Read a word, then a sentence, then a whole book. Pass exams. Go to college. Graduate with a good degree. Find The One. Get married. Have babies. A successful career. A nice house. A designer kitchen. A great sex life. An empty laundry basket. A set of abs.

It's just exhausting. No wonder we want to lie down. *But no, get up!* You should be out there living your best life! Setting challenges, and running marathons and learning a new language. Which of course, means you're constantly doubting your own life and your own choices. Am I doing it wrong? Am I getting it right? Should I be doing more? Is this enough? You can't be lolling on the sofa, or in an OK relationship, or pulled over on the hard shoulder of life, trying to figure things out.

Nell says: Pressure comes at us from all angles. It's like being in a video game and we're constantly being fired at by our personal life, our work environment and, of course, the voice in our head. Expectations, ambitions, responsibilities, comparisons. In recent years social media has put a huge pressure on people to have these seemingly perfect lives, which is why I started my podcast, to tell it like it really is. For me, anyway. Case in point, a few months ago I was supposed to be getting married and felt under such pressure to plan the perfect wedding and be the perfect bride, but sadly it all ended in disaster.

Cricket says: I was expected to lead a conventional life as a wife and a mother, but I fought back to become an actress and resisted marriage until I was in my seventies. But still it doesn't stop. Now, in my eighties, if it's not the pressure to get over the loss of my late husband, it's to be doing the splits. I keep seeing videos on Facebook of women my age skateboarding and practising gymnastics. Apparently they're supposed to be inspirational. I have a different word for them but apparently it's unprintable in a national newspaper.

Our advice: Pressure is everywhere, but that doesn't make it right. Learn to say no. Have the courage of your convictions. Take the path you want to take. Follow your heart and no one else's. Remember #livingyourbestlife is different for everyone. So stop scrolling. Open a bottle of wine or put the kettle on. Call a friend. Stroke a dog. Loosen those trousers. Oh, and f**k the splits.

Wednesday Evening

It's just after 8 p.m. and I'm lying on the sofa with Arthur, reading – and no, it's not a book, but the online comment section underneath our first column. It's a few days now since it came out but it's taken me this long to pluck up courage to read them. I've been super nervous about the response. After all, everyone knows about the dreaded keyboard warriors. But so far, most of them are really lovely and positive, and the only brutal one I read is from **Ihatetheworld** so I'm not taking it too personally.

Better still, Sadiq just texted to say his editor is really pleased.

> Well done, Nell, seems you're not such a fuck-up. Please pass on
> the congrats to Cricket.

I pick up my phone to call Cricket to tell her the good news. We spoke earlier. She'd just finished FaceTiming with Jack – they FaceTime quite regularly now – and was popping out to the shops, as she was out of maraschino cocktail cherries.

As you do.

But just as I'm about to dial her number, my phone starts ringing and I see she's calling me. Isn't it funny how that often happens?

'Great minds think alike,' I laugh, as I pick up. 'I was just about to call you.'

'Is that Nell?'

I'm expecting to hear Cricket laughing at the coincidence, but instead it's an unfamiliar male voice.

'Er, yes – who's this?'

'You don't know me.'

I feel a sudden alarm. 'Why have you got Cricket's phone?' My mind suddenly throws up the memory of a man standing outside her window and her fears of having a stalker. I'd dismissed her, saying it was just a dog walker, but what if I was wrong?

'Cricket? I'm calling from Catherine's phone.'

It takes a moment to register. Of course, her real name.

'Is she OK?'

'I'm afraid she's had an accident. She's fallen. She was unconscious when I found her outside her flat, so I called an ambulance—'

'Oh my God.' Shocked, I sit bolt upright on the sofa. I feel a cold-blooded panic.

'The paramedics have just arrived. They're going to take her to a local hospital . . .'

'Right . . . yes.'

'I called the last person she spoke to on her phone.'

'I'll be right there.' Standing up, I start moving around my flat . . . keys . . . shoes . . . coat . . . pulling it on, my mind kicks in. 'Sorry, who is this, who am I talking to?'

I feel the person on the end of the line hesitate before they answer.

'I'm Theo . . . Monty's son.'

APRIL

#noonegetsoutofherealive

No Bones Broken

A lot's happened since that phone call.

Immediately afterwards I jumped in an Uber to the hospital. My mind was all over the place. It didn't make sense. Monty didn't have a son. But I couldn't think about that now. All I could think about was Cricket. It brought back painful memories of Dad and his accident and how we'd nearly lost him. I don't remember much of the journey. Only that I felt the same fear. And the kind words of my driver.

'It's my friend. She's had a fall,' I said to him.

'Don't worry. The NHS is wonderful. They'll take good care of your friend.'

His eyes met mine in the rear-view. I nodded in agreement, grateful for his attempt to reassure me; a total stranger who just got in the back of his car, white-faced and scared.

The thing is, Cricket was my friend. My vibrant, witty, fearless friend, who wore silver plimsolls and dungarees and a leopard-print bicycle helmet and loved true-crime podcasts, and cocktail hour and taking risks. With her outrageous taste in interior decoration, graffitied coffin and rebellious spirit, she refused to be hemmed in or labelled by any of society's normal parameters.

But she was also eighty-something.

I never thought about it when we were together. It was just a number. Isn't that what they say? Cricket wasn't old. Not like the frail, elderly people you see with their stooped shoulders and shuffling walks and fading memories. And yet, she hadn't fallen, she'd had a fall. At what age does that change? Just saying it felt like a betrayal. Only old people have A Fall.

On arrival at the hospital the nurse at reception asked me if I was her daughter and when I said no she said something about her next of kin. I told her I was her in case of emergency person, she told me about hospital regulations. I think I started crying at that point. A mixture of panic and frustration. Please. I just want to see her. To know she's OK. It's the not knowing, that's always the worst. The space in between. That's when the real fear gets you. When your mind goes to places it shouldn't. When you feel like you can't breathe.

'Nell?'

And that's when I turned and saw him. An older man, late fifties, maybe sixty; his dark hair greying at his temples, the distinctive nose and cleft in his chin. He looked just like the photograph of Monty that Cricket kept on her mantelpiece of when they'd first met. That was in black and white and the man before me was in colour, but there was no mistaking the resemblance.

'I'm Theo. The person who found Catherine and called you.'

'Hi.'

We both take a moment to take each other in. I have so many questions swirling around in my head, but for now they have to wait.

'I came to look for you.'

'Where is she?'

'They've taken her up for a CT scan of her brain.' I must have shown the shock on my face, as he reached out and placed his hand on my arm in support. 'Don't worry. They know what they're doing.'

'What happened?'

'We don't know yet.'

'But she's going to be fine, isn't she?'

With his hand still on my arm, his eyes met mine. I knew he couldn't answer that question even as I was asking it.

'Look, why don't you sit down, I'll get us some bad coffee.' He managed a smile. It was just like the one in the photograph and, unexpectedly, I felt reassured.

'OK.'

Time slowed and dragged. We drank a lot of bad coffee. And we waited. The hands on the clock barely moving. Until finally after midnight a doctor appeared and shook our hands with the kind of professional sensitivity that makes your heart stop. The results were sobering. Brain scans had shown that Cricket had suffered a transient ischaemic attack. The doctor called it a TIA or 'mini stroke' and said it was caused by a temporary disruption in the blood supply to part of the brain. He thought it must have happened when she was leaving her flat, causing her to lose her balance and fall down the front steps and onto her path.

'From what we can gather she lay there quite a while, until she was discovered by a passer-by who called the ambulance.'

I think I broke down at that bit. Thinking of Cricket, lying alone and injured, while I sat obliviously at home in my safe, warm, flat. It was too much to bear.

'Hey, come on –' Theo squeezed my arm '– it's no one's fault.' He turned to the doctor. 'I was the person who called the ambulance.'

'Sorry, yes . . .' The doctor pinched the top of his nose, circling his fingers underneath his glasses and down the sides of his face. He looked exhausted. When someone you love is rushed to the hospital, the world shrinks. You feel as if it's

371

ALEXANDRA POTTER

only happening to you, but hospitals are full of frightened friends and relatives. We were just one case in many that the doctor was dealing with that evening.

'It was lucky you were passing. Especially with this unusual cold snap; temperatures are due to drop below freezing tonight.'

I glanced at Theo. He gave nothing away but now I was suddenly reminded of the figure that Cricket said she saw standing under the streetlamp, watching the flat, her reports that she thought someone was following her.

'Was that you?'

'I'm sorry?'

I realized I'd spoken aloud and both the doctor and Theo were looking at me. I shook my head. 'Nothing. I mean. Yes. Lucky.'

'The good news is that while the symptoms are similar to a stroke, a TIA doesn't last as long, the effects last a few minutes to a few hours and tend to fully resolve themselves within twenty-four hours.'

I feel a wave of relief. 'So she can come home?'

'We're going to keep her in tonight for observation, but all being well she should be able to go home tomorrow. Fortunately for Mrs Williamson, there are no bones broken. Which, considering her age, is quite something.'

'She is quite something,' I say and the doctor's solemn expression gives way to a smile.

'Clearly,' he agrees and I feel a sudden fierce pride for my friend. 'Now, if you just want to wait here for a few minutes, I'll get someone to come and take you to where she's resting.'

And now we're here in the ward and the nurse is drawing back the curtains and the first thing I see are the bruises. Large, angry purple ones on her temple and her cheeks.

372

'I bet I look like I've been in the wars, don't I?' Lying in bed, in a hospital gown, Cricket grimaces and puts a hand up to her face. I notice the cut on her lip and gash on her wrist. 'They won't let me look in the mirror.'

'You look fabulous.' I quickly reach for her hand, careful to mind the cannula and drips, squeezing it tightly, feeling her fingers in mine, the rush of relief that she's still here.

'They said I'd fallen.'

'Yes, I know, we spoke to the doctor, he explained everything, you're going to be just fine.' I try quickly to reassure her.

'We?' Cricket cocks her head slightly, trying to see Theo, who's hanging back behind me. We'd both agreed not to say anything about his claim to be Monty's son, now was not the right time, it would be too much of a shock. Not that I knew any of the circumstances. I'd been too worried about Cricket to ask him about any of the details or even what he was doing outside her flat.

'This is Theo. The man who found you and called the ambulance, he wanted to make sure you were OK.'

I don't know why I thought we could hide it from her, when it was so obvious to me. But as he steps forward to say hello, her face is transformed, like when you find the person you thought you'd lost in a crowd and would never see again.

There's a pause, but finally she speaks.

'Lovely to meet you, Theo.'

Theo

Life is funny. Some weeks you just trundle along, not much happening. Others, it's like you pack an entire lifetime of emotions into one day. Yesterday was one such day.

I'm still trying to process it all as I take Arthur for his morning walk. It's now April, but it's still unseasonably cold. Winter has outstayed its welcome, like one of those annoying guests at a party who don't know when to leave, and is ignoring the signs of birdsong and flowers. It's early in the morning and I'm wearing fingerless gloves and drinking hot coffee that I made at home, while Arthur runs ahead on his lead, sniffing in bushes and barking at squirrels, impervious to the temperature in his thick fur coat.

But my head is elsewhere. With each footstep, my mind spools backwards in time to the early sixties as I replay Theo's story, his voice filling my head . . .

'My mother worked front of house at the Theatre Royal in Brighton; they met when he was touring with one of his plays and they had a brief affair. Apparently it was only some weeks after they'd broken up and the play had moved on that she discovered she was pregnant.'

Cricket is back home, and yesterday Theo had paid a visit to her flat. This time he didn't have to loiter outside under the lamppost, being mistaken for a stalker, but was invited inside.

'Did she ever tell him she was pregnant?' I asked, so Cricket doesn't have to.

'No.' As Theo shook his head, I felt relief this wasn't something Monty had known about and kept from Cricket. They hadn't met until decades later, but still. 'My mother was already married with a son, my older brother Julian. She and Dad agreed between them that he would bring me up as his own and nothing more would be said of it. It was 1962. Things were different then.'

'So how did you find out?'

Theo gave a small smile, almost an apology. 'I look nothing like my dad, or my brother. We were close, but I was so different to them, sometimes I would wonder . . .'

It was late afternoon and the three of us were all sitting together in Cricket's living room. Weak sunshine was filtering through large sash windows, catching the chandelier and bouncing prisms of light off the silver-framed photographs of Monty displayed on the mantelpiece.

I watched as Theo's eyes flicked towards them and wondered how strange it must be to see your face reflected back at you. Their likeness was quite staggering.

'After both my parents died I was clearing out their house and found some old photographs and newspaper cuttings, there were a few from the production of the play, taken in the theatre, Mum in her uniform, front of house, pictured with the playwright, Monty Williamson . . .' He trailed off, almost embarrassed.

'The resemblance was undeniable, so I showed them to my aunt, my mum's sister, and that's when she told me the truth.'

I glanced at Cricket, who has been sitting across from him on the velvet sofa, studying him while he spoke. Initially I'd been worried about how she'd react to these revelations, but their meeting at the hospital had been remarkable for its sense of inevitability. 'You always wonder,' she'd said simply, after they'd been introduced. 'It was the sixties . . . And then when I saw you. It was like seeing Monty again.'

Now with the story laid before her, I waited for her reaction. Her stoicism in the face of unexpected events has never ceased to amaze me and yet I was still both nervous and fiercely protective. I didn't want her to be upset.

'I was worried about intruding, after all these years, I wondered if I should let it lie, sleeping dogs and all that . . .' continued Theo.

'No such thing as sleeping dogs,' she replied without missing a beat. Their eyes met, but I couldn't read her expression. 'So you decided to become my stalker.'

'Good Lord, is that what you thought?' Theo looked appalled. 'I'm sorry if I scared you, that wasn't my intention at all.'

'Dear boy, I'm only teasing. Forgive me.' Reaching across, Cricket patted his corduroy knee, which was as unexpected as it was amusing, considering now we'd discovered Theo was actually sixty. 'To intrude is to be unwelcome and you are very much welcome.'

She smiled then, a slow smile that reached her eyes, and let her hand remain for a few moments, like you do with a treasured belonging that you don't want to misplace. Initially surprised, Theo relaxed and seemed to gain confidence.

'I discovered his obituary and read about his widow, but I wasn't sure if me turning up out of the blue would be welcome or not. I didn't want anyone jumping to the wrong conclusions—'

'The wrong conclusions being you're after my money?' said Cricket bluntly, and Theo blushed with embarrassment. 'Well, that's lucky, because I'm afraid there's not an awful lot left in the coffers.'

'Please, let me reassure you, that wasn't my intention at all, I just needed to get a sense of the situation, of what kind of person you were . . .'

'And did you?'

He smiled then. 'Not everyone would welcome a secret lovechild turning up out of the blue.'

'Cricket isn't everyone,' I interjected, finding my voice. I couldn't help it, and Theo nodded.

'I can see that,' he said and Cricket pretended to bat away the compliment, but I could tell she was secretly pleased.

'What was your mother's name?' she asked a few moments later.

'Betty. Betty Foster.'

Cricket nodded in acknowledgement, then looked down at the arm of the sofa, smoothing the worn velvet with the flat of her hand. She looked deep in thought.

'My husband had quite the reputation you know. He was an incorrigible flirt. He loved women his whole life.' She paused, her fingers tracing the rope stitching on the seam, her mind casting back. She'd once told me the sofa was one of the first things they'd bought when they first met. They'd disagreed on it, as they disagreed on many things, but there it still remained, all these years later, and loved, despite its flaws, like so many things in life.

'I'm surprised there haven't been more of you, Theo, but I'm so very glad there is one of you . . .' She looked up and smiled. 'And I'm sure he was completely taken with your mother during their time together. The sixties were a lively time, but he was never mean, or unkind, he would never have wanted to cause her distress.'

'That's very kind of you . . . under the circumstances,' said Theo quietly.

Witnessing this exchange, I couldn't help but be reminded

377

of the campaign to #bekind but how, behind the public hashtag and the posturing, it's so often forgotten in daily life. And yet here is Cricket, the very personification of it.

'I'm just sad that you never got to meet him, and he never got to meet you.'

Up until this moment, there had been a detachment to Theo as he told his story, most likely born from necessity, but now he looked emotional.

'Monty had secrets, but you would never have been one of them.' Cricket's gaze was as unwavering as her voice. 'He would have been so proud to be your father.'

A look of gratitude flooded Theo's face, and he took a deep exhale. 'Thank you.'

'You have nothing to thank me for,' replied Cricket, without missing a beat. 'I'm the one that should be thanking you. If you hadn't have found me, goodness knows what would have happened.'

'You found each other,' I say and they both turn to me. By their expressions, it's obvious they'd forgotten I was even in the room.

There's a pause and then they both smiled.

'Yes,' they both replied, looks passing between each other; two strangers with so much in common, brought together by an unbreakable bond. 'Yes, I suppose we did.'

No One Gets Out of Here Alive

'I feel like I'm on CCTV.'

'It's for your own safety.'

'What do you think I'm going to do? Shoplift my own silver spoons?'

It's only been a couple of days, but playing nurse to Cricket is proving difficult. Before she was discharged from hospital, the doctor had made enquiries about her living arrangements. On discovering she lived alone, he'd suggested visits from social services. There'd even been talk of sheltered housing.

'Over my dead body!'

Cricket, unsurprisingly, had not taken the suggestion well.

'Well, hopefully not, Mrs Williamson,' joked the doctor, in an attempt to appease her. 'As long as you take your prescription for blood thinners, you should be fine.'

But Cricket was not for appeasing. She was thankful and grateful to all the amazing NHS staff who had taken care of her, but she was also independent and strong-willed. What journalists, when interviewing someone of the older generation, often describe, quite patronizingly I always think, as 'quite a character'.

In other words, they've still got all their marbles and no one is going to come along and start telling them what to do. Either that, or bloody-minded.

So at the advice of the doctor, I've installed a couple of those little security cameras, one in the living and one in the bedroom, and downloaded the app on my phone. This way I can remotely keep an eye on her and check she's OK and hasn't fallen or anything.

'It's just a precaution, that's all. In case you run into any trouble,' I say, climbing down the stepladder, screwdriver in hand.

'Chance would be a fine thing,' she tuts.

'Where should I put this?' I gesture to the ladder.

'Behind the cocktail cabinet.' She gestures into the far corner of the dining room, where her coffin stands upright, its shelves displaying champagne coupes and, rather aptly, I can't help thinking, a selection of spirits. 'Though I might be making use of that soon enough.'

'Nonsense. The doctor said you were fine,' I say dismissively, handing her the screwdriver as I fold up the stepladder.

'But for how long?' She looks at me squarely. 'I'm not getting any younger.'

'I thought you said I shouldn't worry about getting older,' I challenge.

'Who said anything about me being worried?' Putting the screwdriver away in the small, metal toolbox, she turns to me. 'From where I'm standing, you're the one that's worried about me. I'm just being realistic. I'm in my eighties.'

'So?' I'm defiant.

Her face softens, a mixture of fondness and pragmatism, the face of someone telling you something you don't want to hear.

'None of us gets out of here alive, Nell.'

She looks at me and I feel that familiar wrench of anxiety that I'd felt that night at the hospital. Over the last few days I'd tried to put it to the back of my mind. Cricket was fine. It wasn't a stroke, it was a 'mini' one. With blood thinners and some recuperation, she would be fine. But truthfully, I was shaken. And yes, we all know that there are no guarantees in life. I knew that more than most; I write obituaries for a living. I wrote an obituary for Samantha, Joe's sister, and she wasn't even forty.

But the fact remained that one of my best friends was eighty-something, and you didn't need to look far to see that stuff happens in your eighties. Worse still, unless it's a loved one, no one is particularly shocked if someone elderly dies. People express their condolences and talk about how they lived a good life, as if it's plenty long enough, but it's not. Not by half. And especially not when it's your best friend that you can't imagine life without.

'Well, just try not to die any time soon, OK?' I say firmly.

'Roger that.' She gives me a mock salute. 'And you mustn't fuss. I'm not going to be on my own the whole time, I'm expecting a visitor.'

'Theo, again?'

'No, he's back home with his family in Bristol, but we plan to keep in touch. I want to go through some of Monty's things . . . for him to have something . . .' She trails off then, her mind going somewhere.

Earlier we'd spoken about Theo, about him turning up like that, out of the blue, but if I'd been expecting Cricket to privately admit her shock to me, it never came. To be honest, knowing Cricket, I wasn't surprised. I don't think I've ever seen her shocked by anything.

'Monty had a whole other life before he ever met me, and I did too,' she'd said simply. 'It changes nothing about what we had together. I'm just sad for Theo. He never got to know how wonderful his father was. He looks just like him, you know,' she added, then chuckled. 'I wonder if he has his terrible temper, too? Did I ever tell you about the time he threw a whole camembert out of the window in France?'

And then along with the laughter came the tears, which

381

reminded me of when the sun is shining and it starts to rain, and how life can be both good and sad. After which she blew her nose and wiped her eyes and we smiled at each other. And I thought, this is when the rainbow appears.

'Jack is coming to visit.'

'He is?' I snap back.

'Well, I finally told him about . . . what happened.' Cricket still can't bring herself to say the word. 'Of course he got all beating of chest and wanted to jump on a plane and come to my rescue. Honestly,' she tuts. 'He still thinks he's in the movies.'

But while she's acting all irritated, I can tell she's flattered.

'I told him firmly that I didn't need to be rescued, but it would be quite nice to have company. He arrives from Los Angeles on Friday.'

'Well that's great.'

I'm delighted for my friend and she smiles, looking pleased at my approval, but I can't help noticing she touches her wedding ring, absently twisting it with her fingers like worry beads.

'No one will ever replace Monty.'

She says it more as a statement, out loud, as if to both reassure and defend herself.

'I know,' I nod and our eyes meet.

'But meeting Jack again, it was so unexpected. It felt like a gift.' She looks faintly embarrassed then. 'And who returns gifts?'

'Well, once I got some windscreen wipers. I wouldn't have minded, but I didn't have a car,' I say and she hoots with laughter.

I feel the tension release, like air out of a balloon.

'So, tell me, how's our leading man?' she asks, easing herself down on the sofa. She's still a little bruised from the fall.

'I wouldn't know, I haven't called him back yet,' I reply, joining her. Earlier, I'd told her about the exhibition and the coincidence that wasn't a coincidence.

'And have you spoken to Edward?'

Resting back against the velvet, I shake my head. 'It's complicated.'

She observes me, her face thoughtful.

'You know, when we are young, we are taught to believe that love should be effortless. That we shouldn't have to work at it, and if we do, there must be something wrong.'

The French windows are open and the afternoon sunlight shines in, catching the chandelier above us, reflecting light from the crystals against the walls. Absently, I watch them dancing.

'But should it be this hard?' I reason, turning towards her.

'Why on earth not? I was born during the war and everything we cared about was a hard-won fight.'

Her eyes shine brightly as they meet mine.

'Ask yourself. Why should love be any different?'

Success

When my business went bust and I moved back to London, broke and out of work, I felt like a complete failure. Now, at least when it comes to my career, I feel like I'm succeeding. I have a new column as well as my freelance job writing obituaries, which means I've finally been able to pay back all of the loan from Dad, clear my credit card debt, buy some new clothes and do my weekly shop without checking all the prices. I can even afford organic!

Then of course there's my podcast, which holds a special place in my heart. When it first went viral and I got lots of publicity, I quickly hit ten thousand downloads, which was pretty amazing for a little independent podcast like mine. Since then the numbers have kept growing and I now have a loyal following. I've even got a new sponsorship deal. Better still, it's a paid partnership with a brand of coffee, so I don't have to pretend to love the product when I promote them in my ad break, I actually really do.

That said, it's not like I'm some mega famous celebrity, so it's not some huge deal. But to be honest, I was never in it for the money. I'm in it because I love my listeners, both old and new. I love hearing and sharing their stories and showing people they're not alone. And, without sounding corny, that's pretty priceless.

Yet, more and more I find myself thinking success – like so many things in my life – doesn't look anything like how

I imagined it would look. When I got my first job, success to me was being able to afford an almond croissant *and* a coffee (trust me, publishing didn't pay very much), as I got older it felt like being able to afford to go on nice holidays and out to restaurants.

And now? Now, success means staying up till 2 a.m. to meet a newspaper deadline. Sitting at the little table I've shoehorned into the corner of my flat, working on a new obituary, replying to lots of emails from my listeners and thinking I'm going to have to work over Easter. Because, while I'm super grateful to have a job and be doing what I love and earning money, sometimes success just looks and feels a bit like stress.

My inbox is open on my screen and an email pops in. Oh God, it's Annabel's latest newsletter that I was forced to subscribe to at her life-coaching retreat. I'd forgotten all about it. Feeling irritated, I go to delete it, but not before I've seen the headline –

How to achieve work/life balance. Work less. Live more!

– and a photo of Annabel doing tree pose in a leotard on a beach somewhere.

At which point I think *Sod This* and slam my laptop shut.

Easter

'Will you look at you, there's nothing of you!'

I'm standing in the kitchen at Mum and Dad's, having caught the train from London to the Lake District first thing this morning. It's the first time they've seen me since Christmas and Mum is trying not make a fuss, by fussing.

'Mum, please, there's plenty of me.'

Over my shoulder I catch her mouthing, 'The Heartbreak Diet,' to Dad and pursing her lips, as if they're Les Dawson and Roy Barraclough in a Cissie and Ada sketch.

'No Arthur this time, eh?' says Dad.

'No Arthur,' I shake my head as looks fly between them. Neither of them dare mention Edward. I feel a stab of guilt and do it for them. 'He's with Edward.'

At the mention of his name, it's like everyone's been holding their breath and now they can exhale.

'Oh, how is Edward?' Mum tries to sound all breezy. She looks hopeful.* And now the guilt twists like a knife. I keep doing this to her, don't I? One broken engagement is bad enough. But two? Poor Mum. I can only imagine the village gossip about her daughter. The Vegan,† who lives in London and writes about dead people and didn't give poor Carol and

---

* Some might say desperate.

† A vicious rumour which started when I was spotted buying Linda McCartney sausages at the local corner shop.

Philip any grandchildren. Worse still, she does one of those pod*thingys* AND IT HAS THE F WORD IN IT!

'Hello, Granny and Grandpa.'

Luckily they have their son, The Golden Boy, who visits regularly with his gorgeous young family in his shiny new electric hybrid. When he's not busy toiling at running his own business and making everyone proud, of course. #notbitterreally #lovemyannoyinglittlebrother

'Incoming granddaughter!'

He appears in the kitchen carrying a large Easter egg, a bunch of motorway service station flowers for mum, and little Evie, who we all immediately go ape over. My brother might be annoying, but he also gave me my adorable niece and for that all is forgiven.

'Hey, look who's here.' He spots me as we all take turns in scooping her up and having Evie cuddles. 'It's the runaway bride.'

'Hello, Rich. Nice to see you're as sensitive as ever,' I reply, ignoring him and doing Big Auntie Eyes to Evie and making her laugh so she reveals her wide baby-toothed smile.

'Oh c'mon, it's only a joke, sis.'

'Wasn't that a film with Julia Roberts?' Mum pipes up, as she puts her flowers in water. She's absolutely thrilled with them. In fact, she seems way more thrilled with a bunch of artificially-dyed-blue daisies, wilting chrysanthemums and a few twigs sprayed with silver glitter, than with the gorgeous bouquet of fresh, seasonal spring flowers from a boutique florist that I sent for Mother's Day.

'Where's Nathalie?' I ask, trying to change the topic.

'Oh, she's just bringing in the bags,' says Rich cheerfully and then catches my eye. 'What's wrong with that? I'm all about gender equality.'

OK, I take that back about all being forgiven.

'Hang on. Wasn't that called *My Best Friend's Wedding*?' Dad looks confused as he attempts to break into the Easter egg.

'Goodness, she did a lot of wedding films, didn't she?' Mum holds her vase proudly aloft like an Olympic torch and snatches the egg out of Dad's hands.

'More weddings than our Nell,' chortles Rich, and I want to kick him in the shin, but I'm holding Evie and that wouldn't be very auntie-like, now would it? Instead I smile serenely.

'I know, let's ask Alexa,' suggests Mum brightly.

It's going to be a very long weekend.

I'm grateful for:
1. *Dad's allotment, where I seek refuge and he confesses that he's been cheating – though thankfully only at his diet – and where he keeps his stash of contraband chocolate and crisps, which we work through in comfortable silence.*
2. *Spring, for showing me that everything comes back to life; if you get banks of gorgeous daffodils from dried-up bulbs, there's hope for dried-up old me.*
3. *Mum's nightly routine of instructing Alexa to 'delete everything' so we wake up to a clean slate and no more talk of weddings. I wish we could do that in real life, Just imagine, hit delete and start afresh the next day.*
4. *The app on my phone so I can check on the security cameras in Cricket's flat and make sure she's OK. Gosh, they are so brilliant, I can flick between the living room and the bedroom and even zoom in. Hang on, is that her and Jack— ARGH!*
5. *Being able to delete the app.*

Taking the Next Step

Back in London and on Monday morning I wake early as I have my appointment at the fertility clinic in Harley Street. Just the thought triggers so many memories. After my failed IVF with Ethan, I swore I'd never go back to one again, that I was done with all those drugs and needles and tests. That I'd firmly closed the door behind me and I was never going to open it again.

But here I am again, and there's a moment when I stand outside on the pavement and almost turn around and go home. *Almost*. But I don't. Instead, taking a deep breath, I press the buzzer and as the receptionist asks for my name and the door is released, I push it open and walk inside.

I'm grateful for:
1. *The doctor for not freaking out because of my age and past history, but instead calmly talking me through my options and sending me off for various blood tests and scans, which he jovially calls 'a fertility MOT'.*
2. *My credit card and Arthur, for being there with their unconditional love and a 0 per cent balance transfer.**
3. *Facing my fears.*

---

* Because in life, everything comes at a price, and at forty-something, it would appear fertility costs an absolute bloody fortune.

You've Got Mail

Remember when it used to be a fun, flirty nineties rom-com? Now it's a three-word text from Edward informing me I have post at his house. I text back to say I'll collect it when I pick up Arthur, but when I arrive he's not there. Instead his son, Ollie, answers the door.

'Nell, it's you.' He's barefoot and half-asleep, a bowl of cereal in one hand, a roll-up in the other. 'Phew, I thought it was Dad.'

'He's not in?'

Hearing my voice, Arthur comes barrelling to the front door to greet me and I drop to my knees as he gives me a slobbery kiss.

'No. He left a note about going to yoga. I just woke up.'

Smoothing the flat of his hand over his forehead, Ollie pushes back his heavy fringe to reveal his bloodshot eyes.

'Big night, was it?'

He grins then, a long lazy one that turns into a yawn and he lifts his T-shirt and scratches his non-existent belly. Oh, to have the metabolism of an eighteen-year-old boy. 'Uni's broken up for Easter. I was catching up with some mates.'

'How's Manchester?'

'Mad.'

I laugh, fondly. 'Glad to hear it hasn't changed.'

'Do you want to come in?'

'No, it's OK. I'm just picking up Arthur and your dad said that I had some mail.'

'Umm . . . I dunno . . .' He peers blearily at the side console where we used to keep our post, but there's nothing there. 'Do you want to come in?'

I hesitate. I haven't entered the flat since we broke up and I moved out. It feels forbidden. Weird. *Tempting*.

My curiosity gets the better of me.

'OK. Just for a minute.'

I enter the hallway, closing the door behind me, and begin following him down the corridor towards the kitchen. Arthur runs ahead to see if any treats have miraculously appeared in his bowl. The first thing I notice is the rowing machine is back as I trip over it and bang my shin.

'Ow,' I yelp, and Ollie turns around.

'Oh yeah. The charity shop called Dad and asked him to take it back. Said they couldn't sell it and it was taking up so much space . . .' He pulls a face.

'Well, it's his house, he can do what he wants,' I shrug, rubbing my shin. I can already feel a big bruise appearing.

'Luckily for us, someone bought the framed rugby shirts.' He looks at me, his mouth twitching with amusement. We both smile. It feels conspiratorial. 'Thank God you made him get rid of those. Me and Louis were worried he was going to leave them to us as part of our inheritance.'

He shakes his head, laughing, his mouth full of cereal. Which in turn makes me laugh, and then immediately I feel guilty, like I'm betraying Edward. I shouldn't be making fun of him, not when he's their dad, so I stop laughing and try to be serious, but really, it is quite funny.

'Maybe if I just have a quick look in the kitchen,' I gesture, making an attempt to be all official and ex-fiancée-like and striding past the bedroom without even a glance, even though the door is open, and focusing on the kitchen.

It looks exactly the same.

I think that's probably worse. My eyes sweep over the gas hob, where I used to stand every morning, waiting for my stove-top espresso pot to boil; taking in the pedal bins, where we would have our Recycling Wars. Edward had once built a little moat of plastic containers and cans when we were just flatmates; going on about washing them out properly, and nearly choking when I admitted to just chucking in anything that was plastic, because frankly, *all plastic* should be recyclable. And there's the frying pan, left out on the side, that I once used to make pancakes and Edward had taught me how to flip them . . .

A wave of affection and nostalgia wells up inside of me, and I have to swallow it down. Honestly. What I am like? I'll be getting all sentimental over the loo roll next. I turn my attentions to the kitchen table.

'Found what you're looking for?'

Ollie hangs back in the doorway. Mistaking the look on my face as a reaction to the detritus of torn-up Rizla packets, roaches and a suspicious package in the ashtray, his eyes go wide.

'Oh, shit, please don't tell Dad.'

'No . . . no, of course not.' I shake my head, quickly. To be honest, I hadn't noticed it until just now. 'Just get out the air freshener and open some windows. Your dad's got a nose like a bloodhound.'

'Totally.' He nods, gratefully.

'Here, use this.' I dig out a little bottle of orange-and-tea-tree hand sanitizer from my bag and hand it to him. Taking it from me, he shifts awkwardly.

'You know, I liked it better when you lived here,' he says, after a moment. 'You were a cool stepmum.'

'Oh . . . thanks,' I nod, slightly taken aback. I wasn't expecting that at all and I feel ridiculously touched and ridiculously sad all at the same time. 'You and your brother were pretty cool yourselves.'

'Some of my mates have pretty terrible ones. Stepmums and stepdads, I mean.'

'Oh right.' I pull a face. 'That can't be easy.'

'No.' He shakes his head. 'But you were always more like a mate.'

It's like a sucker punch. I feel my eyes well up and I blink them rapidly, not wanting him to see. All this time, I didn't think he and Louis paid much attention to me. I was just their dad's girlfriend. Someone to be constantly filling the fridge and making them food and clearing away their endless empty cups and plates when they came to stay. I wanted them to like me, for us to have a good relationship, and I think we did, for the most part.

But I never felt particularly important, or needed, and why should I be? They had a mum already and I wasn't trying to replace her. Instead, mine was a trickier path to navigate. When Edward and I told them we were getting married, they seemed pleased, but largely uninterested. Too wrapped up in their own busy lives to pay us two oldies much attention. Both were on the verge of adulthood; Ollie at uni and Louis in Paris. Just as they were leaving the home, I was entering it. We were at different stages of our lives. All we had in common was their dad.

And yet, now I realize my presence was valued more than I ever dared hope.

'It's not the same around here now.'

Our eyes meet.

'Dad smiled more.'

There's a pause and, caught off-guard, I don't know how to respond. I feel like I owe Ollie an explanation, but I don't know where to start. In all of this I'd never realized just how

ALEXANDRA POTTER

attached I'd become to him or his brother, or how much I missed them both. Edward and I might not have had a child together, but now standing here in the kitchen it dawns on me that we'd still had a family together.

'I'm sorry that you got caught up in the middle of all this . . .' I begin lamely and then I spot the brown envelope on the side, with my name on it. 'Oh, this must be the mail he was talking about.'

'Right, yeah.'

Stuffing it in my bag, I notice it's from HMRC. I grimace.

'Well, I'd best be off.' I grab Arthur's lead and harness as he stops sniffing the floor and begins bashing my legs with excitement. I think he's the only one that likes this arrangement. Two kitchen floors to hoover up for the price of one.

'I'll tell Dad you called.'

'Maybe don't mention I came inside, I don't want him to think I was snooping or anything.'

'Right, yeah, course,' he nods.

'Lovely to see you, Ollie.' Swallowing down a lump in my throat, I go out into the hallway, glancing into the bedroom as I make my way to the front door. I can't resist.

'Bye, Nell.'

'Bye.'

Only later am I reminded of Ollie asking me if I'd found what I was looking for. I never answered him. I wouldn't know how.

I'm grateful for:
1. *An unpaid tax bill from HMRC for saving me from answering.*
2. *He kept the white bedding.*

Sh*t Happens

Life is a mixture of big, momentous things and small, inconsequential things. Throw them all together and it's a bit like
pick'n'mix, you never know what you're going to get next.
One minute you're dealing with the huge, life-changing stuff
and the next you find you're faced with something much smaller.

In fact, it's so little, it's the size of a tiny pink sapphire.

Like the one in my engagement ring.

I'd taken my ring off when Edward and I broke up, but lately,
I've been thinking I should give it back. I don't know what
the rules are with engagement rings. When my relationship
with Ethan finished, I offered to return it, but he wouldn't
hear of it, so now they both sit in a drawer. I'm building up
quite a collection. Which sounds funny, but really it's not.
Anyway, I feel I should do the right thing.

So, a couple of days ago, after I got home from picking
up Arthur and seeing Ollie, I took Edward's ring out of the
drawer and carefully opened the little velvet box. It was even
lovelier than I remembered, and before I knew it I was taking
it out and trying it on again, walking around the flat and
holding up my hand, wiggling my fingers so that it caught
the light. Which made me feel weird and sad and a lot of
complicated emotions I really didn't want to unpack, so I
quickly took it off again.

But instead of putting it straight back in the box, I decided to clean it first (top tip: washing-up liquid and a toothbrush) and rinsed it under the kitchen tap, then left it on a tea towel on the counter to dry. Where I forgot all about it, until later when I went to grab the towel to take something out of the oven, and the ring went flying. Worse still, I didn't realize at first as I was listening to the radio.

When I did realize it was missing, I quickly looked for it and found it – phew – on the kitchen floor. Honestly, I'm so clumsy. Except, hang on a minute – I stared at it in dismay. The sapphire was missing. Bollocks. The stone must have come loose from its setting.

Dropping to my hands and knees, I searched high and low for it. Where on earth could it be? And then I saw Arthur. Arthur loves the kitchen, it's like a treasure trove for him. As usual his nose was glued to the floor, going around the bottom of the cabinets, hoovering up anything he could find. He will eat anything. A piece of rice. A rogue strand of spaghetti. *A tiny pink sapphire.*

I looked at Arthur. He looked at me, tail wagging happily. Oh shit.

As it turned out, that was quite an apt response, as when I called the vet they told me that if I thought he'd swallowed the whole ring, they'd suggest bringing him in for an X-ray. But as it was just the stone, to 'wait and see'.

'If it's tiny, he should poop it out in a day or so, so just monitor it. Lucky for you, your fiancé didn't buy you a huge diamond,' said the vet, cheerfully.

Lucky me.

So now, for the past twenty-four hours I've been staring at Arthur's backside every time he goes to take a dump. And then, with my hands in a poo bag, picking it up and sort of breaking it apart with my fingers and inspecting it.

Sorry, TMI. I know, it makes me gag too. Oh the joys of dog parenting.

But still no stone!

OK, buddy, this is your last chance.

Saturday afternoon and it's our third walk of the day so far. If it doesn't appear this time I'm taking him to the vet and insisting on X-rays. Enough is enough. I've turned the flat upside down. What if it's got stuck inside him, or something?

We set off walking. It's a nice day and I head towards the river, where there's a good bit of grassy verge next to the footpath and, as any dog owners know, dogs love a bit of grassy verge. As expected, Arthur soon gets down to business, while I hover on the sidelines, like an expectant father, waiting. Which is when I notice the open-air cafe just to my left and two people sitting in the sunshine, their heads bent together, deep in conversation.

Edward and Annabel.

I'm so taken aback that for a moment I stand frozen . . . until suddenly my arm is almost yanked out of its socket as Arthur, having finished, spots Edward too, causing him to bolt and me to accidentally drop the lead.

'Nell?'

As Arthur charges over, barking delightedly, I see Edward immediately look up. The split-second expression of bewilderment, before he spots Arthur – and then me, still standing on the grass verge. Meanwhile I'm caught between the shock of seeing my ex-fiancé enjoying a cosy cappuccino with a woman who a few years ago tried to steal my best friend and now appears to be trying to steal my ex-fiancé – and the mortifying realization that I need to scoop up Arthur's crap and quickly inspect it.

Seriously. Kill Me Now.

'Hi there.'

And now Annabel is looking up and waving and they're both getting up and walking over with their take-out coffees and activewear and yoga mats slung casually over their shoulders. Edward's holding Arthur's lead, looking all square-jawed and handsome, while Annabel's beaming a mega-watt smile, her hair bouncing on her shoulders in slo-mo. They look like one of those attractive couples you see in adverts.

Shit. Literally. Shit. *Where is it?*

Meanwhile I am scanning the grass like a demented treasure hunter. Desperation spiralling. Honestly, you take your eye off the turds *for like a second*, and they just disappear into the grass.

'Yoo hoo.'

Oh phew! There it is!

I quickly scoop it up, just as they reach me.

'Oh, hi,' I reply, trying to appear casual and not like I am holding a poo bag that could contain the sapphire from my engagement ring and that I have a million things going on in my head right now.

'Arthur doesn't know his own strength.' As Edward hands me back the lead we exchange glances. It's the first time I've seen him in ages and it feels awkward. Meanwhile Annabel is beaming like a homecoming queen.

'Fancy seeing you here,' she's saying now, ponytail swinging.

'Fancy,' I nod, wishing I'd put on a bit of make-up and pulling down the peak of my baseball cap. Annabel lives on the other side of town. It's pretty obvious what she's doing over here. I shift uncomfortably.

'I thought you didn't drink caffeine?' I gesture to her take-out coffee.

'It's decaf,' she fires back.

Of course.

'Aren't you going to put that in the bin?' She gestures to the dog-waste bin that's just a couple of feet away.

'Um . . .' Caught, I falter. I don't know what to do. This reminds me of that time I lost my glittery shittery glove* on the driveway when I was picking up Arthur's poo. At the time it was hard to imagine anything worse.

No longer do I need to try to imagine. This is worse. *Much worse.*

'I can take that for you.' Edward, as always, tries to be helpful – it's the Boy Scout in him – and reaches out his hand. I'm touched by his kindness, things have been more than a bit frosty recently.

'No, it's fine. Thanks.' I smile politely, but don't hand it over.

'It's not a problem—'

'No problem!' It comes out a bit strangled and high-pitched.

I can see them both looking at me like I'm bonkers. And who can blame them? I'm hanging on to the dog-poo bag like I'm hanging on for dear life.

'I mean . . . it's no problem for me, either,' I gabble.

I suddenly feel like I'm having one of those out-of-body experiences, where you look at your life and can't believe this is happening. I mean, seriously how has it come to this? Just a few months ago I was getting married to the man I loved, in a couture wedding dress at an exclusive private members club in Mayfair. And now here I am, about to engage in a tug of war over a poo bag with my ex while being watched by Little Ms Perfect and her vision boards.

'Actually, I think I'll just take it home.'

---

* For anyone that might not have this memory seared on their brain (like me) this is a reference to the first time I ever walked Arthur and his poo bag burst all over one of my glittery (now *shittery*) cashmere gloves I'd got for Christmas. Worst still, the aforementioned glove was later returned to me, freshly washed, by a man who later ghosted me. And there I was foolishly thinking I'd come a long way since then. *Not.*

'Home?' Annabel looks at me like I've lost my mind.

To be honest, I think I might have.

'Yes . . . to compost.'

'Isn't that dangerous?'

'Well, um, actually it's a huge misconception that dog waste is not compostable,' I say, totally winging it and trying not to look at Edward, who I know is probably going to correct me.

But actually, it's the opposite.

'Yes, Nell's right,' he says in agreement. 'It's not safe to use as compost for any kind of edible vegetables because of the bacteria and potential parasites, but it's safe for flowerbeds or landscaping when it's composted properly and to strict guidelines. In fact, thousands of tonnes of dog poo is thrown away every year, so by composting we can seriously reduce the amount of waste in landfill.'

'Goodness. You learn something new every day,' replies Annabel. She looks put out.

I glance across at Edward, feeling grateful to him for rescuing me, but he steadfastly avoids eye contact. Of course, that wasn't him being nice, that was just him being knowledgeable. If I thought there was some kind of connection there, I was wrong. I feel a tug of disappointment.

'Right, well, I'd best be off. Nice seeing you both.'

But I'm determined not to show it, and with my head – and the poo bag – held high, I quickly walk off with Arthur.

I'm grateful for:
1. *Getting out of there.*
2. *Rubber gloves and determination (Cricket's advice, thanks Cricket).*
3. *Finding the sapphire under the cooker and having the stone reset.*
4. *Not having to look through any more shit.*

Suspicious Minds

So today something really weird happened. I went to get my watch fixed as it needed a new battery, and afterwards I found myself right by the museum where Fiona works. So I texted her to see if she was free to meet for lunch. When she didn't reply, I thought I'd pop in and surprise her.

It's been ages since I've been in a museum and as I walk through all the different rooms, past Ancient Roman mosaics and Early Asian armoury, on my way to find the Greek Byzantine section, I think back to all those school trips, trailing around, bored rigid, and how now I'm an adult, it feels like an absolute treat. They're amazing, and all free too. And seriously, who doesn't love a gift shop?

It's only when I'm leaving, five minutes later, that I spot a figure walking across the courtyard outside, where people are having lunch. From the back it looks just like Fiona. I peer through the window, trying to see, when briefly she turns. It *is* Fiona!

I'm about to call out and knock on the glass, when I see her walk up to a man at a table in the far corner . . . and something makes me stop. He's been waiting for her, and as I watch the intimate way they embrace each other, I feel my insides freeze. And now she's laughing, and they're smiling at each other, in a way I haven't seen her smile at David in a long, long while. I quickly turn and leave.

Later, when I'm on the bus, a text pops up. It's from Fiona, saying sorry, she just got my texts, but she's been in a meeting and couldn't get away. *'Totally boring work stuff. Yuk.'*

'No *problem*,' I text back. *'Some other time.'*

I'm grateful for:
1. *Not jumping to conclusions and assuming my best friend is having an affair.*

Phone Call with Max

'Hi, Nell, is that you?'

'Of course it's me. You just rang my number.'

'Sorry, yes.'

'Your voice sounds all echoey. Don't tell me you're hiding in the loo again,' I joke, but he doesn't laugh.

'Listen, I need you to do me a favour.'

'No. Max. I am not helping you with another school disco.'

'It's not that—'

Max and I always banter around. He throws a wisecrack, I return a one-liner. It's the way we've always communicated. But not today.

'Are you OK? You sound serious.'

There's a pause.

'I've been arrested.'

'Oh my God, what's happened? Are you OK?'

'Yeah, I'm fine . . .' He quickly reassures me. 'I got caught driving the wrong way down a one-way street and got pulled over by the police.'

'And they've arrested you for that?' I'm hotly indignant. 'God, that's ridiculous—'

'I was over the limit.'

I fall silent, taking this in. There are so many ways to react. I go for practical.

'Where's Michelle?'

'Away on a business trip.'

'So where are the kids?'

There's a beat.

'That's just it. They were in the car too.'

MAY

#forbetterforworse

The Fallout

The coffee signals it's ready by bubbling loudly on the stove. I turn off the gas ring, inhaling its aroma.

Some famous perfumier really needs to bottle that – forget all those floral top notes, there's no better scent than morning espresso – honestly, they'd make a fortune.

Pouring it into two cups, I add the hot milk, then pad barefoot into the living room, where the blinds are still drawn and there's a man, fast asleep, in a sleeping bag. I'm reminded of when we backpacked around the Greek islands, all those years ago. Only now the curly hair popping out his sleeping bag has turned grey, and instead of being on an idyllic beach in Crete, he's on my sofa.

'Max, wake up, I've made coffee.'

He doesn't surface. Instead a hand appears, reaching out of his sleeping bag like a periscope from a submarine. I manoeuvre the handle of the cup into his fingers.

'Don't you dare spill it.'

There's a groaning noise from deep within, then the cup is lowered back down and disappears inside. Evidently, Max is not ready to face up to things yet.

It's been three days since Michelle came back from her business trip and threw him out. Three days that he's been sleeping on my sofa, watching Netflix until 3 a.m. and trailing around my flat, staring slack-jawed at his phone to see if Michelle has replied to any of his texts. She hasn't.

'She was so mad, I thought she was going to kill me,' he confessed, when he'd first turned up late at night and sat across from me at my tiny kitchen table, his head in his hands. I'd made tea. It had gone cold.

'You could have killed yourself. And the kids.'

'I wasn't drunk.'

'You were over the limit.'

'I'd had a couple of beers at lunchtime, that's all.'

'Max, can you hear yourself?'

'Michelle said she'd be back from her business trip in time to pick the girls up from their play date.' He's determined I hear his side of the story. 'Freddy was at a sleepover. Tom was at his grandparents'. I was off the hook for once. Then, at the last minute she called to tell me something had come up at work.' He looked at me then, his face angry. 'It was the same at Izzy's party. Something always comes up at work.'

'This isn't about Michelle.'

'Why not? Why does it always have to be my fault?'

'No one's saying it's *always* your fault,' I tried reason. 'This is about what just happened.'

But it's like he couldn't hear me.

'Yes they are. I can't get a job. I can't support my own family. I'm a fuck-up. A *fifty-something fuck-up*.'

'Max, that's rubbish.'

'No, it's not, I know what everyone's thinking. My mates. My parents. Michelle. All the other dads doing school drop-off before they head off to another "Very Important Meeting".' He pulled a face.

'That used to be you, remember.'

'Thanks for reminding me. So you think I'm a loser too.'

'Oh, Max, stop feeling so bloody sorry for yourself,' I gasped, finally losing it with him. 'And stop making excuses.'

I watched his jaw set, as his startled expression quickly turned mutinous.

'Right, well, I'll just go then,' he said gruffly, scraping back his chair and grabbing his backpack. It reminded me of the only other time we've ever had an argument, over whose turn it was to pay for the pedalo in Greece. He ended up storming off then too.

Now, the stakes were somewhat higher.

'Go where exactly? You've got nowhere else to go.'

I watched as common sense waged a battle with his stubbornness. Finally it won and he sat back down again. 'I'm sorry, Nell.'

'It's not me you should be apologizing to.' Our eyes met across the table. 'You can have the sofa for as long as you need.'

'Thanks.'

'And for the record, I don't think you're a loser.' I stand up to find him a spare toothbrush. 'But if you don't stop drinking and be honest with your wife, you're going to lose everything.'

'What time is it?'

An hour later and he emerges from the bathroom.

'Time you got up and sorted out your life.'

'I'm trying. Michelle won't reply to my texts.'

'That's the best you can do? *Texts?*' From the kitchen table, I look at him, over the screen of my laptop. That's how small my flat is. It's then I notice his eyes are red. Like he's been crying.

'I don't blame her. I fucked up . . .' He trails off, his shoulders sagging. 'I miss the kids.'

Old friends. You love them. However much they fuck up.

I think about calling Michelle. I don't want to get involved, but I am involved.

'Jesus Christ, Nell. *Is that a coffin?*'

I snap back to Max staring at my coffin, which is leaning on the wall next to my bookcase. Shortly after Sapphire Shit-Gate, Edward had texted to say he was de-cluttering and he'd found it stored under the bed, along with a few more items of mine. I'd used it to keep jumpers in. Well, it's meant for storage.

'Oh. Yes, it is,' I nod. 'I made it.'

He looks at me aghast. 'And you think *I've* got a problem?'

'There's nothing wrong with making your own coffin,' I say, defensively. 'It doesn't make you die any sooner.'

'I know you like to be organized, but Jesus, Nell. I think there are some things you can leave to the last minute.'

'I don't think you should be giving me life advice right now,' I snap, then collapse onto my elbows. 'Edward dropped it off. Along with the last of my stuff.' I pause, remembering the stilted conversation. 'It felt really final.'

'The final nail in the coffin,' deadpans Max.

Which makes us both laugh, despite it all, and then we're interrupted by the buzz of my intercom.

'You expecting anyone?' he asks as I go to answer it.

But it's not for me, and hearing a familiar voice on the other end, I turn to him.

'It's Michelle.'

Fertility MOT

So today I got the results of my blood and hormone tests and scans from the private clinic. Now I know why it's called a 'fertility MOT' because at this age you're basically told your bumpers have fallen off, your windscreen wipers don't work, your suspension is knackered and your tank is running on empty. In other words, this old banger has well and truly failed to pass.

I'm grateful for:
1. *Good news! We have a long list of expensive fertility treatments and assisted reproduction services available that offer great success rates but no guarantees, and will test you physically, mentally and financially.*
2. *Gallows humour and a bumper box of tissues.*

411

A First Class Funeral

I was worried the service at the crematorium might be really sad and depressing, all fake plastic flowers and piped organ music in the grey, brutalist building in South East London. But as it turns out there are lots of gorgeous fresh flowers and his friends and relatives gave some really lovely speeches. In fact, the one from his daughter was such a funny and touching tribute, she had us all laughing and crying at the same time. Which made me think how everything said at funerals should be said at birthdays.

'And I liked that they played Elvis Presley's "Return to Sender" at the end,' I say as we gather afterwards at a local restaurant, where they've laid on a buffet spread in a private room upstairs.

'Good song choice,' agrees Cricket. 'Especially with him being a retired postman.'

The news of Derek's death had come as a shock to the members of The Toodlepip Club but not, apparently, to his family, who'd known of his numerous heart attacks over the years, but which he'd chosen not to disclose to us.

'It feels weird now, to think of him next to me making his coffin.'

Cricket nods. 'Though I still don't think he used the right screws, I'm sure he should have used Phillips, not flatheads.' She sips on her rum punch, made, apparently, to Derek's famous recipe. 'All through the service, I was terrified it might fall apart at the seams. Can you imagine?'

We both look at each other, imagining.

'I felt enormous relief when they did the final curtain call.'

After several weeks of recuperation, Cricket appears to have put her TIA behind her and is back to her old self. Helped, no doubt, by the company of Jack.*

'I don't want to get married or live with someone, but it is nice to be able to ask for a table for two again,' she'd confessed earlier, when I'd asked how things were going with Jack staying with her. 'Though it is rather strange having a man around again,' she continued. 'Finding a razor in the bathroom. Shoes by the door. It helps that I knew him before, it feels less of a betrayal, somehow.'

'Monty wouldn't want you to be on your own,' I protested.

'Oh yes he would. He was terribly jealous.' She broke into a smile. 'He'd want me to still be wearing mourning dress and looking desperately sad.'

'You're not serious.'

'Perhaps that's a slight exaggeration. He wouldn't have wanted me to be sad and he never liked me in black – apart from the little black dress I wore when we got married – but there was none of this, "I want you to have lots of boyfriends after I've gone." If he knew I had a man under my roof, he'd be furious.'

She'd fallen quiet then, her face filled with affection at his memory, before looking conflicted.

'What are the rules for dating at my age?'

'That there are no rules,' I replied and she smiled gratefully.

'You know, Jack used Monty's favourite cup the other morning. He had no way of knowing, of course. Yellow, with

---

* I haven't dared look at the security camera app on my phone since.

413

blue painted swirls around the rim. From a little pottery in Spain we once went to. I broke the handle once, and Monty glued it back on. I can see him now, at the kitchen table, tongue sticking out in concentration, readers perched on the end of his nose. I told him to throw it away, buy another, but he wouldn't hear of it.'

Abruptly her eyes filled with tears.

'It was more than a cup,' I said quietly.

'It was more than a cup,' she nodded, and sniffed sharply.

'But a cup can't take you out for dinner or hold your hand, can it?' I added, and our eyes met and we shared a smile.

'Golly, the food looks delicious . . . mango salad, fried auber- gine, spicy chicken . . .'

And now, here we are, shuffling around the buffet table, plates in hand. One thing's for sure, Cricket's certainly got her appetite back.

'Do you want any stir-fried rice?' She holds out the spoon.

'I'm actually not that hungry,' I shake my head, blowing air through my fringe. 'Is it just me, or is it hot in here?'

'I think it's you.' Cricket helps herself to a chicken drum- stick.

'I must be having my first hot flush,' I groan, fanning myself with the funeral order of service.

'Oh, I remember those,' says Cricket cheerfully. 'I used to carry a fan I brought back from holidays on the Costa Brava. I used to snap it open like a flamenco dancer.'

'You make it sound fun,' I grumble, 'instead of really depressing.'

'Good heavens, girl, it's not depressing! On the contrary. It's the beginning of something wonderful.'

Now, I love Cricket's take on life, but this is where I draw the line.

'Look, I'm all for trying to be all body positive when it comes to getting older. Trust me, I know ageing is a privilege,' I add firmly, lowering my voice and side-stepping one of the mourners as we move away from the buffet and towards the dining area. 'But there is nothing wonderful about hot flushes, brain fog and this weight around my middle.' Clutching at my waistband, I try to breathe in. 'I thought this was because of lockdown, but apparently perimenopause is a thief. Not only does it rob you of your youth and fertility, it's bloody stolen my waist.'*

With her plate piled high, Cricket sits herself down at the end of one of the tables and waits for me to join her. 'Waists are seriously overrated,' she remarks, picking up her fork and tucking in.

Usually Cricket can always make me smile, but today my mood weighs heavy. To be honest, I'm still a bit upset and depressed from the results of my fertility MOT.

'It just feels like The End.'

'What does?'

'The menopause,' I gasp, sitting down opposite. 'It's just sitting there. Waiting for me. Like some big dead end.'

In the middle of eating, Cricket puts down her fork and rests her elbows on the table. 'You know, in my day, we used to call it The Change,' she states matter of factly. 'We were taught to be ashamed of it. It was all hush-hush . . . something that happened but no one ever talked about. Almost like a death.'

At the mention of the word 'death', several other mourners glance over at us and Cricket smiles politely and lowers her voice.

'But what no one ever told us, is that while change can be frightening, it can also be wonderful. It leads you on to new

---

* Otherwise known as 'The Thickening', which sounds like a horror movie.

ALEXANDRA POTTER

things. Better things. Brilliant things. It gave me a freedom I
never imagined. Not just from all those years of painful
periods, and spoiled underwear and holidays ruined by having
to lie in bed with a hot water bottle –' she gives a little
shudder '– or all those years spent terrified of accidentally
falling pregnant, of being pressurized by your parents to make
someone a good wife. But also of worrying about what other
people think and wanting to be liked.'

She shakes her head, remembering, then smiles.

'I'll let you into a secret, Nell, it might feel like the end, but
that's only because women are never told the rest of the story.
So let me tell you mine.' She leans across the table towards
me, until her face is close. 'It was liberating,' she confides, her
eyes shining. 'Like a new beginning. I felt like I used to before
all those hormones held me hostage for years. Before I cared
about what boys thought, or how my hair looked, or if anyone
found me attractive. Because I was no longer looking for their
approval. I didn't give a damn.'

'I can't imagine you ever giving a damn.'

'Oh, I did. When I was younger. And what a terrible waste
of time that was.' She shakes her head, her face regretful.

'Here's to not giving a damn.' I raise my glass of rum punch.

Broken from her thoughts she suddenly laughs and leans
back in her chair.

'I'll drink to that,' she agrees, raising her own glass.

'Wasn't it a smashing send-off?'

Interrupted by voices, we both look up to see Elaine, with
Diane and Rosie, from the club, balancing plates of food and
smiles as they join us at our table. Diane has dyed her pink
hair a striking shade of electric blue and matched it with
some long beaded earrings. When I compliment them, Rosie
informs me they're a result of their new jewellery class.

'Yes, wonderful,' I nod.

416

'I thought his coffin looked amazing,' continues Diane.

'All those stamps. It was literally covered!' Elaine shakes her head in admiration, then turns to Cricket. 'What did you think of the funeral?'

All eyes upon her, Cricket dabs her mouth with her napkin and refills her glass. 'Like Derek always wanted,' she smiles. 'Absolutely first class.'

I'm grateful for:
1. *Listening to Cricket's story; it certainly makes me feel better about what my own will be.*
2. *Derek's screws held up.*

Life Goes On

After a bit of a gloomy start to May, Sunshine and her backing singers, Blue Skies, finally take centre stage and in full Spring Clean Mode I fold away jumpers, throw open windows and fill bags for the charity shop. This time of year always brings with it a renewed sense of energy, but also urgency, and I spend the rest of the week not just cleaning up my surroundings, but tidying up my life.

Thankfully I have the flat back to myself. Max is no longer sleeping on my sofa, but is back home with Michelle and the kids. After Michelle had turned up at my flat, I'd gone out to give them some privacy, and returned to find they'd left together. And a note from Max. '*I O U big time. Will call in a few days.*'

It's been a few days but he hasn't called. I don't expect him to. When everything falls apart, you need more than a few days.

Still, he knows where I am if he needs me. I always think friendship is like traffic. It's always there, but how often you speak and see each other ebbs and flows, depending on the weather conditions and if there's been an incident. I haven't seen Holly since the party, but we text regularly. She's finishing her treatment next month and she's grateful and relieved, but mostly just exhausted.

As for Fiona, we haven't spoken since that day at the museum. I've called and sent a few texts, but she's gone really quiet. She didn't even respond to a funny meme I forwarded. I have a feeling something's up, but then again she could just be really busy. Not wanting to jump to any conclusions, I resolve to just keep trying her.

That said, if she is busy, she wouldn't be the only one. At the weekend I attend a virtual adoption event. Sitting at my laptop, waiting to join the meeting, I feel absurdly nervous. I'm not so much worried about what to expect, but what is expected of me. But as it turns out, everyone is so welcoming and I get to ask questions, gain lots of information and listen to social workers and adoptive parents talking about their experiences and the powerful love they have for their children. I leave the meeting with my head and heart buzzing.

Then, this Monday morning, I travel into town to meet with an accountant to sort out my unpaid tax bill. Turns out when you work for yourself you're supposed to know the very important percentage rule of 'spend a third, save a third, invest a third'.* Who knew? Sadly, not me, as I was taught other really useful things in maths like trigonometry and logarithms and if Mary bought twelve DVDs at fifty pence each and Peter bought five pounds' worth of DVDs at a 50 per cent discount, they would have lots of DVDs that are now completely and utterly worthless. Like I said, lots of really useful stuff.

Fortunately, my new accountant sets me up with a monthly payment plan to pay off everything I owe in instalments, and I leave their office, feeling broke but relieved. Heading towards the tube home, I walk up the high street, passing all the expensive designer shops and peering in windows. I can't afford anything, but I need something to wear for the opening night of Monty's play next month.

Next month! I still can't quite believe it's finally happening!

---

* And not to ignore letters in brown envelopes.

It's crazy how it was on hold for so long and now it's come around so quickly. I spoke to Cricket last night and apparently it's going to be this big showbiz affair and there's going to be a red carpet and photographers. And of course, Joe will be there—

'Hey.'

A voice cuts into my nerves and excitement and I snap back to see I'm passing my favourite bookshop. Reflected in its window I spot a figure behind me. I turn quickly around.

'Joe!'

Standing across from me on the pavement, he's leaning against a street sign, phone held outstretched in his hand, mid-scroll. I suddenly get that feeling that I've conjured him up, like you do when you're thinking about someone and the next thing you know you're bumping into them.

'Hi, how are you?'

Oh crap. So this is a bit awkward. I never called him back.

'Yeah, great, busy with rehearsals. How've you been?'

'Yeah, fine . . . busy . . .'

I can feel us falling down the rabbit hole of pleasantries. Oh Sod It. I can't ignore it any longer.

'I'm sorry, about not calling you back. It was really rude of me.'

'No worries,' he shrugs.

'I always say that and I've got loads of worries,' I laugh, in an attempt at a light-hearted joke, but he looks at me blankly. I shift uncomfortably, feeling the need to explain. I owe him that at least. 'Look, I want you to know that I had a really nice time with you at your sister's exhibition, it's just that I recently came out of a serious relationship . . . well, I suppose it's not that recent, and I still—'

But he cuts me off. 'Seriously. It's no biggie. It was just dinner. I thought it might be fun.'

'Fun. Right, yes.' I nod, feeling vaguely embarrassed. Did I misread the signs?

'Sorry, babes, there was a queue.'

We're interrupted by a willowy brunette who comes out of the bookshop and walks straight over to us.

'Hey, babe.' Slipping his hand around her waist, Joe kisses her.

It all happens so fast, that for a moment I just stand there. Frozen. If I was embarrassed before I'm mortified now.

'Sorry . . . Emma, this is Nell. Nell, this is Emma.'

Emma, who doesn't appear to have noticed me up until this point, turns to me with the same kind of bored interest I see in my godson Freddy when I try to tell him about the days before the internet. Actually, I'm not sure Emma, in her denim cut-offs and Dr. Martens, is old enough to remember the days before internet.

We exchange polite hellos and she flashes me a *Love Island* smile, while I pray for the pavement to swallow me up. She's actually really sweet and shows me the book she's just bought. It's not her fault I could be old enough to be her mother.

'Well, lovely to meet you, Emma, bye Joe, see you at opening night.' And quickly saying my goodbyes, I leave them holding hands and scoot off.

I'm grateful for:
1. *Not being born yesterday; I didn't misread the signs. Joe's idea of Fun included a different kind of F word.*
2. *Never calling him back; not because he's dating a woman half his age, but because any man who chooses to stand outside the most wonderful bookshop in the world, scrolling through his phone, instead of going inside, is not the man for me. But then I always knew that anyway.*

Tik-Tok-Tik-Tok

OK, so I'm all for embracing my age and ignoring the wrinkles. So what if I have saggy knees, a deafening biological clock and those lines between my eyebrows that dermatologists call Elevens (not to be confused with Eleven*ses* which are a lot more fun and involve scones and cups of tea) – growing older is a gift.

But I'll be honest, the results of my MOT and bumping into Joe yesterday with his much younger girlfriend, have left me feeling a bit old and depressed. So I've decided: I need to GET WITH IT. Whatever IT is. So I downloaded a bunch of the latest social media apps onto my phone.

I think it's important to keep up with the times and not turn into one of those old people that haven't a clue what all the coloured heart emojis mean and just randomly choose any, still don't know the difference between reels and stories, get slightly freaked out by some of the videos and can't see their phone without their glasses anyway.

Er hello.

I'm grateful for:
1. *Algorithms.*

One Plus One Equals One

So I've been thinking, maybe I'm just not cut out to be in a relationship. Maybe this is the universe telling me something. After all, every romantic relationship I've ever had has failed. Well, not failed, because I don't believe a relationship is a failure because it doesn't last for ever, but maybe I'm lacking in the gene that makes them go the course.

I mean, it can't be everyone else's fault. Over the years my girlfriends have cheered me up and cheered me on, calling them idiots, or losers, or bastards. His loss not yours! Plenty more fish in the sea! It'll happen when you least expect it! But what's the common denominator here?

Exactly.

So maybe being single is better for me. I know society likes to put us together in pairs, it's been that way since the animals went into the ark two by two, but maybe I'm better one by one. No stigma. No pressure. No heartache.

Except, there's just one problem. One fly in the ointment of this whole argument.

Edward. And the fact I happen to still love him.

Shit.

A Very Special Guest

'*Hi, and welcome to* Confessions of a Forty-Something F##k-Up, *the podcast for any woman who wonders how the hell she got here, and why life isn't quite how she imagined it was going to be.*'

Armed with my coffee and headphones, I'm recording this week's episode of my podcast from my newly created vocal booth. Which sounds *very fancy*, but in reality, I've repurposed the tiny walk-in closet in my hallway, well, it's more of an understairs cupboard really, which I've wallpapered with acoustic foam tiles. It used to house my ironing board, and various mops, brushes and a vacuum cleaner, but now they're all shoved in the kitchen and I'm squeezed in here instead with my desk and microphone and this week's guest.

'*I used to think I was the only person struggling to recognize their messy life in a perfect Instagram world, but since recording my first episode I've received so many messages from listeners telling me how much they relate, that now I regularly invite guests onto my podcast to share their stories.*

'*Because, if you're anything like me, you're a bit bored of only hearing interviews with famous women: celebrities and trailblazers and living legends, who I'm sure are all really lovely and interesting, but who I just can't relate to. What about all those other women who are quietly going about their lives? Ordinary women, who are no less extraordinary*

*for facing life's challenges and triumphing not just despite,
but because of them. Strong, brave, incredible women we can
all relate to.*

*These are the women who truly inspire me and in these
honest, heart-breaking, heart-warming conversations, they get
to tell it like it is, with all the laughter and tears that come
with it. Because the truth is everyone has a story.'*

I stop talking and pause to look at my guest who's sitting
across the desk from me. She looks tense behind her microphone and I give her a reassuring smile.

'*My guest on this week's episode is a woman who on paper
looked to have it all. Four beautiful children, a happy marriage
and a successful business. But then it all fell apart. Today
she's here to tell us what happened. As usual, in the spirit of
a show that began as an anonymous podcast, we don't use
any names. So, without further ado, hello to our guest and
welcome to the show!'*

There's a pause, and for a split second I wonder if she's
going to change her mind. I know how nervous she is. But
also how determined.

'**Hi, thanks for letting me come on and share my story.**'

Michelle's voice doesn't waver and I feel a blast of love
towards my friend for being so brave. When she'd called me
a few days ago, to ask if she could be a guest on my podcast,
I'd been taken aback. Was she sure? While I was both flattered and honoured (of course I'd *love* to have you on the
show!) I was worried it might be too soon. That things might
still be too raw. Too difficult.

But she was resolute. She'd gained so much strength and
solidarity from listening to my other guests relating their
experiences, that she wanted to share hers, in the hope that
it might help someone feel less alone. So here we were, two
friends, sitting across from each other in the most surreal of

circumstances, about to have one of the most honest conversations of our life.

'No, *thank you. Yours is an important story, and I think there's going to be a lot of listeners out there today who are going to resonate with your experiences . . . So first, let me start by asking you the question I ask all my guests: Is your life how you imagined it would be? And if not, what's different?*'

There's a moment's silence as Michelle absorbs the question. I notice she's wearing the silver heart necklace Max gave her when they first met. She fiddles with it, rubbing it between finger and thumb, and then she replies.

'*I didn't expect to get pregnant in my forties. My husband and I already had three children and we thought we'd completed our family. The youngest were out of nappies. I was finally getting my life back.*

'*When I found out I was pregnant I cried. I was devastated. Everyone talks about happy accidents, but I didn't want another baby. The thought of going back to sleepless nights filled me with dread. I confess I thought about a termination, and that's something I felt I couldn't admit to anyone.*

'*When my son was born I loved him of course, like all my children, but I still grieved for what little independence I'd had while the kids were at school. Then my husband lost his job and the pandemic happened and that's when I started sewing masks from my kitchen table. This led to me setting up my home furnishings business, and with my husband still out of work, and the business becoming more successful, it made sense for him to look after the kids and become a stay-at-home dad.*'

'*And did you discover unexpected joys because of this?*'

'*Oh absolutely, yes, so much joy.*

426

'*I loved the freedom and independence it brought me. To be able to leave the house with just my phone and a credit card. To be with adults having adult conversations and to be taken seriously as a person, and not just in my role as a mum. It was the most liberating feeling. Don't get me wrong, I love my babies, but my business is my baby too, and I love that too.*'

She pauses, considering her answer.

'*I also felt a huge pride and satisfaction in being the main breadwinner for the first time, for being able to financially provide for my family. But, if I'm honest, it also provided so much for me. I mean, just putting on smart clothes to go to a meeting and not being in a sweatshirt covered in sweet potato puree—*' She breaks off, laughing. '*My son's a messy eater.*'

'*And how did your husband feel about your success?*'

'*He was really pleased, he knew how much it meant to me. But while he was supportive, he was also struggling.*'

'*How so?*'

'*My husband loved his career and he was good at it – being made redundant was a major blow. He tried not to let it show, but I knew not being able to find another job really affected his self-esteem. He became depressed. He started drinking too much. We'd go to a party and he'd have one too many. I'd find empty beer cans in the recycling. He never just wanted one glass of wine. And the worst part was I knew if I confronted him, then we had a problem, and I was scared I would have to give up my new life. So I pretended we didn't have a problem.*'

'*So what happened?*'

'*I'm ashamed to say I ignored it. Until one day it all came crashing down. My husband had gone to pick up the kids because I was late back from a business trip and he got arrested for drink driving. I was so angry, so furious at him. But really, I was more angry and furious at myself. It's not like it came as a surprise, but I'd put my own desires before the safety of my kids. What kind of failure as a mother does that make me?'*

Michelle meets my eyes across the table and as she blinks back tears I want to reach across the table and hug her. I think about that evening Max called me upset from the police station after his arrest and his later confession that he felt like a fifty-something fuck-up. Two people who I love, both locked in a cycle of blaming themselves.

'Well, I happen to disagree. I think that makes you a very real and honest and brave one,' I say in admiration, 'and I think most people listening will agree. Which brings me to my next question, which is one I ask all my guests, and that's if you've ever felt like a fuck-up. But I think you've answered that one . . .'

My voice is full of kindness, but it's also tinged with a humour we both share, and despite it all, Michelle's face splits into a smile as she nods in agreement.

'Oh yes, I've definitely felt like that. After the arrest, social services got involved, but it was a wake-up call for both of us. Because you know, from this terrible thing came a wonderful thing. My husband and I talked. We talked properly for the first time in for ever and while it was ugly and hard and painful, it's brought us closer together than I think we've ever been.

'We're in a much better place now. My husband's in AA. I've scaled back work and hired a manager. We are spending more time together as a family. It's early days and I'm not pretending everything is perfect, because it's not, but it now feels like we're part of the same team and everyone's a lot happier.'

'That's wonderful, I'm really happy for you all.'

'Me too.'

Along with my listeners, I wasn't sure how this story was going to end. As much as Max and Michelle are my friends, I haven't wanted to intrude, so I'm so *so* relieved and pleased by this news.

'Something our guests talk about a lot is the pressure of social media, comparing their lives with those on their phone and struggling to recognize their own messy ones in the perfectly curated images. Has that ever affected you?'

'Well, I remember seeing a photo of some celebrity mum with her bikini body. We'd had our babies at the same time and I think it was supposed to be inspiring but I just felt so intimidated. Instead of joining the gym, I just ate more biscuits.'

As Michelle makes her confession our conversation dissolves into laughter, and more talk about biscuits, specifically the chocolate-covered teacake ones, that are her favourite.

'But you know, I can laugh at it now, but it actually made me pretty depressed. So did all the photos of everyone's kids looking angelic in clean, freshly ironed clothes in neat, tidy houses, whereas my house was just chaos and the kids were feral . . . I've given up trying to get to the bottom of my laundry basket, I think I've more chance of flying to the moon . . .'

Michelle shakes her head, half laughing, half grimacing.

'But seriously, there were times when I'd be at home with the kids and I was really jealous of my husband being out at work. It could be really lonely and, a lot of the time, pretty boring but that's not what you see on social media. I just thought, am I the only one who feels like this? And what's worse is I didn't want to admit it because I was worried that people would judge me, which is silly really

but . . .' She trails off. *'I just wish we could be more honest.'*

'Well, THANK YOU for being so honest today and sharing your story. I can't believe we're nearly out of time. But before we go, I always ask my guests the same final three quickfire questions. Are you ready?'

Michelle nods.

'Hit me with me them.'

'What's your superpower?'

'Having eyes in the back of my head.'

'What advice would you give someone?'

'There's no such thing as the rhythm method.'

'What would your hashtag be?'

'#themorethemerrier'

I look across at Michelle and we share a smile that says, you got this, girl.

'Those are so brilliant. Thank you so much. I've loved our conversation today and thank you to everyone for listening. You can hear a new episode of the show next week, when we'll have more confessions.'

The Letter

My partner and I used to have a great sex life, but now when
we get into bed we can't wait to fool around with our phones.
Google is always up for it and scrolling is our new foreplay.
Last night I was online shopping and practically had an orgasm
over a pair of pink espadrille wedges. Help!

I finish reading out the email and turn to Cricket. 'What
advice would you give?'

Cricket puts down her teacup and looks thoughtful. 'Always
buy a bigger size. Those espadrilles sound fabulous, but you
know how your feet swell in the heat.'

We're sitting at a cafe in Holland Park, sharing a pot of
Earl Grey and going through the letters that have been sent
to us from readers. Every week we get together to choose
one for our column. Apparently there's quite a lot as the
column's proving really popular, so the assistants at the newspaper sieve through them and send us a selection.

Usually we meet in Cricket's flat, but Jack is visiting, plus
the weather is lovely, so this week we choose to sit outside
at her favourite pavement cafe. It's close to her old house
and on the way we stopped by the free little library that
we built on her gatepost and later inspired her to set up a
charity in her late husband's name. Fortunately the new
owners keep it well stocked, but still, every now and then
she likes to check up on it and perhaps add a slim volume

of her favourite poetry, or a new hardback she's read and wants to pass on.

In fact, when it comes to Monty's Mini Libraries, Cricket's a bit like a doctor doing her rounds. Often she'll catch a tube or the bus to visit ones that have since sprung up in front gardens and on fences and in disused phone boxes across the city. Sometimes if they're local, she'll ride her bicycle, but she always carries a backpack containing a few prized books that she scatters across the capital like magic.

'Books shouldn't be a luxury, but since the local library closed, not everyone can afford them,' she replies when I ask her why she's so committed. 'We need these free mini libraries more than ever.' The library is now being developed into luxury flats and whenever we walk past the familiar red-brick building where her late husband used to write his plays, she always shakes her head and tuts, 'We need more books, not bankers.'

'What advice would you give?' Cricket peers at me now over the teapot.

'To be honest, I'm not sure I'm the right person to be giving out relationship advice, after the mess I've made of mine,' I confess, pouring us more tea.

We've been catching up and I told her about bumping into Joe, to which she simply replied darkly, 'Well, he is an actor.'

'Nonsense. Most marriage counsellors I've met are divorced.'

'When did you see a marriage counsellor?'

'Before I was married,' she laughs. 'We went out for dinner a few times. Nice chap. Not for me.'

I smile and pass her the milk. 'Maybe that's how we should look at all our relationships that don't work out? Think of all the years of angst you'd save. Just, "Nice chap, not for me."'

'Now that is good advice,' she beams, stirring in sugar. 'OK, let's have a look at the next letter—'

My phone beeps, interrupting us. It's on the table and I glance at my screen. It's a text from Fiona. I feel a beat of surprise.

Are you free to talk?

We haven't spoken since that day at the museum. I've called and left messages, but she's either not replied or made some excuse about being busy. If she wasn't such a good friend I'd think she was avoiding me. It's because she's such a good friend, I *know* she's avoiding me. And I have a horrible feeling I know the reason why.

I'm with Cricket, can I call you in an hour?

Oh don't worry if you're busy. I don't want to bother you.

It's no bother. We're just going through letters for our column. Should be finished soon. We just need to choose one.

There's a pause and then a text beeps up.

I've got one . . .

I can see the ellipses that indicate Fiona is typing. I wait. It takes about a minute, and then a long text appears.

What would you say to a woman who is married with two children and has grown apart from her husband. Who didn't expect to meet someone at work and for their friendship to turn into something more serious, but who is now terrified and confused and doesn't know what to do. And is desperate to talk to her best friend but feels ashamed and guilty and fearful of being judged.

'Sorry, do you mind?' I say to Cricket and gesture to my phone. 'I need to make a phone call.'

'Is everything OK?'

'I don't know.' I reply. 'But I'm about to find out.'

It's Good to Talk

'I'm sorry I've been avoiding you.'

'It's OK.'

'No, it's not.' She shakes her head. 'None of this is OK.'

It's the next day and I'm sitting in another cafe, only this time it's on the other side of London, and the person sitting across from me isn't Cricket – it's Fiona. Yesterday when she texted me, I called her straight back, but in the space between someone had walked into her office, so we arranged to meet for lunch instead. That way she could talk freely.

Only we've been here for twenty minutes and there isn't much talking going on. The waiter has been to take our order. Food and drinks have arrived. We've both commented on the weather and the traffic. Meanwhile I've been waiting for Fiona to begin the conversation, but it's almost as if she's had second thoughts and done that thing where you regret revealing too much and try to pretend you never said anything.

'You said you wanted to talk to me.' I finally tire of watching her fiddling with her omelette that's gone cold.

'I do.' She nods. 'It's just—' She breaks off, and I can see an internal battle raging within. 'Oh Nell, I don't know where to start,' she bursts out and her eyes brim with tears.

'How about the beginning?' I encourage.

I see her hesitate. Even now she can't bring herself to talk.

'You know, I came to the museum.'

She looks at me blankly.

'That day I texted you about lunch and you said you were busy. I popped by, on the off-chance . . . I saw you but you didn't see me.'

'Oh God.' As the realization of what I'm saying dawns, she covers her face with her hands. 'You saw me with Andrew,' she whispers.

'Is that his name?'

With her head in her hands, she nods.

'Do you love him?'

'Of course not,' she protests, looking up at me, and I'm surprised by my wave of relief. 'We haven't slept together.' Her voice is urgent, her body defensive. 'It was just a kiss.'

Our eyes meet across the table but her face betrays her.

'Except it's never just a kiss, is it?' she adds quietly.

I look at my friend. I've known her since university but I've never seen her like this before. Fiona has always been so steady; happily married, two gorgeous kids, loving husband and a lovely home, she's so settled in her comfortable, family life, that often I would feel like she lived in an entirely different universe to me. Her new job at the museum was the icing on the cake. And while recently I knew she and David were having a few problems, they seemed more like bumps in their steady road. But now it's like watching her unravel, as if she's come undone.

'So what is it then?' I ask.

'It's an escape.'

She sighs deeply and stares out of the window, bracing herself, and then it all comes out, about everything she's been feeling these past eighteen months.

'Every marriage has its problems, but it's much easier to ignore them when you only see each other a few hours a day,' she confesses. 'David spent his whole life at the office. For years it was just me and the children. But then, suddenly he was working from home all the time and all those little

436

things came into focus and I realized how much we'd both changed after all these years . . .'

She looks upset, but I don't say anything. I just listen.

'It's not David's fault,' she adds quickly. 'I don't want you to think I'm blaming him, because I'm not.'

'No, of course not.'

'It's just . . . oh I don't know. We were so young when we started dating. Remember when we first met? It was on my birthday, at that bar in Chelsea.'

'You spilled a drink on him and he asked if he could buy you another.' I smile at the memory.

'Ever the perfect gentleman,' she smiles, only she looks sad.

'You two have been together a long time.'

'It feels like a lifetime,' she nods. 'We've done a lot together. Marriage, babies, promotions, house moves, renovations.' She breaks off, rolling her eyes. 'We did a lot of those.'

'Didn't you remodel the kitchen about three times?' I tease.

'It would've been four if I hadn't gone back to work,' she admits, with a flash of humour. 'I was so frustrated and desperate to use my brain, and David was so supportive when I got the job at the museum.' And now she looks stricken with guilt. 'You must think I'm awful.'

'No, of course not,' I shake my head.

'You know, I never expected to meet Andrew. I wasn't looking to meet anyone. He was a colleague. We began having lunch together and discovered we have the same backgrounds, same interests. He was so easy to talk to, we'd have these conversations, at first it was mostly about work, but then it became about all kinds of things. He was so interesting and interested in me . . .'

I watch her face flush as she speaks about him.

'Andrew really listens . . . he makes me laugh.' She looks suddenly sheepish. 'God, that sounds like such a cliche.'

'So what are you going to do?'

'I've told him we can't see each other any more, but it's difficult, we work together. Maybe I can transfer to another department, I don't know,' she shrugs.

'But that's good isn't it? That you've ended it.'

I try to be encouraging, to try to make my friend feel better, but Fiona still looks worried.

'But that's just it, it's not ended.' She shakes her head. 'Because the truth is, it's not about Andrew, not really. It's about me and David. We don't have anything in common any more, except the children, and they're growing up fast. Before you know it, it will be just me and David rattling around in the house together. We'll be like one of those retired couples you see that sit at restaurants and have nothing to say to each other—'

'I think you've got a few years yet.' I try to make light of it, but I can see the panic.

'Because I tell you, Nell, the thought terrifies me.' She gives a little shudder.

'Have you talked to David?'

'No! I mean, not yet, I know I have to . . . we can't go on like this . . .'

'Maybe David is terrified too.'

She falls silent and looks at me in surprise.

'I mean, look, I'm not particularly close to David so I'm just guessing, but maybe that explains the sudden desire to move to Cornwall and learn how to surf? Wanting to shake it all up.'

She looks at me then, the thought sinking in.

'You know, when Edward and I were breaking up, he told me that a marriage can't work unless you want the same things. But maybe you and David have got more in common than you think.'

438

'And you two didn't?'

And so then I tell her, about finding Simone's pregnancy test and everything that followed, and when I've finished she reaches across the table for my hand and squeezes it in hers.

'Oh Nell, why didn't you tell me all this before?'

'I don't know,' I shrug. 'Maybe because our lives are so different. I worried you wouldn't be able to relate. That you wouldn't understand. And that would just make me feel worse.'

As her eyes meet mine I know my worries are unfounded. I feel closer to my friend than I have done for years.

'You know, I could ask you the same question,' I say, after a moment. 'Why didn't you tell me all this before? About everything?'

Fiona shrugs. 'Because I was worried you wouldn't understand, and that would just make me feel worse.'

For a moment we look at each other across the table. Two old friends. Then we both burst out laughing because for some reason we find this hysterically funny. And we keep laughing until our sides hurt and our eyes water, and everything feels better. Even if it's just for a little while.

I'm grateful for:
1. *Fiona: because it turns out that while our lives are very different, our friendship (and sense of humour) still remains the same.*
2. *Old friends; because you never laugh as hard as you do with the people with whom you've gone through so much, and who can remember you from when you wore crop tops, blue eyeliner and permed your hair. Or have the photos to blackmail you with.*

JUNE

#thebestisyettocome

WhatsApp from Tia, Liza's Wife

She's here! Our gorgeous daughter Grace Penelope was born this morning at 4.45 a.m., weighing 8lbs 2oz. Mom and baby are doing well. We can't wait for her to meet her namesake.

Ringing the Bell

Today is a milestone. Holly is due to have her final session of radiotherapy, which will signal the end of her treatment. I always say I don't believe in happy endings, only happy beginnings, but this is something that needs celebrating and, in many ways, it is a beginning.

'Adam wanted to come, but I was worried he'd get all weepy,' she admitted, when she called me a few days ago to ask if I'd go with her. 'He's been a bit of an emotional wreck, knowing this is the end of my treatment.'

'So you thought you'd ask your heartless friend,' I deadpanned and she gave a throaty laugh on the other end of the phone.

'That's exactly why. I need someone I don't have to worry about. I end up being the one comforting Adam, not the other way around. And I can always rely on you to make me laugh,' she added.

'OK, well, I'll try to do my best.'

'Thanks, Nell. I appreciate it. See you Tuesday.'

So now it's Tuesday and I'm at the hospital with Holly, sitting in the patients' waiting room, drinking bad vending machine coffee and waiting for the nurse to call her in for her last session.

'So Adam's brother has said we can have his house in West Wittering for a couple of weeks at the end of June,' she's telling me now. 'It's right by the beach.'

'Wow, that sounds lovely. I didn't think Adam got along with his brother.'

'He doesn't really, but I think he feels bad we had to put our plans on hold to move to the Cotswolds.'

'Cotswolds adjacent,' I correct, mimicking Adam and she laughs.

'And to be honest, it's more of a smallholding and I think he needs someone to look after his animals when he's away on holiday. He's got chickens, and a couple of donkeys. Olivia is beside herself about the donkeys. Even more than getting permission from the headmistress to take her out of school early for the summer.'

She holds out her phone to show me a photo of them with their big brown Disney eyes and furry ears and I go wide-eyed at how cute they are. 'Oh wow, I can't stand it. *I'm* beside myself about the donkeys.'

'Well, why don't you come down? He has a field you could camp in, all you'd need is a tent. We were thinking of inviting a few friends for the weekend. It's only a couple of hours' drive from London.'

'Try to stop me.' I smile.

'Though I'm not sure I can imagine Fiona camping.' Holly rolls her eyes. 'She's more glamping.'

Remembering my own conversation with Fiona from a few days ago, I feel a beat of concern. 'Have you spoken to Fiona?'

'I just sent a text, inviting her and David and the kids. Why?'

'Nothing, I just wondered,' I reply vaguely.

We're interrupted by a commotion outside. A bell ringing and lots of clapping and cheering.

'What's going on?'

'That's the bell a patient rings to signal the end of their

treatment.' A nurse appears from the next room and overhears me. 'It's a tradition, to acknowledge what you've been through,' she explains. 'A lot of patients invite their families and friends. It can be quite a celebration.'

'Are you going to do it?' I turn to Holly.

'Oh, I don't think so.' Holly shakes her head firmly. 'It's not really my thing.'

'There's no pressure, it's every patient's personal choice.' Smiling kindly, the nurse looks at Holly. 'We'll just be a few more minutes, we're preparing the room for you.'

'Thanks.'

As she leaves, I turn to Holly.

'Are you sure you don't want to?'

But Holly is adamant. 'I just want to walk out of this hospital, and get on with my life. I don't need to mark it by ringing a bell.'

At that moment a door opens to the waiting room and another woman enters. We say our hellos. She looks really nervous.

'First time?' asks Holly.

'Yeah, I'm just starting my treatment.'

'Don't worry. You'll get through it.'

'Hope so.' She gives an anxious smile and sits down. 'The end seems a long way off.'

'That's what I thought, but there is a finishing line,' reassures Holly, then she pauses, her expression thoughtful. 'Actually, today's my last day. I'm just about to go in for my last session. Do you want to come watch me ring the bell afterwards?'

The woman's face brightens. 'Really? Oh, congratulations, that's amazing.'

'Ms Holly Jackson? We're ready for you now, so if you'd like to come through . . .'

As her name is called, Holly stands ups and I give her a smile of encouragement. And in turn she passes on her own to the woman sitting across from her. 'Soon it will be your turn to ring the bell.'

I'm grateful for:
1. *My brave, brilliant friend for changing her mind and ringing the bell, not for herself, but for all the other patients that are just starting their treatment and giving them the greatest gift of all: hope.*

A Weight Is Lifted

'It's very bijou.'

Cricket is at my flat. It's the first time she's visited as I usually go over to hers, but this time she's made the journey across town as I needed some advice. She's walking around, eyes darting everywhere. I feel like the people on *Grand Designs* when Kevin McCloud turns up at the end.

'I love what you've done with the living area, but have you thought about a bold colour for the kitchen? How about a peacock green? It would go wonderfully with all the plants.'

'I need a new kitchen,' I sigh. 'It's ancient.'

'Nonsense, just give it a lick of paint. Hang a chandelier. A nice portrait would look wonderful over that fridge.'

'A portrait? In a kitchen?'

'Why not? Kitchens are just another room. We used to have a piano in the kitchen of our first flat. Monty would play it very badly, while I made my famous spaghetti bolognese.'

God, I love Cricket.

'Debussy, "Clair de lune" . . . Mozart, Piano Sonata No. 16 . . . J. S. Bach, Minuet in G Major . . .' She trails off, her mind casting back. 'Classic FM just isn't the same.' She shakes her head in disappointment.

'I can barely find space for my cutlery, I don't think I'd fit a piano in my kitchen,' I say and she laughs.

'Well, it probably wasn't a good idea, all the steam eventually buggered up the keys.'

448

'I'll bear it in mind,' I nod, 'but I didn't invite you over to give me interior design advice.' I lead her out of the kitchen and into my tiny bedroom. 'I need your advice as to what to wear for the opening night. I've bought about a dozen new outfits, and seriously, I have no idea!'

It feels like one of those pinch-yourself moments. I still can't quite believe that the opening night is finally here, just a week away now. After all the delays and unforeseen setbacks, largely due to the pandemic, Monty's play is finally going to open in the West End to an audience of celebrities, theatre critics and the general public. It's incredible to think back to that moment in Cricket's kitchen, when over bowls of steaming moules frites, she first gave me her late husband's unfinished manuscript, and the seed of an idea was born.

And now here we are, nearly three years later. So much has happened since then. For a while, it looked like it might never happen, but Cricket was always determined. She always kept that light alive and never wavered. She never gave up. The play is testament to the belief she had in her husband and her belief in his play and talent as a playwright. And her belief in me that I could help finish it. In some small way I played a part in all of this. I've never felt more proud, or excited.

But not as much as my mother, who is coming down to London with Dad next week to be my special guests. She's beside herself at the thought of being at the opening night of a West End play written by her daughter. Which is how Mum is describing it to all her neighbours, even though I keep trying to tell her I only played a small part. 'Nonsense, your name is in the theatre programme!' she keeps saying breathlessly. There's even been talk of a hat. I think I might have been forgiven for calling off the wedding to Edward. At least I hope so.

As for Edward, it's weird to think he won't be there. I always imagined he'd be with me on the opening night, to share it all with me. Part of me wondered if despite us breaking up I could still invite him, as a friend, but then we're not friends, not really, are we? I don't know what the dictionary definition of a friend is, but I don't think we qualify. We've broken up and the only time we speak is via text or when it's Arthur's changeover day. Though to be honest, even that's less and less. In the last few months we've both started leaving a key. It's easier this way, more convenient. Much easier to avoid each other.

Cricket's guests include Theo and his wife and their grown-up daughter, and Jack, of course. Jack's still staying with her and they seem to have grown closer than ever. She doesn't say much about their relationship. Cricket is not of the over-sharing generation. There's no endless analysis of their conversations or discussions about where this relation-ship is going to lead, because, like she says, why does it have to lead anywhere? In navigating this new, unexpected chapter in her life, she seems happy and grateful and without expect-ation. She's taken to referring to Jack as 'the icing on the cake'. Maybe that's how we should all view love when, and if, it finds us. The icing on the cake.

Having hung all the clothes over the back of my wardrobe, I try each outfit on while Cricket sits on the end of my bed, instructing me to turn this way and that.

'So what do you think?'

'I think they're all perfectly fine,' she announces finally, after I've spent over an hour trying on outfits and am exhausted from all that twirling around and getting things stuck over my head.

'But I need to make a decision,' I sigh in frustration.

She studies me, her face thoughtful.

'Yes, you do, Nell,' she says quietly and as my eyes meet her bright blue ones I know we're not talking about my outfits any more.

'It's not my place to interfere, but you need to move forwards in your life, one way or another,' she says gently. 'It's time.'

Life weighs heavy on my shoulders and I sit down on the bed next to her. 'I wish someone would just tell me what to do.'

She smiles then, and at such kindness I feel tears spring up.

'No one can do that,' she says, quietly.

'But I feel like I don't know what I'm doing. Like there's so much pressure to make the right choice, in case I get it wrong and regret it.' I brush away a tear that's escaped down my cheek.

'Oh, my dear.' Reaching out for my hand, she squeezes it in hers. 'There is no right or wrong.' She looks at me, her face imploring. 'Nobody knows what they're doing, and when you realize that, it gets so much easier.'

Our eyes meet and I feel such a sense of gratefulness and relief that I knocked on her door, on that cold January day, more than three years ago. I can't imagine what my life would have been like if we had never met.

'I just feel like I've made a mess of everything.'

'But that's what you're supposed to do!' She lets out a throaty laugh. 'Life is meant to be messy. It's how we discover things and evolve and learn. How can you do all that without breaking things and making mistakes? After all, you can't make an omelette without breaking a few eggs.'

Listening, I give a little nod, encouraged.

'Life's not meant to be all neat and tidy, packaged into little squares and given a flattering filter and a snappy hashtag.'

I look in surprise as she pulls out her phone.

'You're on Instagram?'

'Well, I don't know about *on*. I haven't posted any photos yet,' she confesses. 'I thought I'd join after my accident. Well, I had a lot of time on my hands and I wanted to see what all the fuss was about.'

'So, what do you think?'

She frowns, considering her answer. 'You know, back in the day, we used to have to go round to a friend's house to watch their holiday slides. The curtains would be drawn and there'd be a projector and a white bed sheet strung up on the wall. Thankfully, people served drinks as it was *torturous*. I'll never forget Margaret and Lionel's yearly trips to Lytham St Annes. Endless hours of photographs of plates of food and boring views, each of them taking it in turns to stand in front of tourist attractions like wooden puppets. Worse still, then came the invention of the home video and we had to suffer their Nordic cruises.'

Rolling her eyes, she gives a little shudder and I stifle laughter.

'Well, anyway, it reminded me a lot of that. Only people choose to do it voluntarily now, which I do think is rather strange . . . but maybe that's just me . . .' She trails off and peers at her phone. 'You know, I do seem to have already amassed rather a few followers. Though, it's rather odd, as they're all random men with their shirts off,' she frowns, scrolling through, which makes me smile, despite myself.

'Maybe you should delete those.' Now it's my turn to give advice.

'Perhaps later,' she beams mischievously and I laugh, despite my situation. 'But anyway, back to my point. Life is meant to be messy. The best meals always come from the messiest kitchens.'

'But I haven't made a meal, I haven't made anything, least of all a decision,' I sigh. 'And the worst part of all this, is I still love Edward.'

I raise my eyes to meet Cricket's and, putting her arm around my shoulder, she pulls me close. 'You know, Nell, what I don't think you realize is that sometimes in life, not making a decision is still making a decision,' she says gently.

And just like that, a curious thing happens. It's like a weight is finally lifted.

Thanks for the Memories

We're always being told to stay in the moment. *Live for the Moment! The Present is a Gift! Don't Look Back!* But it's not easy when your phone keeps creating memories and dragging you into the past.

Only this evening I was sitting on my windowsill with the sash flung wide open, doing a bit of joy scrolling* – when out of nowhere my phone threw up a selfie of me and Edward. Suddenly I was yanked out of my blissful reverie of cute cat videos to watch a movie made up of a montage of photos and videos of the two of us, taken from my photo library, all set to music.

Me and Edward, in woolly hats and scarves, on Hampstead Heath. Edward grinning like a loon in his Christmas jumper. Arthur looking bemused in reindeer antlers. Me up a ladder with a paintbrush and a gin and tonic, more paint on me than on the walls. Edward flipping pancakes, me *eating* pancakes. A close-up of the scary, huge spider Edward saved me from and my terrified expression. Me laughing my head off when he and Arthur both fell in the river playing fetch, Edward emerging with the stick in his mouth, Arthur wagging his tail like he's demented.

Random, seemingly inconsequential moments, that strung

---

* As opposed to doom scrolling, this involves lots of adorable animal videos that bring nothing but joy.

together make up a life shared. Up pops that evening with Edward on Richmond Hill, when we toasted to the future. I had no idea that just a couple of weeks later he'd propose. Hard to believe that was almost a year ago . . . Reminded, I feel suddenly quite teary. And horribly depressed. FFS and this music! Talk about the saddest soundtrack you'll ever hear. It's positively sadistic!

Fumbling with my screen, I swipe up and down and left and right in an attempt to get rid of it – memories, it seems, are persistent little buggers – and quickly open my Rightmove app. House porn always cheers me up and depresses me in equal measure, but I know that looking at someone's west-facing garden and terrible taste in soft furnishings will take my mind off the total cock-up I've made of everything. Oooh, and look at that dream kitchen! It has a cherry-red Aga and everything.

Forget mindfulness, this is my idea of self-care. Sometimes I like to set the price range into the millions and imagine I've won the lottery and am shopping for a detached house with a swimming pool and one of those circular gravel driveways to swing my sportscar around on. Though what's crazy is there are still some houses I wouldn't want to live in. Trust me, money does not buy taste.

Idly punching in postcodes, I look to see if Fiona's house is still for sale. We haven't spoken since our long conversation, other than to exchange a few texts. I know things have been tough. She and David have met with a marriage counsellor. They've talked about separating. No one's mentioned divorce. *Yet*, she added. To which I replied that I was here if she or the kids needed me. If I've learned anything, it's that we can't fix our friends' problems, all we can do is support them.

A flat pops up that looks like Edward's. Hang on – peering

closer at the exterior photo, I suddenly realize I've set the radius to five miles from Fiona's postcode – *it is Edward's*!

> 'Added today. New to the market, a beautiful, light and spacious three-bedroom Edwardian maisonette in one of London's leafiest suburbs. Interior photos coming soon.'

My mind goes into freefall. Today! No wonder he needed to de-clutter his flat. He's selling up and moving! But where? Away from London? And what about Arthur? A million questions whirl around my head; implications multiplying, hard truths hitting, a new reality dawning.

So this is it. The End. It's really over.

It's like hitting the ground at a hundred miles an hour, limbs flying, heart shattering. I do the only thing I can think to do. I burst into tears.

A Moment of Truth

I wake up early and make coffee. Grinding up the beans, I add a few extra spoonfuls to my little espresso pot. I need it to be extra strong. This morning I'm going to record the last in the series of my podcast and it's going to be an extra special episode.

After talking to Fiona, I've been thinking a lot about being truthful. One thing I've always wanted to be is honest. To tell it like it is. Even when it's scary. *Even more so* when it's scary. Because it's only by being vulnerable that we discover a sense of connection to other people, and in doing so, find our real strength.

And I thought about how we talk a lot about living an authentic life, but what does that really mean? I think it means facing up to the past, accepting our regrets and forgiving ourselves our mistakes. It means Stop. Beating. Yourself. Up. It means figuring out what's important to ourselves and embracing it – even the shitty bits – because it's those bits that made you the person you are now.

It means being truthful to yourself. And to others. Even when it's really fucking hard.

This past year, I've talked about a lot of things and to a lot of amazing women; inspiring, hardworking, all-feeling women who all have a valuable story to tell. You don't have to wear a cape to be a superhero and I'm so proud of our important conversations about feeling flawed and confused, of dealing with whatever it is life throws at you, and finding hope and joy in the unlikeliest places. About the very real, daily struggle to recognize your messy life in a world of perfect Instagram ones and not feel like a bit of a fuck-up.

And I've continued to tell it like it is with my weekly confessions and tales of Motherfucking Monday, We're Nearly There Wednesday, and Sod This Sunday. Acknowledging all the trials and tribulations of this thing called life, with its sad bits and funny bits, wonderful bits and hard bits. But now, I feel I owe more to my listeners.

Armed with my coffee, I sit down at my microphone. Putting on my headphones, I do all the usual checks. Just like I do every week when I record a new episode. Only this episode is going to be different.

You see, I've never been able to talk about this subject before. It's something I've stayed firmly away from. I thought I was protecting myself by keeping it private, but more and more I've begun to feel like an imposter. As my audience has grown, so has the number of amazing messages I get from my listeners. Messages telling me I'm an inspiration, that for the first time in their life they feel seen, related to, better about their lives, *not alone*. And yet, I don't feel like an inspiration, I feel like a fake.

Because if I'm asking people to be honest and to bare their souls, I have to bare mine. To my loyal and amazing listeners. To my family and friends. To the man I hoped to share the rest of my life with. Edward has never listened to my podcast, so I know he'll never hear this, but it doesn't matter. I know I've lost him for ever. But I've got to say it anyway.

My heart thumping, I clear my throat. My stomach twists. I'm terrified.

And yet, I've got to get this out there, into the universe, because it's telling the truth that sets you free. It's the start of everything. I thought I'd let this go on a hilltop in Spain, when I held the grainy ultrasound in my hand and let it be carried away on the wind. That I'd changed my narrative from one of fear and failure.

But this past year I've realized that life is ever-changing and so are we. That our feelings are like waves, constantly ebbing and flowing, along with our experiences. Triggering us, soothing us, surprising us, confusing us. And you can think you've left something behind, only for it to return when you least expect it.

I swallow hard. I don't know where to start. If I'm even brave enough to record this confession. Doubts begin to multiply. So then I do what I always do when I haven't a clue what I'm doing. I just say *Sod This* and dive in.

I press record:

'*Hi and welcome to* Confessions of a Forty-Something F**k-Up. *To mark the end of the series, I want to record an extra special episode. Today's confession is something I've never publicly spoken about before. Something I've kept hidden from most of my friends and family . . .*'

I take a deep breath, screwing up my fists underneath the desk, gathering my courage.

'*But I want to talk about it today, because you see, I've lost the man I love because I couldn't share my story. Because I thought I'd let go of grief, but it turns out grief has to let go of you. And because I hope that me finding the strength to be my most vulnerable will help shine a light into the darkness of anyone listening who's gone through this too.*

'*Statistics say one in four women will suffer a miscarriage within the first three months. But my pregnancy loss wasn't a statistic. It was my baby and their name was Shrimp. And in this extra special confession I want to honour their memory and tell you all about them . . .'*

Opening Night

Photographers. Celebrities. Flashbulbs. Crowds.

I mean, seriously, could it be a more pinch-me moment?

It's the opening night of Monty's play, *The Paris Raincoat*, and I'm walking the red carpet at the Prince Regent Theatre in the West End. It's so exciting and nerve-wracking and I'll be for ever indebted to Cricket. It was such an honour to be asked to finish his play. It's also completely and utterly surreal. This kind of stuff doesn't happen to people like me. It happens to other people. Glossy people you see in magazines, with hair and make-up and six-inch stilettos and designer frocks and famous husbands.

Not forty-something fuck-ups with their Spanx and rental dress and Mum and Dad.

'Don't look now, but there's whatsaname off the telly,' gasps Mum, eyes wide like saucers.

'Where?' says Dad loudly, head swivelling. 'I can't see anyone off the telly!'

'Yes, you can, it's that famous actor!'

'What famous actor?'

Argh. My parents. I love them dearly but they are not subtle. Thankfully Cricket comes to the rescue.

'Carol and Philip, come this way,' she says, appearing between them with a vibrant smile. Cricket first met Mum and Dad when she was my plus-one at my brother's wedding and later that year we all spent Christmas together, so it's been lovely for them to see each other again. 'Let's all have a photo together.'

Looping an arm through each of theirs, she gently leads them over to the roped-off area by the entrance where Jack is standing, along with Monty's son, Theo, and his wife and daughter. I follow behind gratefully and together we form a group for the pack of press photographers.

Everyone looks slightly stunned by it all, except of course for Cricket and Jack, who are old pros at this sort of thing and look thoroughly at home as the flashbulbs begin popping. There's Jack, square-jawed and absurdly handsome, looking like a legend with his California tan, white beard and black tux, exuding that old-school Hollywood glamour that you don't see any more. And Cricket, sporting lots of black eyeliner, a canary-yellow trouser suit and gold plimsolls.

They look so cool and funky and vibrant, it's hard to believe they're both in their eighties, but then what do your eighties look like any more? Certainly not how I used to imagine before I met Cricket. I guess, it's whatever you want it to look like.

After having our photos taken, we move inside the foyer of the theatre, which is buzzing with journalists, ticket-holders, celebrities and anticipation.

'OK, so who's the daughter here and who's the mom?' asks Jack, making Mum blush to the roots of her up-do and go all teenage giggly.

I glance across at Cricket and give her a little smile of approval. When your best friend meets someone you always feel protective, it doesn't matter if your friend is eighteen or eighty-plus. But not only does he plainly adore her, I'm so impressed by how sensitively he's navigating their relationship.

Cricket is here as Monty's widow, but the fact she came with Jack is both personally and publicly symbolic. She's honouring the past while embracing the present. Showing both herself, and the world, that your heart is big enough to hold both.

'So, Catherine Williamson, who are you with tonight?' A journalist stops her in the foyer as we're being shown to our seats and Cricket gives a beatific smile.

'My family and friends,' she replies proudly and I watch Theo's face flood with emotion. There's been no public announcement that he's Monty's son, and there never will be, in consideration of the memory of both his parents. Him being here tonight with his own family, included and a part of all this, is acknowledgement enough.

'Nell, love, this is bloody amazing,' whispers Dad, squeezing my hand as we climb the staircase to the dress circle.

'Thanks, Dad. I know it's not a wedding . . .'

'Wedding, schmedding,' tuts Mum dismissively, as we're shown to our seats in the loge, which gives us the best view in the house. Along with all my friends, she listened to the special episode of my podcast; beforehand I was nervous of their reaction, but everyone has been so kind and supportive. I should've done it years ago, but I wasn't ready. Timing is everything.

'Weddings are ten a penny, but now this—' She breaks off as we look out at the packed theatre stretching out before us, all red velvet and gold trimming, steeped in history and grandeur. 'Now this, is something special.'

'If it wasn't for your daughter, we wouldn't be having an opening night,' says Cricket, finding her seat in front of me.

'Oh, I don't know about that,' I say, embarrassed.

'Well, I do,' replies Cricket. 'We wouldn't have a finished play to be performed.'

I shoot her a grateful, but embarrassed, look, and quickly sit down beside Mum, who leans across and smooths a rogue piece of hair behind my ear, just like she used to do when I was small. It's surprisingly touching.

'We're very proud of her,' says Mum, 'aren't we, Philip.'

It's a statement not a question and Dad nods.

'That we are, Carol.'

It's amazing how just a few words can carry so much weight, and all at once I feel the force field of their love. And the realization that the only person that's ever been disappointed in me has been myself.

A few moments later, and the performance is about to start. The atmosphere is electric. The press and celebrities are in attendance. I can almost feel the adrenalin coming from the actors backstage and I feel jittery with nerves and anticipation. I know the past week of rehearsals has been tough and stakes are high. Live theatre isn't like film. It's a living, breathing thing and anything could happen. But that's where the magic happens. As I look out into the theatre I can see there isn't a single empty seat.

Except for the one next to me. We're in a row of four and there's only three of us.

It must be a spare.

And then I see him. That tall, familiar figure in his favourite dark suit. Hair that grows like a weed, and forever needs cutting, hanging over his black-rimmed glasses. I watch as he walks down the steps towards me, and now Edward's here, standing beside me, and I'm looking at him with disbelief.

'But how?'

I glance at Mum and Dad's blank faces, and then at Cricket.

'What can I say?' she shrugs. 'I'm an interfering old woman.'

'Quiet, please,' instructs a voice over the loudspeaker, and as the theatre goes dark he slips into the seat next to me and

I turn to him, to say something, but he presses his finger gently against my lips.

'Ssh, we're about to begin.'

And as the curtain rises and the lights come on, it feels like he's talking about more than just the play.

Later

The applause nearly brings the house down. We stand and we clap until our hands hurt and our faces ache from smiling. I think the standing ovation lasts about five minutes. It could be longer, I can't tell, I lose track of time. Euphoria does that to you.

Afterwards we go backstage to see all the cast and crew in their dressing rooms. Everyone is high on adrenalin and it's a blur of congratulating, hugging, high-fiving.

In the middle of it all, Edward and I look at each other and I'm reminded of the time Cricket told me about making a French exit. It's the perfect time.

Together we slip away. Outside, darkness has fallen and the city is warm and sultry. We start walking in no particular direction.

'So, I have a confession.'

He speaks first.

'I listened to your podcast.'

I look at him in astonishment. 'You never listen to my podcast.'

'I thought I should start. I downloaded and listened to them all. Including the special bonus episode.'

We look at each other, the reality sinking in.

'So you heard everything,' I say finally.

'Yes,' he nods and as our eyes meet he holds my gaze. It conveys so much.

466

'And you still showed up tonight.'

'I'll always show up for you.'

His voice is quiet but steady and I'm suddenly reminded of that morning in the hospital car park. When Dad was hovering between life and death and Edward drove all the way up from London without being asked. Just to be there for me. To show me I could lean on him in the most desperate of times and I wasn't alone.

'When Cricket got in touch and asked me if I'd come tonight, I was worried you wouldn't want to see me. But it was a chance I was willing to take.'

We pause on the pavement and he turns to me.

'I've missed you.'

'I've missed you too.'

'Look, I'm sorry about everything I said—'

'Don't.' I cut him off. 'We both said things we didn't mean . . . things we should have said ages ago . . .'

I look at him, my face full of apology, but he simply reaches for my hand.

'Remember that time at your parents', when your dad was in hospital and I was leaving.'

'You were stripping the bed and wouldn't let me help.'

'I seem to remember having a fight with the flowery duvet cover,' he admits, his face serious.

'And I said I was too emotional and you said you were a deeply repressed public schoolboy,' I add, interlacing my fingers through his.

'Good to see some things haven't changed,' he nods and a look passes between us. 'But we also said that from now on we should always say what's on our minds. It doesn't matter what it is.'

I nod, remembering. 'Even if it's my murderous thoughts over the thermostat.'

'Even if it was your murderous thoughts over the thermostat,' he nods and then smiles.

'We didn't do a very good job of that, did we?'

'No, I guess we didn't.'

'How about we start again now?' he suggests.

'OK. You go first,' I reply.

'OK.'

And so the conversation begins. It's funny how it's often so hard to start talking about something that weeks and months and years can go by with so much unsaid, looking for the right moment that you can never find, and yet once you take that first difficult step, it's like turning on a tap. As the words flow freely we lose track of time, meandering through a maze of back streets, past the city's landmarks, in no real direction, moving forwards, growing closer, wondering why it was ever so hard.

Of course we start with the easy stuff first – the mix-ups and misunderstandings; after six months apart it's a process of peeling back the layers before we can get to the difficult stuff underneath. Talking about other people, instead of ourselves.

'Annabel wanted to meet me to talk about Pazza . . .'

'Pazza!'

'Yes, they've been seeing each other, didn't you know?'

'No, I didn't!'

'Oh dear, perhaps that's a secret, it's still early days. She ended up giving me some life-coaching advice as I told her about how lost I was without you.'

You were lost without me? I think, but instead say, 'So that's what you were doing the morning I saw you with your yoga mats? I thought you were acting weird.'

'I thought *you* were acting weird,' he replies, and I suddenly remember The Lost Sapphire and The Poo Bag, which sounds a bit like a new Disney movie, and decide that we don't need to share everything.

He mentions the hashtag #oldflames. He thought it meant I'd seen Ethan, that we'd reconnected in LA. I tell him it was in reference to Cricket and I thought he didn't look at social media. He reminds me of his teenage sons who are never off social media and follow me. Lots of things start to make sense.

'Still, I can't believe you're moving away, that you didn't tell me,' I say, and when he pretends not to know what I'm talking about, I tell him about the ad I saw on Rightmove and his face floods with comprehension. 'You mean the flat above me.'

'Above you?'

'Yes, the flat above me is for sale.' As he's talking I realize there weren't any interior photos. I'd just jumped to conclusions.

'I thought I'd lost you, that you were leaving,' I tell him.

'Why would you think that, when I'm right here?' he replies.

Put it this way, there's a lot to unpack.

And then, finally, we get to the hard stuff. Because you can walk around London holding hands, and being honest, and missing each other. But it still doesn't change why we broke up. Why we're broken up.

'When I found the pregnancy test, it brought it all back. It was so unexpected. So confusing. I thought I'd let all that go a long time ago. Made peace with it. But it's not that simple. When you said you didn't want any more children, you were so certain, but I wasn't. I needed to find out what I wanted.'

We've reached the river now and we pause on the bridge,

turning our backs to the traffic and staring out across the water. It feels weirdly intimate, just the two of us, while the city rumbles around us.

'And what did you find out?'

I look at Edward, my mind casting back over this last year, and I think how I've discovered and learned so many, *many* things. How do I start to make sense of it all? For so long I was told a successful life looked a certain way. You fell in love, got married, had kids, a nice house, a good job, thighs that didn't meet in the middle. And all by the age you were forty. It was a paint-by-numbers life.

And there was me with my messy one that didn't fit. Trying to navigate a mid-life marriage, teenage stepkids, an ex-wife, a few different jobs, a dog that chased squirrels and ate engagement rings, only it turned out he didn't, and a best friend in her eighties.

It's a life that looked different to the one I thought I was going to live, but I loved it. I chose it. And yet, for a moment there I wondered if I was getting it wrong. If there was something missing. If there was something else that I wanted. And I was filled with confusion and doubt.

And I found out that grief isn't linear. That it comes in waves and you can be fine one minute, and not the next. That life is complicated. That there is so much pressure to have it all, when all you need is enough. That I love you, Edward. That I don't want to do it by myself. That life is fragile. That none of us gets out of here alive. That ageing is not for sissies, but it's a privilege denied to many. That everything we take for granted we will eventually lose. That I'm lucky. That there is no right or wrong choice.

That I have amazing friends. Brave friends. The best of friends. That everyone is dealing with their own shit. That everyone feels like they're fucking up. That you can live an brilliant, meaningful, fulfilled life and not be a mother. That there are incredible, wonderful people who adopt, but that wasn't to be my journey. That it can be difficult being a mum. That it can be difficult not being a mum. That I still feel like a mum, even though Shrimp only existed for nine weeks. That I didn't want to bring my loss into my relationship, but I realized I couldn't leave it behind.

I found out that I was scared. That I didn't want to make a fuss. That it's difficult to talk about. That I carried a lot of blame. That I needed to forgive myself. That grief made me avoid motherhood. That I was too afraid to try and fail again. That I was afraid to hope. That I'll never forget. That you can't let go of grief, you have to wait until it lets go of you. That I can grieve the absence but at the same time feel joy.

That when I see you with Evie I feel like my heart's going to burst. That I love Ollie and Louis. That I already had a family, it just didn't look how I thought it was going to and it took me some time to realize that. That I'm grateful for everything I've gone through because it's made me the person I am now. That I'm stronger. That I'm not scared any more. That I still don't know what the hell I'm doing and probably never will. That you have to keep filling up the tank. That you have to keep finding the courage to embrace the life that was meant for you. That you have to keep choosing it. That you have to keep committing to it. That what I have is enough. More than enough.

I look at Edward. He's still waiting for me to answer. I think all of these things, but when I finally speak, all I say is this:

'That sometimes you have to get lost to find yourself again.'

'And have you?'

'Yes . . . I think so,' I add, looking at him uncertainly. 'But by doing that I fucked everything up between us.'

'You?' Edward's face, so close to mine, looks incredulous. 'No, I did that.' He shakes his head. 'I fucked up. I fucked it all up.'

It's almost comical hearing Edward swear. But it's also powerful.

'No, you didn't.'

'Yes, I did. I lost you.'

His eyes never leave mine and I feel the breath catch in the back of my throat.

'Do you want to know the reason I came to the theatre tonight? It was because I wanted to tell you that I can't lose you. That I love you. That I want to make you happy. That I don't want you to have to choose, I want you to have it all. And if you want to try and have a baby, then let's try.'

A gust of warm wind comes from nowhere, blowing around us, and I turn my head to gaze out across the River Thames. The water is inky dark, its embankments strung with fairy lights. The skyline is illuminated. In the distance I can see the London Eye. It feels both familiar and exhilarating.

'You know, there's a saying, "It's not getting what you want, it's wanting what you've got,"' I say, finally turning back to him.

'Penelope, that sounds like a fridge magnet.'

'Actually, I think it was a fridge magnet.'

Edward looks at me underneath the streetlamp and we both start to grin at each other. *This*. This is what I want. This is what I've missed.

'So what happens now?'

All that other stuff seems to disappear and it's just the two of us again, right back where we started.

'You asked me that once before, remember?' My mind casts back to New Year's Eve, and those early hours when we first got together.

'And what did you say?'

'I said I don't know,' I admit, 'and then you kissed me.'

Wrapping his arms around me, he pulls me towards him.

'I still think that's a good answer,' he says, kissing me. 'But I've got an even better one.'

I look up at his dark eyes. 'Oh, yeah?'

Breaking apart, he hails a passing cab. 'Let's go home.'

And then he's holding open the door of the black cab and I'm climbing inside. And as he slides next to me on the back seat I sink into his lapel, feeling his arm around me as I lean against his chest. His familiar body. I breathe him in. Exhausted. Tearful. Happy. Safe. I let my eyes close as we begin our journey. A wise person once told me we are conditioned to believe that love is effortless. But love is hard and difficult and complicated and frustrating. Loving someone is the hardest thing you will ever do.

It's also the best.

A Paris Raincoat Review – He Saved the Best Till Last

Monty Williamson is a legend in the world of theatre. As one of our most gifted playwrights, he inspired an entire generation with his vision, social commentary and exploration of human relationships, and his death was mourned by audiences and critics alike. So when rumours began circulating of the discovery of an unfinished play, followed by an announcement by renowned director Christopher Chepstow that it was to go into production, the theatre world was set alight.

Written during Williamson's time spent living in Paris in the fifties, the manuscript was heavily annotated and his widow, whom he affectionately nicknamed Cricket, entrusted the task of completion to her close friend, journalist and podcaster, Nell Stevens. A highly unusual choice, it seemed to many an impossible task for even the most seasoned of playwrights to try to recreate the genius that was Williamson. Later, a series of setbacks and delays caused people to wonder if the play would ever go into production. Some privately wondered if it might be a blessing.

But a blessing it was tonight, when the curtain finally went up on *A Paris Raincoat*. With an inspired cast, visionary sets and direction by Chepstow, the energy is electrifying. Lloyd G Joseph is astonishing in the lead. After a decade out of the limelight, he roars back onstage in his raw portrayal of a disillusioned writer embroiled in an affair with his married landlady. The betrayal is further complicated by an illicit love affair with his co-worker Diego which, in a world where same-sex relationships are still illegal, adds tension and poignancy.

Set over three days, the exciting performances explore the tangled web of relationships; it couldn't feel more timely. The dialogue is at once brilliantly funny and heartrending, but always profoundly truthful. We see ourselves in these characters and their lives and as the curtain falls we are left heartbroken yet hopeful. To all the doubters who thought this play wouldn't pull it off, Stevens has done a remarkable job and it will be exciting to see what's next for her. Book your tickets before it sells out.

Monty Williamson certainly saved the best till last.

At the Prince Regent Theatre, until 10 September.

P.S.

A week later in New York. It's a Tuesday. The sun shines. The taxi's late. Edward wears his best shirt, I wear my favourite sundress. It's pink with white stripes and I look like a candy cane. Edward tells me I've never looked more beautiful. I tell him he's a keeper. Traffic's terrible. I don't notice. Two strangers agree to be our witnesses. Mum is going to kill me. We can't stop smiling as we say our vows. Just the two of us. No fuss. Cricket was right. Sod the big dress and the disco. Feel so happy. You can now kiss the bride. What took us so long? Life. Luckily love is patient and they have an umbrella as it's started to rain. Selfies on the steps of City Hall. Edward's thumb over the lens. Biodegradable confetti (of course) and Michelle's bunting strung up in our hotel room. Toasting ourselves in the bar with Manhattans. When shall we tell everyone? Not yet. Let it just be ours for a little while. I love you. I love you too. Later, jetlagged and back in London, walking Arthur along the river. Wow, look at the sunset. An old married couple and their dog. Holding hands and never letting go. We did it. We did it. We did it.

WhatsApp Group: Summer Get-Together

Holly

Just a reminder it's our get-together next weekend. Satnav can be dodgy so I'm sending you directions to the farmhouse you can print off. Beach is five mins so bring swimming costumes but don't forget wellies in case it rains. It is England! Can't wait to see you all.

Fiona

Can anyone help me put up a tent?

Don't worry, Edward will do it.

Fiona

Thanks!

He's so excited we're going camping, he's been testing all his kit. Last night he put the tent up in the living room and tonight he's cooking dinner on the camping stove.

Fiona

Sounds like you're living with Bear Grylls.

Boy Scout more like.

Michelle

Least you're prepared! Max joked that with our lot it's going to be Five Go Mad in Dorset with a Toddler. Least I think he was joking.

Holly

It's not Dorset, it's West Wittering.

Michelle

Shit. Yes, God, me and directions. We'll still be going mad, tho!
ANYWAY WE HAVE MARSHMALLOWS AND TOASTING FORKS.

Hurrah! Can't wait!

Annabel

Can Edward help with my tent too?

Up she pops. But not to worry. I already knew that Holly had invited her and Pazza. In fact, it was actually my idea. When I found out she'd started dating Edward's best friend – having met at our barbecue, they'd bumped into each other at a farmers' market and he'd asked for her number – and that they were now ready to go public, I thought I'd better start practising forgiveness and generosity. I've even taken to hugging crystals. And you know what? I think it might be working; Annabel's not that bad, really.*

---

* Of course this is all absolute bollocks and it's just the crystals talking.

Summer Lovin'

When it decides to pull out all the stops, there's nothing like an English summer. Endless skies the deepest shade of lavender. Scudding white clouds forming shapes and faces. Hedgerows filled with wildflowers and kaleidoscopic butterflies. Whizzing along country lanes underneath a canopy of leaves with the windows wound all the way down as lush green fields give way to the sea.

'You know there's a name for that,' says Edward, gazing steadfastly ahead, both hands on the wheel. Edward is the best kind of driver. Having a *somewhat* anal husband is annoying when it comes to recycling packaging, but when it comes to being behind a wheel, it's wonderful.

'Name for what?' I ask, glancing at the wedding ring on his left hand, relishing that little joyful spark of astonishment and pleasure I get every time I look at it. It still hasn't quite sunk in yet.

'Pareidolia. It's the science behind seeing faces in everyday objects.' He gestures to the clouds ahead.

'You mean there's a science behind why that cloud looks like Elvis?'

'There's science behind everything,' he nods. 'And that's not Elvis, it's Boris Johnson.'

'Boris Johnson!' I gasp in protest. 'Are you crazy? It's Elvis!'

Furrowing his forehead, Edward leans forward over the wheel, then shakes his head. 'Nope. Boris.'

I swat his shoulder and he smiles good-naturedly. 'Are we having our first row as a married couple?'

'Yes, and it's over whether a cloud looks like Elvis or Boris,' I grin, and then we almost pee ourselves laughing.

Holly's directions are right (of course) and soon she and Adam are wafting us through the five-bar gate and into the field where we're going to pitch our tent. The rest of the gang have arrived already and all the kids are running around, thrilled to be released from their postage-stamp-sized gardens in London into all this open space, while all the parents are busy setting up camp.

As we pull up into a grassy corner I notice Edward looks a little stricken. No doubt he's worried that the best spots will be taken, but he seems quickly reassured by my motley crew of friends' efforts. Not everyone was in the Boy Scouts it seems.

'Thank God you made it,' calls out Fiona, waving her instruction booklet like a white flag while her tent lies crumpled on the floor, pegs strewn everywhere. 'I was beginning to get a bit worried.'

'We took the scenic route,' I grin, clambering out of the car and opening the door for Arthur who charges over to Coco and they begin running around excitedly, playing chase. I think there might be a bit of a love affair going on there. Either that or he's mistaken her for a fluffy squirrel and is trying to eat her.

'No, I wasn't worried about you,' she laughs. 'I was worried about me and the kids having to sleep out in the open. Seriously, I have no idea how to put this thing up. It's worse than IKEA.'

Which makes *me* laugh, as I don't think Fiona has set foot in IKEA since we were students, she's a strictly John Lewis girl now.

'A night under the stars might be rather nice,' pipes up

Max and I glance over from unpacking the boot to see his own tent is absolutely ginormous. In fact, it's less tent and more Eden project.

As he waves hello, Michelle appears from inside one of the compartments carrying a large cooler. 'I thought I'd set up the refreshment stall,' she says, putting it on the grass and opening up the lid. 'Wine, beer, prosecco, fizzy water, fancy tonics, gin, ginger beer . . . anyone?'

'Ginger beer? It really is like the Famous Five,' I say and she laughs.

'Fizzy water's great, thanks,' says Max and I see a look pass between them. I know they're still working things out but they both seem happier than they have been in years. I think Max even mentioned something about an interview for a job.

'And we've got nibbles,' pipes up a voice and I turn around to see Annabel emerging from one of those swanky, top-of-the-range camper vans, looking like she's dressed for Henley Regatta, with a tray of hors d'oeuvres. I'd been wondering whose that was, I should have known she wouldn't be in a tent. 'Oh hi, Nell,' she spots me and waves.

'Nice camper van,' I nod.

'Yes, isn't it? It's got a loo and a power shower and it's fully electric.' She looks over at Edward for his approval, but he's still busy unloading the car. He's taken 'Be Prepared' to whole new lengths. 'In the end I didn't think I could do a tent.' She gives a tinkly laugh.

'Come take a look around,' calls Pazza, appearing from behind her.

'Actually, do you think I could borrow your toilet,' says Max. 'I've got a bit of a stomach ache. I knew I shouldn't have had chilli last night . . .'

'Careful, darling,' says Pazza, quickly catching Annabel as

481

she nearly faceplants down the stairs and Max throws me a wink. He knows all about my previous feud with Annabel, though like I say, now she's dating Edward's best friend we're practically best mates now.*

'Right, OK, I think that's everything,' says Edward finally, shutting both the boot and the Thule roof storage and together we troop over to our spot, laden down with all the stuff. 'I'll be right with you, Fiona.'

'Oh, no rush.' Abandoning her attempts at trying to figure out her instruction booklet, she charges over to help with some of the bags and gives both me and Edward a hug.

Everyone is really pleased we're back together again and this weekend seems the ideal time to break the news of our elopement. We told our parents before we left and they were all really happy for us. No one seemed to mind it was just the two of us. Dad made a joke about me saving him a fortune and from having to put on a suit and tie. Even Mum insisted hers were happy tears.

I also FaceTimed with Cricket. She flew back to LA with Jack after the play. A last-minute decision. I don't know when she'll be back. Travelling without a plan she calls it. We were both equally delighted for each other.

But before we have a chance to say anything, Fiona notices our wedding rings and gives a little scream.

'No way! Did you two . . . ? Are you two . . . ?'

She seems unable to finish her sentence, so I help her out.

'I think the word you're looking for is married,' I say as Edward slips his arm around my waist, while still holding the camping stove and tent poles and we both start grinning. 'Yes, we are.'

A split-second pause, followed by –

---

* Please note: practically is a word that's very open to interpretation.

'NELL AND EDWARD GOT MARRIED!'

It's like a klaxon going off. I don't think I've ever heard Fiona yell so loudly but suddenly all my friends are crowding around us, smiling and whooping and congratulating. How? What? When? Engulfing us in a group hug and firing us with questions. You dark horses! This is amazing! I can't believe it! Thank God, I don't have to buy a toaster! What do you mean, you didn't want any fuss? This *demands* fuss! Quick, anyone got any champagne? I've got lots of prosecco!

As friends start popping bottles and filling glasses, Holly passes me a glass.

'Sorry, I hope you didn't think I was hijacking your weekend. This was supposed to be about celebrating the end of your cancer treatment.'

'Don't be silly, this weekend is for everyone. This just means we have more to celebrate, much more, and how can that be anything but a good thing?' She gives me the biggest smile. 'Oh Nell, I'm so damn pleased for you, this is just bloody brilliant.' And she throws her arms wide and gives me a big hug, almost suffocating me, which is quite something as Holly is not a hugger.

'I'm so pleased for you, Nell,' says Fiona, clinking her glass against mine. 'Edward's lovely.'

'Thanks,' I smile, 'he still drives me nuts though.'

'Welcome to married life,' she laughs but I can see the sadness behind her eyes. I know this weekend is hard for her. It's just her and the kids. David has chosen to stay in London. If I needed any reminder that marriage is a leap of faith with no guarantees, it's seeing one of my oldest friends struggling in hers. She and David seemed rock solid. But then nothing is rock solid when the earthquake comes. I guess we just have to live in the moment. No guarantees and all that.

*

As Holly moves off to find Adam, I look over at Edward who is being backslapped by his friend Pazza while Annabel hands out glasses, hors d'oeuvres and napkins. She's right about her hostessing skills, they're really quite something.

'Congratulations, Nell,' she coos, coming over and greeting me with the double-cheek kiss. 'So pleased to see my life-coaching advice to Eddie paid off.'

'Right, yes,' I smile, but her comment rankles. Truly, she is the queen of the back-handed compliment.

'And I just wanted to say me too.'

'Sorry?' I look at her, confused.

'I listened to the special bonus episode of your podcast.' She pauses, as if summoning up courage. 'We called him Sebastian, after Clive's grandfather. He would have been Clementine's little brother. He still is.'

A look passes between us and for that brief moment all the gloss and the steeliness is stripped back and all I see is a sister in arms.

'I light a candle on his birthday every year. It helps.'

'Thank you,' I smile.

And then she slips away.

We drink all the prosecco, celebrating not just our good news but the end of Holly's treatment. Seeing all my friends and the challenges they've faced, I feel a fierce pride. Life hasn't gone to plan for anyone, but they've all handled it with courage and grace and laughter and sheer bloody-mindedness. Who knows what's going to happen in the future, but we've made it this far. Clinking glasses, we do endless toasts, until Max cries, 'OK, so enough of all this celebrating, who's for a swim?' And there's a roar of approval as we all grab our things and head to the beach.

But not until Edward has finished putting up our tent and

Fiona's, which he does with the kind of practised precision of someone who knows how to do a Rubik's cube with just a few flicks of their wrist. It's seriously impressive and extremely attractive. Gone are the days when I would be impressed by a man driving a convertible.

Now it's a man who can lay ground sheets, rig up fly sheets, inflate Swiss air mattresses and unroll sleeping bags to create a bed more comfortable than the one we have at home. And all while producing a portaloo so I don't have to climb outside the tent at night to pee.

I mean seriously, there's nothing sexier. Even Fiona looks impressed by the portaloo and compostable bags, and she's Strictly Glamping.

We're just leaving the campsite when the sound of a car engine causes us to turn around, just as a local taxi is pulling up at the gate.

'Who's that?' I ask, trying to see who the passenger is inside.

'Daddy!' yell Lucas and Izzy, as the door opens and David emerges with a holdall.

As the cab reverses down the single-lane track, they set off running excitedly towards him, and he drops his bag and bends down to scoop them both up, which is no mean feat as they're getting pretty big now. Lifting one up in each arm, Izzy's arms dangling around his neck, Lucas clinging on to him, he walks slowly towards us. I glance at Fiona. This whole time, she's just been standing, watching.

'I didn't know you were coming . . .'

'Neither did I.' He looks at Fiona. 'The house felt empty without you and the kids. I missed my family. I missed you.'

'No surfboard?'

'There wasn't room for it on the train.'

They smile at each other.

485

'Is there room for one more?' asks David.

'It's a six-man tent,' says Fiona.

Edward and I turn and leave them to it.

The beach is wide and surprisingly empty. We've missed the solstice by a week, but it's still very much midsummer and the days are gloriously long. Later we're going to have a bonfire and Edward's boys are due to arrive with their new girlfriends. Well, I say boys but they're practically men. They both just passed their driving tests and Edward bought them a years-old Prius to share. You can imagine the arguments. Still, that will be fun, all of us together.

Taking off our trainers, we go to join the others, who are further along the beach. Arthur runs in and out of the waves, barking with delight, while Edward and I laugh at him. The sun is shining, dipping in and out of the clouds, as we walk slowly, holding hands, our bare feet on the sand, the hems of my jeans getting wet, our footprints behind us getting smaller.

That New Year's Eve, when Edward and I first got together, I realized I'd fallen in love. Not just with him, but with my life. But what I didn't know then, is that I had to *keep* falling in love with it. That every day I have to get up and actively surrender that 'imagined' life – and embrace the life I'm living. It's a daily practice. Just like writing my gratitude list.

Because life will continue to test you. To challenge you. To make you feel like you're fucking up and failing. You can never reach that fantasy, faraway land on the other side, where everything is perfect, because it's exactly that: just a fantasy. You might think you have, but then something will come along and de-rail you. A break-up. An ex getting married. Your colleague at work getting that promotion. A pregnancy announcement. The loss of someone you love. A diagnosis. An unexpected item in the baggage area. *Life*.

There's a reason why Hollywood films end when the couple first kiss and walk off together into the sunset. Or, in our case, the sunrise. Because that's when real life starts. Falling in love is the easy bit, it's staying in love that's the hard bit.

A wave comes rushing in and we try to outrun it, but it's too late. My jeans are soaked. Edward's glasses are covered in spray. He laughs at me. I have to laugh too.

Edward says sometimes it's got to all fall apart so you can put it back together better. Maybe it's like Kintsugi. Maybe our relationship fractured and fell apart so we could build it back stronger. And the cracks and the breaks and the flaws and the imperfections are what gives us our strength and what makes it more beautiful.

I like that idea. Though ask me again when we're having a row about the central heating. I smile as I watch him run ahead to join Arthur and they chase each other in circles along the beach.

We've decided we're not going to try and have a baby. But we're not going to try not to either. So, I don't know what's going to happen, and that's OK. Life doesn't go to plan, so why make one? Either way, what we have is enough. More than enough. Not just with Edward and Arthur and the boys, but with my podcast and column and the obituaries and the play . . . and Cricket and all my friends and family. It's bursting full of enoughs. That doesn't mean there won't be moments when I feel sad or grieve for what might have been, but at the same time I know I'll feel happy and joyful for what we have. And I'll light a candle.

I feel a raindrop on my cheek and look up at the clouds. The sun is still shining but it's started to rain and I turn my face to the sky, feeling the warm rain on my forehead.

Because while my life is brilliant, it's also messy and complicated. I used to wish it was straightforward, but it's not. It's not black and white. But it's not shades of grey either. It's every colour of the rainbow.

'Look.'

I hear Edward's voice and turn around to see him pointing, as one magically appears in the sky. Huge and iridescent, it arches above the shore. I stare at it, mesmerized, then break into the widest smile.

And rainbows are amazing.

Epilogue

If the last twelve months have taught me anything about life, it's that I'm still learning and I always will be. More than ever, I know there is no destination you finally arrive at where everything is figured out, fixed and sorted. All the amazing women I interviewed on my podcast and letters to our column are testament to that. None of us know what we're doing, but we're doing it anyway. Life, like us, is a sum of moving parts. And while there will be brilliant, joyful, life-can't-get-better-than-this moments, there will be moments that bring you to your knees.

I remember once, when things were particularly tough, talking to Cricket. About all the messy stuff. The scary stuff. The hard bits. The bits that don't go right, or won't fit, or feel broken. And how when things feel like a struggle or we're fucking up and failing we're always told to look for the silver linings, but what if you can't see one?

'What if there isn't one?' I asked.

And she just looked at me and smiled, as if the answer was obvious. Because, when you think about it, it is.

'Oh Nell, my dear. Life *is* the silver lining.'

And last but not least, if anyone needs this . . .

Reminders to Self When Scrolling

* It took about thirty photos to get that bikini shot.
* That dress cost an absolute fortune, she only wore it once and now she's trying to sell it on eBay.
* The sunset is filtered – trust me, the saturation slider is *right up there*.
* And that was the only photo because it rained most of the time.
* They argued. A lot.
* In fact #darlinghusband was sulking before he was made to smile for that photo.
* She's breathing in.
* Boyfriend got mad and told her to put down her phone.
* Kids spilled chocolate ice cream all down those lovely white summer outfits straight after the photo was taken.
* Total meltdown tantrums don't make the grid.
* Neither does greasy hair and spots or wrinkles and cellulite (let's start a trend!).
* Best-Daddy-Ever-love-heart-emoji posts are by the same woman who never stops complaining to her friends about how her partner does sod all to help with the kids and she's HAD ENOUGH.

* That famous person is using a ring light and it's on full beam.
* The difference between you and her is about two hours of hair and make-up (I should know, I had my photo taken for my column and even my own mother doesn't recognize me).
* Smoke and mirrors is such a brilliant saying for a reason.
* That gorgeous new kitchen makeover you saw on their stories = builder hell for six months (not on their stories).
* And now they're getting divorced.
* When they posted that reel they were not out there partying and living their best life, but tucked up on the sofa in their pjs thinking TFFT.
* Glastonbury looked better on the telly.
* THINK OF THE PORTALOOS.
* Those are hair extensions.
* They had to wait for ever to get that shot in Santorini because really it's like Piccadilly Circus and will you move please, you're ruining my selfie!
* Oscar Wilde never said that.
* No, really, it's a great quote, but he didn't.
* Underneath we're all just the same, everyone's winging it and everything looks better with a starburst filter.
* Nobody knows what they're doing and it gets easier when you learn that.
* This is someone's highlights reel.
* Everyone knows comparing and despairing is bad for us.
* We all do it.
* None of it is real (well, maybe the cute kitten videos).
* *Sod This.*
* It's called doom scrolling for a reason.

* Your life is brilliant because it's all yours, even if it's nothing like you thought it would be. Because I have a confession, nothing in life ever is . . . and guess what? That's what makes it such a wonderful adventure.

Acknowledgements

I have so many people to thank in these acknowledgements, but let me first start with my wonderful editor, Trisha Jackson. Not only is she the best in the business and an absolute joy to work with but it was when we were catching up over a coffee one day, chatting about what I'd like to write next, that she smiled and said, 'I think we could do with a bit more from Nell and Cricket, don't you?' and the idea of *More Confessions* became a reality.

So, thank you Trisha, for letting me hang out with two of my favourite characters again (I'd missed them!) and for allowing me to spend another year and more with the rest of the gang – creating more stories, going on adventures and discovering there are plenty more truths to be told, lessons to be learned and joys to discover – while hopefully entertaining my readers!

I also want to thank the rest of my incredible team at Pan Macmillan for all their hard work, skill and support. It really does take a village to publish a book and I am so very lucky to have such a talented village: Joanna Prior, Lucy Hale, Sara Lloyd, Stuart Dwyer, Rebecca Lloyd, Jon Mitchell, Mairead Loftus, Anna Shora, Hannah Geranio, Rosie Friis, Chloe Davies, Becky Lushey, Maddie Thornham, Claire Evans, Jamie Forrest, Holly Martin, Andy Joannou, Stella Moore, Ellen Morgan, Katie Jarvis, Alex Hamlet, Alex Ellis, Alice Smith, Emma Oulton, Carol-Anne Royer and Kieran Devlin.

It's a long list but every single person deserves a thank you. I hope I haven't forgotten anyone, but rest assured if I haven't mentioned you by name, I thank you from the heart. I so appreciate everything you do.

A special mention to Charlotte Tennant; thank you for all your skill and patience in expertly guiding me through every stage of this manuscript to finished pages and for working to such a tight schedule. It's so reassuring to always know my novel is in such safe hands.

Also, huge thanks to Rebecca Kellaway for championing my books and making me smile every time I go to the airport! And to all the amazing people in sales that get my books out into the world, onto the shelves and into readers' hands. I am forever grateful.

As always, a huge thank you to my brilliant agent, Stephanie Cabot, who saw something in me when I was a young, twenty-something writer with just three chapters and a big dream. Here we are fourteen novels (and a few more years) later: I am forever grateful. Thanks also to the rest of the team at Susanna Lea Associates.

I also want to give very special thanks to my friend and fellow author, Laura Price, for helping me with a very sensitive and important storyline. One of my characters is diagnosed with breast cancer and Laura's advice was invaluable. Thank you so much Laura for your time, patience and kind words – any mistakes or inaccuracies are all mine!

It's a funny old job being a writer. I spend a lot of my life living in an imaginary world, talking to imaginary people, so it's lovely to have such brilliant friends when I step back into the real one. Thank you to all of mine.

And to my family, well, I couldn't do any of this without you. All my love, as always, to AC for being my glass half-full;

thanks for all the laughter, adventures and being by my side (and mixing a mean Manhattan).

To Kelly, aka The Best Big Sis Ever; thanks for the fab times in LA, the fab times in Ibiza, the fab times in . . . well, basically all the fab times whenever we're together. And, of course, for constantly being that voice in my ear, telling me to keep writing when I first had the idea for *Forty-Something F**K Up*. See, I always listen to you.

And last, but certainly not least, thank you to my brilliant mum Anita, for giving me everything – including the last line of this novel. I love you.

Finally, but most importantly of all, to my readers all over the world, I want to say the biggest thank you. I have been blown away by the outpouring of love and support for the first *Confessions* novel and I'm so grateful for all your wonderful messages and photos. You have no idea how happy it makes me to hear how much you enjoyed reading about Nell and her story and it's been such an honour to hear your own stories. Thank you for taking Nell and Cricket into your hearts and I hope you've enjoyed reading what's next in store for them. Here's to lots more adventures and a lot more confessions . . .

I'm also grateful for:
1. *Finishing this novel so now I can go on holiday – yay!*
2. *A week spent eating my own bodyweight in pizza and pasta.*
3. *Never having to post a bikini selfie.*
4. *All of it.*

WHEN LIFE FEELS LIKE A F##K UP ALL YOU NEED IS ONE GOOD THING

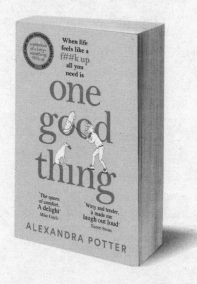

'Wise, warm, witty and
wonderful'
Milly Johnson

'The queen of comfort.
A delight'
Mike Gayle

'Witty and tender, it made me
laugh out loud. I loved it'
Karen Swan

Liv Brooks is still in shock. Newly divorced and facing an
uncertain future, she impulsively swaps her London life for
the sweeping hills of the Yorkshire Dales, determined to
make a fresh start. But fresh starts are harder than they look
and, feeling lost and lonely, she decides to adopt Harry, an
old dog from the local shelter, to keep her company.

But Liv soon discovers she isn't the only one in need of a
new beginning. On their daily walks around the village, they
meet Valentine, an old man who suffers from loneliness,
Stanley, a little boy who is scared of everyone, and Maya, a
teenager who is angry at pretty much everything.
But slowly things start to change . . .

Utterly relatable, this is a novel about how when everything
falls apart, all you need is one good thing to make life
worth living again.

'Enchanting and uplifting'
Chrissie Manby